# GENA SHOWALTER
# JEWEL OF ATLANTIS

HQN™

Recycling programs
for this product may
not exist in your area.

ISBN 13: 978-0-373-77530-9

JEWEL OF ATLANTIS

Copyright © 2006 by Gena Showalter

All rights reserved. Except for use in any review, the reproduction or
utilization of this work in whole or in part in any form by any electronic,
mechanical or other means, now known or hereafter invented, including
xerography, photocopying and recording, or in any information storage
or retrieval system, is forbidden without the written permission of the
publisher, Harlequin Enterprises Limited, 225 Duncan Mill Road,
Don Mills, Ontario M3B 3K9, Canada.

This is a work of fiction. Names, characters, places and incidents are
either the product of the author's imagination or are used fictitiously,
and any resemblance to actual persons, living or dead, business
establishments, events or locales is entirely coincidental.

This edition published by arrangement with Harlequin Books S.A.

® and TM are trademarks of the publisher. Trademarks indicated with
® are registered in the United States Patent and Trademark Office, the
Canadian Trade Marks Office and in other countries.

www.HQNBooks.com

**Printed in U.S.A.**

Dear Reader,

Since the first title in my Atlantis series, *Heart of the Dragon,* was published in 2005, I've been asked how I thought to combine the lost city of Atlantis with the creatures of lore. The answer is simple: what if. What if the gods hid their greatest mistakes inside Atlantis and that's why it's buried under the sea?

That single question branched into a thousand others, each more intriguing than the last. What if a dragon shape-shifter is forced to guard the portal that leads to his home, tasked with killing anyone who enters—even the woman of his dreams (*Heart of the Dragon*)? What if a modern man is sent inside the forbidden city to steal its greatest treasure... who just happens to be a beautiful female he can't resist (*Jewel of Atlantis*)? What if the king of the nymphs can seduce everyone he encounters—except the woman he loves (*The Nymph King*)? I hope you'll join me on these journeys through Atlantis, where the creatures of myth and legend walk, peril lurks around every corner and forbidden passions ignite. Even readers familiar with the books might find a few new surprises in these slightly revised versions!

And be sure to check out *The Vampire's Bride,* my newest tale of Atlantis, where I answer the question readers have been asking for years: What if the villain in all those earlier stories, the vampire king who has tortured and hated and warred, got a story of his own?

Wishing you all the best,

*Gena Showalter*

To Max—my babe.

To the ladies who help make all my dreams come
true—Tracy Farrell, Donna Hayes,
Loriana Sacilotto, Dianne Moggy,
Margo Lipschultz, Keyren Gerlach,
Marleah Stout and the amazing HQN
art department. (And everyone else
I stupidly omitted. Sorry!)

To Merline Lovelace—a woman who generously
and warmly gives of herself without reservation.

To Debbie Splawn-Bunch—
who wouldn't let me title this book
*His (Hard and Shiny) Family Jewels.*

# JEWEL OF ATLANTIS

# PROLOGUE

THE GODS NEVER MEANT to create them.

For centuries they paced throughout the heavens, wailing their need for beings to guide, nurture and rule. They longed fervently for a kingdom overflowing with loyal, grateful, obedient subjects.

And so, the idea of Man was born.

The king of gods was sacrificed, his blood melded with land, air, sea and fire; living creatures were formed. But the elements were unstable, the measure of portions flawed, and the outcome atrocious. The beings they created were not what the gods had envisioned, in appearance or temperament. They were not loyal or grateful, least of all obedient. These Dragons, Minotaurs, Vampires, Nymphs, Formorians—and too many others to name—were powerful rivals, potential usurpers to the royal, immortal throne.

Fear erupted in the heavens.

In a panic, the gods cursed each ghastly creation to a life under the sea, to live forever bound to a city known as Atlantis. The only reminder of their presence was *The Book of Ra Dracas,* detailing the creation and weaknesses of each race. But that, too, was lost.

Centuries passed.

As it always does, time wrapped the gods in an absolution of forgetfulness, burying the memory of their past mistake. They knew only their ever-growing need for fellowship and attempted once more to create Man.

This time they succeeded, and the human race was born.

Soon after, the age of harmony began: the gods meddling in human lives whenever they wished, and Man worshipping the gods. Only one unspoken rule existed. The two vastly different creations, humans and Atlanteans, were never to meet, never to interact, never to fall in love.

Someone should have told Grayson James.

# CHAPTER ONE

IT WAS SUPPOSED TO BE an easy mission. An in-and-out job. A one-day extraction.

His boss had fed him that line of bullshit, and Grayson James had foolishly believed him. Upon first entering this lushly green, sea-kissed land known as Atlantis, however, Gray realized he would have had better luck trying to sell a Frigidaire to a goddamn Eskimo. At a goddamn jacked-up price.

*Atlantis.*

Not a myth. Damn it. He'd hoped otherwise.

He scowled. In one hand, he held a beeping, miniature GPS system programmed from coordinates found on a map. An actual, honest-to-God map of Atlantis his boss had discovered in a missing millionaire's stash. Right now, the GPS signal bounced off the earth's magnetic core, helping him navigate his way through this Atlantean jungle. In the other hand, he gripped a machete. The sharp silver blade hacked at the thick foliage blocking his path.

No, Atlantis was not a myth. It happened to be home to the most loathsome creatures he'd ever encountered. And as an employee of OBI, the Otherworld Bureau of Investigations, he'd encountered plenty.

Made him wonder why he'd even joined the agency.

He knew the answer, though, and it wasn't because he'd (secretly) watched *Star Trek* for most of his teen years and knew how to speak Klingon. "Heghlu'meH QaQ jajvam," he sighed. *Today is a good day to die.*

When he'd learned (to his horrified shock) that there actually were other colonized worlds in the vast expanse of the galaxies, he'd left his job as a detective with the Dallas PD and began searching for a *Men in Black*–type operation. When OBI finally contacted him he'd signed on immediately. He believed fiercely in the need to learn about these otherworlders and protect his own planet from them.

How could he have known that the most fearsome creatures of all resided here, on his own planet? Simply buried beneath the ocean, protected by some kind of crystal dome?

As he dodged a stray limb, he ground his teeth together. "Atlantis," he muttered. "Code name, Hell."

After entering a swirling, gelatinous portal OBI had discovered underwater in Florida, he'd found himself inside an enormous crystal palace guarded by huge, sword-wielding men. Luck had been on his side as he stealthily maneuvered his way past them, unnoticed, and entered this jungle.

That's when he kissed that fickle bitch Lady Luck goodbye.

For the past two nights, a blood-sucking vampire, a fire-breathing dragon, and a hungry, salivating winged demon, aka the Welcoming Committee, had chased him, each sharpening mental forks and knives.

The memories made him feel all warm and fuzzy inside.

He knew the routine now. In less than one hour, night would fall and those…things would emerge again. They would hunt him. They would attempt to fucking eat him. And not in a good way.

His blood ran cold at the thought and not even the hot, humid air could warm him. For fifty-eight hours he'd been stuck in this seemingly never-ending maze, and for fourteen of those hours, he'd followed the exact same pattern: creatures track, Gray evade.

The first night, he'd tried to shoot them with his Beretta. He managed to nail the dragon between the eyes, but his other pursuers dodged the bullets, quickly and effortlessly gliding out of range.

The second night, when the two remaining creatures appeared, Gray utilized his combat skills and slit the vampire's throat. A pleasure, he had to admit, but he hadn't emerged unscathed. Five deep, raw scratch and bite wounds adorned his neck and thigh, throbbing constantly. Not festering, but never quite healing.

How he'd escaped the demon after that, he didn't know. Injured and weak as he'd been, he would have been easy to overpower. Hell, his bleeding body would have made a delicious dinner buffet. Many times he'd wondered if the demon had purposefully let him go, enjoying the thrill of the hunt a little too much.

Well, the demon wasn't the only one who was going to enjoy himself tonight. An anticipatory smile lifted Gray's lips. Smarter now, he wouldn't be caught off guard. Plus, he'd already worked up a plan affectionately dubbed Operation Kill the Bastard. If KTB unfolded successfully, the demon would soon join his bloodsucking friends in hell. If it didn't, well, Gray would resort to Plan B: Operation Oh Shit. He'd sprint like a madman and hide until light glowed once more from the seemingly alive dome above.

His gaze flicked to said dome. There was no sky here, only mile after mile of iridescent, pearlized crystal. Waves constantly washed over the outer side, and multiple-sized and colored fish swam in every direction. He like the naked mermaids best.

A twig slapped his cheek, snagging his attention, slicing skin and adding one more item to his growing shit list. He lost all remnants of his good humor. At least the insects had stopped swarming him. A real silver lining, he thought bitterly. He never should have taken this job.

He veered left just as his wristwatch vibrated. He stopped abruptly. "Just what I need," he muttered. If it wasn't one thing, it was another, and now it was time to check in with home base.

He dropped his backpack, dug inside, and withdrew a small black transmitter, switching it to On. If he failed to check in at least once a day, the cavalry would sweep in and finish his job. He'd never failed a mission, and he wouldn't fail this one.

"Santa to Mother," he said, cringing when he spoke his code name. His unit had thought it was funny as hell, saying he swooped into other worlds and left little presents (like bombs and dead bodies), so the name had stuck. "Do you copy?"

A few seconds of static, before he heard, "Go ahead, Santa." He recognized the voice of his boss, Jude Quinlin.

"I'm still without the package, but all is well."

"Copy that."

"Over." He ended the transmission and stuffed the receiver into his backpack, then kicked into gear again. All was well, his ass. To survive Operation KTB himself, he needed to find a small clearing with ample room to sprint, dodge, and dive for cover. So far, no luck. And he was running out of time, his hour ticking away unmercifully.

When a wall of trees blocked his path, he pivoted right, but the GPS erupted in a series of erratic, high-pitched beeps, a sign he'd taken a wrong turn. Growling low in his throat, Gray spun around and backtracked until the miniature device calmed. Sweat trickled from his temple and dripped onto his military fatigues.

He'd been due a vacation, damn it, a chance to see the brothers and sister he hadn't visited in over two years. He called them regularly, of course, but that wasn't the same as hugging them, laughing with them. *Being* with them. He wanted to play with Katie's children, wanted to make sure her husband Jorlan was treating her like the prize she was.

Working for OBI—which translated into constant planet-hopping through inter-world wormholes—didn't allow for frequent trips home. Hell, working for OBI didn't allow for trips anywhere except alien planets. And now underwater cities. It sure as hell didn't allow for dating and getting laid. Unless he wanted to have a one-night stand with a three-eyed, blue-skinned, slimy alien female.

He didn't.

1. He'd never liked one-night stands, preferring instead multiple nights with multiple orgasms.
2. Three eyes? Slimy skin? Uh, gross.
3. Did he mention that he liked to take his time with a woman, lingering over every nuance of her body, savoring her scent, her taste? That he liked to hear her shout about his unbelievable sexual talents in English?

He grinned at the thought of "unbelievable sexual talents."

Another branch bitch-slapped his cheek, and he lost his grin. *Your fault, man. You shouldn't have let your mind wander into the gutter.* How true. Now was not the time to be thinking of sex and women. Or having sex with women. He blamed the heat for his wayward mind. That, and the fact that he hadn't gotten laid in a long, *long* time. Too long.

Way too long.

Why else would he have lost focus on what was important—his survival—in favor of picturing a naked woman. A naked woman with long, velvet-soft legs that wrapped around his waist and—

Yet another twig popped him, in the eye this time. How many would he have to endure? "Concentrate, boy." It's not like he suffered from ADD. *You're here for a reason, James. Think of nothing but that.*

One moment of distraction could cause a mission to fail. He *knew* that, and was surprised at how easily his mind kept veering. Perhaps being hunted by a cannibalistic demon wasn't exciting enough for him. If that was the case, he needed a total body probe and psych exam ASAP.

"The mission. Think only about the mission." As they had a thousand times before, his boss's departing words drifted through his mind. *We found a book, Gray. The book, actually, titled Ra Dracas. It tells of dragons and vampires and other such nonsense, but the true message is hidden between the text, written in code.*

"The text about dragons and vampires is nonsense," he mocked. Hindsight sucked major ass.

*Once we broke that code,* his boss had added, *we learned about the Jewel of Dunamis, a jewel so powerful it can be used to predict the future. A jewel so powerful it can show who's lying and who's speaking the truth. Whoever holds it will have the ability to destroy any enemy. Conquer any army.*

Small wonder his government wanted so desperately to own it.

Gray was to find and steal this precious jewel, then bring it home. If his mission was compromised in any way, he was to destroy it so that no one else got their greedy hands on it.

It was that simple.

Simple? Yeah, about as simple as routine brain surgery. Gray paused briefly and sipped from his dwindling canteen of vitamin-enhanced water. The cool liquid slid down his parched throat, offering a much-needed burst of energy before he jolted back into motion.

For an eternity he pushed himself onward, never slowing, ever conscious of what awaited him if he didn't find a spot to enable Operation KTB. His gaze darted to his wristwatch, the digital red light barely visible under the dirt and grime covering him. Twenty minutes until showtime, so he had to find a workable patch of land *now*. He scowled and—

*watch out for the quicksand.*

His eyes jerked swiftly across his surroundings as he searched for the speaker, a woman. He didn't duck for cover, didn't stop walking, preferring instead to be mobile. Plus he didn't want to scare her with any surprising movement. That's how trigger-happy fingers were created.

He did tighten his grip on the machete. The odds were fifty-fifty the woman had a weapon, and even higher that she'd actually use it. Still. A man couldn't be too careful.

*Are you listening to me? I said, watch out for the quicksand!*

The husky, heavily accented female voice slammed into his mind once again, so richly sensual and commanding he acquired an instant, unwanted, and surprising hard-on—before he promptly began sinking into a large pool of quicksand.

"What the hell?" Instinctively he attempted to raise his legs, which only caused him to sink farther and faster. He stilled and glared at the ground, watching it slowly rise, covering his feet…his ankles.

*Now you've done it.* Exasperation clung to the edges of her words. She might even have added, *Dumb ass,* but he wasn't sure. *I tried to warn you.*

"Where are you?" he asked, using his gentlest, most reassuring tone as he eyed the lush green bushes circling him. The leaves here were thicker than any he'd ever encountered, barely moving in the gentle wind.

There was no hint of person or clothing peeking from the shrubbery, still no rustle or snap to indicate movement. She'd tried to save him from the quicksand, so she hopefully meant him no harm. God knew he needed all the help he could get right now.

"You can come out," he said. "I won't hurt you. You have my word."

*Think for a moment, Gray. You don't hear me with your ears, but with your mind.*

"How do you know my name?" he asked sharply. Then he blinked, shook his head, blinked again. The voice remained, echoing from each corridor of his brain. She was right. Her words were actually inside his mind.

How was that possible?

How the hell was that possible?

"I'm schizo." The statement burst from his mouth, too shocking and surreal to keep inside. "I've finally jumped over the ledge of sanity with thousand-pound weights tied to my ankles." He'd seen some weird shit in his lifetime, and it had finally caught up with him.

He should have known it would come in the form of a split personality. A sexy as hell female personality, at that. Her whisky-rich voice…he'd never heard anything quite so erotic.

Down, down he sank as the sand covered his calves with its gooey wetness. The scent of stagnant water and decaying—he wrinkled his nose. He did *not* want to guess what was decaying.

Insane or not, he hadn't survived two days and nights of torture to die by stinky sand. No matter what he had to do, he'd save his life—or rather, lives—from this mess.

God, this sucked.

Unwilling to lose a single supply, he tossed his GPS and machete to dry ground. Careful not to jostle too much or too quickly, he removed his backpack and tossed it beside the blade, wishing to God his propel wire hadn't been lost during a battle with the Welcoming Committee.

He scowled for, what…the thousandth time in as many hours? The expression well represented his views of Atlantis. Meanwhile, he continued to sink, slowly, slowly, the wet sand working its way past his knees, up his thighs. The thick liquid grains were cold, and his body temperature fell a couple hundred degrees. His blood pressure was the only thing on the rise.

Amid the popping and gurgling of wet suction, he searched his surroundings again, this time looking for a lifeline. No branches, no vines were nearby. Only a large white rock, but it was too far away to reach with his hands.

*Take off your shirt,* the sensual, I-want-you-naked-and-in-my-bed voice said.

He snorted derisively. He was sinking toward death,

and his new female personality wanted him to strip. Why wasn't he surprised?

"Want me to remove my pants, too?" he asked dryly. At least he'd picked a hot, nympho chick to be his mind-companion and not a nasally old man.

*Idiot!* she huffed, a blush dripping from her tone. *Take off your shirt, clasp the opposite ends in your hands, and hook the material around the rock.*

His eyes widened as he studied the distance of the rock again. That might actually work. For the first time in days, he laughed with genuine amusement. He might be schizophrenic and teetering on the brink of total insanity, but he was also a freaking genius.

The woman—it was hard to continually think of such a distinctive, seemingly real voice as merely an extension of himself—sighed. *Why did the gods have to pick you?*

Her dejection caused his smile to grow. "I could ask myself the same question, babe."

Reaching behind him, he gripped the neck of his shirt and tugged it over his head. With one end of the camouflage material in his left hand and the other in his right, he leaned forward and tossed the looped shirt at the rock. He missed.

He tried again and missed.

Okay, so he seriously needed to increase the hours he spent at target practice.

The sand now reached his waist. He continued to lean and toss until the shirt finally anchored solidly. He gave a hard jerk and stopped sinking.

*Now pull.*

"I know what to do." He pulled, using all of his strength. His arms burned from the strain. The sand grasped at him like strong, greedy fingers, holding him in place.

Grimacing, he continued to hoist up his two hundred pounds of muscle. His shoulders popped, the weight straining sockets and bones. The sand continued to tighten its embrace, burning the wound in his leg. The teeth marks in his neck throbbed against the exertion, perhaps even split open because he felt a trickle of something warm and wet on his skin.

Just a little more…almost…there. The sound of ripping cotton and poly filled his ears. With a final yank, his body landed on dry, solid ground. He sucked in a relieved breath.

*Now, run. Hurry. The demon has already begun to stir.*

Ignoring her, Gray rolled to his back before easing up and into a crouch. As he glanced at his wristwatch, a soft, salty breeze drifted past him, reminding him of the beach vacation he so craved. This area would be as good as any other, he supposed. He'd run out of time.

"Let Operation KTB commence." He slipped on his shirt, unzipped his backpack and rooted inside.

*What are you doing? Run, you fool.*

"You need a name," he said, ignoring her demand and continuing his search inside the bag. Didn't all split personalities have names? If he was going to be insane, he might as well embrace it fully. For now, at least. Once he returned home and told the captain about his new friend, he'd be poked with so many needles it would make an alien probing seem like a sensual massage.

Maybe he'd call her Bunny. Or Bambi.

*Please,* she cried. *You need to hide. If you don't, you'll be hurt again and—*

"I'm not running. I'm going to kill it."

She paused, absorbing his words. *Listen, Gray. You aren't insane. I'm not a figment of your imagination or a personality inside your mind. I'm very real, and I can help you. I know Atlantis and the creatures here. Listen to me and you just might live for one more day.*

Now it was his turn to pause. Her claim made a weird sort of sense. Throughout the years, he'd seen and experienced all sorts of strange things. "Can you prove it?" he almost said, but stopped himself.

Though he hadn't actually spoken, she heard him and uttered a frustrated hiss. *You are such a human. Prove this, prove that. Humph! I'm speaking with you, aren't I?*

Several alien races communicated psychically, so he already knew it could be done. He just hadn't known it could be done with *him*. Fact is, he was relieved his brain hadn't experienced full meltdown.

"Where are you?"

*Hades, it seems.*

He grinned. "Yeah? Me, too. Want to tell me how you know my name?" He resumed his search inside the bag. "And how are you getting inside my mind?" That bothered him, a lot, but he had too many other things to worry about right now.

*Do you really wish to discuss this now? Time is your enemy.*

Again, she was right. He truly didn't have long, perhaps five or ten minutes and he needed every second. "I'll let those questions slide, but there's one thing I've got to know. Why are you helping me?"

Pause. *It would be a shame to mar your pretty face.*

Good answer. Dare he say irrefutable?

"You know how to take down a demon?" Myths claimed garlic, a stake through the heart, or holy water would do the trick. Wait. Those killed vampires. What the hell killed demons? *The Book of Ra Dracas* might have very well provided step-by-step instructions, yet he'd paid no attention, seeing the script merely as camouflage for the hidden code about the jewel. Stupid.

*There is no reason to fight. I can lead you to safety.*

"Poison? Dynamite?" As he spoke, he lifted the items in question.

Heavy silence blanketed his mind.

"I'm not going anywhere, honey, so you might as well tell me."

*His neck,* she finally said on a trembling catch of breath. *You have to—well, you know.*

"Yes, I'm afraid I do." He bypassed the grenades; he might need those later, and withdrew four sticks of dynamite, as well as his night-vision goggles.

*That dynamite won't help you. Demons are strengthened by fire.*

"I'm hoping the force of the explosion will slow him down so I can get close enough to him to…you know." He slapped a clip into his gun and slid a load into the chamber. This was his last round of ammunition, so he had to make the most of it.

*Be careful. Please, be careful.*

So many emotions layered her words. Terror, regret, hope. Concern. Emotions he didn't understand and didn't have time to ponder.

*Promise me.*

"I give you my word," he answered, and then he tuned her out completely, unwilling to let her distract him from his purpose. If he wanted to win, he had to get in his zone—and stay there.

Sensing his needs, she said, *I won't speak again until this is over.*

Forming a large circle with the dynamite, Gray planted a stick next to each of the towering trunks. The breeze intensified, prancing with renewed life. Darkness approached steadily, threading gnarled fingers through the thickness of the trees. Adrenaline thundering through his veins, he anchored his night goggles over his eyes, the world dimming to reds and grays.

Dynamite in place. Check.

Gun in hand. Check.

Bullets loaded. Check.

Knife. He lifted the machete and hooked it to the waistband of his pants. Check.

All that remained was covering his body with a blanket of leaves, camouflaging him from the demon's view. But as he bent to gather the first leaf, a whiz sounded next to his ear, followed by a sulfur-scented wind and taunting laughter.

Too late.

The demon had arrived.

Mentally cursing, Gray crouched low and tightened

his grip on his weapon. As he lay there, sweat dripped from his forehead and onto his goggles, momentarily shielding his line of vision. His head moved slowly, his eyes scanning from side to side, looking for a telltale blur of heat. Where the hell was it? *Come on, show yourself.*

Not finding a hint of the creature on land, he flicked a glance upward—and saw a figure speedily diving toward him, down, down. He didn't panic as it came closer. Closer still. No, he grew eager, anticipatory.

Almost here… Gray rolled out of the way a split second before contact. The demon crashed into the ground, and an evil hiss slithered through the night. Unfortunately the creature was up and hidden in the trees before he could fire off a shot.

"You want to play hide and seek," he shouted, "we'll play hide and seek. Come and get me, you ugly bastard." Gun pointing straight ahead, Gray jumped to his feet and ran. Ran toward the first cluster of dynamite, praying the demon followed. When he heard the rustle of a cloak and felt the warmth of breath on the back of his neck, he smiled with satisfaction.

Oh, yeah. The little shit had followed him.

As Gray passed the tree, he whipped around and aimed his gun. *Boom!* The bullet nailed the dynamite. Instantly fire spewed, and the tree exploded. The blast lifted Gray into the air, then slammed him onto the ground, shoving the air from his lungs. It did the same to the demon, and amid its howls of pain and fury, wooden shards and charred leaves rained.

He'd hit him, Gray knew, fighting for breath, but had he slowed him down?

An acrid stench and black smoke billowed around him as he pushed to his feet. Gray launched into a sprint, closing the distance between himself and the second cluster of dynamite. Infuriated, the demon followed once more; no longer playful and taunting, it stayed close on his heels. Saliva dripped from the too-white, too-sharp teeth, and onto Gray's neck.

Gray spun around and fired. *Boom!* The second cluster exploded, lighting up the shadows with orange-gold flames. A blast of pure heat swept over him; he went airborne again, but this time he expected it and hit the ground rolling. The demon propelled into another tree trunk, shrieking in rage and renewed pain, growling curses in a language Gray didn't understand.

Gray jolted up and started running.

*Now!* the female shouted inside his mind. *Fire now!*

He hadn't passed the third cluster yet, was just in front of it, in fact. If he fired now, he might barbecue himself. He aimed and fired anyway, diving for the ground.

*Boom!*

The impact threw him backward, and he covered his head with his hands. Waves of heat rolled over him, hotter than before, burning his clothes, his skin. A loud *thump,* then a gasp for breath echoed in his ears.

Unfolding from the ground, Gray readied his knife. He raced to the demon. The ugly bastard had slammed into another tree and now struggled to right himself. His eyes glowed a bright, eerie red. Horns protruded all over his scaly body. Without pausing for thought, Gray raised the blade and struck. Blood splattered.

Silence greeted him as the scent of rotting sulfur filled the air.

Remaining in place, Gray moved his gaze through the clearing. The smoke was thicker now, heavier, and billowed around the remaining trees like angry clouds. Bits of bark and foliage continued to fall from the sky. His goggles had come off sometime during the fight, and his eyes watered. His nostrils stung, but most of all his joints ached.

He jerked the bandana from his head and smoothed the material over his nose, blocking the foul, heated air.

*You won,* the woman said, awe and joy laced in the undercurrents of her voice. *You really won.*

"I never doubted it," he lied. Without any hint of emotion, he carefully stretched every vertebra of his spine, working out the kinks and bruises. He was getting too old for this shit.

After replacing the camouflage bandana, he kicked through the rubble until he found the GPS system, his goggles and his backpack. Each was burned around the edges, but essentially unharmed. He flipped the safety on his gun and stuffed it in the holster at his side before hooking the pack over his shoulder. That done, he cleaned his machete and sheathed it at his side, as well.

"Now," he said, knowing his adrenaline rush would soon wane. Best to finish his business with the woman before he crashed. He leaned against a thick, splintery tree trunk and rubbed the throbbing wound on his neck. "Let's you and me have a little chat, shall we? I want to know who and where you are. I want to know the real reason you helped me. As much as I hate to admit it, there's got to be more to it than you like the look of me."

She sighed, the sound heavy and long. *This isn't the time.*

"Sure it is." Patience was for priests. Gray damn sure wasn't a priest.

*I'll tell you anything you want to know. Later.*

"That's what you said before. And by the way, I'm not sure I like this role reversal thing we've got going on. Woman love to talk and share every detail of their lives. Men don't. But look at us? I'm wanting to talk and you're wanting to shut me out."

*I'm sorry, it's just...Gray?*

"Yes?" he prompted when she slipped into silence. He shifted from one foot to the other, not liking how quickly she'd lost her happy timbre.

*That was only the beginning.*

# CHAPTER TWO

*THAT WAS ONLY the beginning.*

The warning echoed through Gray's mind, ominous and dark. A malevolent tempest gusting straight toward him. He forgot his need to question the woman, to know her name and her true reasons for helping him.

"What do you mean that was only the beginning?"

*Danger still lurks here. You need to reach the safety of the streets.*

"What kind of danger?"

*Other demons are nearby. Vampires, too. Once they learn of their friend's death, you will once more be a hunted man.*

His inner child perked up immediately, thinking: all right, I get to blow more stuff up. His adult self groaned in protest, suddenly too fatigued and too sore to play anymore, wanting only to take his toys and go home.

"This jungle is a real who's who of Atlantean crap, you know that?" As he'd feared, his adrenaline rush was quickly dissipating, the explosions and heat taking their toll. He needed to find a safe place to crash.

For some dumb-ass reason, though, he didn't want the woman to know how winded he was. He wanted her to think of him as strong and invincible. So he kept his breathing slow and even, kept his shoulders straight and his expression firm.

"Can you get me out of this jungle?" His fingers flexed around the machete's hilt.

*North. Head north.*

His feet heavy, he plodded through the ash, rocks and twigs until he came to a grove of white trees. They swayed like ghosts. He didn't recall seeing them before. He plucked one of the white leaves, the woman's sexy voice leading him past them. Soon he found a pair of footprints and realized someone else had once taken this same path.

*Those are your footprints.*

"No way," he said in disbelief.

*Take a look.*

He bent down and studied the dirt etchings. Sure enough. They matched his size and shoe type. He scowled. He'd been here before, but he'd obviously gone the wrong way. "How close is this to the exit?"

*You'll see,* she laughed.

He emerged five minutes later.

Gray cursed under his breath. He stood at the edge of a cobbled path, winding away from the forest. So simple. So easy. The darkness was growing thicker, but without the density of trees hovering around the road, ribbons of the crystal dome's soft golden glow slipped free.

Frowning, he released his grip on the machete and fisted his hands at his sides. It had only taken him three miserable days, three explosions and a goddamn Invisible Woman to get out.

"I could have found it on my own," he mumbled for pride's sake.

The woman laughed again, a sound so lush and sexual his body instantly responded. Most likely she could have cursed him to everlasting hell and he would have lusted after her. Would have hardened for her, ached to touch her. She sounded *that* sexy.

He didn't like how quickly and easily she affected him. Wasn't used to it, in fact. As much as he loved and treasured women, as much as he enjoyed savoring and pampering them, they always came to *him,* had to work to gain *his* interest. He'd never responded so potently to a specific one; there were just too many to choose from.

*The only way you would have made it out of that jungle without me, was if your dead body had been dragged out between that demon's teeth.*

"Smart-ass," he said, but he found himself grinning.

*The creatures never would have found you if you hadn't doused yourself in insect repellant.*

"You're kidding me? That repellent is supposed to be scentless."

*For insects, perhaps.*

He lost all remnants of his grin. If the label had said one word, one freaking word about attracting demons and vampires, he never would have used it. Disgusted, Gray stopped and sipped from his canteen, the coolness of the water soothing his ashy throat.

"Where do I go from here? I need a hot meal—" the energy bar in his bag wouldn't cut it this time "—a bath and a soft bed." A willing woman wouldn't be amiss, either. Preferably the one eavesdropping on his thoughts.

She cleared her throat. *Yes, well, just follow this path.*

He chuckled and jolted into motion. Perhaps it was folly on his part to trust her so completely, but trust her he did. She'd saved his life. Twice now.

Maybe that was part of a diabolical plan, but he just didn't care. At the moment, she could have lead him straight into a human stew pot and he would have willingly gone.

His boot struck a cluster of pebbles, skidding them forward and tripping him. He righted and rubbed the wound on his thigh. Every action increased the pain there.

*You need to clean that, as well as the one on your neck.*

"As soon as I find shelter, I'll use the first aid kit in my bag." Not that the antibacterial ointment would do any good. He'd been using it for two days to no avail.

*You received these wounds yesterday, yes? From the vampire?*

"Yes."

*And they've only grown worse? That is not good. Not good at all.*

He caught the underlying foreboding in her tone. "Do I need to worry about morphing into a bloodthirsty phantom of the night?"

His dry tone raised her hackles. *You should not joke about something so serious. Did the demon bite or scratch you today?*

"Are you kidding? The bastard barely got near me."

She sighed. *Neither of us has reason to worry, then. For now. Besides your monstrous ego, you should be fine.*

He was tired, though. God, was he tired. He hadn't lied. He needed food and a bed as soon as possible or his legs were going to give out on him. The bath and the woman were optional at this point.

A cool wind wafted past him, gentle and welcome, offering a bit of comfort to his stiff muscles. Darkness was reaching the point of total black, like a tomb, where he wouldn't be able to see a damn thing.

Down the road, he noticed a slash of white against the shadows. After a moment, he realized that slash was actually a person, slowly padding in the same direction he himself traveled, just twenty paces ahead of him. Gray tensed and reached for his gun, never slowing his gait. He had two bullets left in the clip.

He'd only need one.

*You may rest easy, Gray. The nymph will not bother you.*

"Nymph?" He paused briefly, the word dancing through his mind. "An actual nymph? As in a female with such a high sexual drive, she leaves her partner in a coma of pleasure?"

*Will you get serious?*

"I *am* serious. Do you know her? Can you introduce us?"

She growled low in her throat. *For your information, the surface legends are wrong. Most nymphs are males.*

Male? "No way."

*Look closely and see for yourself.*

He did, his gaze probing deeply into the creature's back, taking in the small details. Broad shoulders. A masculine gait. Large, booted feet peeked out from the robe's hem.

A shudder raked Gray, and all thoughts of pleasurable comas vanished. "That man needs to die simply for ruining my fantasy."

*He will not be as easy to kill as the demon. Nymphs are the greatest warriors in the land, stronger even than dragons, though they never strike first. As long as you leave him alone, you'll both walk away unscathed.*

"I'll remember that." The closer Gray came to the nymph, the taller he realized the creature was. Taller than him, actually. An amazing feat considering Gray stood at six-five and usually towered over everyone he encountered. Keeping his weapon ready just in case, Gray maintained a wide berth as he passed.

The imposing white-robed male grimaced, glanced over at him, and waved a hand in front of his surprisingly feminine and starkly beautiful face. He barked something in a deep, guttural language.

"What did he say?" Gray asked as soon as he was a safe distance away.

*That you reek of ash and death.*

"Well, aren't I the special little boy today." Nearly eaten alive, then aromatically insulted. He sniffed himself, and his lips pursed. Okay, so he *did* smell a little.

He delved deeper into the shadows, listening for telltale signs of footsteps or the cock of a weapon. As his mind-companion predicted, the nymph left him alone.

Only when he'd gone a mile farther, however, did he relax his guard. He breathed deeply and let his gaze wander. The beauty here amazed him. Dew sparked like diamonds atop the brilliant green foliage. The whisper of waves created a melodic rhythm, and the scent of pineapple and coconut fragranced the air. Throw in a La-Z-Boy recliner, a fridge loaded with ice-cold beer, and a dozen dancing hula girls—naked of course—and he'd be in heaven.

*can you think of nothing besides women and sex?*

"Sure I can," He jumped over a pile of rocks, never breaking stride. "Why don't you take off all your clothes and tell me who you are and why you're helping me."

At first her only reaction was a gasp, and he would have given anything to see her expression. To see *her.* He suspected she was blushing. Would her blush color only her cheeks, or would it spread, delving further, along her collarbone…her breasts?

He swallowed against the sudden lump in his throat.

*we can discuss that later,* she finally said.

"You keep saying that, and to be honest, I'm sick of hearing it. I don't even know your name."

Silence.

"A name is such a simple thing. Surely you can tell me yours."

*I can't.*

"Yes, you can. Open your mouth and let sound come out. Try it, you might like it."

*No, I truly cannot tell you. Because, well…because I don't have one,* she admitted reluctantly, shamefully.

His brow furrowed. Not have a name? Everyone and everything had a name. Was she lying, perhaps? No, he decided in the next instant. Her shame was too real. Which left the question: why didn't she have a name?

Instead of pressing for more details, he said, "Why

don't I call you Babe? It's short, easy, and perfect for you."

*I am not an infant,* she said, clearly offended.

"In your case, the word means hot and sexy."

*Oh. Ohhh.* He imagined her smiling dreamily. *Still, I think I prefer something less suggestive. You may call me...Jane Doe.*

"Now it's my turn to nix." He chuckled. "I'm not calling you by a name I use for dead female bodies I can't identify."

She sighed. *Will you call me Jewel?*

He experienced a jolt of surprise that she had picked *that* name, since it was the whole reason he was here. *Is that why she chose it?* he wondered suspiciously. Probably. Clearly, she could read his mind, as well as toss her voice inside. He'd have to be more careful about what he considered. "Jewel it is, then." He rolled the name across his tongue, savoring its taste. He hadn't seen her face, but anyone with such a flat-out sexy voice deserved a flat-out sexy name, and Jewel did fit the bill.

He skirted around a pile of rocks. "Why did you help me, Jewel?"

She exhaled slowly, and the breathy trickle caressed his nerve endings, tickling like the tip of a feather. *I need your help.* She sounded defensive. Unsure.

"Help doing what?"

*Saving me. I've been imprisoned again and I—*

"Again?" He stopped and his backpack slammed into his spine. "What the hell for?"

*For being me. I believe you surface dwellers would say everyone wants a piece of me.*

The scolding edge in her voice made him laugh, and he jolted back into motion. "I'd like to help you, babe, but I'm kind of pressed for time."

*I know.* Bitterness hardened her tone. *You're after the Jewel of Dunamis.*

The moment she spoke, the muscles in his shoulder tensed. Oh, he wasn't surprised she did, in fact, know— she could read his thoughts, after all. But hearing her say the words… He didn't want to have to find her and silence her (permanently) because she knew something she wasn't supposed to. Could *tell* someone she wasn't supposed to.

He drew in a breath and slowly released it. "What I'm doing here isn't relevant to you."

*I can take you to the jewel, Gray. That's why I picked the name Jewel for myself. I am the only one who can lead you to it.*

"Please. I can find anything, anywhere. That's why my boss chose me for this mission. Besides that, I work alone." He enunciated each word, wanting no misunderstanding of his refusal. "Always."

Still she persisted. *You'll never find it without me. This I swear to you.*

He shook his head and his bandana fell askew. He shoved the material back into place. "This little baby says I can," he said, patting the GPS system he'd hooked to his belt, the quiet, steady rhythm of its beep soothing.

She snorted. *So that little baby helped you out of the*

*jungle, did it? That little baby helped you defeat a demon? Let me tell you something. You will not successfully navigate or survive Atlantis without me.*

His fists clenched at the reminder—and the threat, veiled though it was. "You'd say anything to get your way."

*Yes,* she replied truthfully, surprising him. *I would. In this case, however, I'm not dancing around the truth. We need each other.*

His teeth bared in a scowl, and he kicked a large rock with the steel toe of his boot, sending the white stone skidding down the path. Jewel might have proven herself trustworthy, but he preferred to rely only on himself. People got scared, did stupid things. The last partner OBI had given him abandoned him in a weapons compound at the first sign of trouble, leaving him at the mercy of an infuriated alien warlord. Only Gray's long-standing seduction of Lady Luck helped him escape alive. That, and a two-pound package of C4 explosives.

But if Jewel *was* the only way to reach the gemstone, he needed her. Period. He'd be wasting valuable time by *not* going after her. And Gray hated wasted time almost as much as he hated feeling helplessness.

*I feel the same.*

"I can do without the commentary," he told her dryly.

*Don't forget I saved your life. Twice.*

"That's debatable," he said, even though he'd thought the same thing only moments before.

If she were with him, he could make sure she didn't

tell anyone about his mission and compromise him. But if he rescued her and she conveniently "forgot" to help him find Dunamis, if she tried to harm or stop him… He sighed.

*I would never harm you.*

He was going to liberate her, and he knew it. No use trying to talk himself out of it. He'd save her and force her to help him, if need be. And he'd do it for reasons that had nothing to do with that I'm-waiting-for-you-to-find-and-fuck-me voice.

*I am not!*

At her outrage, he lost some of his anger. To be honest, he was looking forward to seeing Jewel and hearing her voice in person, to coming face-to-face with the woman who could read his mind.

The cobbled path twisted sharply to the left, scattering his shadowy cover. He quickened his pace until he maneuvered back into the deepest darkness. Up ahead, the road stretched for miles.

Maybe he'd get lucky and stumble upon a massage parlor. "Do I have to walk this entire road to get to you?"

At first, she said nothing. Then, *You're going to help me?*

"We're going to help each other. Isn't that the deal?"

*Yes. Yes! Oh, thank you. You won't be sorry.*

Joy and shock and excitement radiated from her words, and he imagined her dancing…wherever the hell she was, wearing nothing but a skimpy black leather halter top and a smile.

Another bout of silence erupted, before she *humphed*

and said, *I'm wearing a long white robe that covers me from head to toe, if you must know.*

"Way to ruin the fantasy and cause Private Happy to hide." He tried to sound stern, but his amusement seeped through. He'd never had this much fun teasing a woman. "I think we picked the wrong name for you. I think I should call you Prudence."

*Do it and your Private Happy will receive a proper introduction to my knee.*

A rich, husky laugh escaped him. "Ah, Pru, we've got to loosen you up a bit. Show you the advantages of being wicked. I'll add that to my 'To Do' list."

*Yes, well, you can be here in two days,* she said, changing the subject.

"Two days?" He so did not want to endure another two days in this hellhole.

*Just go around the far hill, past the sheep farm—*

"Over the river and through the woods, then down the yellow brick road. I know." He exhaled. "One thing at a time, babe. One thing at a time." Maybe two days wasn't such a bad thing. It would give him a chance to rest up, rebuild his strength. "I'm still needing that hot meal, bath, and soft bed."

*Oh, yes. Of course. The sheep farm has everything you need.*

Three hours later, the darkness waned and Gray reached the farm. He performed a perimeter check and discovered the owner asleep in his bed. The man/thing possessed the top half of a human, and the bottom half of a chestnut horse, complete with tail and hooves. Dear God.

*Don't hurt him. Please.*

Silently Gray withdrew a tranq-filled gun from his backpack and with a quick shot to the horse-man's neck, injected him. The creature jerked, then stilled completely. This was the only tranquilizer Gray had brought, and he hated to use it now. At this point, however, he would have injected his own father if it meant eating a hot meal without interruption.

When Gray was assured the creature wouldn't awaken for hours yet, he strode into the kitchen and dropped his backpack on the freshly polished wood floor. The place reminded him of a country cottage, complete with straw beds, wood-burning stove, and fresh, home-cooked scents.

He filled a clay basin with water, stripped to the skin, and washed himself as best he could, taking care around his wounds. He slathered those with antibiotic ointment before slapping bandages over them.

*Be gentler, please. You're making me cringe.*

He arched a brow. "Can you see me?"

*Only through your eyes.*

How prim she sounded, he thought, smiling, just before he looked down.

She gasped.

He chuckled. "I think General Happy likes you."

*Yes, well... I thought his—its—name was Private Happy.*

"He seems to be the one in command lately, so he's come up in the ranks. Got a nice promotion." His throat clenched as he fought to contain his guffaws of laughter. "Wishing I'd look down again?"

She remained silent, and his smile grew.

Clean at last, he redressed in his mud-caked fatigues. He hated wearing dirty clothes, especially now that he was clean, but he wouldn't leave them behind. After he devoured a bowl of fruit and nuts and a plate of some sort of meat pie, he pilfered a royal blue robe and a yellow toga from the creature's closet. He slipped the first over his head and shoved the second in his bag.

"Why do centaurs wear robes?"

*They don't. The clothing is for visiting sirens.*

Sirens. Women who lured men to their deaths by singing. Of course. He should have known.

*You can sleep here. The centaur will not mind.*

"I prefer to find a spot in the woods." Solitude was always safer. A long length of rope caught his eye, and Gray stuffed it into his backpack. "He wouldn't happen to have bullets lying around, would he?"

*No. No bullets.*

"It was worth a shot." He hiked his way back to the cobbled path, feeling more energized than he had in days. Darkness had faded even more, making way for a bright golden glow. Flowers opened their petals, carpeting the ground with all shades of pastels, from the barest lavender, to the daintiest yellow. Trees swayed with renewed life.

He spied several similarly robed people, their faces covered by their cloaks. Again, his first instinct was to whip out his knife and strike.

*The sirens are as harmless as the nymph. Simply block their voices from your mind.*

Gray strode past the small group, and he met a woman's gaze. She was pretty in a delicate, protect-me way, with pale skin and mossy green eyes. Despite her prettiness, he felt not a shred of attraction toward her. She opened her mouth, about to speak to him, and he quickened his speed, not about to let the sensuality of her voice lure him to his death.

When he was out of hearing distance, he said to Jewel, "You told me everyone here wants a piece of you. Now tell me why."

*I'm special,* she evaded.

He opened his mouth to press her for more details, then closed it with a snap. She sounded so forlorn, on the brink of tears, and that knowledge unbalanced him for some reason. Made his stomach twist into several painful knots. Made his chest tighten and ache. She'd been impudent and bold up to this point.

"Do they hurt you? These people who hold you captive?"

*I don't want to talk about this.* Her voice wavered.

Which meant, yes, they did. Fury pounded through him, scalding hot and blistering. Gray had done many unsavory things in his life, all in the name of patriotism, but he had never hurt a woman. He would if he had to, yes, had even considered silencing Jewel on his own, but he did not like the thought of anyone else hurting her. She seemed soft and delicate to him, in need of protection. Anyone who hurt a woman like that deserved pain. Lingering, torturous pain.

He'd already decided to spring Jewel from her prison, but his determination intensified, reaching new heights. No way in hell would he abandon her now. He'd save her or die trying.

*There will be no dying on your part. Promise me.*

"Of course there won't. You might have missed the memo, but I'm invincible."

*Yeah. Right.*

Another hour passed, this one in silence as they each mulled their own thoughts. All the while he climbed up a steep, dangerous mountain, fast losing his bout of energy.

Finally—God, *finally*—Jewel uttered the magic words his tired, exhausted body longed to hear.

*You'll be safe here.*

Gray immediately tossed his bag onto the ground and made camp. Only when he lay atop his bedroll, the stolen yellow toga acting as his pillow, did he allow himself to drink in the scenery. He was perched atop the highest ledge of the mountain, overlooking a breathtaking vista of trees and flowers, and a waterfall that glistened like liquid pearls. So clear it was, he could see the mossy bottom.

Exotic birds with bright, colorful feathers soared around him, calling to one another in a symphony of squawks and cries. This was, quite possibly, the most beautiful sight he'd ever beheld.

Above him arched the crystal dome, so close he had only to reach out to touch the glistening, jagged fixture. Seawater churned in every direction, splashing one way, then another, before dancing away. Foam and mist lingered determinedly as schools of fish swam past.

*I'll warn you if anyone approaches. Sleep well, Gray.*

"I won't let myself sleep deeply. I'll know if anyone comes close to me."

*whatever you say.* A soft melody drifted through his mind, Jewel's sexy voice lulling him to deep, deep sleep.

His eyelids grew heavy against the dawning brightness, and he yawned. Why fight it? Slowly he surrendered to nothingness, one final thought drifting through his mind: if today was only the beginning, getting to the end was going to be one hell of a ride.

# CHAPTER THREE

"OUT OF PARADISE and straight into purgatory," Gray muttered as he maneuvered through a thick, cackling crowd of…people. He used the term loosely. Around him meandered bull-faced men (with actual fur!), women with skin that glowed and glittered—and who also dressed in scanty, see-through robes with more cleavage than a *Playboy* centerfold (which he only flipped through for the articles). They reminded him of the siren he'd encountered last night, pretty and delicate.

Giant, one-eyed Cyclopses shook the ground as they walked, and griffins, half lion, half bird, raced on all fours, growling and snapping at each other, their tails whipping from side to side. Overhead, birds flew—no. Not birds, he realized. They possessed grotesquely misshapen faces, female torsos with large—very large—breasts, and the body of a bird. Talons, wings and all. Harpies, that's what they were. With beautiful breasts. Had he mentioned those?

He was truly hard up if female birds were turning him on. Maybe it was time to renew his subscription to *Playboy*. For the articles.

There were a few centaurs, half man, half horse like the sheep farmer, and each of them carried long, thick clubs. A pack of giggling horned children darted past him, throwing rocks at each other as they ran.

Jewel had navigated him down the mountain and into *this*—whatever it was. Town? Freak fest? He'd already checked in with home base, and now gripped his knife, careful to keep the dark metal hidden within the folds of his robe. Heat stretched from the crystal dome above like a too-tight rubber band, ready to crack and break at the first sign of pressure. Still, he was glad for his robe and hood. They blended him into the crowd quite nicely. And if anyone sensed his human blood, they gave no notice.

*You made it,* Jewel said, breathless with excitement. *You really made it.* The last was barely a whisper. The closer he'd drawn to this area, the more desperate she'd become for him to reach her.

"Finally," he muttered. "Where am I?" A salty breeze at last stirred, whisking his hood around his face.

*This is the central agora—market—for the outer city.*

Only then did he notice the vendors selling their wares. Gleaming linens, sparkling jewelry and—slaves. His eyes widened. A man with green scales instead of skin and red-rimmed eyes paced in front of a line of naked humanoid men, shouting about the merits of buying them, he'd bet. What he wouldn't give to speak Atlantean. The slaves were well muscled and streaked with dirt and whip marks, and they each wore expressions of dismay, their cheeks flushed with humiliation as they stared down at the ground.

Gray's hands flexed and relaxed, flexed and relaxed. He wanted to cut them loose, at least try to save them, but that wasn't his mission and he couldn't afford to draw attention to himself. Maybe, after he found the jewel, he'd come back for them.

*Those men are rapists, killers and thieves.*

"Then they deserve what they get," he said, losing all traces of pity. He turned away from them. The scent of fresh, succulent meats taunted his nose, and his mouth watered. Having eaten only one decent meal— the rest being fruits, nuts, and tasteless energy bars— in the past five days, he craved steak, so rare it mooed, with another steak on the side.

*With a sexy serving wench, I'm sure.*

"You got that right."

She snorted. *Since dragons control and protect the Inner City, outcasts and the more bloodthirsty races stay in this area. It's why everyone here carries a weapon. No one trusts anyone else.*

Gray intensified his guard. He even let his robe drop from his wrist, revealing the long length of his machete. Jewel was right. Everyone else had a weapon, and they weren't afraid to show it. He'd stand out if he *didn't* showcase his blade.

Someone pushed past him, jostling the backpack that was hidden under his robe and causing him to stumble forward. He growled, knife raised, ready to strike, but the bull-faced man never turned to engage.

*Follow him. He'll lead you to me.*

Gray quickened his step, elbowing figures out of his way as he clambered past a tall, stone gate and toward a black crystal castle that swept a towering apex toward the dome. His gaze remained on the bull-man's back. Anticipation unfurled in his stomach, then quickly spread through his veins.

This morning he'd finally admitted to himself that his desire to reach Jewel had less to do with his mission, and more to do with seeing her in the flesh. More than anything, he wanted to save this woman who had been his only companion for two days.

"Where are you?" he muttered quietly, not wanting the creatures surrounding him to hear his foreign tongue.

*I'm at the top of the palace steps. Hurry. Gray, please hurry. I will only be here a few moments more. I want to see you and know I'm not dreaming. That you're really here.*

He finally reached the bull-man and shoved him out of the way. Sweat beaded across every inch of his skin, trickling down and wetting his robe. He would have preferred to hold his gun, but there wasn't much two bullets could do in a crowd this size. Since he hadn't used the grenades, he had those, and would use them if necessary. He only hoped it didn't come down to that kind of destruction.

Several beings grumbled when he continued to shoulder his way closer to the castle. Almost there. He'd see her any moment….

"What am I up against, Jewel? You never told me." Even as he spoke, he scanned the area, searching for any signs of trouble. Searching for her. Someone stepped directly in his path, and he barreled into the man's back, propelling him forward. Damn it, would this crowd never part? Would he never reach the steps?

*I can feel your presence.*

Strangely, he could feel hers. A warm, feminine energy pulsed inside him with greater intensity every step he took. Faster, faster, he strode, only then realizing she hadn't answered his question.

And then, he forgot about his need for answers.

He was there, standing at the front of the crowd, his feet hitting the bottom of the steps. He stopped, but his gaze still moved, roving, searching, climbing the dirty, blood-soaked staircase. Where was she? His heart hammered inside his chest, nearly cracking his ribs with its fierceness. He couldn't see her.

The centaur beside him pointed to the top left and whispered something to his female companion. Gray shifted his attention—and sucked in a shocked breath.

There she was.

He knew it was her, knew it was Jewel. And she was a stone fox. A bound stone fox, and seeing her arms tied over her head, the ropes anchoring her to a towering column, pissed him off royally.

A pristine robe draped her slender body, knotted at her right shoulder and just below her stomach. The long material hung loosely, both hiding and showcasing her curves as it billowed against her frame. Silky, jet-black hair cascaded down her back, a startling contrast against her virgin-white clothes. Even from here, he could see the creamy, flawless purity of her skin, skin that seemed to glisten like a pearl.

His stomach tightened—right along with the rest of him. In ever-growing anger at seeing her bound. In arousal at simply seeing her. Her face was as smooth and pure as his mother's antique cameo. Not classically beautiful, but somehow so exquisite he ached simply from looking at her. Her lips were full and pink, deliciously pouty.

She was familiar to him, but he didn't know where he'd seen her before. He only knew that he *had* seen her at some point in his life. How was that possible?

A black-robed man knelt in front of her, his head bowed. Too busy scanning the masses for Gray, she ignored him.

"I'm here," Gray whispered. "Toward your left."

Her chin snapped up and turned in his direction.

Their gazes collided.

He sucked in another breath, this one burning his lungs with the force of its sizzle. Her eyes were large, so large they dominated her face, and they were amazingly blue. Startlingly blue. Otherworldly blue. A shade so clear and deep he could easily lose his soul in their depths—and thank her for the loss. They hypnotized him.

"My God," he said, unable to hold the words inside.

Her buttercup lips lifted in a dazzling smile, and that smile rocked him to the core, nearly laying him flat. Her teeth were straight and white. Perfect.

*You're even more handsome than I realized.*

And she was lovelier than he ever could have guessed.

He watched as a scaled, yellow arm reached from behind her and nudged her in the shoulder. Her grin quickly faded. *I'm sorry. I must finish my day's work.* She turned her attention to the kneeling man. Her rosy lips moved as she spoke to him, but Gray was too far away to hear what she said.

She closed her eyes, paused for a long, protracted moment, then spoke some more. The man was jerked up and hauled away, sobbing in relief.

Gray's eyes narrowed, and his temper sparked to life. What was going on here? He forced himself to study the little details he had missed in his haste to see Jewel. A trio of demon guards stood behind her. Two small, sharp horns protruded from each of their scalps. Their noses were beaked, and their skin pulsed with a yellowish, scaly hue. Evil red eyes stared out at the crowd. None of them held a weapon, but then, they didn't need weapons. Gray knew from experience that demons relied on their superior strength and speed, as well as their razor-sharp teeth to defend and attack.

A wave of shock worked through him as he realized exactly what he was seeing. *This* is what Jewel had meant when she told him it was only the beginning. She needed him to save her from an army of demons. Sure. No problem. Whatever.

Shit. "How many are there?"

She needed no explanation. *More than I can count. I can make an escape plan for us, but I must wait until I'm alone.*

Gray wasn't sure he had enough firepower to beat such a large army. But damn it, he was here, and he wasn't leaving without Jewel. He also knew he wasn't going to wait on Jewel to make the escape plan. That happened to be one of his specialties.

A guard cut her ropes, and she sank into a heap on

the ground. He yearned to race up the steps and sweep her away, but she was quickly scooped up and carried inside the castle.

"What's going on? Where are they taking you?"

Silence.

"Jewel!" he shouted, and he didn't care who heard him. "Answer me."

Again, silence.

Damn it! He didn't like this. Didn't like not knowing. Didn't like the feeling of helplessness working its way through him.

The crowd began to disperse, and he soon found himself alone, staring up at the black castle through slitted eyes. He released a heated sigh. "Be ready, babe. I'm coming in."

"WHAT KNOW YOU of a portal that leads from Atlantis to the surface world?"

On her perch at the edge of the bed, Jewel blinked up at Marina, Queen of the Demons, and prayed her expression remained blank. "A portal?" She phrased the words as a question, though she already knew the answer.

"Darius of the Dragons has taken a human bride. I've heard the woman came to him through a portal located below the dragon palace." Marina's arms were crossed, and she drummed her long, sharp claws against her scaled forearms. The scent of sulfur emanated from her. "You spent several years with the dragons, so you should know if the portal exists. Does it?"

Lying, for Jewel, brought great physical pain. She

didn't know why, she only knew that it *did* happen. Horrendous, agonizing pain. The information Marina wanted was not information Marina needed. If she told the truth, bad things would happen to the dragons, a race of creatures she adored. But if she lied, bad things would happen to her.

Silence would not work. As always, Marina would threaten to kill an innocent for every minute Jewel remained silent. She would simply have to trick Marina into believing something different.

"Do you truly believe a cold and merciless warrior such as Darius en Kragin, King of the Dragons, would discuss a secret portal with me, knowing I would one day be stolen from him?"

Marina leveled a narrowed glance at her. "I'm onto your ways, girl. Answer with a question and your words are never lies. Not this time. You will answer me with a yes or a no. Understand?"

"What did I lie about?" she said, lifting her hands. "Darius *is* known throughout the land as a warrior whose only joy is killing. Tales of the deaths he's inflicted abound. You know that as well as I."

"That is not the information I wished from you, and well you know it. I'll ask once more, and do not answer me with generalities and misdirections or you will suffer for it. Did Darius discuss a portal with you? Specifically," Marina added, "a portal that leads from Atlantis to the surface world."

Jewel frowned, gauging her next words very carefully. "I can honestly tell you that he never willingly supplied such information to me."

The queen growled low in her throat, and the sound rippled menacingly from the walls. Marina paced, hands fisted at her sides. Her sheer, transparent robe revealed every outline of her body, every horn protruding from her back. Her green and yellow scales pulsed, and her eyes glowed bright red.

The woman was pure evil.

"You think you are so clever," she grumbled. "Have you ever *seen* a portal?"

"I have never seen a portal with my physical eye."

She paused midstride, catching Jewel's meaning. Unfortunately. "Does that mean you have seen one in a vision?"

Trying again to lead Marina down a different path, she said, "If I had seen a portal in one of my visions, don't you think I would have done whatever was necessary to return to the dragons? To find and enter the portal? I am tired of being stolen from one leader to the other. I would love to enter the surface world and lose myself in their masses."

"Once again you refuse to answer as you were told," she growled. "Because of your refusal, one of the prisoners that was released today will be found and killed. That will be your punishment. Now, do you care to rephrase your last answer?"

"Please," Jewel said softly, regret, helplessness, and anger working through her. Of all the ways to be controlled, this was the worst. Knowing other lives, others' suffering, revolved around her cooperation. "Please, do not do this."

"I'll take that as another refusal. Two will die this

night. And know this, little slave. You do not have to worry about being stolen again because I plan to keep you for eternity. Whether that eternity feels as if you are in Olympus or Hades is up to you. Think on that, and we'll speak again in the morning." Marina stalked from the room, slamming and locking the door behind her.

The threat lingered in the air long after she'd gone, and a shudder racked Jewel. Marina always found a way to get what she wanted. Jewel longed to call her back, but pressed her lips together. The knowledge she possessed had the potential to destroy all of Atlantis.

She leapt to her feet and paced the confines of her chamber. Or rather, prison. A prison fairly bursting with anything and everything a woman could desire. Fluffy pillows spilled from the gold-wrought bed; brilliant sapphire-and-emerald dyed lambs' fleece carpets adorned the marble floor. A large, heated bathing pool, canvas and paints, and a table piled high with mouthwatering food. All were here to keep her occupied, keep her thoughts away from escape.

She might have luxuriated in the room and its offerings if she were allowed an ounce of freedom. Instead, the queen kept her sealed inside. Jewel was only allowed out to hold court with the queen's supposed enemies, where Jewel herself judged them friend or foe. Oh, she *had* tried to escape. Many times. She had always failed miserably—and others had been punished for her efforts. Still, she kept a satchel hidden and ready, just in case an opportunity arose.

"Just in case" might actually be tonight, she thought with a slow grin. Gray had promised to come for her, to save her. She needed to plan their escape route. Should have done it already, but had had no time alone.

There were no windows here, but she knew darkness had already fallen, for sentinels marched outside her door. Their boots thumped against the floor, blending with the sound of her own pacing. Her silky white robe wisped at her ankles, as delicate as clouds.

*Be ready, babe,* he'd said. *I'm coming in.*

With every step, Gray's words echoed through her mind, bringing with them a wealth of emotion: joy, excitement, hope. His arrival almost seemed too wonderful to be true. How long had she waited for this day?

The answer was simple. Forever. She'd waited forever.

*He will be hurt.*

The warning suddenly echoed through her mind with the force of a tempest, swirling and churning, consuming. Her joy and excitement were instantly replaced by dread. Her eyes widened in horror. Oh my gods, what had she done? Her premonitions were never, *never* wrong. If Gray entered this palace, he would be hurt. The knowledge now burned inside her as hot as flames, and she covered her mouth with a shaky hand.

What if she'd led him to his death?

If something happened to him, she'd never forgive herself. The demons were a vicious race, always happy to kill and maim. And now, with knowledge of the portals apparently spreading, the demon queen would desperately need Jewel's aid. She wouldn't hesitate to kill Gray in the most painful way possible. A tide of apprehension slammed into Jewel.

"What have I done?" she whispered brokenly.

She never should have led Gray here, no matter how desperately she needed him. The demons would smell his human blood. They would find him and rend the flesh from his bones.

The consequences of her actions rose full force in her mind. Jewel rubbed a hand over her forehead and briefly closed her eyes. A dark, dangerous inner storm threatened to flood and drown her; *she* was responsible for this. She should have known better, she thought, laughing bitterly. She of all people should have known better than to ask someone to help her. Especially Gray.

He had always been a part of her life. Her earliest memories were filled with him; throughout her life, she'd had visions of him, of his path from child to man, of his silly antics with his siblings. Of his kill-or-be-killed missions. Of his numerous—too numerous, to her way of thinking—women.

Quite simply, she'd always loved him.

His image formed in her mind, though it didn't soothe her as it usually did. No, her fear increased. Wonderfully tall and strong, he was muscled like the fiercest warrior. He had pale blond hair and slate-colored eyes fringed by spiky black lashes, and he glowed with unflinching life and vitality. He fairly sparkled with it.

His lips were pink and lush like a woman's, but perfect for his masculine features, softening the rough edges and providing an utterly arrogant smile that promised absolute pleasure. For years she'd imagined those lips all over her, tasting, sucking…

A shiver trekked along her spine. His body was a work of art, bronzed and roped with sinew and scars. So many times she'd longed to somehow breach the vast distance between them and touch him. Trace her fingers over him and assure herself that he was real, flesh and blood, not an exotic figment of her imagination.

As if she needed another reason to stand out to the creatures of this land, her connection to Gray provided one. Having observed him and the people of his world for so many years, she knew their language, their attitudes, and their humors. She hadn't meant to, gods knew, but she'd adapted herself to their way of life instead of her own.

She'd known Gray would one day enter Atlantis, and she should have resisted the urge to lead him to her. She'd foolishly allowed her desire for freedom, her craving to learn about herself, her abilities, and her father, to color her actions and thoughts. But more than all of that, she'd simply longed to see him. To see Gray. Not as a dream, but as a man. Real and warm. Touchable.

She had to do something, anything, to prevent him from entering this palace. She would find a way to escape on her own.

She closed her eyes, pressed her lips together, and fought a tremor of regret. "I've changed my mind, Gray," she said, projecting her voice into his mind. "Do not enter this palace. Just…go home. Go home and forget about Dunamis. Forget about me."

He didn't respond, but she knew he heard her. "Gray!" she shouted. "Answer me."

*Not now, Jewel.* His hard voice growled inside her mind, and it was the most beautiful sound she'd ever heard.

Frustrated by his lack of concern, she crossed her arms over her chest. "You better be packing up and heading out."

*As if.*

"I'm appointing myself your commanding officer, and I command you to go home."

His only reply was a derisive snort.

"Did you hear me, soldier? I told you to lea—"

*Boom!*

She gasped and tumbled to the ground, the explosion rocking the very foundation of her room. Her heart skipped a beat; her ears rang—and that ringing soon blended with the sound of demonic screams and racing footsteps.

Gray was here. Damn him, he was here.

*Where are you?* he demanded.

Stiffening with helplessness, horror and fear, she gritted out, "Do not enter the palace, Gray. Bringing you here was a mistake. You'll be hurt!"

*I'll get there faster if you tell me. Otherwise, I'll end up wandering these damn halls and searching every damn room.*

Too late to send him away—he was already inside. How could she protect him? Shaken to the core of her soul, she quickly rattled off directions. "Be careful," she whispered.

*Always.*

Her limbs trembling, she climbed to her feet. *Nothing*

*would happen to him, nothing would happen to him, nothing would happen to him.* She'd protect him, somehow, someway.

A lump formed in her throat, and hundreds of sharp knots twisted her stomach. She didn't know what to do. Seconds passed without a word from him. She yearned to call out to him, to ask him where he was and what he was doing. Too afraid to distract him, she remained silent. She merely stood in the center of her room, helpless and racked with guilt and worry.

Minutes passed.

Even more minutes passed, becoming longer and more torturous.

Another explosion rocked the palace.

Jewel gripped the bedpost, holding herself upright. Her blood ran cold and hot, alternating between the two as demons hissed and wailed beyond her door. Her limbs shook violently.

"Please, let him live," she prayed. "Bring him to me unharmed."

The gods didn't respond, but then, they never did, preferring instead to pretend the people of Atlantis did not exist.

*Get away from the door, Jewel.*

Her eyes widened, even as hope and excitement flared to life inside her. "I'm already away."

*Cover yourself with something. Anything.*

He sounded so urgent, so forceful. Bending down, she crawled under the bedframe. "I'm covered."

*Boom!*

The third explosion nearly burst her eardrums. Wood

chips and marble chunks crashed onto the floor, raining around the bed like hail.

"Jewel!"

This time, Gray's voice wasn't inside her head, but inside her room. Nearly crying with the force of her relief, she crawled from under the bed, pushing past plumes of smoke. She winced when her knee slammed into a broken shard of glass.

"Here," she shouted, waving a hand in front of her face to clear the haze. "I'm here." Her gaze darted around the destruction until she found him.

He wore his green and black clothes, his robe nowhere to be seen. His shirt was tight against his bulging muscles, and his pants were ripped at the thigh. A cloth made of the same material as his shirt anchored his hair, hiding the paleness of the strands. He'd painted his face green and black, but beads of sweat had lightened the colors and now streaked his forehead and temples.

He looked so beautiful.

He scanned the room, searching for her. And when their gazes collided, locked, hot awareness stole her breath. Her heart skipped a beat. He was strength and life epitomized just then, and he was here for her.

Slowly his lips lifted in a tender smile completely at odds with the fiery carnage behind him. "Hello, Prudence."

She nearly melted.

"And just so you know, you are so not the commanding officer in this relationship. Now let's go."

## CHAPTER FOUR

JEWEL'S HEART THUNDERED in her chest as she raced behind Gray through a maze of darkened rooms. She remained alert, ready to lash out if someone tried to hurt him. More than once, she'd attempted to take the lead, but he kept her firmly shielded by the width of his body.

Her satchel of stolen goods was tied to her waist, and the heavy burden banged against her thigh with her every movement. Flames flickered sporadically, licking the walls, offering momentary visions of crimson remains.

Gray's steps were eerily quiet amid the tormented screams of dying demons, and he blended so well with the shadows she might not have known he was there if she hadn't been able to smell the masculinity of his scent. Hadn't felt the heat radiating from him and enveloping her.

He stopped abruptly, pivoted, and leveled her with a hard stare. He towered over her, the size and width of him nearly swallowing her whole. She'd known he was tall and big, but not like this. Seeing him in person brought to light the sheer maleness of him, the vitality.

Placing one finger over his green-black painted lips, he motioned for her to be silent. She nodded her understanding.

One of his arms wrapped around her and pulled her deeper into the shadows, deeper into his body. This was her first true contact with him and even though danger lurked all around them, she found herself yearning to melt into him, to wrap herself around him and slide her lips over his skin.

"Stay here." His warm breath fanned her ear. "I'll be back."

Truth. His words held only truth. He *would* be back.

Her gift to hear beneath the actual words and know beyond any doubt the speaker's true intention was usually a curse. Not today. When Gray slinked away in the next instant, she didn't race after him. Following him would have proved impossible, anyway. He was like a mist, barely visible one moment, an ethereal phantom the next, lost from her sights completely. She pressed against the too-warm, jagged wall behind her. Where had he gone? What was he doing?

Seconds dragged by, and a slow panic began to burn in her belly as a sickening thought occurred to her. Gray intended to return, true. Sometimes, though, intentions mattered little. He could be ambushed. Hurt. She gulped. *Killed.* After the premonition had warned her of his being hurt, why had she let him leave her?

Fighting a rising tide of terror, she tried to open her mind to him, to find him in the chaos and guide his steps, but she continually stumbled against a mental barrier and saw only darkness. Was it his barrier? Or her own? Having never encountered this type of resistance before, she didn't know the answer. Frustration joined ranks with terror, heating her panic to boiling.

She drew in a long breath, hoping to calm herself, but the overpowering odor of sulfur and smoke stung her nostrils, making her gag. Bands of fiery heat permeated the air as flickers of light continued to illuminate the shadows. Her gaze scanned the hallway for any sign of Gray. Instead, she saw the dead demon bodies that littered the floor, their scales sizzling.

A noxious breeze ruffled her hair when a hissing demon whizzed past her, his wings gliding frantically. The creature didn't spare her a glance, but she caught the feral, pained glaze in his eyes, the wildness of his expression.

She quickly untied her satchel, dug inside, and yanked out a jeweled dagger she'd stolen from Marina. Sensing her, the demon whirled around and pinned her with a deadly glare, hunger washing over his features. Marina's minions were never to hurt or touch her without permission, but Jewel doubted this one cared about such an edict now. He craved blood and death. Saliva dripped from his fangs, as he moved toward her.

Her heart skipped a beat before reclaiming its frantic tempo. In her visions of Gray's life, she'd seen him fight. She'd seen him kill. He performed each feat with ease, such grace and agility, never questioning his choices. *I can do this. I can.* Nothing mattered except survival. Determined, she raised the weapon.

Sensing her intent, the demon abandoned his slow stalking and launched himself at her.

Her mouth went dry and time slowed. Closer and closer he came. As his claws elongated, preparing to rip through her, she sank to the ground, shoved her knife up and into his stomach. An unholy screech vibrated in her ears.

"Bitch!" He spat the profanity, hissing wildly. His body jerked and spasmed; his legs kicked out.

She rolled away from him but wasn't fast enough. His foot slammed into her middle, knocking the breath from her lungs and doubling her over. Panting, she jolted to her feet. The demon tried to remove the knife, but couldn't get a good grip on the handle. He thrashed and moaned and writhed.

*Run,* her mind shouted. *Hide.*

She didn't. Couldn't.

Very soon Gray would return here, and she couldn't leave this demon alive, placing her human in unknowing danger. A weapon. She needed another weapon. Jewel sprinted through the hallway, searching for something. Anything. Only dead bodies greeted her.

Gray suddenly appeared at the opposite end of the hallway like an avenging angel, his features hard and cold. His legs were braced apart, and his hands fisted at his sides.

He spied the infuriated, injured demon, then darted his gaze throughout the long, narrow space until he saw her. His eyes were winged with soot, making the silver irises appear all the more steely and as dark as a winter sky.

"Stay where you are," he commanded her, returning his attention to the creature. He still held his knife, the silver now drenched with crimson. Steps slow and sure, he approached, his muscles clenched and ready for attack.

As Jewel watched him, four words pounded inside her mind. Gray. Danger. Blood. *Death.*

No. *No!* "Stop," she screamed, bolting toward him. "Not another step!"

Too late.

The demon had gained his bearings, had waited until Gray drew close enough, and used his wings to vault forward. Before Gray could dodge him, the creature sank his razor-sharp fangs into Gray's upper arm.

Gray howled in surprise and pain. "Motherfucker!" He slashed at the demon with his knife, but its teeth retained a tight grip, buried deep.

The moment she was within reach, Jewel kicked up and struck the demon dead center in the face. His head whipped to the side, and his teeth tore out of Gray, dripping with blood.

With a growl, Gray leapt to the creature and sliced its throat. When it stopped thrashing, when its screams died, the room too became still. Silent.

"Want to touch her now?" Gray barked, kicking it. Then he stopped, shook his head and seemed to lose the sharpest edge of his fury. He jerked her blade from its belly, wiped the tip on his pants and handed it to her.

"Thank you." She sheathed the weapon at her side with a shaky hand and fought the urge to throw herself into his arms. To slather his face with kisses. He was so fierce, so much a warrior.

He wiped a streak of red from his check with the

back of his hand, but only managed to smear it further. "Were you hurt?" His voice was hoarse, cracked and layered with tension.

"No." Her gaze dipped to his newest wound, watching the slow trickle of blood pooling at his elbow. "But you were. I'm sorry. So sorry." More sorry than he might ever know. If not for the vampire bite he'd received days ago, he would be fine. Because of that bite, his blood was already tainted. When the demon and vampire saliva combined, they acted as a deadly poison.

Gray had one hour, maybe two, before his body reacted and he collapsed.

*This* is what her premonition had warned her about. "I'm sorry," she said again. She had to get him out of this palace.

"I've had worse," he said dryly.

He wasn't thinking of the vampire who had bitten him, but of the women he'd bedded, the women who had bitten him sexually. Their images flashed through his mind—blondes, redheads, brunettes, their bodies open for him. Eager.

Jewel saw the images, too, the block from earlier gone. Her sympathy and concern for him dwindled. The debaucher! He had the dirtiest mind she'd ever read. Motions stiff, she bent down and retrieved her satchel, then retied it to her waist.

"Let's go." Gray grabbed her hand and tugged. "I found a clear pathway that leads outside."

Incredulous, she ground her feet into the marble floor, holding herself immobile. She ignored the delicious tingle racing from her hand and up her arm. "That's why you left me?"

"Yeah." Another tug. "Now let's go."

"Escape routes are *my* specialty."

His brows arched, two sandy slashes on his forest-colored forehead, and he offered her a sexy grin. A born rogue and charmer, he was. He released his hold on her and spread his arms wide. "Then lead the way, baby. I'll follow."

"I will need a moment."

He sighed. "It's not like we've got a pressing need to save our lives or anything. Take all the time you want."

"I will, thank you," she responded primly. Eyelids drifting closed, she pictured the palace, sweeping every corner and hollow. She saw exactly where the demons lurked, where they donned blade-resistant armor around their necks, gearing for war. They hungered for human blood. Smelled it. Craved it.

Were determined to have it.

*You, to the front entrance,* Marina commanded her strongest minions. *You, to the back. I want that human snack captured immediately. Do not let him leave.*

"Your path will not work," she said, opening her eyes. "We must go that way." She pointed in the opposite direction.

"You sure?"

"Very."

He didn't ask how she knew, but intertwined his fingers with hers. The feel of his callused hand once again tingled up her arm, renewing her ever-present awareness of him as a male. He pulled her behind him and bolted into action. "I'm sorry you had to fight the demon without me," he threw over his shoulder.

In her shock, she missed a step and stumbled. An apology. He was giving her an apology. He'd come for her; he'd saved her. He owed her nothing, while she owed him everything.

"What's wrong? Are you hurt?" He didn't wait for her answer; he whipped around, bent until his shoulder made contact with her belly, then effortlessly lifted her.

Jewel gasped. "What are you doing? Put me down!"

He shot back into motion. "You're too slow."

"This puts you at a disadvantage." She slapped at his hard, muscled bottom. "Put me down this instant or I'll stab you in the back!" Truth. She'd stab him with her nails, but he didn't need to know that.

"I hadn't realized you'd be so bloodthirsty." He chuckled. "You wouldn't let me hurt the centaur or the nymph, but you yourself attempted to kill a demon, and now you want to draw my blood. And if you don't settle down, your feet are going to bruise my favorite body part."

"Your penis?"

He made a choking sound in the back of his throat, and his feet nearly tripped over themselves. "Watch your mouth, Prudence. You shouldn't talk like that."

Watch *her* mouth? Watch her mouth! "Penis, penis, penis," she muttered, but she stilled, her body bouncing over his shoulder.

Stone chips were scattered across the floor, and Gray kicked past them to rush through the wide, jagged hole that used to be a wall. He settled into the shadows whenever a demon flew past, doing his best to keep them out of view. When they found themselves alone again, he would jump back into motion. Her satchel pressed into his stomach. She directed him toward the center of the palace, toward the demon queen's private pool.

Three sentinels awaited them.

Gray spied them and quickly settled her on her feet. "Stay here."

She was getting sick of those words.

He sprinted in front of her. The guards' evil red eyes narrowed hungrily. He didn't slow. Gray grabbed a small, round object from a side pouch in his pants, pulled something thin and silver out of it with his teeth, then tossed it at the creatures.

"Down," he commanded Jewel, turning and diving on top of her, propelling her to the ground. The moment she hit, Gray's heavy weight crashed into her, and cut off her air supply.

*Boom!*

More jagged pieces of stone rained over them. More dark plumes of smoke. More hisses of fury as the demons were tossed into the air like play toys. Before they even hit the ground Gray was up and running toward them. Fire flickered around him, licking dangerously.

Coughing, eyes watering, Jewel shoved to her feet and raced after him. When the demons landed, Gray expertly killed two. Jewel didn't hesitate. She knew what needed to be done. She gripped her knife and killed the third.

Demon blood splattered her clothing.

She'd never killed before. She'd attacked the other demon, yes, but she herself hadn't been the one to render the deathblow. Now that she had...she stared down at the lifeless body. She expected to feel guilt or remorse; she'd always fought for the survival of the Atlantean races. But she felt neither of those emotions. Instead, she felt empowered. Like she had finally taken control of her life.

Gray grabbed her by the arm and whipped her around, his gaze dipping over her, scanning for injuries.

"Did you see me?" She couldn't stop the slow grin that spread her lips. "I killed him. I really killed him."

"Yeah, and you surprised the hell out of me." Grudging pride laced his tone. He plucked the bloody dagger from her hand and sheathed it in his belt. "We can't stay here. We need to find an exit. Fast."

"We'll use the pool."

His gaze shot to his right, at the debris-covered water dappled by pinpricks of light from the flickering flames.

"We can swim to safety," she said.

He frowned. "I hate to break it to you, babe, but I'm guessing that pool is only seven feet deep. All we can do in that is swim laps." *And have sex,* his mind added, never far from the subject.

Hearing his unbidden thought, her cheeks warmed and her stomach knotted. This time he hadn't been imagining any woman except her. *Her.* He'd pictured her naked and rosy, skin covered with droplets of water waiting to be licked away.

Tendrils of pleasure curled inside her veins, spreading like the fire around them. When she spoke, her voice cracked. "There's a hatch on the bottom. A door that leads into the forest."

He paused, considering her words. His frown deepened. "If the demons follow us inside the water—"

"I'll make sure they do not."

His mouth opened to ask how, but he shut it with a snap, changing his mind. "All right. We'll swim."

He stepped to the pool's ledge, Jewel still close to his heels. Before he entered, he turned to her and said, "Take off your clothes."

Her head snapped up, and she met his stare with wide eyes. "The demons will sniff you out soon and you want me to get naked?"

His mouth twisted in one of those wry smiles of his. "Silly girl. Can't you read my mind?"

"Not always," she grumbled. Like before, he had erected some sort of wall she couldn't breach. It had to be him, but how he managed it, she could not fathom.

"Just so you know, *Prudence,* that thick material of yours will weigh you down in the water. Take it off." As he spoke, he began removing his shirt.

She'd seen him naked a hundred times before, perhaps a thousand, but those visions of him had always been in her mind. Seeing him now, in the flesh, was so much more potent. She forgot her surroundings, forgot the danger, focusing only on the bronzed strength of his muscled, sinewy chest. His abdomen was chiseled into perfect rows of hardness.

"You can look all you want. Later," he added. "Right

now, Pru, you need to get naked." He dropped his shirt and withdrew his dagger.

Her gaze still locked on him, she brought her shaky fingers to her waist and tried to untie the satchel.

"No time." He sliced the ties with his knife. The satchel dropped to the ground with a thwack. In the next instant, he cut the shoulder straps of her robe. The white material swished to the floor, joining the satchel and leaving her in only a thin chemise.

Bending down, Gray grasped the robe and said, "Step out of it."

The moment she complied, the robe was stuffed inside his bag, followed quickly by her satchel. All the while, he perused her up and down. His eyes were heated. What did he see when he looked at her? She gulped, too afraid to try to probe his mind to discover the truth.

His hands reached toward her and she felt their warmth as they neared her skin. What did he plan to do? He stopped just before contact.

He shook his head, and his gaze grew cold. Empty. "We need to get the hell out of Oz. Can you swim?"

It took a conscious effort to tug herself out of the sensuous spell he'd woven over her, but force herself out she did. "Yes." Swimming was one of the few memories she possessed of her childhood. Frolicking many hours in sunshine and water. Laughing. Enjoying the day. Over the years, she'd forgotten how to laugh and enjoy, but she'd never forgotten how to swim.

"Just try to keep up with me," she said, proudly tilting her chin.

His lips twitched. "Can you hold your breath for long periods of time?"

That, she didn't know. "We'll just have to see, won't we?"

"I'll take that as a no," he muttered. "Listen, I've trained in water. The key is to stay calm, to slowly release the air trapped in your chest. Understand?"

"I will not let you down." She'd prove herself worthy and strong if it killed her.

Jewel entered the water with Gray right behind her. The wet warmth lapped at her skin, seeping past the thin garment she wore, making her shiver. A cloud of red swirled around Gray, his open wound coloring the water.

"I want you holding on to me at all times once we leave the pool," he said. "Don't let go for any reason."

"I'll do my best."

"No, you'll do it." His voice whipped out like a king instructing a servant. "I want to know you're with me every second we're down there."

"Yes, sir."

He shook his head at her impudence. Without another word, she dragged in a breath and dove underwater.

She kicked her way to the bottom. Marina often used this secret doorway to sneak into the city undetected, commit her crimes, feast off unsuspecting creatures, then return. The queen thought she herself was the only one who knew. She should have realized long ago that with Jewel, there were no secrets.

Once they reached the bottom, Jewel grabbed for her

dagger. When her hand encountered only wet cloth, she nearly panicked before she recalled Gray had taken it.

She jerked on his pants to gain his attention. A few bubbles slipped from his mouth as he faced her, and he nodded as she slipped the weapon from his belt. Gliding away from him she inserted the tip into a tiny crevice. Marina used a key, a key Jewel did not possess. She pried at the opening, making it widen slowly.

The water stung her eyes, and lack of air soon caused her lungs to burn. Her dark hair floated into her line of vision like curling ribbons. Gray worked feverishly beside her, his strong hands pushing the slab of rock farther and farther apart.

Both she and Gray had to go up for air before the opening was wide enough for them to slip through. Jewel wanted to swim to the surface one last time and steal another gasp of precious oxygen, but when she pushed up, she saw a horde of demons had entered the room. They spotted her and cried gleefully.

Ice filled her veins, and she sliced her way back to the bottom and pointed up. Gray saw them and tried to wrench her through the opening, but she violently shook her head. *I have to keep them from following us.*

He stilled. Had he heard her, or was the block still in place? Gray, deciding to trust her, released her and held his palms up. *Do your thing, baby.*

Thank the gods, no block. She closed her eyes, her thoughts directed at the creatures above. *No one is in the water,* her inner voice suggested to them. *You do not see the human; you do not see the girl.*

She'd never attempted to direct so many at once,

never tried so valiantly to keep a being from knowing she'd entered its thoughts.

The shouting demons pressed their lips together, going silent. They stared down at the water, shaking their heads, their eyes glazing as they accepted her plea, but they didn't leave the room. They looked around, confusion flittering over their expressions.

Why wouldn't they leave?

Jewel's strength was quickly depleting, and her hold on them began to lessen. Gray must have sensed her need for him because he yanked her through the opening and worked swiftly to close the hatch.

Whether the demons had seen them there at the end or not, Jewel didn't know, and she no longer had the strength to find out.

She held a firm grip on Gray's pants. Her lungs burned, and she desperately needed air, and even though her strength was nearly depleted, she kicked her legs and lowered her free arm, trying to increase their speed. A thick fog soon wove its way through her mind.

*I can't...need...to breathe...*

Gray wrapped his arms around her, holding her close to him. His eyes met hers and the connection managed to strengthen her. Calm her. She'd been thrashing, she realized, but settled as his hand snaked around her neck.

Slowly he drew her face to his and their lips met. *open,* he commanded. His voice filled her head, bringing with it a wealth of hope and confidence she eagerly embraced.

She did so without question, parting her lips wide.

He blew air into her mouth, precious air her lungs accepted with relief. The warmth of his breath curled through the rest of her as her black tresses floated around them, a dark cloak that wrapped them in a private haven. Time seemed to slow. She savored his sweet essence.

All too soon, he drifted a few inches away and met her gaze. *Better?*

*Better.*

*You can do this. I know you can.*

She nodded, praying he spoke true.

## CHAPTER FIVE

JEWEL'S HEAD BROKE the water's surface, her lungs screaming in pain. She gulped in great gasps of oxygen, her arms and legs flailing to keep her afloat. Pitch-black greeted her eyes, an unholy darkness filled only with phantomous shadows. Every inch of her burned for more air, and the burning eased only slightly with each intake. In, out, she breathed, as fast as her lungs would allow.

The choppy, frantic sounds must have disturbed nearby wildlife, because the clatter of snapping limbs, rustling bushes and pitter-pattering hoofbeats rang in her ears.

"Gr—Gray," she called between pants, swallowing a mouthful of water. The liquid slid down her throat, cool and sweet, but it was too much, too fast. She choked and coughed.

"Don't," he said, his voice labored and hoarse as it sliced through the void. "Don't try to talk. Just breathe. Slowly."

Where was he? She'd lost her grip on him somewhere along the way. The darkness around them wasn't thinning and she couldn't feel him near her. "Tr-trying."

"You're talking again. Stop," he demanded.

"I need you," she croaked. "Where are you?"

He must have followed the drum of her voice, silently treading through the restless water until he found her. His arm brushed her stomach, and she shivered, resisting the urge to grab onto him and ascertain he truly was there.

"You okay? Since you won't obey a direct order, you might as well give me the info I crave."

"Yes." The sound of lapping water beat between each syllable. "You?"

"I can't see shit, but I'm fine." He sounded relieved, concerned and angry all at once. "Think you can make it to shore? Wherever the hell the shore is," he added darkly.

"Of course." Determination rode her hard, and she said, "I can make it." The words were for her benefit rather than his.

She must not have sounded convincing. His arm snaked around her waist, pulling her into the curve of his body. "Just keep breathing, and I'll do the rest."

"No, I—"

"Save your strength for an argument you can actually win."

The feel of him holding her, his strength surrounding her, was a heady thing, but the thought of lying back and allowing him to do all the work… No! She might love the feel of his arms around her, and she might teeter on the brink of total exhaustion, but she kicked and paddled with him, adding to their speed.

"Sometimes," she said between breaths, "an argument…can be won…without words."

"Smart ass. Don't you know you're making me look bad? I, man, do the rescuing. You, woman, do the eager accepting."

Jewel grinned, loving the way he teased her. It made her feel normal, accepted. As if she was his friend, not just a woman watching him from afar, wishing she were part of his life. Besides, set apart from the Atlantean races as she was, she'd never had a true friend before. But she'd wanted one. Gods, she'd wanted one. At times, the ache had been so fierce, it had almost been a living entity.

"That is not how our rela—" Sharp pains shot through her calf like a thousand knives cutting through bone. She jerked and cried out.

Gray's arm tightened around her, and they ceased moving forward, his leg movements the only thing keeping them above water. "What's wrong?" he demanded, concern in the undercurrents of his voice.

"Just a cramp," she gritted out, her leg already relaxing.

Expelling a relieved breath, he jolted back into motion, his muscles bunching and straining. "You're doing great. But listen to me this time, and stay still." He spit out a mouthful of water. "I've done this kind of rescue before, and with a two-hundred-pound man no less. Featherweight that you are, I can get you to shore, no problem."

"I *will* help."

"Damn it, Jewel."

She forced her arms to swim more quickly.

"Stubborn woman," he muttered. "Have it your way."

"I will. Thank you."

His legs kicked out and brushed hers. His free arm pushed at the water and skimmed over hers. Because of the danger, such an innocent contact shouldn't have affected her, but it did. Currents of something dark and light, hot and sweet, floated through her blood as swiftly and surely as the river flooded around her, giving her added strength.

"Thank you for coming for me," she said, swallowing more liquid. The words whispered from her, soft and raspy, husky with her gratitude.

"I wish I could say it was my pleasure, but so far the adventure has sucked like a Hoover."

She laughed heartily.

The water slapped as if he'd whipped his head to face her. She wished there were at least a kernel of light to reveal his actions and features, but the darkness was simply too heavy.

He squeezed her waist. "I didn't expect you to get that. Do you even know what a Hoover is?"

"Well, yes. I know a lot of things about the surface."

"You ever traveled there?"

She heard his true question: do Atlantean creatures travel to the surface? "I've never been, no. None of us have. It's forbidden, not to mention impossible. I've only seen it in my visions." Visions of *him*. She'd wondered why she'd been gifted with glimpses of his life, but the answer had never come. Finally she'd stopped wondering and just accepted the fact that he was meant to be part of *her* life. They were connected.

He huffed out a moist breath. "Impossible how?"

"Just impossible," she hedged. "I admit I've always

dreamed of visiting the surface." She couldn't hide her edge of wistfulness. "You have so many fascinating things there."

"Yeah? Like what?" Fatigue was beginning to layer his words, making them drag slightly. "Exactly what does Prudence Merryweather find fascinating? This I've got to hear. Wait. The water is becoming more shallow," he said. "We're almost to shore. See if your feet touch."

Her legs sank toward the bottom until her feet hit a soft, mossy foundation. "Yes! I can touch." Limbs almost too weak to support her, she labored onto the sand, trudging step by step.

Finally she collapsed atop a soft bed of foliage. Water poured from her as she smoothed sopping hair out of her eyes. Gray dropped beside her. The ragged sound of their breathing blended with the gentle rush of the river. Gods, they had made it.

They had escaped the demons.

Several minutes passed in raw silence. She could have closed her eyes and drifted to sleep—*would* have drifted to sleep, if Gray hadn't picked up their conversation where they'd left off.

"What do you find fascinating about the surface?" He was only a little winded. "This land of yours is amazing. It's littered with evil incarnate, true, but the sheer beauty of the terrain is awe-inspiring."

She shivered as a wave of cool air brushed her. "I'd trade every flower and tree for the chance to sit inside a theater and watch a movie. To anchor myself in a hoodless car and soar down the road, the wind in my hair. To wiggle on a waterbed and smoke a cigarette. To taste a—"

"Whoa, there." He chuckled, the sound rich and smooth with his amusement. "Back it up a minute. Waterbed? You *live* in water, in case you hadn't noticed, and you think a waterbed is cool? And why the hell would you want to smoke a cigarette? They taste like a demon smells."

Her cheeks heated with a blush, and she was suddenly glad for the darkness. Gray hadn't thought cigarettes tasted so horrible the night she'd seen one of his women smoke one. He'd just finished making love to her, and the two had been lying on a waterbed, the sides lapping around their sweat-soaked limbs. The woman's pretty features had been totally relaxed, euphoric even, as the smoke wafted around her. Gray had appeared equally sated, not the least disgusted by the supposedly ashy fumes.

"I'm waiting for some type of explanation, Smoky Smokerson."

"People seem to enjoy them, that's all. And as for the waterbed, well, I'd like to know how it feels to lie on a bed of liquid and never sink."

"They're hell on the back."

"Who says I'd be sleeping?" she said primly.

He snorted, and she had to curb the urge to kick him. Did he think she couldn't tempt a man? That she couldn't seduce one into loving her body madly and passionately?

"My guess, *Prudence,* is that you'd be bundled up in a neck-to-ankle body stocking, complete with chastity belt and semiautomatic trained on any man stupid enough to try and get into your panties."

"That's not true! I'd have a lover with me. And we'd be naked," she added with a defensive edge.

"Would you now?" He drawled the words slowly, dragging out each syllable, making her feel achy inside. "And what would the two of you be doing, being naked and all?"

She knew Gray liked to linger over a woman's body, taking his time and learning every nuance, every scent. Gods knew how many times she'd seen him do it, wishing it were *her* he was pleasuring. She drew on that knowledge now, the only sensual knowledge she possessed.

Trying for a casual tone, she said, "I'd caress my hands over his chest and back, of course, while he kissed me. With tongue. His fingers would slide between my legs, sinking inside me, moving in and out while I arched my hips. And I'd be so, so wet. And when I screamed his name, begging him to fuck me—"

"Did you just drop the *F* bomb?" he asked, incredulous, cutting her off.

"Yes. He'd lick my breasts, sucking my nipples into his mouth, and impale me with his thick, hard penis. I would wrap my legs—"

"That's enough!" Gray's body couldn't take much more. He was rock hard and tense, ready to explode. Just from her words. When had *that* ever happened? He cleared his throat and flopped to his back. "Christ, I get the picture. And I'm seriously considering renaming you Blaze Champagne."

There, she thought smugly. Now he'd never again call her Prudence or assume she wouldn't know what to do with a man in bed. "What kind of name is Blaze Champagne?" She already knew the answer. She wanted him to say it, though, to hear the words aloud.

"The naughty kind reserved for porn stars, that's what. Fuck me, indeed."

A wide smile lifted her lips. "Have I offended your innocent ears? If so, you can just fuck off, *Mr. Monk*." Being naughty was more fun than she ever could have imagined. She hadn't felt so lighthearted in—ever.

"Jesus. Do you kiss your mother with that mouth?"

"My mother's dead." She said it simply, merely stating a fact.

"God, Jewel, I'm sorry." Contrite, he reached out and wrapped his fingers around her forearm, squeezing gently. The heat of his grip banished any lingering cold caused by the wind. "I never would have said that if I'd known."

"It happened so long ago, I barely remember her."

"Still, I shouldn't have said it and I'm sorry."

His hand left her, and she heard the zip of his bag, a rustle of movement, a crack—almost like glass breaking. A golden glow of light erupted, surrounding them in a luminescent halo. Gray held a long, thin tube, she saw, eyelids closing to half-mast to dim the bright rays.

"What is that?" The object fascinated her, as she'd never seen its like. It looked as if he were holding pure fire in his hands.

"It's got a technical name, but I just call it a glow stick." Gray's gaze met hers, and *he* claimed her fascination. The cloth he'd worn on his head had slipped off, so his pale hair was plastered to his scalp. Streaks of green and black paint remained on his cheeks, but most of it had washed away.

Droplets of water trickled from his forehead to his nose, then onto the leaves. His lashes were black and spiky, his eyes a liquid silver, as mesmerizing as the water itself. Her gaze devoured him.

He smoothed away a dark strand of hair from her cheek. His fingers were callused but, oh, so gentle. The night air should have made her miserable by this point, but the chill barely touched her wet body. A growing sense of warmth and lassitude wove through her, starting exactly where he'd touched her.

As he studied her, his lips dipped into a frown. "Have we met before? I mean, sometimes when I look at you, I'd swear I've seen you before."

She'd dreamed of just such a circumstance, of meeting him; she'd wanted it, craved it, but the answer was an unequivocal no. "I promise you, we have never met in person until this night."

"Still." He shrugged away the mystery. "Be honest. Are you really all right?"

"Yes. Promise. How do *you* feel?" She longed to reach out and trace her fingers over his face.

Had the poisons begun weakening him yet?

The question popped into her mind, reminding her that they had not yet escaped all danger. Had the demon and vampire poison already begun to interweave, clashing together, fighting for dominance? Destroying Gray little by little?

Nausea churned in her stomach, rising to fill her throat. She could *not* let this wonderfully alive man die. There had to be a way…something to do…but at the moment, no miraculous answer came to her.

Arms stretching over his head, he twisted each vertebra of his spine. "I'm good to go. Stronger than ever."

He *did* look healthy and capable, his skin bright with color, his eyes sparkling. Maybe the venoms wouldn't affect him, she thought hopefully. Maybe she worried for nothing.

"Come on," he said. "We've hung around here too long. We need shelter ASAP."

He pushed to his feet with the agility of a jungle cat and readjusted his bag over his shoulder, one hand continuing to keep the glow stick elevated, lighting the surrounding area.

She, too, pushed up, her movements a bit slower and less sprightly than his. As she shifted her weight to her feet, her knees shook. Dizziness struck her, and she massaged her fingertips into her temple.

Gray wrapped his arm around her waist, holding her up. "Lean on me."

"I'll be fine," she said, stepping from him. Gods, he'd felt so good, but she would not be a hindrance. He'd had enough of those in his life. At last her vision cleared, and she said, "I can lead us to shelter. Follow me."

"With pleasure. Your robe is sticking to your skin, so I can see the outline of your a—"

"Gray!"

He chuckled.

"Your gaze better remain straight ahead."

"Ah, come on. Cage Prudence, and let Blaze come out and play."

Smothering a laugh, Jewel moved in front of him, her hands covering the object in question. "We'll need to stay along the river's edge."

"Take your time. I'll just be enjoying the view. Your fingers don't hide anything, baby."

"Incorrigible," she muttered with a falsely grim shake of her head. He wasn't like this with everyone, only his family and coworkers. For everyone else, even his women, he usually presented a gruff, take-no-prisoners persona. The fact that he favored her enough to tease her delighted her. "This way."

Time passed in agonizing slowness as they maneuvered through trees, bushes and thick, wet sand. Knowing Marina would expect her to avoid civilization, Jewel led them toward the Inner City.

The breeze soon dried her clothes, making the material stiff, unbending. But at least they weren't sticking to her bottom! Insects were eerily silent, and night prowlers stayed away.

"Jewel," Gray said softly, suddenly. "Something's wrong with me."

She glanced at him over her shoulder, then stopped abruptly. His eyes had lost their teasing light, and now blazed with pain, the lids lowering slowly, then snapping wide open as he struggled to remain awake. His normally bronzed skin was pale and pallid, with a greenish tint. Sweat dripped from him.

It had begun.

Intense fear raking her, she said, "We're almost there. Focus on me, on my voice, and I'll lead us to safety."

A wave of dizziness must have hit him because he swayed on his feet. He closed his eyes and pressed his fingers into his temples. "What's wrong with me?" His voice emerged as weak and unsteady as his legs.

She didn't answer, but she did race to him. He was so tall, the top of her head barely brushed over his shoulder, but she wrapped a supporting arm around him, opening her mind to his. The wall she'd encountered inside the demon fortress was still gone, and his thoughts instantly slammed into her. *The pain. Can't give in to the pain. Must get Jewel to safety.*

The vampire and demon poisons battled inside him, and she knew his blood heated to a boil. His limbs ached with the sting of a thousand needles. His head throbbed and pulsed like a war drum.

"Lean on me," she coaxed.

"No. No help." He tried to tug from her clasp, but didn't have the strength. His arms fell weakly to his sides, the tube of light stretching its rays across the twig-laden ground. "I…can do…it on my own."

She knew multiple betrayals at his job had conditioned him to rely on no one. One partner had abandoned him, another tried to kill him. Another had left him behind to save himself. In his weakened condition, that ingrained, self-reliant instinct surfaced with renewed force. She knew that, and was determined to destroy it.

"Gray," she said softly, gently. With her free hand, she claimed the glow stick and held it up, encompassing them in golden brilliance once again.

He didn't speak. Lines of tension bracketed his face. She sensed the panic growing inside him, heard his thoughts of, *Don't fall. Don't fall. Get Jewel to safety,* and tightened her hold on him.

"Gray," she repeated firmly. "The only way to get me to safety is to let me help you. Lean on me." Using all of her strength, she stepped forward. "Now walk."

He gave no indication he'd heard her until he moved forward, carefully placing one foot in front of the other. Always beside him, Jewel absorbed most of his weight. Her limbs and back soon burned from the strain. All the while, she retained a steady, albeit one-sided, conversation, hoping her voice would keep him awake. If he were to fall into slumber… She shuddered at the thought.

"I only have one memory of my father, and that was the first and only time I met him. I remember how big and strong he was, how his shoulders dwarfed me when he drew me to him for a hug. I didn't get to spend much time with him, probably five minutes. When he released me, he waved goodbye and my mother carried me away. I didn't know it was the last time I'd see him. My mother was killed soon afterward, and I was all alone." Panting now, she continued her monologue. "All I've ever wanted to do is find my father again. Well, that and—" She fumbled, realizing she couldn't admit she'd wanted *him.* Gray.

A grove of white trees filled her line of vision, and she ground to a halt, drawing in a shocked breath. "We're here." She hadn't expected to reach the alcove so soon. At her side, a waterfall crashed into the river, falling from a towering cliff.

Gray moaned. His shoulders were slumped, and his breathing shallow. Though they were headed toward the Inner City, they were closer to the Outer. Noises reached them, footsteps and conversations blending with the rush of the water. Scents of freshly baked bread and dewy fruits wafted on the breeze.

"Five more steps and you can rest, Gray."

"Rest," he repeated, the very word brought forth on another moan of pain. He shook his head. "No rest! Protect Jewel."

"We're safe here. I'm safe," she promised, urging him forward, toward the secluded glen. When they finally reached it, Jewel eased Gray to the ground. He collapsed onto the bed of leaves with a grunt.

Few creatures dared enter this area. The Forest of Dragons belonged to Darius en Kragin, Dragon King and Guardian of the Atlantean Mists. Fierce, blood-thirsty warlord that he was, only the most desperate of people tempted him to anger by trespassing.

"I'll take care of you," she said. "Don't worry." She dug her satchel out of Gray's bag, amazed that the contents inside were completely dry, and withdrew her robe. After ripping several strips, she strode to the river edge and soaked them in the pink sand.

Thankfully she no longer needed the glow stick. Above them, the crystal globe approached its dawn cycle and swept thin, golden fingers of light over the forest.

Cloth heavy with the healing sand, she hurried back to Gray and wrapped it around his arm wound. He didn't make a sound. He didn't move. Her fear and apprehension grew, and she fought against a sting of tears. He'd saved her life, only to die himself? No. *No!*

This was her fault. She had guided him to her, had convinced him to rescue her. She *had* to save him.

But he looked so pale, so near death…. She pressed her lips together to cut off a sob of terror. *He's stubborn,* she reminded herself. When he accepted a mission, he succeeded. Always. Whatever the cost. Whatever the consequence.

"You have to beat the poison, Gray, or your mission will fail. Do you want to be a failure?" She shouted the last, desperate for him to hear her.

No response.

"Do you want to be a failure?" she repeated brokenly, shaking him this time.

Not even a flutter of his eyelids.

With a growl, she ripped two more strips from her robe, filled them with sand, and used them to bind the bite on his neck. The vampire cut on his thigh had opened and now oozed a thick, black blood. She bound that with sand, too, fighting back a rising sense of hysteria.

She couldn't lose him. He was a part of her, had always been a part of her. But what more could she do to help him?

She watched the slow, shallow rise and fall of his chest. She possessed so many gifts, that of knowing truth from lie, the ability to sometimes see the future, the ability to read minds, and yet none of those could help Gray.

Her eyes widened in horror as he gasped for air—then stopped breathing altogether.

# CHAPTER SIX

WHAT THE HELL was happening to him?

The panicked thought tumbled through Gray's mind with dizzying speed. He tried to search his surroundings, but he couldn't open his eyes. He couldn't fucking open his eyes.

The knowledge hit him, and his body jerked; his lungs seized. Sharp needle-pricks stung his chest, and he realized he didn't even have the strength to draw in a single molecule of air. My God, he was going to die.

Every survival instinct he possessed screamed for him to fight, to take action. To do something. Anything. All he needed was one breath. As seconds passed and he didn't get it, the lack seared him with fire. The flames ate at him, consuming him. Devouring him. Colors flashed through his head, so many colors, all too bright in their intensity.

But with the colors came calm. Not acceptance, never that, but a sense of knowing his pain would vanish completely if he sank into the never-ending void of darkness that awaited him, beckoning. How beguiling the void was, like the last cold beer in the Sahara.

A part of him longed to simply fall into the peaceful

abyss. The other part, the part that refused to be a failure…failure—was that Jewel's voice he heard? He fought to reach her, grinding his teeth together, clenching his muscles, and squeezing his hands into fists.

Where was she? He needed to ensure her safety.

Hissing voices and grunts of fury suddenly echoed in his ears, claiming his focus; his own death dripped from each timbre, the evil sounds chilling his every cell. And with the sounds, a need to taste blood, warm and living blood, grew inside him. He yearned to drink sweet, crimson nectar from someone's throat. Yes, he needed to, would die if he didn't.

What the hell was happening to him? Around him? Inside him? His eyelids remained heavy, too heavy to open and look. He heard the clang of…swords? Claws? The louder the intonations became, the weaker he became. His chest constricted, making him all the more aware he needed to breathe but couldn't.

"Gray." The gentle beseeching drifted above the chaos encompassing him, drowning out the horrifying battle sounds. "Gray."

Jewel.

He recognized her sexy accent. She seemed closer than before. Reachable. The need for tasting blood abandoned him, replaced by a need to see Jewel. With every ounce of strength he possessed, he finally managed to pry open his eyelids—no, not his eyelids, but his mental eye—the very act more excruciating than taking a bullet.

In a flash of white light, Jewel materialized.

Dark walls surrounded her, and he realized they weren't in the forest. They were in some sort of shadow land.

"Your mind," she said. "We're inside your mind."

He saw her float toward him, her hips swaying seductively. Her sheer white robe whispered around her ankles, a vivid contrast to the silky black hair cascading down her back. She looked like an angel.

Her rose-petal lips eased into a sweet smile. "Gray," she said again. "Breathe with me."

*Can't,* he wanted to tell her. His mouth refused to obey.

"Breathe with me," she repeated, the command sharp. "In. Out. Open your mouth. In. Out."

Never had anything been so impossible. The paralysis affected both mind and body, leaving him completely frozen.

"Perhaps there is another way, the way you helped me in the water." Jewel closed the remaining distance between them, crouched down, and pried his mouth open with her fingers. She fit her soft, soft lips over his. Her hair hung like a curtain around them as she blew her very essence into his mouth. The sweetness of her breath seeped down his throat and little by little, his lungs accepted the offering.

The fragrance of sea-storms and magic wafted to his nostrils. Jewel's scent. So lovely. So necessary.

"In. Out. In," she said when he began breathing on his own. "You're doing wonderfully."

With her face hovering over his, his lips tingling from the touch of hers, he couldn't help but remember

how turned on he'd been when she'd talked about
having sex on a waterbed—how he'd wanted to be the
man doing those naughty things to her, touching
between her thighs, sinking his fingers into her hot, wet
sheath. Bringing her to climax while she shouted his
name.

Two hissing black plum clouds flew past his
shoulder and slammed into the far wall of his mind. The
moment they hit, Gray's body jerked, his muscles
spasming. The little bit of air he'd managed to draw in
evaporated, and darkness once again crept insidious
fingers around him. Images of Jewel faded.

"What's happening?" he croaked.

"Don't worry about that right now." She smoothed
a gentle hand over his brow. "Concentrate on me."

*Yes,* Gray thought. *Jewel. Think only of Jewel.* His
gaze met hers, silver against fathomless blue, and he
was overwhelmed by a compulsion to do whatever she
asked. She was his lifeline.

Behind her, in an obsidian swirl of sulfur and blood-
scented evil, the dark clouds whirled and gelled until
two separate creatures formed, circling each other. One
vampire—fangs elongated, saliva dripping from its
mouth. One demon—claws sharpened, eyes glowing
bright red.

Shock chilled him from head to toe.

The two creatures leapt at each other, oblivious to
everything except the other's destruction. As they
sliced, bit and kicked, it was *Gray* who experienced
pain. Gray who felt the sting of each blow.

Their combating forms maneuvered toward Jewel,

and for a long, protracted moment, she was wrapped in a cloak of malfeasance, shielding her from his view. When Gray lost sight of her beautiful face, his body cramped horrendously. Sharp. Like knives slicing him. He fought against the pain, determined to save Jewel.

Growling low in his throat, pushing past his injuries, he leapt to his feet and attacked full force. He used the only weapons he currently possessed—his fists and legs. But each time he punched or kicked, the cloud darted away with a violent, taunting laugh.

"Step away from them," Jewel commanded.

"Get out of here." As the battling pair whizzed past him, he jumped onto the demon's back, wrapping the winged creature in a chokehold.

"Gray," she shouted, frantic. "You cannot beat them alone, but I can do nothing while you are in the middle of them. Let me help you."

The demon threw him off. Gray immediately sprang up and launched himself atop the vampire, ripping at its throat. All the while teeth and nails sliced at his back. His breath grew ragged, unsteady. Any moment, he would lose the ability to inhale again. His limbs shook with increasing lethargy. He'd spent his entire life protecting those weaker than himself, first prowling the streets of Dallas as a police officer, then as a detective, then stalking other worlds as an OBI agent.

He wouldn't stop now. He'd kill these hell-bound bastards if he had to die to do so.

"Please," Jewel cried, the sound distant. "Please step away from them, and let me help you."

Her desperation and fear penetrated his killing rage,

but he refused to do as she asked. If he released the creatures, they might attack her and that he would not allow. Not knowing what else to do, he used the last of his mental strength to shove her out of his mind.

He would not risk her.

"Leave. Now!" he shouted.

A burst of white light erupted, and she disappeared.

A hint of sadness lingered where she'd been, making his chest constrict. His deepest male instincts wanted only her happiness. Wanted to grant her every wish. But if her wishes put her in danger, he'd refuse her every time.

Using his distraction to their advantage, the creatures closed over him, cutting at him, drawing blood.

ABRUPTLY JEWEL JOLTED UPRIGHT.

Panic thundered inside her, panic she could not subdue. Gray had actually shoved her from his mind, and she'd been unable to maintain her hold. Right now his physical body lay at her side, jerking every few seconds as the creatures ravaged him.

The golden stick still glowed, chasing away lingering hints of night's shadows. As she forced her heartbeat to slow, she studied him. His skin carried the greenish hue of sickness, and several cuts on his face and chest bled profusely. Bruises curved under his eyes.

How much longer he had, she didn't know. Not long, though.

The dire warning echoed through her. *Not long.*

Hand shaky, she reached out, wrapping her fingers around his wrist. His skin was cold, his pulse weak.

Before her eyes, a cut appeared on his forehead, slashing from brow to hairline. Every wound he received internally appeared externally.

All her life, he'd been her anchor and her only source of happiness. Watching his life unfold had been her greatest joy. If she had any hope of helping him, she had to find a way back inside his mind.

*Think, Jewel. Think.* How could she slip past his mental shield?

There was no magical answer, really, she realized a moment later. She'd just have to try harder, to force her way back inside, through the one method guaranteed to get his attention.

Jewel drew in a deep breath and as she released it, she eased herself on top of him, her legs straddling his waist. She tangled her fingers in Gray's pale, silky hair, and the pulse at the base of his neck leapt. He sensed her touch!

She closed her eyes and dragged in another breath. The air boasted summer scents, dewy foliage and blooming flowers. Mocking, all. Very slowly, she lowered her head until her lips met his. Her tongue pushed past his teeth and into his mouth. His masculine flavor consumed her senses, caused her blood to heat, her thighs to ache.

His nostrils flared, his mouth widened, and he kissed her back.

As their tastes blended, her sense of awareness traveled into Gray like a storm cloud moving from one city to another. Physically, her hands and feet grew cold, her stomach numb. Spiritually, she grew warmer.

On a soft, almost glowing exhale, her conscious mind abandoned her body completely. On a strong, forced inhale, it entered Gray's.

Jewel swept into his mind for the second time, tearing at the barrier piece by piece. Her eyes widened as she watched his essence combat the creatures. He was noticeably weak, his punches and kicks ineffective as he swayed on his feet.

"Gray." She had to get him away from the combatants.

He spun around, facing her. "Jewel." His gaze narrowed. "Leave. Before they come after you."

"Come here," she said, using her most seductive voice.

"I told you to leave, woman!"

"Come here." She licked her lips, mimicking an action the women of his world used to draw a man's attention. "I want to kiss you."

"Now is not the time." He shook his head and—reluctantly—turned back to the dark fog, slapping at it with his fists.

"Kiss me. Now is the perfect time." If he wouldn't come to her, she would go to him, hopefully forcing him to meet her halfway to keep her from the action. One step, two. "I thought your philosophy was anytime, anywhere. And right now I want your tongue in my mouth."

Something hungry and hot flickered over his expression. Something cold and hard at the same time. Then the creatures swirled and laughed around him like naughty children, and he kicked out his legs. He missed, earning another laugh from his enemies.

"You're in danger here," he growled to her. He sounded stronger, more like himself.

"My nipples are hard just thinking about our kiss. There's an ache between my legs, and I *need* to feel you there, touching me."

For a moment he stopped fighting and turned his back on the fog, leveling her with a hot gaze that traveled the length of her body, lingering on her breasts, on the juncture between her thighs.

He took a step toward her, then stopped himself. "No. No." With a growl, he spun back to the battling vampire and demon, tendrils of their darkness wrapping around him. He swung out his arms and slammed his fist into the demon's face.

The creature flew at him, tossing him backward, chomping for his throat. Jewel gasped and almost fell to her knees in fear. Thankfully the vampire launched himself into the demon, rolling him away from Gray. Saving Gray's life.

"Soldier," she called desperately. "I command you to kiss me."

Former military, the urge to follow a commanding officer's commands was ingrained. Her tone gave him pause, and he shook his head, as if trying to clear his thoughts, to focus. He stood. The fight continued around him.

"Everything feels surreal." He massaged his temples. "Illogical and out of sync."

"I can make it better. You just have to trust me."

He grimaced and grabbed his side, hunching over, suddenly gasping for air. "It's almost like…I'm viewing a Dali painting where the world…of reality melts and turns inward on itself. What's real? What isn't?"

"I'm real. Touch me and see."

"I want to, God, I want to, but I can't," he said raggedly. "I can't. Must…stop them. I'm an OBI employee and I will…fight to protect you."

She curbed the urge to cover her face and cry. His protective instincts were buried so deep, she might never breach them. If so, he would die. Desperation clamped sharp claws around her, cutting deep. Her eyes narrowed. He could resist her promise of a kiss, but could he resist a naked female form?

She quickly untied the shoulder straps of her robe. The material fell to her waist, revealing her breasts, her beaded nipples, and the flat plane of her stomach.

Gray's eyes widened. "You're flashing me. You're seriously flashing me."

"Touch me."

"No, I'm an OBI employee and I will fight to protect you. I'm an OBI employee and I will—stare at the most beautiful pair of breasts I've ever seen." He shook his head, but his gaze remained locked on her. "I'm an OBI—your breasts will fit perfectly in my hands."

Her skin warmed. "Why don't you make certain?"

He slowly closed the distance separating them, limping the entire way but never stopping. When he was in front of her, his arms reaching out to caress her breasts, Jewel shivered with anticipation. She wanted so badly to accept his touch, but she couldn't. Not yet.

And so, she did something she never thought she'd do. She hooked her leg around Gray's knee and shoved him, hard. Weakened already, he fell, his expression shocked as he landed. He winced, staying on the ground, trying to orient himself.

With Gray out of the way, she closed her eyes and raised her hands, willing the creatures to slow. Battle sounds receded, the air around her thickened and ceased all movement until there was only utter stillness.

Her eyelids fluttered open, an astonishing scene greeting her. The demon and vampire continued to war with each other, yes, but they moved in slow motion, their every action sluggish. A drop of black blood trickled from the demon and splashed onto the floor. She saw every inch of movement.

"Now, Gray," she shouted. "Kill them now." She was afraid to move her arms and help him up, afraid the creatures would leap back into lightning speed.

Gray rose determinedly, albeit shakily, to his feet. He rubbed a hand over his eyes in an attempt to clear his vision before he hobbled to the creatures. Then, with a deft, ingrained ability, he attacked. The creatures hissed and bit at him, even drawing more blood, but he fought, snapping both their necks and dropping their bodies.

He stood there, panting, his wounds open and bleeding.

Wave after wave of relief and joy swept through her. "You did it," she said, awed, her hands dropping to her sides.

"No, *we* did it."

Her lips lifted in a grin, and a sudden flash of desire filled his eyes—eyes that were staring at her chest. Her own desire sparked to life—it had never really died—and she gasped, realizing her breasts were still on display.

"If I'm remembering correctly," he continued, stronger by the second, "you promised me a kiss before dropping me on my ass."

She ached erotically at the thought of his lips on hers. Of his hands moving over her. Perhaps rolling her nipples between his fingers. "You're not too weak?"

"For a kiss? Never." He stalked three slow steps toward her. "Are you too weak?"

"Of course not."

He chuckled at her affront. His skin color was growing rosier, more bronzed. "You once said humans demand proof in everything. Well, you were right. Prove it. Prove you're strong enough to handle me."

She gulped, not knowing where to begin. By touching him? Tasting him? Perhaps both? Her words might have been bold today, but she'd never been with a man before. Her fingers itched to move all over him. Her mouth watered, yearning to lick every inch of him.

"Are you going to kiss me or not?"

"I don't know where to begin," she admitted.

His liquid silver eyes radiated the very hunger that rocked her. His head lowered. "We'll start here," he said, tracing his fingertips over the seam of her lips, "and work our way down." Two of his fingers circled her nipples, making them harden all the more.

Her lips parted on a gasp of sheer pleasure.

And then he was there, his arms locked around her waist, his lips meshing into hers. Because her mouth was open, he easily swept his tongue inside. He tasted of heat and man and the flavor intoxicated her. She liquefied against him, his shirt deliciously abrading her chest, his touch fueling her dreams. Forging her fantasies.

"Kiss me back," he muttered.

"I don't know how. Exactly." She whispered the confession, unable to look at him. She'd seen kisses, but never experienced one herself.

He pulled slightly away, tilted her chin up, and stared into her eyes. Possessiveness radiated from him. "Just move your tongue against mine. Suck on it. Lick it."

Erotic shivers danced through her. The image his words elicited was heady, enthralling. Moistening her lips, she dropped her gaze to his mouth. "I'm ready."

"You sure?" He uttered a strained chuckle before softly brushing a kiss against the tip of her nose, her chin, the edge of her mouth. Each touch scorched her, weaving a seductive web in her mind.

"Let me have your tongue again," she said, desperate. Achy. Needy. "I want to suck it, just like you said."

"God, I like an eager student." He complied and once more his tongue swept into her mouth.

She moaned at the first touch. His erection rubbed between her legs, thick and hard. She wanted him; she'd always wanted him. He'd become an obsession over the years and now his very closeness wrapped her in a cloak of sensuality.

As their tongues danced and sparred, she arched

against him. He kissed her as if he was completely absorbed in her, as if nothing else mattered but holding her and giving her pleasure. His hands found her breasts and kneaded them. Pure heat lanced to her deepest core. Her blood electrified. How she longed to shout her love for him, but too easily did she recall his reaction when surface women had done that. He hadn't been able to get away fast enough.

"See. They do fill my hands."

"Take off your clothes," she whispered. "I want to feel your skin against mine."

This time, *he* moaned. Her desire became more intense, drowning her with sensations sweeter than the richest honey. Then...

His thoughts filled her mind. *I want her. God, I want her. She tastes so damn good. I need her. I— What the hell are you doing, James? She's not for you. Push her away. Push her away. She's dangerous.*

Jewel jerked from his clasp, her breath ragged. The words *she's not for you, push her away* echoed in her head. Hurt, she covered her swollen, moist lips with her hand, then quickly tied her robe, shielding her nakedness. Gray's pending rejection stung and battered her pride. If they'd been flesh and blood just then, she might have slapped him—or kneed his precious General Happy.

So many times she'd watched him kiss other women. He'd never pulled away—never thought to pull away. He'd always lingered and savored, moving slowly, prolonging the pleasure for as long as possible.

Why could he not be the same with her? Why?

His hands gripped her forearms, his breath just as

ragged as hers. "Why did you stop? I'm not done with you."

So he wouldn't see her hurt expression, she turned away from him. "You will live now, Gray. Your body has already begun healing. It's time for me to leave this place."

Silence.

Silence so heavy it weighed upon her shoulders. No protest, no begging her to fall back in his arms. Why did she have to love this man? Why did he have to mean so much to her, when she obviously meant so little to him? He thought her dangerous, of all things. As if she would ever hurt him.

"My God," he gasped, releasing her completely and stumbling back.

There was such horror in his tone, she whipped around, gaze dragging over him. "What's wrong?"

His eyes were wide, the lines around his mouth taut. "I can read your mind."

## CHAPTER SEVEN

MARINA, QUEEN OF THE DEMONS, studied the vast expanse of the forest, her extraordinary gaze cutting through thick foliage and mounds of dirt and rocks. Flames from her army's crackling fire illuminated the surrounding trees, casting shadows and light in every direction. Smoke billowed toward the skydome, a curling, scented stream of ash. Frustration gnawed at her with the determination and frenzy of a hungry beast.

The murdering human was nowhere to be seen. More important, her favorite slave was nowhere to be seen.

"Damn this," she growled, hands tightening into fists, sharp claws biting into her skin.

Calling a halt to the search and commanding her army to make camp here had not been easy. Not when she was desperate to regain possession of the girl. Yet with every minute that passed, Marina lost more and more of the girl's scent. Morning was due to arrive at any moment, and while the harsh rays of dawn would not kill her, her people hunted best in the dark, their eyes too sensitive for the day.

Now she would have to wait, and the knowledge curled her lips in a scowl. Where was the slave? Where had the human hidden her? Humans. How she loathed them. The gods used to amuse themselves by sending some to Atlantis and watching the ensuing chaos. But one human should not have been able to steal her slave.

*Where were they?*

Would the pair beg protection from another race? she wondered, but discarded the idea almost instantly. Her slave always lauded the merits of freedom and would not risk enslavement from another kingdom. Easily recognized as she was, she would have to avoid the cities.

Which was why Marina was so far from the city. Her gaze continued to search, but she saw nothing out of the ordinary. She uttered a low snarl in the back of her throat, the sound of it reverberating throughout her entire body. Where were they?

A gentle, metallic breeze kissed the back of her neck and Marina whipped around, knowing her solitude had just been interrupted. Her eyes narrowed at the handsome intruder standing before her.

"Hello, Marina." The silky male voice floated across the short distance.

"What do you here, Layel?" The question emerged on an angry growl. Had this been one of her men, she would have struck him down instead of demanding an answer.

The vampire king lifted his dark brows, giving them a dangerously seductive slant. "That is no way to welcome an old friend."

Old friend? Ha. "You didn't answer my question." As she spoke, her claws elongated, preparing to strike. Why *not* strike him down? While the demons and vampires were not enemies, they were not friends, either. And she'd wanted to destroy this smug, haughty bloodsucker for many years. Every time she looked at him, she was reminded of the time she had begged him to love her—and he had denied her.

How dare he approach her now? He deserved pain, and she would be the one to give it to him. Vampires were fast, unnaturally fast. She'd have to take him by surprise. As she slowly inched toward him, her gaze drank him in. He was tall and lithe, a creature who radiated power and sex. A lethal combination. Many an Atlantean queen, no matter her race, had fallen prey to his deadly charms. He possessed pale skin, perfectly sculpted features, and crystalline eyes that usually revealed only mocking amusement. At the moment, he was as still as a night stalker.

"You are not welcome here," she drawled, claiming another inch closer.

"Of course I am." He chuckled, the sound rich and husky in the night. "This is *my* hunting field."

She stilled. Only her gaze moved as she reassessed the milieu. The trees were taller than those on her own land. Lusher. Greener. The sweet scent of ash and sulfur so prevalent to her kind *did* fragrance the air, but underneath it was the scent of flowering blooms and sea salt.

It *was* his land, which meant the vampire's own army skulked nearby, hidden and silent. Waiting.

Her claws retracted into her nailbeds, and she scowled. How had she missed them? Another failure on her part, obviously. Her scowl deepened. She might be able to kill Layel right now, but she wouldn't live long enough to gloat; no, his army would emerge from their hiding place and attack and slaughter.

"Well?" Layel prompted, his eyes narrowed. Instead of menacing, the expression made him appear all the more sensual, all the more erotic.

"I'm looking for a human," she finally said. "A man. Have you seen him?"

Layel grinned. "The human who decimated half of your palace and decapitated several of your guards?"

She gritted her teeth at the reminder. She didn't understand how one man, a human at that, had wreaked such desolation. All she knew was that she would not rest until she caught him. And when she captured that human bastard, she would feast off his body for days, prolonging his suffering and enjoying every moment of it.

"How do you know of his actions?" she demanded, her voice so sharp it could have cut glass.

"Word travels fast here. *That,* you should know."

A movement to her right caught her attention, and Marina remained silent as one of her sentinels glided toward her. The demon camp behind him buzzed with activity. Pitching tents. Sharpening weapons. Consuming dinner—a satisfactory array of squealing pigs.

The guard, a handsome male with a profusion of horns on his arms and legs, and long raven hair that cascaded down his back, held a goblet in each hand. He offered the first to Marina, then presented the second to Layel with an alluring smile. Her jaw twitched. Even her males were susceptible to the vampire.

"I saw you here and thought you might be thirsty," he said, his words for Marina, but his gaze remaining on Layel.

"Do not come this way again," she snapped. "Remain at camp or it will be *you* the army has for dessert."

Expression panicked, the demon rushed to obey, the long length of his wings flapping erratically. Leaves and twigs floated and danced in his wake, before dropping back onto the dirt.

Alone with the king once again, she gripped her goblet, watching him over the rim, studying him, considering. He was so pale, so exotic. She sipped the rich, crimson liquid, wishing the animal blood were sweeter, warmer. His.

"Darius en Kragin has a new bride," she said, leaning against the rough bark of a tree trunk. The tips of her horns pierced the top layer. An idea began to form in her mind, overshadowing her desire to destroy the king. For now.

Layel arched a dark brow. "I know. I have seen her."

"Then you know she is human."

"Of course." He drained his goblet, his gaze never leaving hers, and unceremoniously dropped the cup. He slowly closed what little distance there was between them, gliding over the dirt and limbs in his path. When he was just within reach, he stopped, his cool breath caressing her cheek. "What does she have to do with the human male? Why do you even mention her?"

A single drop of blood trickled from his lips. She leaned forward and captured the droplet with her fingertip. Then she licked away the drop with relish.

Perhaps she and Layel could help each other. For the time being.

Yes, she thought, a wave of giddiness destroying her sense of failure. It would be perfect. Together, they would be all-powerful. Together, they could destroy anything. Destroy anyone.

She dropped her cup to the ground, letting it clatter against his. Instead of answering his questions, she asked him one of her own. "What do you know of a portal that leads from Atlantis to the surface world?"

He laughed, his husky amusement irritating her. She scowled. Marina was not a woman to be mocked.

"The gods would not be foolish enough to give us a doorway to their precious surface kingdom," he said. "They hate us. They want us to remain here, forgotten."

"Of course they would erect a doorway to the surface. If there is a way in, there has to be a way out."

"True, but a doorway would place the human world in danger, and... No, the gods would never do such a thing." His words dismissed her, as did his tone.

"Then how did Darius bring his human bride here? She was not sent by the gods. My spies claim Darius left Atlantis and brought her here."

Layel frowned and stroked two fingers over his jaw as he considered her. "The portal is not for your use, Marina."

She jerked her chin up. "So you know it's there? You know it exists, and yet you tried to pretend it does not?"

He gave a negligent shrug. "I know everything. And yes."

"You are not the Jewel of Dunamis," she said, her eyes slitting. "You cannot possibly know everything."

"Ah, Dunamis." He dragged out each syllable as if they were a caress to his senses. "A thing no longer yours to command," he said with a smirk.

The razor-sharp points of her teeth gnashed together. Every sovereign in the land had owned the jewel at some time or another, and Marina had possessed it all too shortly. "I will get it back, I assure you."

His wide shoulders lifted in another shrug. "I do not have to be Dunamis to know that the portal brings only death to Atlanteans. If you enter, the gods will kill you."

"Darius survived. Besides, the gods do not care what we do. They will not harm me, I assure you." She paused, a heavy silence encompassing her as Layel's warning echoed through her mind. Even the sounds of the demon camp and the idle chatter of her men drained away. She might sound assured, but she did not feel that way.

What if the vampire was right? The gods had ignored them for so long, had made their preference for the mortals so clear...

No. No. She wouldn't let the *possibility* of their anger affect her decision.

"I do not like that you have known about the portal and never thought to tell me," she said with deceptive calm, traipsing her finger over the seam of her lips.

"Perhaps it amused me to think of your ignorance."

"Are you frightened of the gods, Layel?" She smiled slowly. Innocently. Mockingly. "Do you fear their wrath? You must, you poor, poor baby. Otherwise, you would have used the portal to find yourself another human bride."

Though his expression remained neutral, impassive, and still revealed not a hint of his emotions, his teeth elongated and sharpened. He must be furious, she thought with a smug inner grin, for the man did not like to be reminded of the woman he had loved and lost.

"Best you watch your tongue, demon," he said softly. "Before you lose it."

Her head canted to the side, her own teeth lengthening. "Best you recall whom you are threatening."

The blue of his eyes sparked with flecks of red. "You do not want a war between our people, and you are very close to beginning one."

Marina dragged in a frustrated breath. If she wasn't careful, he would leave, and she would be forced to find her slave on her own. Forced to battle Darius and his dragon army alone, because she wanted control of the portal. Badly. And she would do anything to ensure it.

If only she still possessed Dunamis, she would not need Layel or anyone else. She would know exactly what battle plan would work, would know exactly what her enemy planned.

Oh, how she cursed the jewel's loss!

She did not like this feeling of helplessness. She liked even less the necessity of catering to another creature—especially the seductive and enigmatic Layel.

"We both know you hate Darius," she said, padding

a few steps away from him. His closeness unnerved her. She watched as trees swayed against the breeze to hopefully cover her weakness. "He killed your lover, and you have never had revenge."

Layel didn't answer for a long while. When he did, her gaze was drawn back to him and she saw that his features were blank, revealing no emotion. His voice was thick with dry amusement. "Such subtlety warms my heart. Truly it does."

"You do not have a heart."

"True," he said, his amusement richer. "Tell me something. Why do you wish to travel to the surface? You are a queen, and you possess everything you could ever wish."

"Are you truly so foolish you do not know?"

When he made no reply, she added, "Think of it. On the surface, *we* will be the gods. Not kings and queens, but gods who are worshipped and revered. Humans will be forced to obey our every command and we will drink from their bodies anytime we desire, no longer reliant on animals to sustain us."

"You would risk the gods' wrath for dessert?" He tsked under his tongue. "Silly demon. Can *you* truly be so foolish?"

As the sound of his renewed amusement echoed from the forest, her irritation with him intensified. Bastard. Could he not see the rightness of her fantasy? They'd been hidden their entire lives, considered unworthy. It was past time they proved the extent of their prowess. "You know as well as I that there is nothing sweeter than human blood."

"I have done without for so long, I hardly remember the taste."

She tried another line of persuasion. "Have you ever longed to fly until you see nothing but heaven? I have. Here, we never reach anything but crystal and water. I crave freedom, Layel. True freedom." Never mind she repeated the same words her slave girl always gave her. This was different. This was *her* desire.

Several moments dragged by in silence. Layel liked doing that, liked making her wait for his response. Patience was not part of her nature, and waiting now, when the matter held such importance, proved impossible. "On the surface, you can seduce a thousand human women if that is your desire. You can find another human to love," she added on a whispery catch of breath.

His lips dipped into a wistful frown, giving his features a lethal kind of beauty. In that moment, she knew that she had him. Knew that he would help her in any way necessary.

With a conscious effort, she kept the blaze of triumph from her expression. "Together, we can control the portal. Together," she added, "we can destroy Darius and his army and get inside his palace. That is where the portal resides, isn't it?"

He nodded, one slow decline of his chin.

"Fire kills you. My demons are impervious to it. And your vampires can do things we cannot. Darius will never be able to fight both our armies at the same time."

Utter silence reigned for several long moments. How many times would he do this to her?

Her fists clenched.

"Very well," he said smoothly, as if he hadn't kept her waiting again. He gave another nod. "I will help you."

"You will not regret this decision." That was the truth, for a dead man could not regret anything. Once Layel no longer proved useful... She grinned, happier than she'd been in years. "From this day forward, let it be known vampires and demons are allies."

His lips pursed in disgust, but he didn't deny her words. "My spies saw the human male and a female slave headed for Javar's palace."

She crossed her arms over her chest. "The former dragon king is dead. His palace is empty. Why go there?"

"If there is a portal at Darius's palace, doesn't it stand to reason that there is one at Javar's, as well? The human will want to travel through it. You can kill him and we can take the first and easiest portal, then worry about the other."

Her eyes widened. "You are right. We will kill the human, steal back my slave, and I will take possession of one of the portals. Perfect." And so much easier than she ever could have imagined.

"Don't you mean *we* will take possession?" he asked, one brow arched.

"Yes, of course," she lied glibly. "We."

"I will gather the rest of my army and return within the hour." Offering no other explanation, he disappeared, moving so quickly it was as if he'd never been there.

Marina finally allowed her smile of victory to emerge. Life suddenly seemed so sweet.

# *CHAPTER EIGHT*

LIGHT POURED from the crystal skyline, so bright Gray had to squint to prevent his eyes from watering. Even the trees looked white—wait. They *were* white.

His head pounded, and several minutes passed before he was able to orient himself completely. He lay on a soft bed of foliage. Jewel knelt beside him. The long length of her silky black hair tumbled down her shoulders, caressing his skin and drifting a magical sea-storm fragrance in its wake. She wore an expression of intense concentration as she gently massaged a grainy paste into his arm wound.

The injury burned as if she'd poured molten lava inside it.

"What kind of poultice is that?" he asked between gritted teeth. His voice cracked with each word, his throat raw.

Startled, she gasped. Her hands stilled, and she blinked over at him. "You're awake."

"Seems like it, doesn't it?" Reaching up with his good arm, he rubbed his temples, his neck. The ache slowly receded.

Her gaze bore into his, deep and penetrating, the

otherworldly blue of her irises mesmerizing. "How do you feel?"

"Like shit."

"I've done my best to make you more comfortable."

Maybe he should have lied, he thought, studying her crestfallen features. Told her he felt like spring roses, or some other romantic crap women liked to hear. He'd hurt her feelings, and the knowledge didn't sit well inside him. Plus, he had pride—more than most and more than he should—and he didn't want the woman he planned to bed to think of him as a pansy-assed weakling who couldn't take a little pain.

Gray frowned. Wait. He was not going to bed this woman. Think about it, sure, but that's as far as he could allow it to go. Much as he imagined every touch, scent and sound, every breathy sigh that would purr from her lips as he dragged his tongue over her nipples, between her legs—he cut off that line of thought, hoping to slow the amount of blood pumping into his dick—starting a sexual relationship with a non-earth girl wasn't smart. One, he wouldn't risk pregnancy—did human and Atlantean DNA even mix? And two, he simply didn't do flings.

What's more, a man involved sexually with a woman tended to relax his guard and lose his edge, thinking of nothing but getting the woman naked again. Gray snorted. He hadn't slept with Jewel, but he thought of her naked constantly. Hell, he'd already lost his guard with her. He'd passed out in front of her, for God's sake. The reminder mortified him, but how much more relaxed could a man get?

"You're doing great. My feeling like shit is a good thing," he said grudgingly.

"True," she replied after a moment's contemplation. Her expression brightened, and she offered him a soft, sweet smile. "A man who feels like shit is a man who's alive."

He pressed his lips together to smother a laugh. Hearing Jewel cuss, no matter that the dirty words sprang from such a luscious, made-for-sin mouth, was like hearing his potty-mouthed dad sing a chorus of hallelujah. It just didn't fit with their respective personalities. But damn if he didn't get a thrill every time Jewel talked dirty.

She returned her attention to his arm, once again massaging the grainy, feels-like-fire substance into his wound. "Do you remember anything that happened last night?"

"You mean my passing out like a little girl?" His adrenaline rush must have crashed hard-core. "Yeah, I remember."

"What about after?"

He searched his mind and shook his head. "No."

Tendrils of different emotions curled over her expression: relief, disappointment, resignation. "While you were out, you muttered in Klingon. Something about a Khesterex thath—a screwed up situation."

His cheeks reddened. He felt the burn of it, and that made him all the more embarrassed. "How do you know about Kling—" He frowned. "Never mind. I don't want to know." Passing out in front of a woman was bad enough. Passing out in front of Jewel and muttering in Klingon was an ego killer. He'd tried his damnedest to make her see him as strong, capable. Invincible.

Too late now.

"Help me up," he said darkly.

"You need to remain—"

"Help me up or I'll do it myself."

With a growl, Jewel slid her arm under his neck and applied pressure, helping him rise. The higher his head, the more lightheaded he felt.

"Want to lay back down?" she asked smugly.

"Hell, no." He raised his knees, planted his elbows there, and dropped his face in his waiting hands. "Just give me a minute. Damn injuries." His stomach rolled in protest, and didn't stop rolling. "Yes, damn it. Back down I go."

She eased him onto the ground, remaining at his side. He liked her there more than he should have, liked the feel of her against him. Liked the way her scent encompassed him.

She was beginning to get under his skin.

"You could be a lot worse, you know, and if you don't lie still, you will be."

"Wounds aren't to be recovered from, they're to be conquered. I'm not worried. I've beaten worse." Trying not to wince, Gray motioned to his arm with a tilt of his chin. "The poultice. What is it?"

"Sand," she answered, as if it was the most natural thing in the world to rub a potentially bacteria-infested clump of mud into an injury.

He jerked his arm away from her, his eyes wide with

horror. "Sand? Did you say sand? As in, off the ground, stepped on, spit on, God knows what else has been done on it, sand?"

Confused, she nodded. "Are you hard of hearing, as well as stubborn and foolish? Yes, sand. Now give me back your arm."

"No. Putting dirt in a wound can cause an infection and an infection can cause a limb to rot off. And what do you mean, I'm stubborn and foolish?"

"The sand possesses many healing qualities your body needs." Her shoulders squared, and she pulled her gaze away from him, concentrating on the wound. "Stubborn because you refuse to listen to reason, instead doing whatever you think is right. Foolish for the same reason." As she spoke, she wound a strip of white cloth around the injury.

He didn't protest further. Instead he watched the way she nibbled on her bottom lip as she worked. Images probed at the back of his mind. Dark images, dangerous images. Erotically seductive images. Last night he'd dreamed of battling a demon and a vampire, but what he remembered most was dreaming of Jewel. Kissing her. His lips had moved against hers, savoring the softness. His tongue had dueled with hers, devouring the sweetness. All the while, the soft mounds of her naked breasts had pushed into his chest, her pink, pearled nipples creating a delicious friction.

The pleasure he'd received from that one dream-kiss had astounded him. He still remembered the taste of moonlight and stars. And magic. Yes, she'd tasted of magic and possibilities.

In his dream, he'd known her thoughts. Known she craved him like she craved air to breathe. Known she loved him—loved him more than her own life.

Known, too, that she carried a secret she feared would destroy them both.

What had that secret been? He couldn't remember, and fought to bring the answer to the surface of his thoughts. No luck.

Right now, Jewel's gaze was downcast, her long, thick lashes shielding the otherworldly blue of her eyes he found so fascinating. Perhaps that was best. He didn't have the strength to keep from drowning in them right now. He wondered, though, what thoughts swam through her mind. He couldn't read her as he'd been able to in his dream.

"Time to bandage your neck," she said, cutting into his thoughts. "Hopefully that wound will be better healed." Her sensuous voice swept over him, and he felt himself growing hard. Always hard.

He wasn't a teenager, damn it. He should have better control over his body. Who was master? Him or his dick?

*Me,* his dick said confidently. *As if there was ever any question.*

*Oh, shut up.*

Jewel slapped her hands together, back and forth, causing sand crystals to fly in every direction. "Turn, please."

He shifted to his side to give her easier access, and a sharp pain tore from his neck to his toes. "Damn it," he growled. "A stupid bite shouldn't have caused this kind of damage."

"You're right. A bite like that should have caused much *worse* damage. Be thankful you're alive."

"I'm thankful," he grumbled.

Gingerly her fingers probed at his throbbing neck. She had to lean closer to him, and her female scent again filled his nostrils. More of her hair glided over his bare chest—when had she removed his shirt, or had he done it?—and the lush fullness of her breasts pushed against his chest.

Just like his dream.

If he'd had the energy, he would have jerked her to him and learned if she *tasted* like his dream. Like heaven and hell, sin and deliverance. His mouth watered for her tongue; his body tensed for the weight of her.

*Not smart to fraternize with the locals, James. Remember?*

He felt, actually felt, her nipples harden against him, going from soft to utterly lickable in seconds.

Being smart was overrated.

One kiss didn't a sexual relationship make, he rationalized. Would she even be receptive to him? He studied her expression. Her rosy lips were parted; her breath emerged a little shallow. Twin circles of pink colored her cheeks. She might not know it, she might deny it, but she wanted him. She wanted him bad. All the signs were there.

He almost, *almost* decided it didn't matter that he had no energy. He wanted to kiss her. Only the thought that he'd do a poor job of it in his weakened condition and have her think he didn't know how to pleasure a woman correctly kept him still.

"What do you think?" he asked. "How does it look?"

"Better than I'd hoped." She nodded with satisfaction. "You'll heal with barely a scar."

"Maybe you need to lean in and take a closer look."

Her gaze flicked to his in confusion. When she saw the heat in his eyes, the color in her cheeks deepened prettily. "I'm going to start charging you for your sexual invitations."

"Excellent plan. I'll pay you in kisses."

She chuckled, a throaty purr better suited for bed than banter. "It will only be considered payment if I accept."

"You'll accept," he said, his tone laced with utter confidence. "I have no doubts. I have a feeling you'll even thank me."

She rolled her eyes. Using another strip of cloth, she began rubbing sand into his neck. He tried not to cringe at the thought of bacteria and microbes. All right, he also tried not to shout at the burning pain. "You're one hundred percent positive there are healing qualities in that disgusting stuff, right?"

"Yes. Well." She added hesitantly, "Ninety percent positive, at least."

"What!" He grabbed her wrist, surprised momentarily by the delicacy of her bones, and stilled her hand. "That ten percent of uncertainty could mean you're shooting disease straight into my bloodstream. My neck could rot off, for all you know."

A booming laugh escaped her. "I was teasing. Only teasing. You need not fear the sand."

"You are a cruel, cruel woman." His grip loosened by small degrees, more from wonder at her laugh than relief at her words. Unlike when she chuckled, her all-out laugh had been raw and new, as if she rarely gave way to such unabashed amusement. She'd uttered the same sound while they'd been in the water, swimming to shore. It had affected him then, and it affected him now, warming his every cell.

"I'm the one who cracks jokes in this relationship. You just stick to caring for my every need."

"May I return to my work now?" she asked with a grin.

"No."

"Baby." Her fingers probed at the edges of the wound. As she worked, her nail accidentally scraped a particularly sensitive spot on his scabbed ear, and a sharp pain rebounded through him. He gave no outward reaction, however. He didn't want her to pull away. God knew he'd let her slap, punch and pinch him if it meant her hands would be on him.

Wait. If he didn't want her to know she'd hurt him, he had to stop thinking about it. She would read his mind—if she hadn't already.

He studied her more closely, and his brow furrowed. As he continued to watch her, she gave no indication that she knew what he was thinking. Gave no indication she knew she'd scratched him.

Interesting.

In fact, she'd given no indication she'd heard *any* of his thoughts since he'd woken up, and he'd had some pretty heated ones.

*I want to strip you naked,* he projected, still watching her.

No reaction. Her fingers remained steady.

*I want to crawl over your body, lick every inch of you, and savor your taste.*

Still no reaction.

*I'll start with your lips, then work my way down, and I won't stop until you're writhing in pleasure and screaming for God to deliver you from my tongue.*

Again, nothing.

Interesting, he thought again. Very interesting. Could she no longer read his mind? During their escape from the demon palace, she'd mentioned that there were times she was unable to get inside his head. What prevented her from doing so? Less and less, he liked the idea of this woman knowing his every thought.

"What are you thinking about?" she asked. "Your body has gone stiff."

"Can't you read my mind?" His gaze probed her.

She paused. She drew back and stared down at him. "You sound upset by the very idea. I can't help what I am, Gray. You were thankful for my ability only a few days ago."

On a sigh of regret, he anchored one of his hands behind his head and closed his eyes. "I know."

"If it makes you feel any better," she said grudgingly, "I'm having trouble getting into your head. It's like your mind built up an immunity to me when—" She stopped abruptly.

"When?" he prompted, then his eyelids popped open as her words confirmed his suspicions. "You can't read my mind anymore? Not at all?"

"No." She sounded both annoyed and shocked. "And believe me, I've tried."

He decided to test her one more time. *I won't rest until I've had you in every position possible. And when I'm done with you, your naked, sweaty body will be so sated you'll never again be able to think of sex without picturing my face.*

Nope. Nothing.

"Finally." He sighed with pleasure. "We're on equal footing."

"Then why do I always feel off balance with you?" she asked, resuming her doctoring. When she finished bandaging him, she sat back and eyed the results. "You'll be sore and weak for several more days, and I'm sorry for that but there's no help for it. The important thing is that you *will* heal." As she spoke, her stomach growled.

His grin spread as quickly as the color in her cheeks. "Hungry?"

"Yes." She nodded, rubbing her belly. "Very."

"I have energy bars in my pack."

"Energy bars?"

"Tasteless morsels packed with everything our bodies need to survive."

"Sounds…delicious." Her nose wrinkled, but she leaned over him, meshing her breasts into his chest.

His blood heated as desire rushed through him.

She rooted through the backpack. "I have bread in my satchel."

"Grab that, too. The bars will help us keep up our strength, but they won't do much to fill us up."

"Is this what I'm looking for?" she asked, holding up a brown-packaged rectangle.

"Yes," he said, his voice more hoarse than he would have liked.

She started to pull away.

"Maybe you should dig one out for me, too."

"Of course."

"Just make sure you dig real deep." He wriggled his eyebrows at her.

Her lips twitched, a smile clinging to the edges. She reached deep inside the bag and withdrew another energy bar.

"Oh, yeah. Just like that."

"I suppose this is where I demand payment?" She slid away from him, leaving a trail of heat, and grabbed two pieces of hard, slightly crumbling bread. "I did warn you that I planned to start charging you for your naughty invitations."

He allowed his gaze to sweep over her. The hem of her robe was noticeably shorter where she'd torn the strips for his wounds, revealing the peaches-and-cream perfection of her calves. Smooth and lean, slightly muscled. All traces of amusement abandoned him. Though she'd moved away, he felt the imprint of her nipples all the way to the marrow of his bones.

"I did warn you that I planned to pay with kisses," he said, willing her to close the rest of the distance between them. He needed her tongue in his mouth. Weakened body be damned.

She lost her amusement, too. Her smile disappeared. Desire lit her features, swirling in her eyes. "Yes, you did warn me," she said, breathless.

"Com'ere."

Slowly she moved her face toward his, so close the sweetness of her breath fanned his chin. "I shouldn't."

"You should."

"You're hurt."

"Not too hurt. Kiss me."

"Yes, I— No." She blinked and straightened her back, widening the distance between them. "No. We need to eat," she said, giving no other reason for her sudden refusal.

What had changed her mind? He wanted to demand an answer, but his pride wouldn't allow him. A woman had never pulled away from him before, and he didn't like that one had now—one he wanted more and more as the seconds passed. One he wanted more than he'd ever wanted another.

He ate the bread first, relishing the familiar taste, then tore into his energy bar, eating half in one bite. Jewel, too, ate her bread, then nibbled on the bar, wrinkling her pixie nose in distaste.

The wind kicked up, rustling leaves and gusting tendrils of her hair over her shoulders, onto his chest. It felt like a caress of her hand.

He gulped. "We really should get moving soon. The longer we stay here, the more likely the demons are to find us."

"They'll never find us here. In fact, we're safer here than we would be anywhere else."

"How do you know?"

"Marina fears the owner of this land."

He considered that and wondered if *they* should fear

the owner of the land. "So tell me, Prudence. Where will I find the Jewel of Dunamis?"

Her cheeks paled, leaving her skin pallid. "You need rest. There is no reason to worry about that now."

"You swore to take me to it. Are you planning to renege on me?" He spoke quietly. Deceptively calm.

"No, of course not." The thunderous look Gray was giving her now was the look he usually reserved for his enemies. Ominous. Deadly. "I have every intention of revealing exactly where Dunamis is."

His shoulders relaxed. "So where is it?"

She turned to him, meeting his gaze and holding his stare. The fact that she was still fighting her need to kiss him didn't help matters. But run, she would not. Kiss him, she would not. He might not remember what had happened inside his consciousness last night, but she did. She remembered how he'd thought of her as "not for him." Remembered that he'd intended to push her away if she hadn't done it herself.

If she kissed him now, she wouldn't have the strength to pull away from him, even if she heard him curse her to Hades in his mind. She'd spent the entire night caring for him, bathing him when his fever raged, pouring water down his throat. Sleep had been impossible when his survival depended on her, so shards of fatigue rode her hard, weakening her resolve to remain distanced from him.

"Where is it?" he demanded again.

She pushed out a breath and prayed he took her next words as the answer. "I need you to escort me to the Temple of Cronus." A sense of foreboding swept over her. For her? For Gray? Or the temple? She closed her eyes, trying to center the sensation, to study it, but it slipped out of reach.

Gray bared his teeth in a scowl. "That wasn't the deal, babe."

He hadn't taken it the way she'd hoped; instead, he'd heard the hesitation in her voice, the wistful catch. She couldn't lie to him, but now she'd have to utter a distorted truth he would assume meant one thing, when in fact, it meant another. It's what she had done with Marina, and she hated to do it to Gray, but she *had* to reach the temple.

The only memory she had of her father was inside that temple. His face was a blur to her, but she remembered how he'd descended the long, white steps, coming straight for her, his arms wide.

"I sprang you from prison," Gray said. "You take me to Dunamis. *That* was the deal, and you know it."

"What if I told you that you will discover Dunamis at the temple?"

"Will I?" he asked, suspicious.

"I wouldn't have said so otherwise, would I?"

He remained silent for a long, protracted moment, then relaxed. "If Dunamis is in the temple, that's where we're going. Geez. For a minute you made it sound like they were entirely separate things."

She blinked innocently. It had taken Marina over a year to even suspect that when Jewel responded with a question, the real truth did not lie in the answer. Gray was well on his way to that realization after only a few days.

"Is anyone or thing guarding it?" he asked. "Dunamis, I mean?"

"It does have one protector, yes."

When she said no more, he added, "You want to tell me what I'll be up against?"

How did she explain without lying? "The protector is strong and brave, but he will let you do whatever you wish with Dunamis."

Gray's eyes narrowed. "Just like that?" He snapped his fingers. "The man will give it up just like that?"

"Answer a question for me first. Why do you want it so badly? The jewel, I mean."

"You mean you don't know?"

"All I know is that you do not wish to conquer and rule the surface world, nor do you plan to use it to destroy an enemy."

His silver gaze pierced her all the way to her core. Jewel didn't think a man had ever looked at her the way Gray did, as if she were a platter of some unknown, but delicious-smelling dessert.

"Will my reason affect your willingness to take me to it?"

"No," she said, and it was the truth. No distortion. No dancing around the issue.

He nodded, deciding to trust her. "I want Dunamis because it's dangerous. In the wrong hands, millions of people could be annihilated. I want Dunamis," he added carefully, "because it needs to be guarded by the right people or be destroyed."

Her stomach knotted, sadness mixing with her dread. She'd had to hear that, hadn't she? What would he do or say if he knew that destroying the jewel would destroy *her?* Would he hesitate in his determination, perhaps change his mind? Or would he act without reservation?

"I will answer your question now," she said, forcing the words out. "The protector of Dunamis *will* let you destroy it. Just like that." She snapped her fingers.

"Why?" Incredulity radiated from him.

"He believes as you do, that it needs to be destroyed."

Gray's brow furrowed. "Then why the hell does he protect it?"

"That is a question you will have to ask him yourself."

He opened his mouth, his eyes thoughtful, then he closed his mouth with a snap. Opened, closed. Finally, he growled, "What do you have on under that robe?"

Confused, she blinked over at him. What kind of question was that? He knew what she wore under her robe: a thin white chemise. He'd seen it. Had he planned to ask her something else, then changed his mind?

She sighed. She might have watched this man her entire life, but she doubted she'd ever understand him. Or maybe it was just men she didn't understand. All the other male minds she'd ever read had been focused only on their survival. Some hoping to block her out so that whoever owned her at the time wouldn't know of their crimes. Others had merely been nervous, wanting her to see the truth so she could send them on their way. But for all of that, she'd never taken time to truly explore the male thought process.

"You want to know what I'm wearing under my robe?"

"That's right."

"But—why?" She wished to the gods she could read his mind right now.

"Instead of answering me, why don't you show me?" Gray let out a heavy breath. Damn it. For a moment, when they'd been discussing the destruction of Dunamis, Jewel had looked so lost, so sad, and he hadn't known what caused the transformation. He'd only known he had to fix it.

Thankfully, he had. Color bloomed bright in her cheeks, and her take-me-to-bed eyes sparkled. Desire flared to life, but it couldn't beat past the sudden sense of lethargy racing through him. He gently stretched his arms over his head, arching his back. His mouth widened in a yawn.

"You've already seen exactly what I'm wearing under the robe. Soaking wet, no less."

"Maybe I've forgotten." His eyelids were growing heavy. "Maybe I need to see again."

"No, you do not," she said primly. "What would Katie say about your behavior?"

Hearing her speak his sister's name so easily was disconcerting. Strange and surreal. "How do you know Katie?" His question held curiosity and surprise as he fought to stay awake. "I haven't thought about her since I met you."

"I'm sorry." Jewel nibbled on her bottom lip. "I shouldn't have mentioned her."

"It's okay." He yawned again. "Really. I'm just curious how you know about her."

Agitated, Jewel eased to her feet, but he was unable

to read her expression, unable to figure out what she was thinking. "I don't want to talk about this," she said quietly.

He wanted to push her for an answer, but didn't think that would be wise. She looked ready to bolt and never return. He didn't understand this...or what it meant. "Jewel," he said.

"Sleep," she interjected, cutting off whatever he'd been about to say. He felt oddly compelled to do so. "I'm going to the river to fish. If I never eat another energy bar, I will die complete."

# CHAPTER NINE

J EWEL STOOD at the edge of the river, her robe tucked into her waist, liquid lapping at her ankles, her hands wrapped around a long, sharp stick. She'd removed her shoes, and moss-covered rocks supported her feet. The dome above stretched hot fingers over the land, making her sweat through the thin material of her clothing. She stared down at the clear, dappled water, watching, waiting for a plump fish to swim past. She'd never done this, had never lived off the land before. She only prayed she was successful.

Soon a long, fat swirl of iridescent color darted between her ankles. Her heart skipped a beat. Finally! Her hand tightened around the stick as the fish continued to swim around her, nipping at her ankles. When it tired of playing with her nonresponsive legs, its rainbow fins spanned and flapped, ready to bolt.

She threw the spear.

And missed.

The succulent thing darted away to safety. "Damn it," she growled, sounding very much like Gray.

Over the next half hour, four more delicious-looking fish swam past her, and she missed each one of them, her spear falling uselessly into the water.

"I can do this. I can."

Another fifteen minutes passed. Finally, a plump, incandescent beauty came within her sights. She stilled, even her breathing grinding to a halt. *One, two,* she mentally counted. He was about to swim…three! She tossed the spear.

Success! The tip of her spear cut into the target.

"I did it," she said, jumping up and down, splashing water in every direction. "I did it!" She grinned, holding the stick up for inspection, feeling proud and accomplished as she eyed the flopping treat. No more energy bars today, thank you very much.

She skipped back into camp and leaned her stick against a tree. Gray was still sleeping. His features were relaxed, giving him a boyish quality that warmed her. His pale hair fell over his forehead, and he had one arm over his head; the other rested over his bare chest.

Her hands itched to reach out and trace the hard planes of his abdomen, the ropes of muscles that led down, down—she gulped, forcing herself to gather twigs and grass. After building a sufficient mound, she used Gray's lighter to create a fire. Once the flames crackled with heat, she cleaned the fish as best she could and held out the stick, cooking the meat until it flaked into her hands. Unfortunately the outside charred.

A little while later, Gray yawned and stretched, grimacing as his wounds protested the sudden movement. Then he stiffened, his eyes darting in every direction before settling on her. He pulled himself to a sitting position.

"I didn't mean to fall asleep. Sorry."

"You needed the rest. You look better already."

"I feel better. What's that?" he said with a chin tilt to the fish.

"I've never cooked before, but I have seen it done, so you'll have to tell me how I did." Using a large, firm leaf as a plate, she scooped some of the fish on top, and handed it to Gray.

He accepted with a raised brow. "What if I'm not hungry?"

"You'll eat it anyway, because you don't want to hurt my feelings after I went to the trouble of catching and cooking it."

"Good answer." He took a tentative bite, chewing slowly, his expression unreadable.

She was just about to ask him what he thought, when something in his backpack started speaking. A real, human voice. Jewel jumped, her gaze going impossibly wide.

Gray set his plate aside and dug inside the pack. "Christ," he muttered. He tangled his free hand through his hair. "Check-in time."

"Ah, your communicator," she said, when he withdrew a small black box. She'd seen him use the box on several of his missions. People from his work were able to speak with him, and he to them. Her apprehension faded.

"Mother, this is Santa." He spoke directly into the box. "Go ahead."

"Where are you?" a deep male voice said.

"Pickup has been delayed," Gray responded.

"Should we send another courier?"

He rubbed a hand down his face. "No. I have scheduled a pickup within the next few days. Copy."

"Copy. Over."

"Over." Gray shoved the box into his backpack and picked up his plate. He took a bite, acting as if he hadn't just had a conversation with his box. Or boss. Or whoever. His expression remained blank as he chewed.

She decided not to ask about his work; she could guess. The package: Dunamis. What she couldn't guess was how he felt about the food. She waited beside him, rising on her haunches, ready to hear his praise. "Well?"

"Tastes like chicken," he said. "Thank you for cooking."

Not what she'd wanted to hear because she remembered how he'd complained about chicken in one of her visions. She'd hoped for *delicious, scrumptious,* or *savory.* "It's good for you, so eat it whether you like it or not."

She filled a leaf for herself, sat back and nibbled on the burned flakes. Not wonderful, but not as bad as that energy bar either. "I wish we had pizza delivery here. I've always wondered what one of those gooey round things taste like."

His hand froze midair, hovering just in front of his mouth for a split second before he lowered it. "First you knew about the Hoover, among other surface items, then you knew about my sister Katie, and now you know about pizza, yet you don't know what it tastes like. I know you said you don't want to talk about this, but I have to know. How can you know of them, but not have experienced them? You said you never visited the surface."

She didn't want to answer. She could walk away from him again—she doubted he had the strength to follow—but he'd just bring it up the next time he saw her. Determination seeped from his every pore.

He'd been upset with the thought of her reading his mind, so how would he react to knowing she'd watched his life unfold all these many years?

No matter the answer to that, he deserved to know.

She closed her eyes and gathered her courage, then forced the words to emerge. "I've had visions of you for years." There. She'd confessed, and the rest spilled from her. "I watched you grow from boy to man. Sometimes you'd appear in my night dreams, sometimes in my daydreams, the rest of the world fading from my consciousness."

"What? How?" Those simple single-word questions whipped from him, lashing out.

"I didn't see your entire life," she assured him, "but merely glimpses. And I don't know how, only that it was so."

A moment passed in heavy silence while he absorbed her revelation. "Glimpses of what, exactly?" Now his tone was devoid of emotion, and somehow that was all the more frightening.

"I saw your family, your home. Your," she coughed and glanced away, "women."

"That seems like more than a glimpse to me." Still, no emotion.

"I had no control over it. I tried to stop them, to close my mind to them, but the harder I tried, the more visions I received."

His eyes narrowed. "I don't like being spied on."

"I didn't spy on you," she ground out. "I wish to the gods you'd had visions of me, so that this wouldn't seem so one-sided and wrong."

His eyes widened, and his mouth fell open. "That's it. That's where I've seen you."

"What?" Her brow furrowed. "Where?"

"I've seen you before. I told you that. Remember, I asked you if we'd met?" It all fell into place, and Gray's fish settled like lead in his stomach. Why hadn't he recognized who she was immediately? He'd known she was familiar to him the first moment he saw her.

Over the years, he'd dreamed of her. He'd thought nothing of the dreams at the time, thought they were merely products of his overactive imagination and the weird things he'd encountered, but now he replayed some of them through his mind.

Jewel chained to a wall, her body draped in a blue robe, her black hair streaming around her. Men and women were paraded in front of her, some killed afterward, others spared.

Jewel being held down while someone chopped off her hair. A punishment, the one-armed, knife-wielding bastard said, for omitting details.

Jewel, trying to escape a tower, falling to the ground and breaking her leg.

He shook his head, the images alone sparking fury. Dark, potent fury. This was so hard to take in. Almost impossible, really. He only prayed he was mistaken, that he hadn't dreamed of her actual life.

"Let me see your leg," he demanded softly.

Her face scrunched in confusion.

"Show me your lower right leg." He remembered how the bone had popped through the skin, how she'd cried in pain and hours passed before anyone found her. And then she'd been punished, forced to watch an innocent man slain. Her physical wound somehow had miraculously healed days later, but a scar had remained. "Please, sweetheart. Show me your leg."

Surprise flashed in her eyes, but she stood and lifted her robe.

His lungs constricted, and he scrubbed a hand down his face. There, on her shin, was the scar. His childhood dreams had been real. He'd actually seen glimpses of her life, and he hadn't been able to stop them, either. He'd tried, though. God knew he'd tried anything and everything to rid himself of the haunting images of the dream woman's tragic, tortured life. Therapy. Hypnosis.

Jewel had known one cruelty after another. It had been bad enough when he assumed they were merely dreams, but knowing they were real, that Jewel had truly lived those horrible things, he wanted to gather her in his arms and keep her safe for the rest of her life.

"I've seen enough," he said, his tone cracked. How had she survived? How had she retained such innocence? How could she still see beauty in the world?

She dropped her robe and sat back on the ground, picking up her plate, resuming her eating. "What was that all about?"

"It isn't one-sided," he told her, his tone flat.

She paused, looked at her leg, then at him. "You saw glimpses of me?"

He nodded.

Her cheeks bloomed bright with color, and her mouth formed a small O. "What did you see me do?"

Obviously she didn't like the knowledge that she'd been watched, either. "This and that," he answered vaguely. "What was happening when I saw you that first time as flesh and blood? Those people were being paraded in front of you, then carried away or killed by the demons."

Going pale, she set her leaf aside. "You know of my ability to read minds."

He tensed, because he suddenly knew where she was going with this.

"Whoever owns me at the time brings me their citizens and enemies alike and commands me to ferret out any betrayers. The first time I refused to do this, I had to watch a man die horribly. I've tried to lie, to protect the people, but I can't. Lying cripples me for a reason I don't understand, the words frozen in my throat, so at times I'm forced to admit things about people that I do not want to."

"I'm sorry," he said, reaching for her, wishing there were more soothing words he could give her.

"So many times I wished they would have simply punished me instead. *That* I could have withstood, but no one wanted to hurt the very one who held the answers they so desired."

"Have you always had this ability?"

"Always."

"Was your mother or father—were they like you?"

"Not my mother. She was part of the siren race, and while she was powerful, she could not read minds or tell the future. I'm not sure about my father."

"So you are siren?" Gray searched his mind, but didn't recall any glimpses of Jewel's childhood or family. That explained the sexiness of her voice, though.

"Part siren. I'm not sure what the other half is. My mother and I, we lived in a village of peace-loving creatures and any one of those creatures could have been my family."

"Why aren't you still living in that village?"

"A human army marched through, slaughtering everything and everyone in its path."

"I'm sorry," he said again, helpless to do anything more.

"Thank you."

His brow furrowed. "A human army, did you say?" When she nodded, he said, "How did they get here?"

"The same way you did: through portals. Most Atlanteans believe the gods sent them."

"Are we close to a portal now?"

She nodded. "The dragons now guard them, killing anyone who dares enter."

Gray remembered the guards that had stood at the ready at the palace he'd entered. They'd been big and strong, but had looked human, not dragon. Not like the winged dragon-creature who attacked him in the forest.

He forced down the rest of his fish, even though it

had grown cold and tasted like refrigerated ash. He set his leaf aside. "I wondered how the people here seemed to know so much about humans, yet I hadn't seen many. What happened to them?"

"For the first time since the creation of Atlantis, every race banded together to fight and destroy the enemy, but even if those humans had not invaded our land, we would have known about humans. As I mentioned before, sometimes the gods send us humans they wish to punish. Those criminals serve as a food source for the demons and vampires."

"That explains why I've been so hated and on everyone's shit list." Gray shuddered, recalling all too easily that he himself had been on the menu. "How did you survive the attack?"

"I'm not sure." She laughed, but the sound lacked humor. "I can predict everyone's fate but my own. After the attack, the dragons found me roaming the woods. They raised me for many years before I was stolen by the vampires."

"And what of your father? Did he die, as well?"

"I never really knew him, and my mother rarely talked about him."

Sadness colored her voice and gleamed in her eyes. He knew what it was like to miss a parent, to ache for them. His mother had died when he was barely a teenager. It had been a long, painful death as cancer ravaged her body. He'd tried to be a man about it for many years and pretend it hadn't affected him. But at nights, when he'd been alone with his thoughts, he'd remember her voice, the way she'd sung him lullabies, the way she'd read him stories, and he would cry, wishing her soft arms were around him.

He'd weakened once and tried to talk to his dad about it, but his dad had gone on a weekend drunk. After that he'd never let his dad see his pain, nor had he let his brothers and sister know. He was the oldest child, and he had to be strong. Even if his dad hadn't given him the reminder over and over again, he would have known that he was supposed to be the rock. The man they could lean on and count on to see them through.

To this day, though, he missed his mom with everything inside of him.

"My father will be strong and wonderful," Jewel said, cutting into his thoughts. "And he'll be happy to see me."

Desperate, hollow hope infused her tone. She wanted him to agree, not tell her that the man had wanted nothing to do with her or he would have found her—no matter the obstacles. "I'm sure you're right."

Her shoulders relaxed, her facade of faith restored. "I wonder if I look like him. My mother had pale hair, green eyes, and skin so translucent it glowed."

"Okay, I honestly hope you look nothing like your dad because that would make your dad one hot babe, and that's just not right."

A tinkling laugh escaped her.

As always, the sound of that laugh heated his blood. Reminded him of the kiss they'd almost shared earlier. "You mentioned when you saw glimpses of me, you saw me with my women."

Jewel's expression lost all traces of humor. She pressed her lips together and nodded, her eyes taking on a weary haze.

"What was I doing with them?"

She colored prettily again, and this time the color spread to her neck—and under the collar of her robe. "You talked with them and laughed. You danced and did, uh, other things."

He grinned, the corners of his lips slowly inching upward. There was something about that prudish tone of hers that amused him. "You sound scandalized. Have you never *danced* before?"

Her back went ramrod straight. "For your information, no, I have not."

"Are we talking about dancing or having sex?" He had to smother a hand over his mouth to keep from laughing.

"Both," she answered on a growl.

His smile disappeared. "You're telling me you've never danced with a man?"

"That's right."

"Never been held by a man? Never gotten naked with a man?"

"No." She looked away.

Possessiveness consumed him, joining ranks with his desire. He knew he shouldn't feel that way, knew he should feel sorry for her. God knows, she'd missed out on a lot of stuff. But he couldn't force pity past the need to be her first. He wanted to be the one to teach her, well, everything. Wanted to be the first man to lick her breasts, the first man to taste the passion between her legs. He wanted to be the first man to hear his name on her lips as she came.

Of course, he wouldn't allow himself to actually sleep with her, no matter how much he might want to, but damn if he wouldn't introduce her to everything else in between. No harm in that.

"On our way to find the Jewel of Dunamis," he said, the words hoarse, "will we go into a town?"

"Yes." She sucked on her bottom lip.

His body hardened at the sight. "Does this town have a bar? Music?"

"Yes." This time she drew out the word, letter by letter.

How hesitant she sounded, as if she knew where he was going with this line of questioning but didn't dare hope. He didn't have time for what he was about to suggest, but he could no more shut himself up than he could ignore the ever-persistent General Happy.

*At ease, solider.* "We'll stop at the bar, and I'll teach you."

Blue eyes widening, she said, "Really?"

"Really. How long will it take us to get to the city?"

"A day if we move like lightning."

"What about the temple?"

"Two days. Maybe three."

A surge of anticipation nearly electrified him. Soon he'd be holding Jewel in his arms, teaching her a few of the naughtier pleasures of the flesh. And in two or three days, he'd be holding Dunamis in his hand. Whether he'd destroy it or take it to his boss, he didn't yet know.

Whichever he chose, it would be mission accomplished—on both fronts.

Gray pushed to his feet, wincing at the sharp ache in each of his wounds.

"What are you doing?" she demanded, standing. She rushed to his side, wafting a gentle breeze of sunshine around him.

"I need to work out the stiffness from my body, then pack up so we can head into town."

"You haven't healed yet."

"We need some supplies. Food, more clothing. Weapons."

"Yes, but—"

"No buts. It's my turn to win. You won the last argument. You were stubborn, remember, and refused to relax against me in the water. It's my turn."

She waved aside his words. "We don't have any money. How do you propose we buy those things?"

He held up his hands and wiggled his fingers. "We don't need any money."

"We can't steal. Those creatures work hard. They need every cent."

"And we need the nutrition and the protection. I'll do whatever is necessary to keep us fed and strong."

"I'll fish some more."

"That will take more time than I have to spare. Stop arguing. It's wasted breath."

She hissed in frustration. "Fine. You go stretch or whatever it is you need to do, and I'll clean up camp."

"See how easy that was?" He grinned and lumbered to a nearby tree, throwing over his shoulder, "I'm glad you're starting to see things my way."

Jewel burned their leaf plates, spread the ashes and

embers with a stick. All the while she watched Gray. His skin had more color, so the fish had helped. He had his palms on the tree trunk, his body leaning backward, stretching his arms and sides. When he finished that, he slowly straightened and twisted each vertebra in his back. His blond hair hung around his forehead and temples in complete disarray, that green and black cloth head-covering long forgotten.

Just watching him made her chest constrict with longing. Knowing he wanted to teach her to dance made the sensation all the more intense. She hadn't asked him; he had offered, true desire etched in his voice.

"Have you ever seen the Jewel of Dunamis?" he asked, keeping his back to her.

The question rattled her, but she tried not to show any reaction. "Many times. Why?"

"I'm curious. What does it look like?"

She scrambled for the right words. "Some say it resembles sapphires." Truth. Her shoulders lifted in a mockingly casual shrug. "Others say it resembles a black storm cloud." Truth.

He arched his brows at her cryptic words. "Some say...but what do *you* say?"

Gauging her response very carefully, she said, "I say it looks sad and vulnerable."

"I've never heard a gemstone described that way." There was a catch in his voice, an odd inflection.

Did he suspect the truth? "One day you will have your own opinion about what it looks like." When the fire died completely, she gathered the backpack and satchel, stuffing the latter inside the first, along with everything else they might need. A few sharp rocks, a handful of berries she discovered growing on a nearby bush.

The only thing she didn't pack was the canteen. That, she hauled to the river and filled with water, then strapped it around her neck. She and Gray were truly going into town. The shock of it swept through her, and her hands shook with nervousness; her heart pounded with excitement.

She'd always passed through the cities under cloak of darkness, surrounded by guards of whatever ruler possessed her at the time. The scents and sounds had always amazed and tempted her, those from the taverns most of all. They always bustled with music and laughter.

And now she was going to enter one. Now she was going to dance. With Gray. Her pulse fluttered.

"I'll need a hooded robe," she said. "Otherwise I'll be recognized."

He cast her a quick glance before motioning to the ground he'd laid on only moments before. Something hot burned in his eyes. "Wear mine."

"You'll be recognized as human without it."

"Baby," he said, mouth twitching in a grin, "I stole two."

"Oh." Jewel dug back inside the bag and sure enough, there was another robe, this one a light, fine yellow. She pulled it free and settled the material over her head.

"We have to remember to be careful. We trust no one but ourselves, understand?"

She nodded.

"If we see a demon or vampire, we haul ass back into this forest. As much as I'd like to get a room in town and get us out of the elements tonight, I'd rather deal with the weather than with those bastards from hell."

Gray finished stretching and closed the distance between them. He took the bag and dug out his weapons. Perhaps she shouldn't have packed up quite so efficiently. He strapped a knife to his waist and one to his ankle, then draped the dark blue robe over his shoulders. She was a little worried about his trekking through the forest, but the man was stubborn and there would be no changing his mind.

He looked at her and their gazes met, a charged moment of awareness filling the space between them. "Let's do this."

## CHAPTER TEN

THEY HIKED for two days, leaves raining like emeralds from brown velvet as they brushed past each new grove of trees. Distracted as she was by Gray, Jewel proved to be their biggest threat. She almost led them into a pool of quicksand, then off a staggeringly high cliff, which had added time to their trip. Precious time, according to Gray. Thankfully he jerked her to safety when she messed up, his arms banding around her.

During the last incident, he'd held her longer than necessary, his gaze lingering on her lips. She'd shivered and ached, her mouth watering for a taste of him. His warm, male scent constantly enveloped her, luring her. Tantalizing and mesmerizing her. But she'd at last pulled away. He still bore traces of fatigue, his face pale and his limbs shaky.

He always remained a few steps behind her, his silver gaze focused intently on her back, his arms ready to shoot out and drag her into the hard shield of his body. She wasn't normally so inattentive and uncon-cerned with her surroundings. Knowing he was behind her, however, played havoc with her attention.

"So how do the men around here impress the women?" he asked, speaking for the first time that day.

She flicked him a glance and grinned, grabbing on to the thread of conversation as if it were the most precious thing in the world. "Some men—"

"Eyes on the road," he commanded. He grabbed her robe by the hood and tugged her away from a large boulder.

Gasping, she returned her attention to the forest. *Pay attention!* Tough as these treks were, the nights were tougher. She had to get them into town *today.* Another night, close to him but untouching…it would be too much.

"Good. Now, what were you going to say?"

"Some men kill the woman's greatest enemy and bring the body to her as a gift."

"Then you should be thoroughly impressed with me. I might not have gift-wrapped the demons, but I did kill your enemy."

"Yes, you did."

"What about the other men? The peace-lovers you grew up with. What did they give their women?"

Her lips pursed as she considered his question. She'd never been on the receiving end of a man's romantic attentions, but had witnessed many courtships. "Depends on the creature, I guess."

"Sirens. Tell me about the sirens."

She searched her mind. What had the men of her village given her mother when they'd wished to seduce her? What had her mother liked to receive? Her eyes widened as long-forgotten images surfaced, her mother's tinkling laughter drifting from the far recesses of her mind. "Once, a male centaur wrote a play for my mother. He acted the part of hero and hired others to be his cast. It was a love story about two people giving up everything to be together, and I remember the way my mother sighed dreamily and smiled for days afterward."

Gray's only response was a shudder. Of revulsion? His silence soon began to weigh heavily on her shoulders. "I know you give your women flowers and candy," she said, stomach clenching at the thought of how each one had rewarded him with kisses. Sometimes naked kisses.

"That's easily done and requires little thought," he said darkly.

She stayed the urge to look back at him. Was he irritated with her? Or himself? Before she could ponder the answer, she stopped, a thin layer of bush the only barrier between her and the path to the city. "We're here."

"Don't go any closer until I've done reconnaissance." His hand latched onto the tendon at the base of her neck, massaging gently as his gaze darted in every direction.

Her nerve endings leapt up to meet him, craving more of his touch. She knew he was cataloguing their surroundings, deciding what was safe and what wasn't. Laughing female voices drifted to her ears. Ahead of them on a cobbled path stamped a herd of female centaurs. Each possessed a mane of hair, some red, some brown, some pale, their chests covered by blue cloaks, the color marking which clan they belonged to. Every one of them carried a basket or satchel overflowing with wool.

The women approached an enormous, glistening pearl gate that arched toward the skydome and led straight into the pulsing heart of the city. Jewel's excitement expanded, grew, unfurling through her entire body. She searched her senses for any sign or shiver of danger but felt nothing. She wasn't surprised. She never knew when she herself would be in peril.

"The Inner City is so much different from the Outer City. Here, the people are friendly and honest and hardworking. Notice that no one is carrying weapons."

"None that we can see, that is."

How like him, she mused with a grin, to suspect everyone of foul play. He was a warrior to the marrow of his bones.

"Get ready," Gray said. To their left, a group of robed—what the hell were they? he wondered. They were as ugly as legend claimed Medusa was, with too-big, black eyes, a too-big beaky nose, and hair comprised of serpents. Those snakes hissed and slithered from their heads. Gray slid his hand down, wrapping his fingers around Jewel's. They jolted into motion. Because his backpack was under his robe, he looked like he was some sort of humped-backed creature. That worked in his favor.

"Pull your hood tight around your face," he said, and as he spoke, he fitted the hilt of one of his blades in his hand, covering the metal with the cuff of his clothing. When she complied, he added quietly, "We're going to try and blend in with those snake—things."

"Gorgons," she said. "Do not look directly in their eyes; if your gaze meets one of theirs, you will be turned into stone."

"Ah, shit."

"Why bother trying to blend in with them? No one will recognize us with these robes covering our faces, and we aren't being followed."

"In case anyone is questioned, they won't know that two individuals entered the city at a specific time. Anyone who sees us will think we're part of this group, and I highly doubt the demon queen will make the connection."

Ah, that made sense. If she hadn't been glad to have Gray with her before, this would have convinced her. "I can project my thoughts into their heads and convince them we are not even here."

"That tires you out, and I need you strong."

The Gorgons didn't pay them any heed as they came up behind them. They were too busy discussing—my gods. Her ears perked, and she listened intently, frowning all the while. A cold sweat trickled over her skin. Back and forth the Gorgons threw comments about the demon and vampire armies that had passed through their village, demanding to know if they'd seen a human male and female. Jewel stiffened.

The vampires and demons were working together? How…odd. The two races had never outright warred, but they had never allied themselves, either. What had brought them to mutual terms?

Reeling, she glanced up at Gray. His face was partially shadowed by his hood, but she saw the grim line of his lips. Had he understood them? She projected her consciousness into his mind, but met with that frustrating block.

He squeezed her hand, and she bit her lip. Did he know she'd just tried to read him?

"Where were they headed?" she asked the Gorgon in front of her, using their harsh dialect of the Atlantean language.

All of them skidded to a halt and turned to her.

Gray growled low in his throat, but he kept his head turned.

"Well?" she demanded, pretending she had every right to be among their group and question them.

"Toward Javar's palace," one of them answered, and they all kicked into motion.

Which meant her enemy was headed away from the Inner City. That was good, but… Why journey all the way to Javar's, the former High King of the dragons? Javar had been dead for many months, and Darius, the new king, had sent a legion of his men to protect the palace from invaders.

This made no sense.

The moment she and Gray passed through the city gates, they pulled away from the Gorgons.

"The point was to blend in with those things, not announce we were there and didn't belong," Gray whispered in her ear, his tone fierce. He claimed the lead, but retained a tight grip on her hand.

Three-headed dogs bolted from behind a stone hut and frolicked around her feet as carts and vendors came into view. The scent of sweet pies and meat tempted her nostrils. Her mouth watered. Beautiful, brilliantly colored clothes greeted her eyes, and gems sparkled in the light.

She wanted to taste every kind of food, try on every piece of material, cover herself in the jewelry.

"Look for a weapons dealer."

"Of course," she said, a wealth of disappointment in those two words. "Can we explore the city after?"

"We have to—" He threw a glance over his shoulder, then paused. He turned toward her, facing her fully.

She slammed into him.

When she steadied, the long length of her lashes swept up and her gaze met his. "Is something wrong?"

Silent, Gray stood in place, studying Jewel's face and the eager gleam in her eyes, making them sparkle like sapphires. A smile half curved her lips, and a rosy glow lit her cheeks. There was a palpable air of excitement radiating from her.

She'd never looked more beautiful, more alive— and the sight of her hit him straight in the gut. He was unable to move, could hardly breathe.

He'd thought to get business out of the way first. It had seemed like the most important thing at the time, the smart plan of action. Now, looking at her, the only thing he could think of, the only need inside him, was to make her happy.

During their trek to the city, he'd thought of nothing but giving this sweetly innocent woman the perfect gift. When she'd told him of the romantic play that delighted her mother, he'd heard the wistfulness in her voice and had known she desired the same for herself.

He wasn't a writer; he wasn't an actor. But he didn't want to give Jewel the same things he'd given other women. Flowers seemed cliché and candy didn't seem good enough.

He didn't know why, he only knew that it was important, necessary, that he do something for her he'd never done for another.

She wanted to explore the city, then by God they'd explore the city.

"We've got a little time to play first," he said, his voice rougher than he would have liked.

Her eyes widened. "Really?"

"Just be sure to keep your face hidden and be on the lookout for demons and vampires."

"We're safe from them. They're headed in the opposite direction."

"Sometimes armies hide in the shadows, sweetheart, and sneak inside. Now, where do you want to go first?"

Grinning, she glanced left and right, spun, glanced left and right again. "There," she said, pointing to a booth of jewelry. Something caught the corner of her eye, and she spun again. "No, there." This time she pointed to a table piled high with some kind of fruit and laughed. "Everywhere. I want to see everything at once."

As always, the sound of her rich laughter was like a sensual battering ram, hitting him with thousand-pound force. He'd seen women take pleasure in shopping before, but never like this. Never with a potent enthusiasm that wrapped around him, tightening him in a delicious hold.

"Come on," he said, taking her hand, loving the feel of her soft skin, her delicate bones. He led her to a table of sparkling gemstones. "One thing at a time. We'll get to all of it, I swear to God."

Her gaze lingered on the rainbow of jewels, and she gasped. Her fingers lovingly traced an emerald torque, caressed an amethyst ring, and savored a gold and silver linked chain. The amount of wealth glistening up at him was staggering.

A male creature manned the table and watched them with an assessing stare. Though he possessed the body of a man, he had the face of a bull, with horns jutting from his forehead and fur on his cheeks.

Kind of freaky to see, in Gray's opinion.

"Something you like?" the man—bull—*thing* asked.

It was in that moment Gray realized he understood every word. The bull-man had spoken in the guttural Atlantean language, and so had the ugly Gorgons, for that matter. Gray had understood them, as well, and had listened to their conversation about the demons and vampires. He had simply been too wrapped in their words to realize they weren't speaking English. Now...

How the hell had he learned Atlantean? One day he hadn't understood a damn word of it, and now he knew the entire freaking language.

"Everything is so beautiful," Jewel breathed, cutting into his thoughts. She raised an armband with one hand and raised the sleeve of her robe with the other, revealing several inches of smooth skin. Crystals gleamed from the torque, projecting a vast array of colors. A silver stone rested in the center.

The sight of the rich gold band contrasting with the peaches-and-cream flesh proved more erotic than two chicks making out right in front of him. He wanted Jewel to have it. Real bad. So easily he could picture her wearing the armband—and nothing else.

"That looks beautiful on you," the vendor said, low and gravelly.

Gray wouldn't have minded stealing, but he, well, he didn't want to acquire the item that way. He wanted to gift Jewel with an honest purchase. Something she would look at and always think of him.

"Thank you," Jewel said, but she removed the item and returned it to the table, her sleeve falling back into place. There was regret and longing in her voice, and she gazed at the item wistfully before finally turning her attention to a bloodred ruby headpiece.

"Roasted fowl," someone called. "Only half a drachma."

Her chin jerked to the side. "Roasted fowl," she gasped, skipping to the vendor without a backward glance.

Gray watched her go, then did a quick scan of the crowd and decided she was safe enough for the moment. He half turned toward the freaky bull-man, dividing his attention between his woman and the jewelry seller.

"How much?" he asked, pointing at the armband. Surprisingly the Atlantean language flowed easily from his tongue, as if he'd spoken it his entire life.

"Forty drachmas."

He couldn't ask what drachmas were or he'd look

like an idiot who didn't belong in Atlantis. He merely nodded and pivoted. As he closed the distance between himself and Jewel, the bull-man called, "Thirty-five. I'll let you have it for thirty-five."

Gray pulled Jewel to the side, away from the roasted fowl peddler, a thickly muscled, one-eyed Cyclops. Jewel held two pie tins of meat in her hand. The Cyclops was eyeing them warily, as if he half expected them to sprint away with the goods. She was biting her lip, staring down at the food.

His gaze returned to the Cyclops, and he noticed the man was clad in rags, and had hollowed cheeks despite his oddly muscled appearance. He was dirt poor, and Gray didn't have the heart to steal from him, either.

"What are drachmas?" he asked Jewel quietly.

"Money." She sniffed the food with a rapturous expression, completely absorbed in her task. "Like your dollars."

"How can I earn some?" As he spoke, he saw a group of the freakiest of all the things he'd seen so far. One arm protruded from their chests, and one leg swung from their torsos, and only the wings on their backs kept them upright. They formed a small, laughing circle.

Each *whatever the hell they were* held a good-sized lizard, and each lizard wore a jeweled collar, a different jewel for each different owner. They placed the squirming things in a line, using their only hand to hold on to the lizard's tail.

One of the men shouted, "Go," and everyone released their lizards.

Gray expected the cursed things—he hated lizards, *hated*—to bite their handlers, but they surprised him by jolting into action and racing forward. The green-collared lizard crossed the finish line first and its handler fluttered up and down with excitement, clapping his hand against his thigh.

A heavy-looking pouch was thrown at the thing, and he caught it, opening the burlap sack with his teeth and withdrawing a dull rock. Gray would bet his sub-stantial savings account that dull rock was a drachma.

God love the gambling community.

He brightened. "Never mind," he told Jewel. "I know how." His grip tightened on the blade he held. It was good-sized with a marble handle and worth a small fortune. His brother-in-law, Jorlan, a prince of some distant planet, had given it to him. "You ever gambled?"

"No."

"Today's going to be your day of firsts. Come with me."

"Wait." She replaced the food on the table, and he ushered her through the crowd darting along the street. When she noticed the only possible destination for them, she said, "Uh, Gray, perhaps we should turn around now."

He ignored her, never slowing. Soon the *things'* low voices drifted to them, reminding Gray of something he wanted to ask Jewel. "Would you mind telling me how I now know your language?"

Her radiant sapphire eyes rounded. "You can under-stand?"

He nodded and cast her a glance. He could see

wheels turning and watched her eyes widen as the answer hit her, but she merely shrugged. "How does anyone learn a language, really?"

"With hard work and a lot of studying."

"You could have learned it simply by listening to others speak it."

The woman was good, he'd give her that. She never lied, but when she didn't want to answer a question she had ways of trying to throw him off the scent. "I didn't work at this and I didn't listen closely to others. How did I learn it?" he persisted.

She paused, gulped, then offered, "I have heard some humans learn our language through magic."

Magic. His brother-in-law dealt in magic, and Gray knew firsthand the dangers involved in using it. A man could be turned to stone, while still able to see, hear and feel everything around him. A man could be cursed inside a box, allowed to emerge only when his female master had need of his services. He shuddered.

No, thank you.

"Did you use a spell on me?" Before she replied, he realized she'd never actually said with one hundred percent surety that he'd learned the language through magic. She'd merely suggested it. In fact, she hadn't answered his question in any way.

He gritted his teeth together, stopped, and stared down at her for a long while, making her squirm. "I'm on to you. Magic, indeed. When we're safe in our room tonight, we're going to have a long talk."

*Our room,* he'd said. Jewel swallowed, trying to alleviate the sudden dryness of her mouth. She suspected

Gray understood the Atlantean language because she'd been inside his head and must have left pieces of herself behind. Amazing, surreal, but there it was. Had she, then, taken pieces of him with her?

She didn't know how he'd take to that news when he didn't seem to remember she'd been inside his head at all, so she said nothing, letting him rationalize whatever explanation he would.

Right now, she had other things to worry about. Formorians. She studied them. Their skin was as pale as a vampire's but looked more like dry paper with thin blue lines. They had just finished another lizard race when she and Gray reached their circle. Gray stopped, not saying a word, just watching curiously; she remained at his side, scanning faces, reading minds, ready to warn him if anyone attempted to hurt him. The Formorians had blades strapped all over their bodies. She didn't know why they were here in the Inner City when Formorians usually stayed in the more accepting Outer City. They were a danger-loving race who didn't mind feasting on flesh, preferably while the bodies were still alive and screaming.

"I want to play," Gray finally announced to the surrounding crowd, as if he hadn't a care in the world.

The Formorians whipped around, frowning. "Do you have drachmas?" one of them asked, eyes narrowed.

Gray held out his dagger and gave it, hilt first, to the creature closest to him. The Formorian accepted the glinting dagger greedily, gripping it in his only hand. "I must see who I am dealing with first," he said.

"You see enough of me." Gray's tone had lost its easiness, becoming dark and menacing.

"I will see all of you." He motioned with a tilt of his chin, and another of the Formorians stepped forward, reaching out to push back Gray's hood.

Gray shoved the creature, hard, making him stumble backward. All of his friends growled low in their throats. "You stink of human," one of them spat. "We will see your face."

"And you stink of shit," Gray snapped. "All you'll see is another of my weapons if you don't get out of my face. Now, you accepted my dagger, so deal me into the game."

"You will leave or die. That is your only choice."

Gray stepped forward quickly, shadows covering most of his face. But through the shadows, his eyes were glowing bright, menacing red. "You will let me in your game. Understand?"

Seeing the glowing eyes—demon eyes—they nodded, now eager to please. Formorians feared demons, their stronger counterpart.

Jewel stifled a horrified gasp. The red light in Gray's eyes had already died down, leaving only the silver irises. The changes were happening, then. Gray wouldn't be spared as she'd hoped. Over the coming weeks, he would acquire traits of both the vampires and the demons.

Which traits, she could only guess. How he would react when he discovered what was happening to him, she could only dread.

The leader sheathed Gray's knife at his belt and

handed him the amethyst-collared lizard, the least active of the group. Gray didn't complain, but he did grimace.

"Line up and we will begin. First lizard to cross, wins."

Gray nodded and lined up beside the other men. The disgusted expression he wore would have made her chuckle in any other circumstance. As it was, she didn't trust the Formorians to act honorably, so retained a watchful eye on them.

"Go!" the leader shouted.

The lizards were released and bolted into action. Well, all but Gray's lizard bolted. Gray's began a slow, leisurely stroll. "Go, damn you," he shouted, poking at it with the tips of his fingers.

It turned and ambled in the opposite direction.

All too soon, a lizard crossed the finish line, ending the race. Gray cursed loud and long, then turned to the Formorian leader. "Again," he said.

"Show me payment."

He removed his wristwatch and handed it over. The Formorians gathered around it oohing and aahing, and Gray picked up his lizard. "Let's get this done."

Eager, everyone lined up.

"Go!"

Gray's lizard did a repeat performance, as did Gray. He cursed the entire race, expletives that near burned her ears. Afterward, he demanded another race, handing over his fire starter. A lighter, she knew it was called. The Formorians were salivating to own it, so they quickly agreed.

The men lined up. Gray's lips were taut. Hard lines

bracketed his eyes and mouth. Determination radiated from him. "You better move this time, you disgusting sack of shit," he muttered. "Again. Winner takes everything." He handed over an energy bar, and the creatures sniffed, nodded.

"Ready...go!"

The lizards scrambled forward.

Jewel had never entered an animal's head before, but she did this one. She didn't know if it would work, but she gave it a try, anyway. Anything to help Gray. *Go, damn you. Swiftly.*

Hearing her sharp command, the lizard leapt into action, moving faster than the others, and it inched into the lead. An odd sense of excitement grew inside her. They had a chance of winning this time! She was jumping up and down by the time Gray's lizard crossed the finish line, capturing first place.

Heated silence met the victory, and no one moved, only staring in shock at the amethyst-collared lizard.

"My prize," Gray prompted.

All of the Formorians frowned and hissed as the leader handed over two bags of drachmas, along with all of Gray's belongings. Jewel clapped her hands and laughed, her hood almost falling in her excitement. Gasping, she reached up and secured it in place.

Gray clasped his arm around her wrist. "Nice doing business with you, boys. If you'll excuse us..." He led her away, mumbling, "I knew that little bastard would pull through. With your help," he added with a grin. "How much is this?" He held up the two bags with his free hand.

"Two hundred drachmas is my guess," she said on a laugh, not asking how he knew what she'd done. "We have money!"

He tossed her a wickedly sensual wink. "Let's have us a celebration."

# CHAPTER ELEVEN

LAYEL STOOD at the edge of the forest overlooking the former dragon king's palace. Javar no longer lived, of course, killed by Layel's own hand. He'd relished killing the man, he had to admit. The bastard had been cold and unemotional and should have had more control over his men. If he had, perhaps Susan would still be alive.

A cool breeze wafted past him as he continued to stare at the palace, blocking out the sounds of the armies behind him. Crystal beams stretched to the golden skyline, casting rainbow shards in every direction. The mocking beauty of this place always amazed him.

Some of the most horrendous crimes against Atlantis had been committed in this lush glen, juxtaposing the beauty against the horror.

Humans sacrificed, battles waged until blood ran like a deadly river. Women and children stolen. He'd played a part in it, all of it, and he did not feel guilty. The women and children were now slaves, but they were well cared for. The humans he'd killed had been evil, a means to an end. The dragons he'd fought had thought nothing of raping an innocent female, so they had deserved what they got.

Unlike other races where only one ruled, there had always been two dragon kings. One to guard and protect each side of Atlantis. When Javar died, only Darius remained, and the stupid man had yet to crown another. Yes, he'd sent soldiers here to guard but without a true sovereign in residence, the palace was left vulnerable.

Right now, warriors stalked the parapet of the palace, guarding, watching all that happened below them. With his extraordinary vision, Layel saw them as clearly as if they were pacing directly in front of him. Twelve armored men, perfectly muscled, perfectly bronzed. But they did not possess the telltale golden eyes of the dragons.

His brow quirked to his hairline, and he began to notice another odd detail. Usually dragons flew overhead at all hours. Today, this moment, there was no sky guard. Only a soft, amber glow from the crystal.

Everything was falling smoothly into place.

He grinned slowly.

Weeks ago, Layel had *casually* mentioned to the nymph king that Javar's palace was without a leader, that Darius had left an army of hatchlings in charge and then Layel had gifted the nymph with an array of dragon medallions needed to open the doors. Valerian must have immediately gathered his forces and ambushed the palace, claiming it as his own. For it was the nymphs who walked the parapet this dawning, their bodies bronzed and muscled to perfection, their hair as silky as satin, their faces so luminous they glowed brighter than the dome above.

Word of this victory had yet to spread, for not even he had known. Satisfaction filled him, then dimmed with a single thought. The female slave stolen from Marina probably knew. *She* knew everything. He himself had owned her for a brief time, so he knew her abilities very well.

Would the slave tell anyone of this? Would she reveal his own plans? Would she come here?

No, he decided in the next instant. If she told anyone, she would have to reveal exactly who and what she was, and she would be taken prisoner, a circumstance she would avoid at all cost. She would shun the nymphs just as she shunned the demons. They were a powerfully sensual race, dangerously erotic, and they enthralled everything female. Enslaved them body and soul, until all a woman thought about, all she craved, was her nymph.

Layel's plans were not in jeopardy.

His smug gaze strayed to Marina. The queen would never be allowed inside the palace—and thanks to the nymphs, he didn't have to prowl his mind for a reason they should not enter. He'd led the bitch here under false pretenses, buying time.

No matter what happened, no matter what he had to do, he would make sure Marina never claimed the slave girl again. Too much was at stake.

As if his thoughts had summoned her, the demon bitch rode her horse to his side, its hooves pounding into the ground. She'd stolen the beast from a Gorgon village—after she'd eaten its master. The animal ground to a halt.

Marina's thin, sheer wings flapped behind her like a gossamer cloak, the only elegant part of her hideous, horned body. "Those men do not look like dragons, they look like nymphs. Nymph warriors." Her eyesight was as good as his own, if not better.

"That they do," he said, trying not to allow himself another smile. "They must have fought the dragons and taken possession. Do you think they heard about the portals and want them for themselves?"

She gasped. "That's exactly why they're here. I'd stake my life on it."

He'd stake her life on it, too. Happily.

"How dare they?" she screeched. "The portals are mine. Mine! This place was supposed to be empty!"

"Keep your voice down." Not that he cared, but he had to act the part of concerned friend. "You know how sensitive their hearing is. And don't you mean *ours?*"

"What if they now have my slave, as well as control of the portal?" Panic crested her voice to a high, deafening pitch. "You said she would come here, that the human would need the portal to return home."

"They do not have the girl. Otherwise, a thousand warriors would have been waiting for us here."

"You're right." She loosed her viselike hold on the reins, an air of superiority forming around her. "I don't care who is inside that palace. We ride. If they try to keep the portal for themselves, I'll kill them. And their children."

Before he could utter another word, she leapt into action, and Layel was forced to follow. "Forward," he called, and their armies sprang into a run. His vampires could move faster than the blink of an eye, but they kept a steady pace beside the demons. They knew him well and would not fly into full attack without his express permission.

Both demons and vampires sprinted through the open field, headed toward the towering double doors. This was foolish, he knew it was, but if nothing else, it would prove entertaining. Marina would never get inside, and he would enjoy watching the nymphs shove her from her exalted pedestal.

An arrow suddenly rent the sky and landed at their feet.

Marina's horse reared up, tumbling her backward before she could right herself with her wings. She hissed as she hit the ground, thumping and rolling. Layel laughed heartily with genuine amusement. Something he hadn't done in years. Ah, yes, this would definitely be a day to relish.

Marina jolted to her feet, scowling at him and everyone around who dared laugh. "That animal is—is—"

"A true hero of war?" Layel asked.

"Stay where you are," a nymph called. "You are not welcome here."

Layel recognized that voice. Valerian, King of the Nymphs. He gave the king his full attention, Marina forgotten at his side. Valerian stood on the highest ledge of the palace. Golden hair framed a wickedly mesmerizing face. Perfectly tanned skin, perfectly chiseled features. Lush, pink lips and long, fringed lashes. Eyes so blue-green they were as deep and fathomless as the ocean above them.

Valerian's features should have made him appear

feminine. For some reason, his physical perfection made him all the more masculine, all the more harsh. All the more desired by women.

"Is that how you welcome an old friend? With arrows?"

"You know you are welcome to enter, Layel. The demon, however, must remain outside the walls."

"Alas," Layel called. "Where she is, there must I be, as well. Why do you not join us? We both wish to speak with you."

"Trust a demon enough to enter its midst? I think not." His laugh echoed across the distance, rich and husky, a caress even Layel felt. That was the way of the nymphs. With their voices, with their bodies, with their every glance, they radiated sensuality. "Why have you joined with one such as her?"

He couldn't announce his true reason, and he wouldn't lie to the only man he'd considered friend over the years. Though he knew Valerian would refuse and was glad for it—Layel didn't want him involved any more than necessary—he ignored the question and said, "We wish only to speak with you. You have my word you will leave exactly as you enter."

"I wish to fight you, coward." Marina bandied a claw through the air. She climbed back on her horse. "Bring your army down if you dare."

"Are you sure you can control her?" Valerian said, grinning. "She seems quite determined to place me on her dinner menu."

"Are you afraid?" she spat. "You should be. I plan to cut out your tongue and eat it in front of you."

Layel rolled his eyes. When would the woman learn such words and actions would get *her* killed?

His ears suddenly perked as he picked up the sound of Marina's soldiers readying their weapons for attack. Eyes slitting, he flicked his second-in-command a glance, motioning to the demons with a tilt of his chin. No words were necessary; his man understood what he wanted. If a demon made a single move toward the palace, it would be killed.

"Cut out *her* tongue if you must, Layel," Valerian said, "but shut her up. I'm tempted to come down if only to humble her. As if a female would ever be able to attack me." He chuckled. "The idea of such an occurrence is ridiculous."

"If you want my tongue, come down here and get it."

Valerian's golden brows arched.

"Not another word from you," Layel bit out, hand shooting up and latching on to Marina's thigh. If he hadn't needed her so much, if there had been any other way to defeat Darius, he would have killed her here and now.

*Later,* he comforted himself.

"His every breath insults me," she whispered fiercely. She squirmed against his hold. "He's taunting us."

"Obviously you've never been in the presence of a nymph before. If you go to him or if he comes to you, you will gladly become his slave. You will beg to remain at his side; you will want nothing else in your life but to please him. The nymphs cannot help it. Their very presence causes women to become enslaved to them."

Horror darkened her expression, and her gaze whipped to him. "If you knew that, why the hell did you invite him down here in the first place?"

"I knew he would refuse the invitation. I also knew it would open our lines of communication."

"Why are you here?" Valeran said on a sigh, cutting into their conversation.

"See," Layel muttered. "Now we are communicating."

Marina opened her mouth to reply, but Layel silenced her by strengthening his hold on her thigh. Painfully. Her lips pursed.

"We thought to take the palace, but as you arrived first we will leave it to you. However, now that we are here, I wish to inquire about a human man." As he spoke, hundreds of nymphs lined up beside their king, showing their great numbers. Every one of them was tall and strong with a beauty that surpassed that of any other creature or object. Such exquisite magnificence hurt his eyes, nearly forcing him to shield them.

"Did you also come hoping to find the Jewel of Dunamis?"

Layel shrugged. Valerian knew him very well.

"It's mine," Marina screeched. "Do not think you can keep it for yourself."

"I think I'll do whatever I wish," Valerian said, his sensual timbre laced with amusement.

Marina's hands tightened on her horse's reins, and her green scales drained of color. "Let's destroy him," she whispered. "Let's send these creatures to Hades."

Stupid woman. "We do not have the time nor the re-
sources to war with both the nymphs and the dragons.
You may take comfort in the fact that once Darius is
defeated, we can do what we will with the nymphs."
Not that he'd allow her to attack Valerian, or even that
she'd still be alive at that point.

"I do not want to wait."

"But you will." He cast a glance at the armies behind
him. His vampires stood completely still, halving their
attention between the demons and him, not paying heed
to the spectacle above. They awaited his signal.

The demons, however, continued to shift restlessly
on their feet, licking their lips in hungry anticipation.

That was the difference between trained warriors
and slovenly idiots.

"You know the dragons will attack you for taking
this palace," Layel told his friend.

"Of course. We look forward to their visit. If you've
disposed of the demon by that time, you may come and
aid us." Valerian spoke as calmly as if they were discussing the weather, not a prophecy of war and death.
"Now, if you have nothing more to say—"

"Have you seen the human and the girl?" Layel
called for Marina's benefit.

"They have not passed through this land today or
any day we have been here."

"You're lying," Marina hissed, and Layel saw her
claws elongate, preparing to attack. "We'll fight our
way inside, if we must, and see for ourselves."

Valerian shook his head. "I bid you goodbye, Layel."

"The portal." Her features were desperate as she

turned her attention to Layel. "What of the portal? We cannot leave it in that bastard's care."

Hearing her, Valerian's beautiful face drained of all emotion, all amusement. His perfect lips lifted in a slight scowl. "You can, and you will," he said, his tone dangerous, menacing.

She gasped. "So, there *is* one inside? You've seen it?"

"That is none of your concern."

"All this time." Her snakelike tongue flicked out and moistened her lips. "The portals existed, and I had no idea. Javar's palace—"

"This is Valerian's palace now," the nymph king snapped. "Best you learn the name and use it."

"*Javar's* palace," she continued with a sneer, "Javar's, Javar's, Javar's."

"If the armies come any closer, kill them," Valerian shouted to his men. "All of them."

Layel knew the king, slow to rage, would not hesitate to slaughter them all now that he'd been provoked. Their friendship was the only reason Marina still lived.

"We have the information we need," he told her. "Let us leave. We will head toward Darius's palace. We must pass through the Inner City to get there and will search for the couple on our way."

"No, we can take Valerian. We can slay him."

"I have already explained to you why we will not." He spun around and stalked away from her, before he killed her now, all he'd worked for forgotten. She was forced to follow or die. "I hate Darius. I will help you kill him. But I will not hurt Valerian."

She decided to follow. Her horse whined as she turned it around, and she was soon at Layel's side. "And if the human and the girl are not found? What will we do then, mighty vampire king?"

"We will fight Darius as planned."

"Fight him without the slave at my side?"

"You were perfectly willing to fight Valerian without the slave."

"He is a nymph. He knows how to fuck, nothing more."

Layel stopped and glared up at her. Her green scales were vivid and disgusting in the light. Puffs of smoke and sulfur constantly curled out her nose. "Have you just arrived in Atlantis, woman? Is that why you know nothing of the creatures here?"

"He could be harboring my slave inside those walls."

"He is not." Layel kicked back into motion. "Valerian is many things, but he is not a liar."

"How do you know?" she demanded, keeping pace beside him. "Why do you like him so?"

Their armies followed behind them, and they soon reentered the forest. Limbs stretched long fingers toward them, and twigs snapped under his feet. "If he had her, he would have paraded her across the parapet, showing her to us and laughing. The man has a twisted sense of humor."

"We wasted our time coming here." An irritated statement, not a question.

"We learned the human and the slave have not left Atlantis. They have not passed through a portal, so they are here, waiting to be found and captured."

Perhaps a lie, perhaps not. But she did not question his "logic."

No, she smiled.

Soon, he reminded himself.

## CHAPTER TWELVE

GRAY AND JEWEL SHOPPED for several hours, buying clothing, weapons, trinkets and food. After devouring three meat pies, or whatever they were, Gray felt stronger than he had in days. And he needed his strength. His backpack probably weighed a hundred pounds, stuffed as it was with Jewel's purchases.

He'd watched her skip and laugh from booth to booth like an eager child, simply enjoying her, loving the way her eyes sparkled, the way her cheeks glowed from peaches to strawberries.

So many times he'd come close to jerking her aside and ravishing her mouth, desperate to taste her. One taste, that's all he wanted. One taste, that's all he needed. Just one taste—

Would never be enough.

The words slammed into his head, but he shoved them out with iron-edged determination. Denied them. One taste would have to be enough because that's all he could allow himself. He simply couldn't risk more. Soon, they would part.

"I want this, and this, and this," she sang. "Oh, look at this. I want it."

*I want you.* Only once did he deny her something she wanted. She asked to return to the first table, the one with the jeweled armband. He didn't want her to buy it for herself; *he* wanted to buy it for her. He wanted to surprise her with it. With her mind-reading ability, he doubted anyone had ever managed to surprise her. He would be the first, he vowed.

"We shouldn't go back to that area," he said, the excuse lame but all he could come up with in his excitement.

She accepted his refusal with an adorable pout before racing to a stall overflowing with silks and lace. He scanned the crowd around her and found no hint of their enemies.

"I'll be right back," he said.

Her only reply was a slight nod. He shook his head and grinned wryly. If the woman had to choose between shopping and him, he had no doubt which would emerge the winner. And it wasn't him.

While she haggled over the price of a sexy gold-and-white robe, he snuck off and bought her the armband, burying it at the bottom of his pack so she wouldn't see it.

If she realized what he'd done, she gave no indication as he approached her side. She had moved from the clothes to a table piled high with large, painted rocks. The rocks appeared to be ordinary pebbles found on the ground, but the brilliantly colored scenes painted on their surfaces gave them a breathtaking beauty.

The seller, a female with the face of a bull and the body of a human—God, he might never get used to looking at these bull creatures—wore a dirty robe and paint stained her very human fingers. She didn't try to talk them into buying, just let them look at their leisure.

"I want one," Jewel said.

"They're amazing." Gray was still surprised at the ease with which he spoke the Atlantean language.

"Thank you," the woman muttered demurely.

"You did them yourself?"

She nodded. "I take great joy in my art."

As she spoke, Gray encountered the oddest sensation. Suddenly and shockingly, he smelled her blood. Actually smelled the sweetness of her blood—and he wanted to taste it. Not in a sexual way. His mouth watered like he needed water. His gaze flicked to the woman's neck, at the pulse thumping there.

He ran his tongue over his teeth, repulsed by the desire and trying fervently to squelch it. But her sweet scent remained strong in his nostrils and the need for a taste, a single taste, intensified. What the hell was wrong with him?

He whipped to Jewel, intending to tell her he'd wait for her at a distance. Then he caught a whiff of *her* blood. She smelled of goodness and innocence, too, but also of power and passion. Hunger ate at him, consumed him, *this* need holding an undercurrent of sexuality and making it all the more intense.

That quickly, he almost attacked her. Almost leapt on her and sank his teeth into her neck, filling his senses with her essence. Sweat poured from him as he purposefully locked his muscles in place, holding himself in check.

His wounds were responsible for this craving.

Throughout the week he'd lost a lot of blood, therefore his body wanted to replenish. That's all there was to it. Still...

*Get the fuck out of here,* his mind screamed.

"I'll be right over there," he said, the words a mere croak. "Scream if you need me." He slammed several drachmas on the tabletop and stalked away.

Confused, Jewel stared over at him. He stood a good distance from her, but remained within sight, keeping guard over her as always. His silver gaze now churned a stormy gray, fierce and hard. Taut lines formed around his eyes, and his body vibrated with some kind of pent-up energy.

Had she angered him?

"Your man—tell him I cannot accept so much money," the seller said.

Jewel tore her attention from Gray and met the woman's warm, worried gaze. Unbidden, she smiled. Hearing Gray referred to as her man was...heady. "I've never seen such beautiful work as these. You deserve every bit of money he gave you. Please—what is your name?"

"Erwin."

"Please, Erwin, take it with a happy heart."

Her thin lips grew into a smile as she placed the drachmas in her pocket. "Take as many rocks as you'd like."

Jewel nodded. She studied the rocks. Some had waterfalls, some had forests. Some had creatures painted on the surface. Each scene appeared to be alive, as if it were actually happening, as if the creatures were truly moving.

One had two sapphires painted in the center, and they caught Jewel's eye. She lifted the stone and gasped, realizing it was *her* face she was seeing. In the portrait, her eyes held sadness and her mouth dipped in a wistful frown. She looked alone and vulnerable.

"Do you like it?" Erwin asked hesitantly.

"Why—why did you paint this woman?" She held up the rock, showing the minotaur the features decorating the surface.

"Look at her. She represents the suffering of all of us, desperate to escape the life she was born to."

How true. Except for these last few days with Gray, Jewel couldn't recall a time when she'd been happy with her life. She'd always prayed for a day, a single day, where she could be as normal and unaware as everyone else.

"Maybe one day the woman and I will find our escape," the minotaur added. She reached out and drew a finger over the surface, and as she did, her fingertip brushed Jewel's palm.

Jewel jerked as a vision raked her mind.

A little boy, a minotaur, was ripped from a woman's arms. *This* woman's arms. The seller's. Night had fallen and shadows danced all around a small hut that had been built under a tree. Both mother and child were crying and screaming, but the demon army carted them both away, seeing them merely as a food source.

Jewel blinked her eyes and shook her head, clearing

her thoughts. Her heart was slamming inside her chest, and a cold sweat had broken out all over her body.

"You live nearby," she said.

Erwin's furry bull-face became pallid. "That is none of your concern."

"You have built a shelter under a tree for you and your son."

She gasped and stumbled backward, her hand fluttering over her heart. "How did you—"

"Very soon, the demon queen will march her army past your home. They will take you and your son and both of you will die."

"What? How can you—"

Jewel knew the woman would never believe her, not without proof. Not knowing what else to do, she reached up and pushed back her hood, letting the light shove away the shadows and reveal her features. Erwin gasped again, this time shock and horror dripping from the sound.

"You!" she breathed, both hands cupping her mouth.

"Please," Jewel said, replacing her hood. "You wish to escape your life, as did I. I have done so. Do not take it away from me by yelling out now."

The woman nodded, her eyes wide.

"You know now that I'm telling the truth. You know that if you do not move out of the forest, you will lose your life and your son."

She nodded again. With shaky fingers, she began gathering her things and closing her table. "I will take us both to safety," she whispered, horror coating every word. "Now. Right now."

Jewel's hands relaxed at her sides. "All will be well for you," she assured her. "I know it. And I thank you for the rock."

With that, she went to Gray, craving his nearness, his heat. The daylight was beginning to thin, the air to cool. Darkness would soon fall. It would be best if they were ensconced inside a rented room and not wandering the streets. Or had he wanted to return to the forest?

She didn't want him to know what she was doing, so she threw her arms around him, and while he was distracted, dropped the rock inside his bag. "Thank you for everything."

He hugged her back, lingering a moment, before pulling from her. "What were you two talking about?" He no longer appeared angry. His expression was relaxed, his body at ease. "The woman looked sick and ready to faint."

"She realized her son was in danger and went to remove him from harm's way."

"Is that so?" There was a wealth of meaning in that one sentence, and Gray was able to deduce the entire story. Jewel had a vision of danger and had told the woman. The woman had rushed to save her child.

Jewel...amazed him.

He'd seen her lower her hood slightly and had almost run to her and dragged her back to the forest. But he had remained in place, curious about what she was doing. She'd put herself in danger, risked being seen and stolen by God knows what, to help a woman she didn't know. Such kindness was as wonderful as it was foolish.

"I think you've seen all the shops," he told her. "I haven't seen any sign of the demons, so we can get a room. Are you done here?"

"Yes."

"I'm thirsty. For water," he added for his own benefit. His bloodlust had thankfully calmed, but now his mouth felt dry and parched. "Drink first, room afterward."

"I drank all the water in your canteen. I'm sorry! There's an inn near here. We can have drinks and dinner there, as well as stay the night."

"What kind of creatures run it?" He wrapped his arm around her waist, and they padded down the cobbled street, circling around other shoppers.

"Centaurs and sirens. They are known allies, often protecting one another. If we keep our hoods over our heads, I can pretend to be an average siren and you can pretend to be a—"

"Nymph." He stroked two fingers over his jaw. "I think I'd make an excellent nymph."

Jewel chuckled. "They reek of sex and you, well, you smell of delicious human. Besides, you would have a line of women behind you if you were a nymph."

He gave a faux, mournful sigh. "So I have to be… what? A one-eyed Cyclops? A snake-headed Gorgon?"

"Perhaps you can pretend to be a god," she said thoughtfully.

"Pretend?" He snorted.

She chuckled. "Years and years ago, the gods visited us once a week, always taking a different human form and mingling among our ranks. It's been a long time, but you are tall and handsome enough. As a god, you would be worshipped and no one would dare attempt to harm you."

"That's a plan I can go along with." He hefted his backpack higher on his shoulder. "I've always wanted to be worshipped. How much farther is the inn?"

"About a mile. If we hurry, we'll make it before dark."

He caught the undercurrent of anxiety in her tone. "You afraid of the dark, Pru?"

"This area of the Inner City is for all creatures, but it branches off into different sections, one for each race. If we're in the wrong area at the wrong time… Once we reach the area designated for centaurs, we can relax."

He had to admit, his body was aching, his wounds throbbing, and he was more than ready to find a bed. Hell, he might have signed up for a week-long excursion in Demon Town if it meant catching some Z's soon.

"I already miss the *agora,*" Jewel sighed. "The people, the smells, the food."

"You know," he told her, "when I'm gone, you'll have your freedom. You'll be able to visit the market anytime you want. Shop whenever you want."

Her shoulders straightened; she kept her gaze straight ahead. "That is something to dream and hope for, yes."

Manipulating her words again. When would she learn he would not be swayed so easily? "So you can dream about it," he said, "but you can't actually have it? Is that what you're telling me?"

Jewel's eyes widened. She hadn't expected Gray to fully realize what she was doing. Suspect, yes, but not call her on it. "What's to keep another ruler from stealing me? What's to keep someone who thinks I'm dangerous from killing me?" she added in a whispery, hollow tone.

A muscle ticked in his jaw. "You need to learn self-defense. You need to learn how to evade your enemy."

She snorted. "Evade an entire army?"

"It can be done. Believe me."

"I've seen many of your missions, but I doubt I will ever learn to fight and evade as you do."

"You'll do what you have to do to survive." He squeezed her hip, rubbing his thumb along the curve of her waist.

She shivered.

"I was sent to Gillirad, a planet rife with magical wars. Their armies had spells for everything, from freezing someone in place, to spells of sickness. They were destroying each other, and I found myself in the middle."

"Why were you even there?" she gasped, horrified.

"OBI sent me in. I was to do recon, nothing more. To observe them, find out how they practiced such powerful magic, and leave. I had a team of psychics with me. When one of the Gillradian armies spotted us, they cast some kind of spell over my group, a spell that killed everyone but me."

She grabbed his hand, linking their fingers. "What saved you?"

"I think it was the fact that I was the only nonmagical being there. I had no magical qualities, so their magic didn't stick. They realized that and chased me all over the planet. I overheard one of them say they wanted to study me, to experiment and use me against their enemies."

"How did you escape?"

"The same way I survived when I first arrived in Atlantis. It's all about blending into your surroundings, knowing when to strike and when to back away."

"My face is recognizable. One look at me, and everyone knows who I am."

"Maybe you need to disguise your face. Color your hair."

Her shoulders slumped, and she fought back a wave of gloom. Some part of her had hoped he'd ask her to return to the surface with him. Another part had yearned to hear him vow to stay with her always. "That is no life, hiding my true identify. That is not freedom."

"Is there no one you trust to help you, then? To fight in your behalf?"

"I trust *you.*"

His hand slid up, up, to the edge of her breast. A lump formed in her throat, and she gulped. Fire licked through her, heating her blood.

"Besides me," he said, his voice suddenly hard. "Someone who knows Atlantis and its people."

She tumbled the question through her mind, then shook her head sadly. "I could go to the dragons, I guess, but it wouldn't last long. Someone would sell my location and I would be stolen."

"What about your father?"

"As I told you, I have yet to find him. And when I do, I can't be sure he'll be able to help me."

Gray was silent for a long while. Finally he said, "I'll think of something. I won't leave you helpless."

She paused. "You could take me with you."

Gray liked the idea. A lot. A whole hell of a lot.

He liked the idea of having her in his house, in his bed. Just thinking about it got him primed; it hardened and excited him. He could strip her every night, sink into her warm wetness. He could enjoy her at his leisure.

Be her first man.

His hand fisted at his side as pure, undiluted desire rocked him. He'd teach her the way he liked to be touched, and he'd learn the sensitive spots on her body. They'd make love in every position imaginable—and some positions that weren't.

God, he was tempted. So tempted.

No matter how much he might want her with him, however, he was going to leave her here. OBI would find out about her, take her, experiment on her, and lock her away, just as the people of her own world did. There was simply no way to get her through the portal without their knowledge. They had men stationed outside of it twenty-four hours, seven days a week.

"Sorry," he told her, forcing his tone to be as unbending as steel. "I can't do that. You have to stay, and I have to go."

Her eyelids squeezed shut for a brief moment, and she let out a shaky breath. He knew he'd hurt her, and he hated himself for it. "I wish I could, Jewel, but it's impossible."

"I understand," she said softly. "I do. You don't have to explain."

Frustrated, he raked a hand through his hair. Pain oozed from her voice, and he realized he would rather kick his own ass than hear that again. "You would face the same dangers on the surface as you do here, if not worse. Here, at least, the kings and queens do not hurt you physically."

"Sometimes I think that would be better than the emotional pain I'm forced to bear."

God, she was tearing him apart inside, and she didn't even realize it. "Like I said, I'll teach you to defend yourself. We've got some time. I can whip you into a fighting machine in a snap."

They came to a white stone building, music humming from the doors, a soft melody that seduced. No one was entering or leaving the place, so Gray couldn't get a look past those doors. Intrigued, he stopped and read the sign. "The Happy Hoof."

"A centaur bar," Jewel supplied. "With dancing."

His silver gaze whipped to her, just as his stomach clenched. Electric currents raced through him as he imagined holding her in his arms. Pulling her close, meshing her breasts into his chest, swaying with her to the gentle melody. He forgot about his aching body in that instant, his arms itching to hold Jewel, his palms burning to caress her. To sweep away her sadness. "I promised you dancing lessons, sweetheart, and I'm a god of my word."

# CHAPTER THIRTEEN

JEWEL TRAILED behind Gray as he barreled his way past the double doors and inside the bar. The soft sounds of a flute drifted through the laughter and chatter that permeated the room. Centaurs were scattered in every direction, some sitting at tables, resting on their haunches, others prancing on the dance floor in a tangle of chestnut, blond and carmine fur. Several sirens were also present, their skin glowing incandescently, their dark hair silky and flowing. Then—

Everyone stopped, paused, and turned toward them, staring. Even the music ceased, cutting to quiet. Jewel shifted uneasily on her feet.

Gray stepped forward, and several people gasped, muttering, "Human."

As he jumped wholeheartedly into his role of god, his brows arched into his forehead, and his lips dipped into an imperial frown. He waved a hand through the air. "I have arrived," he said, his superior voice cutting through the silence. "Why do you not bow? Do you dare disrespect me?"

The fluidity of his words, as if he'd spoken her language his entire life, still amazed her. She'd never before considered the abrupt syllables sensual, but when Gray spoke them, a hungry shiver traipsed along her spine.

"You can't truly expect us to bow to you, human," a huge centaur snapped, darting forward menacingly. His arms were tanned and thickly muscled, his chest bare and laced with scars.

Jewel's mouth went dry. The centaur planned to snap Gray in half like a twig. She read the thought so clearly in his mind. Coming here had been a bad idea, she'd known it, but had allowed her desire to be in Gray's arms overwhelm common sense.

"I am Adonis," Gray said, layer upon layer of power in his voice, "and you *will* bow."

That voice…compelling and enigmatic, hypnotic, laced with an all-encompassing authority that left no room for argument. Half of the people in the room gasped and stepped toward him, wanting to touch the god who had stepped into their midst. Hope filled them. *It had been so long,* they thought, their excitement growing, *and they hadn't been forgotten as they'd supposed.*

The centaur wavered in his surety that Gray was nothing more than a human, but retained a firm grip on his doubt. "Prove it," the horse-man snarled.

*His name is Bradair,* Jewel whispered in Gray's mind. She hadn't been able to reach him this way since his sickness, and she had no way of knowing if it worked this time.

"Shall I strike you down with a lightning bolt, Bradair? Shall I turn your flesh to ash?"

It had worked! Perhaps his defenses against her were

down. Perhaps he wanted her inside his head. Either way, she was grateful.

Color drained from the centaur's bronzed skin, revealing a fine trace of blue veins. "How did you know my name?"

*He fears snakes,* Jewel added.

Gray never missed a beat. "Shall I toss you into a snake pit?"

"I—I—"

Ready to end this, Jewel closed her eyes and projected her thoughts into the patrons' minds, willing all of them to think Gray was floating, that fire crackled from his head, and lightning sizzled on his fingers.

Bradair fell to his knees, babbling, "I am so sorry for my doubt, my lord. Please forgive me. I am a foolish man, and I will despise myself for all eternity for daring to question you."

"You are forgiven. Make sure it doesn't happen again."

"Yes, yes. Thank you, thank you."

"Table, chairs." Gray clapped, obviously enjoying his role. "I have immediate need of them."

Centaurs and sirens rushed to please the man, or rather *god,* beside her. A table was quickly cleaned, the contents swept to the floor with giddy eagerness, and two chairs dragged in front of it. "Your table, oh Lord of Lords."

He strode to it with an arrogant swagger, everyone he passed reaching out to touch him. He helped Jewel into her seat, then plopped down next to her. No one seemed inclined to leave; they hovered around the table, their expressions rapt. A female centaur with a silky mane of carmine hair stepped forward. Her chest was bare, and her large breasts bounced with her movements.

Jewel's hands fisted at her sides as she fought the urge to cover Gray's eyes.

"Please allow me to serve you, Divine One. It will be my greatest pleasure."

"Two of your finest." Gray flicked Jewel a glance and noticed her chair was several inches away. He grabbed the edge of her seat and scooted her closer, until their thighs brushed.

She gasped at the hot, electric contact. Her gaze locked with his, and his lips slowly teased in a half smile. Every time she looked at him or touched him, she felt as if her soul were exposed. As if she were raw and vulnerable, and oh so needy.

"That's better," he said to her, then to everyone else, "Continue about your business."

Gradually, reluctantly, they obeyed, though everyone kept a reverent eye on him.

"I never expected you to announce your godliness like that. I thought we'd mention it only if absolutely necessary." She paused. "You're always surprising me."

"Then we're even. Besides, I wanted them deferential, not suspicious."

Jewel tore her focus from the hot intensity of his gaze and glanced around. The walls were painted with beautiful murals of frolicking centaurs, lush meadows, and blooming flowers. The wide array of colors was breathtaking, from the brightest azure to the palest pink.

Their drinks were deposited on their table a moment later. "Is there anything else I may get for you, Glorious One? Anything? Anything at all?" As she spoke, the centaur's finger traced the outline of her nipple.

"Nothing else," Jewel snapped. If anyone was going to invite Gray to bed, it was *her*. Jewel.

Expression crumbling, the female trotted away.

"What was that about?" he asked, lips twitching.

"As if you don't know. Pervert!"

"Sheath the claws, Blaze. There's only one woman I'm interested in at the moment."

Her stomach clenched deliciously, but she barely had time to explore the wonderful sensation before he was pushing a glass at her and saying, "Drink up. We really can't stay here long."

Curious and unsure, she sipped tentatively at the amber liquid. It was sweet with an apple flavor. "Mmm." She drained the rest and despite its coolness, it warmed her inside out.

Gray gulped back a drink, then paused and grimaced. "What is this stuff?" He held up his glass and eyed it suspiciously. He even sniffed the rim. "It's like pure sugar."

"I've never tasted anything so delicious."

His gaze dropped and lingered on her lips, intoxicating and heady.

Her cheeks warmed with a blush, that one look affecting her as strongly as a caress, moving along her skin. Her nipples hardened. What would it be like if he licked her there? What would it be like if his fingers delved between her legs, spread her moisture and glided inside her?

She shivered.

What would it be like to clasp his penis in her hand and gently stroke up and down? Tasting the bead of maleness from the tip? So many times she'd dreamed of those things, prayed for them. Been desperate for them. Would he ever give them to her? Would he ever truly *want* to give them to her?

Her gaze strayed to the centaurs dancing in the middle of the large room. Their arms were clasped around each other, their hooves swaying left and right, their tails swishing, and a deep pang of longing rebounded.

"You ready to begin your dancing lessons?"

"I've been ready for years," she said, then pressed her lips together. She hadn't meant to say that out loud. She didn't want Gray to know how she felt about him. He claimed he preferred relationships over quick, forgotten entanglements, but she'd seen the number of women who had fallen in love with him only to watch his back as he walked away.

He was not a man who accepted ties easily.

Pushing to his feet, he intertwined their fingers and tugged her up. The calluses on his hand ignited an inexorable friction. Everyone watched as he ushered her onto the dance floor. He turned, facing the crowd, his back blocked by a corner, and spun her. He drew her into the hard embrace of his arms.

Her lashes fluttered down. She lay her head on his

shoulder and breathed in his scent. Her hands wound around him, anchoring on his lower back, right above his buttocks and beneath his bag. She felt the strength of his muscles, the heat of his skin, and never wanted to leave that spot.

The music continued to play, soft and slow, and they swayed to its seductive beat. It felt so wonderful to be in his arms. So…perfect.

"You're a natural," he praised, his voice thick. He buried his nose in the hollow of her neck, inhaling deeply. "Hmm, you smell good. Ever heard of dirty dancing?"

"No."

"Want me to show you?" His legs spread slightly, fitting hers between them, and his hips began to rock forward, brushing and retreating, his erection straining against her core.

Shock waves of pleasure shot through her, sizzling like the lightning Gray had threatened to use against the centaur, and she gasped. Every point of contact seared her.

"Move your hips against mine."

She did, moving in the opposite direction and connecting in the middle. "It's—it's—" The words caught in her throat, suspended on a jolt of pure carnality. Faster and faster they rocked, arching into one another.

"Perfect. God, I know." One of his hands strayed to her buttocks, gripping, and the other lifted to her neck, tangling in her hair. He pulled her deeper into his embrace, so deep their mouths were only a breath apart. Gazes locked together with sultry intensity, he moved one of his legs so that the apex of her thighs straddled him.

"Oh, gods." Another gasp slipped from her. If they kept this up much longer, she was going to explode. Already her body rushed toward completion. A coiling of pleasure. A search for release.

"I want you tonight," he said. "I shouldn't, but I do. I want you so much I'm aching with it. I told myself I wouldn't take you all the way, just play a bit, but that's not going to be enough. Not nearly enough. Right now, I can't make the consequences matter. I want you tonight," he repeated.

*I want forever with him,* she thought dazedly. Her taste of freedom today had broken something inside her. An acceptance, a passiveness. She deserved a life all her own, a life of love and happiness. Different she might be, but she possessed a very human heart. She wanted Gray in her life now and always. Wanted to strip him down and welcome him inside her body, over and over, night after night, their limbs tangled together.

He wanted only tonight.

"What do you feel?" Gray asked her, the words a whispered caress. "How does being in my arms make you feel?"

"Fire. I feel like I'm burning all over."

"That's good. Real good." His eyes were liquid silver, alive with…something she was almost afraid to name. It was a look she'd never seen from him, in her visions or in reality, almost brutally tender.

She moved her palms to his chest, placing one over

his heart. His heartbeat thundered, strong if a little offbeat. Fast.

"You're begging to be kissed, sweetheart, you know that, don't you? But we can't. If I kiss you, I won't be able to stop. You're a hell of a distraction, and even though these people think I'm a god, I can't afford to be distracted in here." His hand kneaded the back of her neck. "No one else has ever smelled like you, like moonlight and storms."

"You said I couldn't go with you, Gray, but maybe… maybe you can stay here." She tightened her grip on him, her cheek nuzzling his. "Stay here with me."

His eyelids fell to half-mast, and his lips traced her jawline, his tongue flicking out in hot, determined strokes. "I can't. OBI will send in another agent, perhaps more, and those men will die or kill the people here. I want you, Jewel. I do. More than I've ever wanted another woman, but I *will* leave you. No matter what happens, I'm going home. Never let yourself think otherwise."

There was pure honesty in his voice, a bone-deep conviction. He didn't harbor a single doubt about his words; he believed them with his whole heart. If she allowed him, he would kiss her, perhaps make love with her tonight, but when his mission ended, so did their association.

They would never see each other again. Never speak with each other.

That knowledge cut deeper than any knife.

She'd known he would deny her, of course. The moment she'd spoken, she had known his reply, but hope was a strange, foolish thing.

Only two options presented themselves. Embrace the time they had together or keep him at a distance. Either way, she would end up with a broken heart. One would leave her with beautiful memories that could destroy her. The other would bring regret, but she would survive.

"I've been honest with you from the beginning," he said, softening his tone to ease the sting of his previous words.

"I told you before that you don't have to explain your reasons to me." She tried to mask her hurt, but didn't quite succeed. "I'm very aware of what you're like."

He studied her face. Whatever he saw in her expression angered him because he scowled, grabbed her hand, and hauled her back to the table. His scowl remained as he signaled for two more drinks. He didn't speak until they arrived and the server disappeared.

News of Gray's presence must have spread, because the bar filled with centaurs and sirens, eating away at the space. Every few seconds, someone fingered his hair or caressed his shoulder. For the most part, he ignored them.

"What do you mean, you know what I'm like?" He propped his elbows on the table and leaned forward while she sipped at the ice-cold sweetness. "And before you remind me that I said we can't stay here much longer, answer my question."

She met his gaze dead on, eyes narrowed, blood surging with her own sense of growing fury. "You get rid of your women very quickly."

"That's a lie, honey. I don't do one-night stands."

"Not in your mind, no. You keep women around for a while, but you never give more of yourself than the barest glimmer. The moment they start to get close to you, you leave them."

Gray's nostrils flared. His last girlfriend had lasted six months. Six months of monogamy and commitment. He'd liked her, had enjoyed spending time with her…but the night she told him she loved him was the last night he spent with her, he realized.

He blinked, doing a quick mental replay of his other girlfriends. Goddamn it, Jewel was right. In the beginning, his last girlfriend had been content to see him the few days out of the month he was home and talk to him sparingly on the phone. They'd had a great sex life, one where they both found enjoyment. Then she'd started hinting that she wanted more. More of his time, more of *him*. She'd begun leaving clothing at his house. The shit exploded, however, when he found tampons in his medicine cabinet. Tampons, for God's sake. It had only been at that moment, as he stared at the feminine products, that he'd realized he was in a hard-core relationship.

He'd sweated for a couple days, but hadn't stopped seeing her. He'd wondered, though, why he felt no compulsion to tell her about his life. And why he hadn't wanted to introduce her to his family. If he had, maybe the "I love you" thing wouldn't have sent him flinging over the edge.

He hated one-night stands, or so he'd always told

himself. Basically, that was all he'd ever had. One-night stands that lasted several months. He'd never told a girlfriend he loved her, never lived with a woman, either. Never told a woman about his life, his job, or his family. He shook his head in disbelief.

It wasn't like he wanted to remain a bachelor for the rest of his life. He actually liked the idea of marriage, children, and happily ever after. So what was the problem? Why did he refuse to allow himself to fall in love?

Only one answer sprang to mind. He hadn't met the right woman.

He frowned, considering the validity of that thought. If that disgusting cliché was true, it would mean there was only one person, one true love, for everyone. His dad and mom, he'd thought, had been soul mates. Then his mom died, and though his dad remained single for a long time afterward, he *had* found another woman—one he loved more than he'd ever loved Gray's mom.

Gray didn't resent his stepmom, Francis, for that, but it *had* rocked his views of love. Was he waiting for a deeper connection than he'd had with any of his women? Had he somehow known he couldn't get it from them? Had his dreams of Jewel ruined him for anyone else, because he'd known deep down what she would be to him?

*Yes,* roared inside his mind. He quickly stamped it down, one of the most difficult things he'd ever done. They were from two different worlds, and he could never let himself forget that. Despite his dreams of her, despite her visions of him, they were not destined to be together. They couldn't be. There were just too many complications.

He couldn't deny that he wanted her, though. God, did he want her. Bad. She fired his blood, made him hot and hungry. Made him sweat, willing to beg for it. Made his hormones surge. For her. Only her.

Only Jewel seemed to excite him now and the knowledge mocked his previous denial of their connection. Her kindness continually rocked him. Her smile continually brightened him. He was more aware of her than he ever had been of another. He wanted to protect and coddle her. He wanted to possess her, brand her.

He wanted to keep her.

Gray scrubbed a hand down his face. Fuck, shit, damn. He wanted to keep her with him, now. Always. He wanted to wrap himself around her until he was all she knew. The most primitive part of him demanded he mark her with his essence so she'd never forgot exactly which man she belonged to. So every man would know who she belonged to.

No. *No.* He wouldn't allow that to mean more than a few nights of pleasure. He'd have her—there would be no stopping that, he realized that now, but he wouldn't keep her. Tonight, he would claim her body, satisfy the hunger that ravaged them both, and purge her from his system.

"It's getting late," he bit out. "And it's too crowded in here." The thought of having her was already exciting him, heating his blood and consuming his senses. On the dance floor, he'd been close to coming in his pants like a teenager. She'd felt so damn good, a perfect fit against him. God knew how much better she'd feel naked, under him, her legs wrapped around his waist. "We should go."

She lifted her glass and drained the contents. He dropped several drachmas on the tabletop, then stood, Jewel following suit. He didn't dare touch her right now. He wanted her too much and his control teetered precariously on total annihilation.

Out of habit, his gaze searched for menacing movements and creeping shadows as he stalked to the door. Since joining OBI, he'd lived his life that way, always searching for those who meant him harm. The proclivity had saved him on several occasions.

"Return whenever you wish," someone called.

"I'll make a sacrifice in your honor," someone else shouted.

Outside, he kept his gaze intent as he scanned the empty street. Night had fallen completely. Stone torches glowed from jagged walls.

"The inn is over there," Jewel said, pointing to a building that looked more like a stable than a hotel.

He would have preferred a bed of silk and satin for his first time with Jewel, but he'd take whatever he could get. Besides, he thought hopefully, maybe it wasn't as primitive on the inside as he'd feared.

Wrong.

As he stepped over the threshold, his boots sank into a thick layer of hay. The scent of sweat and animal enveloped him. An aging male centaur with a long silver beard manned the area.

"I'd like a room," Gray told him, sliding the last of his drachmas over the scarred wood surface that separated them.

"You're Adonis," the man gasped. "They said you had come, but I didn't believe them. I beg forgiveness for my doubt."

Gray nodded. Because really, what else could he do?

His money was slid back to him. "It is my greatest honor to house you, great lord. Please, please. Follow me. If you have need of anything, you have only to ask and I will personally see that it is yours. If you wish a morning ride, I will gladly seat you on my own back."

The centaur showed them to a large, cozy room. There was an actual bed, complete with soft blue sheets. There was a bathing pool and enough pillows strewn across the floor to use as a trampoline.

"You may leave us," he said, staying in character.

"As you wish." The centaur backed out of the room, bowing low. "Thank you, sweet lord. Thank you."

Jewel's gaze shifted nervously from Gray to the bed, to the pool, to Gray again. He looked her up and down, imagining his hands everywhere he looked.

She gulped. "Are we going to bed now?"

Instead of answering, he said, his voice rough with the force of his need, "Why don't you take a bath here, while I search the perimeter." He needed to map an escape route, just in case, and she needed time alone. If her sudden nervousness was any indication, she knew what was going to happen, wanted it, but needed time to accept.

# CHAPTER FOURTEEN

JEWEL SOAKED in the bathing pool, luxuriating in the sweet scent of the water. Orchid oil had been poured inside, softening her skin. The air around her was cool, but the water was hot, and the two made an intoxicating combination. She scrubbed from head to toe, washing away the trials of the last few days.

Her gaze continued to shift nervously to the side. She'd placed a screen in front of the pool, so Gray wouldn't be able to see her if he entered. Still…she sank deeper into the water, the liquid lapping up to her neck. A part of her was afraid he wouldn't like what he saw, but another part of her, the wildest part, suspected he'd find her sensually beautiful. Irresistible. He'd take her in his arms—but would she know what to do? Would she please him?

Before he'd left, there had been an intense heat blazing in his eyes. He'd looked at her, his gaze lingering on her breasts and between her legs. She'd felt that same ache she always felt whenever he watched her. Where nothing else mattered but Gray, his voice, his touch.

That ache plagued her now. Biting her lower lip, she

skimmed a hand down her breasts and her nipples hardened. Her fingers lowered, slipping over her oil-slicked stomach, the same way she'd seen Gray touch other women. Her fingers glided back up and circled her nipples. A shiver raced through her.

Her gaze once again darted to the screen. She'd hear him if he came in; there was no reason to worry.

"Gray," she groaned, closing her eyes and picturing the sensual planes of his face. She'd seen him do other things, as well…things that had always fascinated her. She kneaded her breasts, pretending it was Gray's hands touching her. Her blood heated, and she gasped in a choppy puff of air.

*I'll die if I don't touch you,* he said inside her mind.

Her hands trailed down her stomach again, stopping at the small triangle of hair between her legs. What would Gray do to her if he were here? Slowly her hands moved lower. He'd touch her…right… there. She gasped as a shaft of pure pleasure struck her. Her teeth bit more sharply into her lip, and she moved her fingers again, circling this time, slowly, slowly.

She moaned. In her mind, she saw Gray kissing his way up her body. Kissing her behind her knees. Kissing her inner thighs. And licking his way between her legs, his tongue exactly where her fingers moved.

"Ahh," she cried, arching her hips. The water lapped at the sides of the pool, then changed directions and hit her sides, caressing her skin like waves caressing a beach. While she imagined his mouth devouring her, she also pictured his fingers slipping and sliding up her body, pinching her nipples. His tongue circled faster, licking and sucking at her.

"Oh, gods," she groaned. The pleasure was building, already so intense she verged on insanity. "Gray," she whispered. "Gray."

GRAY STRODE DOWN THE HALL, headed toward his room, intent on finding Jewel and at last finishing what they'd started. He'd given her time to get used to the idea, given her time to calm and accept.

That time was over.

After he'd left her, he'd found an escape route, then a place to bathe. His hair was still damp, his robe clinging to his moist skin. Soon he would—

An image of him and Jewel flashed through his mind, and he stopped abruptly, boot raised midair. She was naked, splayed out in a bathing pool, and he was on top of her, between her legs, pleasuring her with his mouth, drinking in her sweet essence.

Instantly his body went rock hard, desire more intense than anything he'd ever experienced rushing through him. He nearly doubled over from the force of it. He could almost taste her in his mouth, and he knew he'd never tasted anything sweeter, hotter. He could almost feel her oil-slick skin beneath his hands, and he knew he'd never felt anything so soft.

In his mind, he glanced up at her. *I'll die if I don't touch you.* Her head was thrown back, her eyes closed, her teeth biting down on her bottom lip. Inky strands of hair floated around her, and her skin was flushed, a bouquet of strawberries, peaches and cream.

He wanted to eat her up.

One of her hands was gripping the side of the pool, the other was tangled in his hair. He'd never seen anything more erotic.

Alone in the hallway, he leaned against the wall. A sheen of sweat broke over him, dripping from his temples. His lips pulled taut.

"Holy shit," he growled. The vision in his mind was so real, it was like he really was there. He could actually hear her moan his name. She arched her hips, and his erection jerked. He rubbed a hand down the long, hard length of himself, wishing it were her hand. Her mouth.

He had to get inside her. In the vision, in reality, it didn't matter. He had to get inside her. Had to…get inside…her.

Gritting his teeth against the pain of his arousal, he stalked down the hall. His fists clenched as he entered the room and shut the door behind him, his eyes searching for her. She was nowhere to be seen, but he could hear the sound of her breathing, shallow and erratic. There was a screen in front of the bathing pool, and he strode toward it without a word.

When he rounded the screen, he jerked to a halt. Sucked in a breath. Nearly came. There she was, splayed out in the water, just like in his vision, her hand between her legs. Her hips were arching, her face glowing with her pleasure. Her nipples were pink and hard and his mouth watered for them. Steam wafted around her, creating a cloudy haze.

She was on the verge of orgasm. But he didn't want her to come without him, nor did he want to come without her. He moved to the edge of the pool, his every nerve on alert, his every cell heating.

"Jewel," he whispered brokenly.

Her eyes slowly opened. "Gray," she said, and she didn't seem surprised or embarrassed to find him there. Her arousal had reached the point of complete consumption. It was all she could think about, all she could feel. "What's happening to me?"

"You need a man. You need me."

"Yes," she said. "Yes. Please."

He jerked off his robe and tore off his military fatigues, his movements clipped and quick, desperate. He unstrapped the blades from his wrists, waist and ankles and dropped them to the floor with a thump. He should have forgone the arsenal after his bath, but hadn't. Now he cursed himself for the time it took to remove them, time he could be touching Jewel.

Finally he was naked, his erection jutting forward as he stepped into the water, liquid heat swallowing his ankles. He sank as though in a dream. Her gaze raked over him, and she moaned, arched her hips, her own fingers still working at her clitoris.

The time had come.

No more thinking about it, no more wondering if it was the right decision. No more worrying about their different worlds. All that mattered was the here and now. All that mattered was being with Jewel, if only for a little while.

He reached her, unable to go another second without her in his arms. He gripped her hand, her pleasure-giving hand, and placed it at the side of the pool. Next he spread her legs and moved between them. He didn't enter her, though. No, he wanted to savor her first. Wanted to touch and taste her like he had in his vision.

But everything inside him screamed to rush, to take her now and take her hard.

"Were you thinking about me when you touched yourself?" he asked, amazed he could even get the words out. He was *that* hungry for her.

She nodded.

"What did you see in your mind?"

"Your mouth," she whispered, "tasting me."

"Here?" His fingers circled her clitoris, and she gasped. He raised her pelvis, bent his head and licked her, sliding his thumb down and pressing it against her core. Her sweet, sweet taste tantalized him.

"Yes, right there." The words emerged as little more than a moan.

If he licked her there again, she'd come. And he didn't want her to come yet. He wanted her to come on his cock. Rising up, he slid a finger into her hot, tight sheath. She felt so good, so damn good. He leaned down, and licked his tongue around one of her nipples, then the other, tasting the nectar of whatever flower flavored the water.

Her hands clenched the sides of the pool, helping to hold her up. "Gray," she panted. "I feel so…hot. Make it stop. No, don't stop. I need more. No, no more. I have to taste *you*. All of you."

Eyes wild, she rose over him and pushed him back before he could utter a protest. Not that he would. Then little Miss Prudence went down on him, sucking his length up and down, bringing her teeth and tongue into play, her hand cupping his ball sac. On and on she continued, until he was shouting, clenching, wild.

Before his body completed the last spasm, he was hard again. Ready for her. Panting for her, as if he'd never come. A sense of urgency built inside of him, again, beating against his usual need for leisure, about to unfurl completely. He always went slowly with women, always took his time, never allowed himself to be quick and hurried. But his blood was heating, near boiling, about to burst, and he suddenly wasn't sure of his control.

He climbed up her body. Water sloshed. His gaze strayed and lingered on her neck, at the pulse hammering there. His mouth watered. What would it be like to sink his teeth in her vein, to let her blood pour down his throat? He kissed his way between her breasts, lingered on her collarbone, then licked her neck.

She arched against him, writhing. Her hands flew to his back, squeezing him, scratching him. He was going to bite her…had to bite her…and he was going to do it while he filled her with his cock. He was disgusted with himself, but he couldn't stop the need from growing. He wanted to enter her and bite her at the same time, taking all of her, all she had to give. The need was so strong, he couldn't control it.

If he didn't bite her soon, he'd perish. If he didn't enter her soon, he'd perish. If he didn't spill his seed inside her soon, he'd perish. So many ways to kill him, yet all reasons to live. He had to have her, *would* have her, nothing could stop him.

"Tell me you're ready. Tell me you can take me."

"Yes, yes. Now. Please now. Pleasepleaseplease."

"Jewel. Mine." He was just opening his mouth, just reaching down, gripping his erection, poising himself for entry, when he heard the door burst open.

# CHAPTER FIFTEEN

PROTECTIVE INSTINCTS ROARING to life, Gray fought through the cloud of lust encompassing his mind and jolted up. A feral rage burned in his chest, spreading, growing hotter. He hummed with it, vibrated with it, was savage with it. A low, bestial growl emitted from his throat.

Water splashed over the pool's edge as he leapt out. His breathing was harsh and ragged, and sweat trickled down his cheeks. Scowling, he grabbed two of his blades from the floor.

Jewel's eyes were glazed with passion and she shook her head, trying to clear her thoughts. She straightened, a look of horror lighting her features. Gray heard no footsteps, only the flutter of wings. He couldn't see past the screen in front of the bath, so had no idea who this unseen enemy was—an unseen enemy that would die painfully for daring to interrupt him.

"Where are they?" he heard a deep voice demand.

He immediately recognized the speaker. A Formorian he'd gambled with—and beaten—at the market. Gray's gaze narrowed. He should have expected something like this, but he hadn't. His only concern had been the vampires and demons. And getting Jewel naked.

"What—"

"Shh," he whispered to Jewel, handing her one of his knives. She took the offered weapon with shaky fingers. "Stay here," he mouthed.

He found another blade buried under his pants and hurriedly grabbed it. With every second that passed, his rage intensified. Yes, someone was going to die this night.

"Find the money," the Formorian barked.

The sound of destruction rose, breaking wood, ripping fabric. He didn't know how many there were, but it was only a matter of seconds before they spotted him and Jewel behind the screen. He preferred to keep the action in the center of the room, away from Jewel.

Unconcerned by his nakedness, he crouched low and peeked from behind the screen, soaking in details. The Formorians used their wings to hold themselves up, their one leg reaching out and knocking everything down, their one arm holding a spiked club. There were five of them. Shit. Shit! He'd been in worse situations, but he would have preferred his gun.

As he crouched there, deciding the best way to attack, any lingering sexual lust mutated into simple bloodlust. He went from white-hot to ice-cold in seconds. His mind shut down, focusing only on war and death. The thick metallic stench of Formorian blood enveloped him.

One, he mentally counted. Two. Three.

War cry blaring from him, Gray sprang from his

position and attacked the nearest creature, determined
to fight it the same way he'd fought the demons. He
might not know these creatures' weaknesses but
nothing could survive a slit throat.

Because of the element of surprise, he was able to
grab the first one-armed, one-legged beast from behind.
The creature jerked, hard, and Gray felt the wound in
his thigh tear. Determinedly he gave a quick slash of
his blade. The creature went limp and dropped his club,
falling to the ground, thick black blood seeping from
his twitching body.

One down, four more to go.

By the time Gray had turned around, two other creatures were flying toward him, fury darkening their ugly
features. Seconds before they reached him, he ducked
low and grabbed both of them by their ankle. They
pulled and struggled against his hold, but he pivoted,
slashed up with his feet, using the creatures' elevated
height to anchor him as he kicked them senseless.

Both dropped to the ground, gasping for breath, and
he cut both their necks at the same time. The leader
screeched an unholy sound that rocked the walls.

"Come and get me," he spat.

Club raised, the Formorian stalked toward him.
Gray's lips were curling into a slow smile—until he
saw Jewel race from behind the screen. His grin died
as a sense of rage and helplessness sprouted inside
him. She'd haphazardly wrapped her robe around her
body and it billowed at her ankles, flapping with her
movements. She had her blade raised, ready to battle.

Her name was poised at the edge of his lips, ready

to scream it out and command her to hide, to return behind the screen. But he didn't want to draw any attention to her. He didn't mind dying himself, but he'd be damned if he'd let Jewel receive even the smallest scratch.

A Formorian sensed her presence and turned around, club raised. The leader was still flying toward Gray, Jewel was still racing toward the other. Gray started running, too, and when he was almost upon the leader, he jumped up and slammed his feet into the bastard's chest, shooting him backward.

Gray didn't slow, but the world seemed to slow around him. An agonizing slowness with a reality that there was only one thing he could do sinking into him. And if he failed, if he missed…Jewel would be dead. He kept moving, sprinting toward her and the final combatant.

The two were almost upon each other. Jewel's attacker was reaching back with his club just as Gray drew back his arm to throw his knife.

He was suddenly grabbed from behind with a single hand. Sharp nails dug into his shoulder, tugging him backward. Gray's blade flew out of his hand, but missed its intended target completely. As he fell, he watched through horrified eyes as Jewel slammed into the other beast. Her knife was raised, ready to strike, but the bastard managed to act first.

His club pounded into her upper arm.

Gray hit the ground, howling in fury, a red haze of rage beating inside him. The leader jumped on top of him, and he rolled over, not thinking about his next actions. He simply opened his mouth and sank his teeth into the Formorian's neck, thick blood sliding down his throat, burning the pit of his stomach. The creature howled and jerked against him, but Gray kept a steady jaw lock, draining the bastard dry.

When he finished, he tossed the lifeless creature aside and sprang to his feet. Warm drops of blood trickled down his mouth, off his chin. He wiped them away. The remaining Formorian had an unconscious Jewel by the hair and was dragging her out of the room. Her blood left a crimson trail behind her. Gray's heart stopped beating and he snarled, the sound raw and animalistic.

He sprinted after them, swooping down and grabbing one of the abandoned clubs as he ran. He hefted its weight in his hand. With another war cry, he raised up his arm and struck, slamming the spiked tip into the back of the creature's head, putting all of his strength behind the blow.

Jewel was released; she thumped to the ground. As the creature spun toward him, Gray hit him again and again, until there was nothing but pieces left. He was panting with the force of his rage. Only when his arms shook and his hands throbbed from splinters did he drop the club.

His gaze found Jewel. Her eyes were closed, her face soft, as if she were sleeping. He knelt and gently gathered her in his arms. Her head fell back, her hair streaming down. A few centaurs were scattered throughout the hallway, gasping at the blood. Gasping at the sight of Jewel.

"It's her," one of them said, his voice reverent. The foolish horse-man took a step toward her, reaching out.

"Touch her and die," Gray snarled. Without another word, he carried her to their room, kicking bodies and debris out of the way. He laid his woman on the mountain of pillows. His fingers found the hollow of her neck where her pulse should…beat… Thank God! His knees buckled in relief. Her pulse was weak and thready, but it was there.

She was alive.

His satisfaction was a palpable, all-consuming force, and in that moment he recognized Jewel as *his* woman, the one woman for him. The one he couldn't live without. He might deny it later, but for now, in this moment, he acknowledged the truth.

He stayed on his knees, ripping off her robe, searching for her wounds. Blood had dripped onto her stomach, and he cleaned it away to ascertain she hadn't been hurt there. That kind of wound was often fatal, but he encountered only smooth, healthy skin.

The only wound he could see was on her left arm. There were dime-sized holes from the club spikes, and the skin was black and blue. As he watched, however, the holes began to close, the bruises began to fade.

His eyes widened. She was healing at a superhuman speed. His unsteady heartbeat slowed and calmed, and the rage in his blood dwindled. The things he'd done only moments before played through his mind. Without any remorse, he'd sucked the blood from someone's neck. And he'd liked it. He'd clubbed someone. And he'd liked it.

Obviously the desire for blood was not because he'd lost some of his own like he'd first supposed. Something was changing inside him, something dark and dangerous. He didn't understand it, was almost afraid to analyze it, but there it was.

Jewel gasped, and her eyelids popped open. "Gray."

"King of kings, more Formorians will arrive soon," one of the centaurs said, stepping into the room. "They will sense the deaths of their brethren and come. We must prepare." Hooves pounded in the background.

"How you feeling?" he asked softly, not moving from his place beside Jewel. An army could invade, and he wouldn't have cared. He wasn't leaving this spot until he was one hundred percent positive of her recovery.

"Stiff, but good." She stretched her arms over her head and arched her back. "Did I kill him?"

"Yes," he lied, knowing that was what she wanted to hear. He smoothed his hands over her face, lingering over the seam of her lips. "How did you heal like that, sweetheart? Do you need extra time to heal internally?"

Her face scrunched adorably in her confusion. "Heal? I remember that he hit me and that it burned like fire, but I feel fine now. He must not have hit me very hard."

She didn't know, he realized. She didn't know the club had cut through to the bone.

"Easy, easy," he said as she jerked to a sitting position.

"Gray, I'm fine—" She glanced down and saw her

nakedness. Gasping, she pulled her robe tight against her. "I thought I covered myself!"

He grinned. His little Prudence would be fine. He didn't understand it. Hell, he didn't understand a lot of the things that had happened lately, but he was okay with that because Jewel would live.

Gray planted a swift kiss on her lips and pushed to his feet. "We have to get out of here." He scrambled around the room, grabbing his backpack, weapons, and securing his robe over his shoulders.

Jewel's cheeks glowed bright as she realized her robe simply wouldn't cover her breasts. The edges were ripped to shreds. She grabbed the velvet-soft sheet atop the pillows and wrapped it around herself. When she finished, she gazed at the room, at the carnage littering the floor.

"I should have sensed them," she said quietly. "I should have known they were coming."

"You told me you can't sense danger to yourself, so how could you have known? *I* should have known they would do this."

"No, I—"

"I'm taking blame for this and that's the end of it. Are you strong enough to walk?"

"I am, yes, but are you? You're bleeding." Concerned, she stared at his face, his hands. A frown tugged at her lips, and she stepped toward him.

"I'll be fine." He closed the rest of the distance between them and grabbed her hand. "We've got to head back to the other side of the forest."

She nodded.

They raced out of the room and into the hallway, pushing past centaurs. Gray followed the escape route he'd mapped earlier, before his bath. He hadn't known at the time that he'd need it, but lived by the "better to be safe than sorry" code, and now he was grateful he did.

The route twisted and turned in every direction, the wall torches becoming fewer in number. He took the narrowest path, the one that led to a staircase. He and Jewel pounded down those steps, and he kicked the door the moment it was within reach. Hinges splintered as the door burst wide open. Cool night air wafted around him.

His eyes quickly adjusted to the darkness, faster than usual. As he raced through the abandoned alleyway, a wave of dizziness struck him. He was losing blood. He'd managed to forget his wounds for a while, but now they throbbed, demanding attention.

"Keep an eye behind us, okay? Tell me if you think we're being followed."

"Formorians work best in the air, but the skyline is clear. They haven't spotted us."

"Good. That's good." The streets were quiet, and he kept to the shadows, moving behind buildings and carts.

What seemed an eternity later, Jewel said, "We're almost there, I can feel it."

Finally tall oaks filled his vision and he raced toward them. Insects buzzed and swarmed him. Dewy green leaves and branches swatted at him. "Cover your face," he said.

"Ow," she cried, reaching up to cover her cheek from the stinging vines.

"Let's find a spot to rest." His breath was burning inside his lungs. His limbs were growing shaky, and a web of lethargy was weaving through him. He'd taken a lot of abuse lately, more than he ever had before, and he was feeling the effects. He refused to pass out in front of Jewel again. "Tell me when you feel like it's safe."

Once he spoke the words, he realized how much he'd come to depend on her for their safety. He trusted her judgement, her senses. He *needed* her.

"Head toward the river," she panted.

He listened for the rustle of water and veered right. When they reached the water's edge, he saw a wide, rocky path.

"Formorians hate water."

"Then we're crossing." Not waiting for her reply, he tugged her into the water. At first the icy liquid only reached his ankles, but as he ran through it, splashing it in every direction, it became deeper. Finally he was swimming, unable to touch bottom.

Jewel swam beside him. It took them about ten minutes to reach the other side, and once they did, they pulled their soaking bodies onto the edge. "We've done this before," he said between shallow breaths.

"Let's hope this is our last time."

"I want to move a little farther away."

She nodded, stumbling forward. He stayed right beside her, crawling through vegetation and sand. How much time passed, how far they actually got, he didn't know. Finally, he dropped his backpack, painfully aware he couldn't go another step. "Here's good."

"Here, yes."

"Take off your wet clothes." As he spoke, he stripped. When he was naked, he dug inside his backpack and withdrew his dry fatigues. He spread them on the ground.

Jewel didn't protest. She shed the velvet sheet and it pooled at her feet. Her arms wrapped around her waist in a vain effort to guard against the cold.

Gray lay down on top his clothing, saying, "Com'ere." He shouldn't allow himself to sleep; he should erect some sort of shelter. But he closed his eyes, feeling Jewel lie down beside him, her body contouring to his. She placed her head on his good arm. He could feel her erratic heartbeat drumming against his chest, beating in sync with his. A sense of contentment settled over him.

He fell asleep like that.

## CHAPTER SIXTEEN

LIGHT PIERCED Gray's consciousness.

He slowly cracked open his eyes and winced. His body throbbed like he'd been thrown into a ring and gone fifty rounds with a heavyweight. Jewel was curled into his side, still asleep. Her features were soft and relaxed and contentment lifted the corners of her lips.

She was naked. He was naked. And his body liked the contact.

God, she was lovely. Her skin was as dewy as a morning peach, her legs long and tapered perfectly. Her waist dipped and her hips flared deliciously.

Fighting the sudden fire in his blood, he brushed a strand of hair from her cheek. Last night's events sped through his mind. He'd almost lost her. This innocent little peach had almost died. Just the reminder made his palms sweat. In their short time together, she'd come to mean a lot to him. More than any woman ever had.

*She's safe now,* he reminded himself, relaxing. That was all that mattered.

From this point on, he was damn well going to do a better job of looking out for her. Gambling with the Formorians had been risky, and he'd known better. He'd just wanted to give her an honestly purchased present and the desire had clouded his common sense. Which proved his reasons for not getting involved were well founded.

The armband rested at the bottom of his bag; he knew it was there. He just didn't know when—or *if*—he was going to give it to her. He had to get focused on his job, and if he gave her the gift now, she might think it meant more than it did. Like he'd stay with her or something. His heart skipped a beat.

"Wake up, sleeping beauty." He wanted to wake her with a kiss, but didn't dare. If he kissed her, he wouldn't stop kissing her until he had her under him, his cock sliding inside her. They had stuff to talk about, and he had stuff to do. It was time he remembered that and put things in perspective.

Jewel stirred and stretched like a newborn babe, purring low in her throat. The sounds drifted over his nerve endings like an erotic caress. She blinked open her eyes, her long lashes fluttering up and down. He was suddenly thirsty for her.

"Gray," she said, gingerly sitting up. "Is everything all right?"

"Everything's fine." He forced his mind to remain on business. "Did last night's adventure throw us off the path to Dunamis?"

She pushed her hair from her face, realized she was naked, and grabbed her now dry sheet, tugging it around her. "We were already thrown off, slower than I anticipated. But the temple is only a day and a half walk from here."

Walking that long sounded about as fun as a full body waxing. He grimaced and worried a hand on his jaw stubble. "I'm going to ask you something, and I want you to answer honestly. Don't answer me with a question. Just tell me the truth, okay?"

Her eyes met his, thoughts spinning in her head. Reluctantly she nodded.

"Why am I craving blood?"

A soft sigh escaped her. A relieved sigh? Had she expected him to ask something else? "When the vampire and demon bit you, they left pieces of themselves inside you."

So, legends had gotten that part right. Revulsion, dread, and rage pounded through him. "I'm becoming like them?" The words were stark, ripped from his throat. He wanted to howl in denial; they were evil, he was not. He believed in truth and justice, protecting the weak. "Exactly like them?"

"Only certain characteristics. We won't know which ones until you experience them."

"And there's no way to stop the changes? I'm going to become evil?"

"No, never evil."

"You say that with such surety, yet you also say I'll change."

"Who you are inside will never change."

He took comfort in that, inhaling and exhaling, then determinedly pushing the subject from his mind. He'd deal with each change as it came and not worry about it beforehand. Right now he needed to radio OBI, let them know he was okay. And he didn't want Jewel to hear the conversation. As he struggled to a sitting position, he pinned her with a pointed stare. "Why don't you go to the river and wash, honey. You've got mud all over you."

"No, you're too weak—"

"I didn't want to say this," he said, cutting through her words, "but you've forced me. You kind of smell." Unlike Jewel, he could lie his ass off. She smelled wonderful; she always did.

Her eyes widened, and her mouth dropped open.

"Come on," he said. Gray pressed his lips together to keep from smiling, humor at her distress overshadowing the darkness inside him. He wanted to laugh out loud at her horrified expression. He pushed to his feet, every muscle and bone in his body screaming in protest. Damn, he hurt. He picked up his backpack after she dug out her underclothes. "I'll escort you down there."

Cheeks flaming red, she squared her shoulders and hugged her makeshift robe more tightly around her.

They lumbered to the river's edge, and Gray did a perimeter search. "Everything appears safe and sound."

"Then you can go back to camp," she huffed. "You are not watching me bathe. And if you need me, well, don't bother yelling. I won't come to your rescue." She stomped away, but paused and turned, facing him. The blue of her eyes gleamed with wicked retribution. "Oh, and Gray? I plan to bathe naked, letting my hands linger on my breasts and between my legs."

Truth. She couldn't lie. "Thanks for that," he said

wryly, already growing hard, delicious images racing through his mind.

"You're welcome."

While she bathed—naked and touching herself in all the places he wanted to touch, damn it!—he trudged a few feet away and eased down behind a bush. Her words brought images of soft, peach-colored skin, lips parted on a breath, dark hair spread like a rain cloud around her shoulders. Nipples hard and begging for his mouth. Legs—

"Damn it." He withdrew his transmitter. "Santa to Mother."

Static, then, "Mother here."

"Will have package in about two days and head home."

"You've got us worried, Santa. Delivery is taking longer than expected."

"Maybe next time you need to rethink the words 'in and out.'"

Pause. "What do you mean?"

"You know the text we discounted? Well, it's true."

"You mean—"

"Yeah. That's exactly what I mean. Read *The Book of Ra Dracas* again and work me up a list of every creature's weaknesses." He didn't know why he hadn't thought of using *Ra Dracas* before. "Have you learned anything else?"

"We found something, but we're not sure we translated it right."

"Tell me anyway."

"Basically, anyone who tries to snuff out the breath of life from the Jewel of Dunamis will earn the gods' darkest wrath." His boss paused again. "How can a gemstone breathe? Is it alive?"

Good questions.

A completely ingenious/dumb-ass idea crashed into his mind, and he stiffened. He blinked his eyes. No. Surely not. But…maybe. "I need to think about this," he said. "Will contact you later for that list. Over."

Gray set the radio aside, intent on finishing his tasks before he allowed himself to work on the puzzle that had presented itself with his boss's words. He checked his GPS system, only to discover the stupid thing was broken. He didn't understand. It wasn't water damaged, wasn't smashed. For a long while, he reworked the wires, reconnecting and tightening, to no avail. Disgusted, he finally shoved the priceless piece of shit into his backpack.

Because he himself wasn't at his best, he needed his equipment to pick up the slack. Obviously that wasn't going to happen. He expelled a frustrated breath. If he and Jewel were going to sleep out in the elements for another night or two, he'd have to build some sort of shelter, preferably something he could hook to his back and carry. Something to hide and protect them.

His gaze scanned the surrounding area, mentally cataloging what he could use. Twigs, leaves, rocks. His camo tent had been destroyed his first night.

Damn Welcoming Committee. They'd messed him up big-time.

Gray lumbered to his feet. His head pounded sharply, and his wounds pulsed. His legs were still weak from blood loss, and his vision swam, but he managed to stay upright. He really, really wanted to stroll down to the river and shock Miss Prudence Merryweather right out of her inhibitions. To catch a glimpse of those long legs that stretched all the way to paradise…that soft belly and rounded waist…those lush, pert breasts and pink-as-berries nipples that begged for his mouth…

"Don't do this to yourself again, man." Too late. His body hardened, and he forgot all his aches but one. But Gray stayed put—and not because of any gentlemanly tendencies. "Damn shelter," he muttered, adding it to his shit list.

Jewel was a walking contradiction, a smart-mouthed, freaky little sex puppet slash shy, innocent virgin nun. Both sides of her intrigued him, and he enjoyed watching the two sides of her nature battle for supremacy. He often found himself wondering which would ultimately prevail. The angel or the tigress? Or a combination of both?

As he forced his attention on his surroundings, the sound of splashing water echoed in his ears as loudly as screams of pleasure. He could very easily imagine droplets of water cascading from Jewel's plump breasts, dripping onto her stomach, gathering in her navel, begging for his tongue, before finally catching between her legs and—

"Not again." He slapped himself across the face. "Concentrate, man." He rubbed his cheek, feeling several days' worth of stubble. "Work. You have work to do."

Holding his stinging side, Gray gathered branches

and leaves, vines and sapling. Over the years, he'd constructed hundreds of hideaways; the actual building was most likely ingrained in his cells. His expert eye quickly found the best location, a spot that provided an escape route yet hid them under a sloping hill and between two trees.

The trees stood roughly five feet apart. Using the rope he'd stolen from the centaur, he tied a long, solid branch to each trunk, reaching as high as possible. He crisscrossed the sapling and vines he'd gathered, working his way down the beam, then did the same to the other side. Sweat trickled down his brow, and he wiped it away with the back of his wrist.

By the time he finished the framework, his arms were shaking and his knees knocking. He hated weakness of any kind—especially in himself. He sipped at the water in his canteen, then jumped back into his work.

After he covered the braided vines with brush leaves and grass, he pulled back and studied the end results. "Not bad," he said with a nod. Not a five-star resort, but it would hide them from their enemies and protect them from the elements. When the time came, he would untie the vines from the trees and fold everything up, hitching it to his backpack.

Deciding to rest while he could, Gray eased to the ground. He closed his eyes. Rocks dug into his back, but relaxing proved easy. All around him, the insects were creating a soft symphony. Who needed an MP3 player when the sounds of nature performed twenty-four seven?

He rubbed his temples to ease the ache. How long would it take him to heal completely? He knew better than most it was best to keep moving, and keep moving quickly, never staying in the same spot long. Less chance the enemy could ferret him out.

"God, I need a vacation." Once he returned home, he'd go to the beach, find himself a woman and rid himself of his growing need for Jewel.

Funny thing, though. No woman appealed to him but Jewel. His body wanted her, and only her. His *mind* wanted her, and only her. The thought of being with another woman felt wrong, and the thought of being without Jewel made him sick. And Gray didn't think a few nights, a month, a year away from her would diminish his obsession in any way.

He hadn't lied to her. If he stayed, OBI would continually send agents inside Atlantis, looking for Dunamis. People would die. Dunamis might end up in the wrong hands. If he tried to take her home, well, OBI guarded the portal, so he could never get her through without their knowledge. The moment they saw her, she'd be poked and prodded and dissected by scientists for the rest of her life. She'd never leave the laboratory—not alive, at least. And she couldn't lie to them, tell them she was a human who had stumbled through. She couldn't lie, period.

He scrubbed a hand over his face, infuriated with his lack of choices. Sweat poured down his back as he realized, really realized, that these next few days were all he and Jewel had. That was it. After that, he'd never see her again. A bitter laugh escaped him. He wanted her in a way he'd never wanted another woman. He wanted her taste, her body, her voice, and he knew she would willingly and passionately give herself to him. He could have her all right, but he couldn't keep her.

"I'm not going with you." Jewel's angry voice tore through his musings. "Let me go. I've killed before, and I'll do it again."

Male laughter floated across the distance.

Instant fury and concern burning inside him, Gray jumped up. Damn it all to hell, not again! Couldn't they rest for a fucking hour before something else attacked them? Ignoring the sharp tongs of discomfort—all right, agony—he launched forward, swiped his gun out of his bag and sprang toward the river. As he ran, he checked the weapon's clip. Only one bullet left. Crap. Had he lost one?

He shoved himself past trees and branches, uncaring as they cut his skin. His adrenaline level kicked up, providing extra strength, causing energy to surge through his veins. At last he reached the edge of the river, gun aimed in front of him. Jewel immediately came into view. She was in the middle of the river, the water up to her neck.

"You'll suffer if you continue with this," she said, her tone hard. "I see your death in my mind."

"Our king desires a word with you," another male said.

Shit. There were at least two of them. Gray's gaze scanned, but he saw no one besides Jewel. Where were—

The two heads smoothly broke the water's surface

and the men were flanking Jewel's sides, only their naked upper bodies visible. Fiery rage mutated into a murderous craze as one of the men reached for her. She slapped at his hands, but he managed to clasp her shoulder. Thankfully, soaked as she was, she tugged free.

Gray growled low in his throat, heat burning in his eyes. He didn't like another man's hands on her. If they hoped to rape her... His growl became a silent, feral breath as he studied his enemies. They were big, their stomachs and arms ripped with sinew and muscle. Clearly warriors, they carried themselves with confidence and an unwillingness to back down.

"Come."

"Your king can go to Hades."

Water splashed. A man grunted. Jewel gasped.

Gray crouched down, keeping his arm steady. Perhaps, with the right angle, he could kill them both with a single bullet. The men closed in on Jewel, gliding through the water effortlessly. So effortlessly, the water never even rippled. It was as if they were floating.

"Come on, Pru," Gray whispered. "Move to your left." At the moment, she blocked his shot.

"You're coming with us. Understand? If you fight, you might be hurt and we do not wish to hurt you."

They continued to close in on her. Gray cursed under his breath. He couldn't risk shooting one and giving the other time to abscond with Jewel. God, he wished he had his rifle and a case of hollow-point bullets. They left a nasty hole going in and a crater going out.

"I warned you," Jewel said. Scowling, she bent her

arm and jerked up her elbow, landing a solid blow to the closest man's nose.

He bellowed in pain, the other guy merely watching in shock as his friend wiped at the blood streaming down his face.

"You hit me. You hit me!"

"You hit him!"

"Well, of course I did. And I'll do it again if you come near me."

"Witch!" The idiot launched himself at her, his intent to hurt evident in the harsh lines of his expression.

Gray squeezed the trigger.

The big guy dropped into the water like a lead weight, a red cloud already forming around him. That red made Gray's mouth water.

"Brackin. Brackin! What's wrong?" When the dying—or dead—man failed to respond, the friend darted a confused look around him. His gaze collided with Gray's, his features narrowed and darkened.

Gray raised the gun as if he meant to shoot again. The man panicked, grabbed his friend and dove under the water's surface. A glistening tail slapped droplets in every direction.

His eyes widened. Tail? Shit. He'd forgotten about the merpeople. He rose. "Get over here, Jewel. Now." He barked the command in the same tone he used for his subordinates, but didn't wait for her to obey. He chugged into the water, heading straight toward her. He'd drag her out if necessary.

She hadn't moved at the sound of his gun being fired, but she whipped around at the sound of his voice.

Her color was high, her eyes bright. He'd expected her to appear frightened. Instead, she appeared excited.

"Did you see what I did?" She grinned. "I hit him."

"Get out of the water," he barked. He wanted her as far away from this river and those mermen as possible. Jewel would be safest at camp. More than that, Gray needed to get himself away from that blood. Before he did something he'd regret.

"Did you hear me? I said get out of the water."

Unaffected by his brusqueness, she swam to the shallow bank, meeting him halfway. As she ascended from the dappled liquid, the white undergarments she wore clung to her curves like a dedicated lover, revealing the pink thrust of her nipples and the dark patch of hair between her legs.

He had to force himself to look away. When she was within arm's reach, he clasped her by the forearm and helped her to shore.

"Don't touch me. I'll make you wet," she protested.

"That's my line," he muttered. "And I'm already wet. Why the hell didn't you scream for me?" Launching into motion, he dragged her behind him. He glanced back and pierced her with the force of his glare, knowing his eyes practically sparked with silver fury.

Her grin faded. "Your wounds are still healing, and I—"

His male pride roared viciously in response to her words. She hadn't screamed for help because she'd thought him too weak to protect her. He scowled. "I'll never be so hurt that I can't protect you. Understand? If something like this ever happens again—" he almost slammed his fist into the nearest tree trunk over that thought "—if something like this ever happens again and you don't shout, I'll, I'll—" Nothing sounded violent enough.

"Next time you're in jeopardy," he said, forcing himself to calm, "at least project your voice into my head to let me know something's happening!"

"I tried," she said.

"What?" He paused midstride and faced her. His sense of urgency immediately started screaming, and he jumped back into motion. "What do you mean you tried?"

"I can't reach your mind anymore." She dragged in a breath. "Inside the bar was the last time, and then I was only able to send my voice, not hear your response. It's as if the ability has weakened with every passing moment and now is gone completely."

They reached camp, and he ushered her to a trunk and sat her down. He crossed his arms over his chest and stared down at her. He never would have let her out of his sight, not in town and certainly not here if he'd known. "You aren't leaving my side. Not for a single moment. Got that?"

"Why are you so angry?" She grinned proudly. "Didn't you see the way I punched him?"

Gray nodded with grudging respect. His hands itched to draw her into his embrace, to hold her close and assure himself she was all right. "You should have told me there were creatures in that water."

She shrugged, kicking at rocks with the toe of her bare foot. "I didn't know they would bother me. They didn't before. The moment I sensed them, though, I dressed. That's why I wasn't naked. I'm not without *some* sense."

He almost cursed as his attention became snagged on her foot. He'd dragged her through the woods without any shoes. He bent down and clasped her ankle in his hands.

"What are you doing?" she gasped.

"I should have carried you." Her bones were small and delicate, her skin soft and moist. He lifted her foot and inspected. No cuts, thank God. No bruises. Just specks of dirt. He didn't want to let her go, but he gently placed her foot back on the ground.

A muscle ticked in his jaw. If he didn't do something to change her future, this hide-and-seek thing was the life she'd be left with, always on the run, always hunted by one creature or another. She'd told him that. He'd known it was true, but the knowledge had never been more real than right now. But what the hell could he do?

Unbidden, his gaze moved over her again. He couldn't help it, really. She was like a magnetic force. Those delicious curves, that smooth skin. She was watching him just as intently, desire in her eyes.

He wanted to kiss her, was almost shaking with the need, but didn't. He'd known it before and he knew it now. He wouldn't be able to stop. And if he didn't stop, the urge to drink her blood would rise up inside him, gnawing at him, consuming him, making him crave the very substance that kept her alive. He'd sink his teeth into her neck, he knew he would. Look how close he'd come to doing just that inside the inn. Look how close he was *now*. Her pulse was hammering wildly.

While he could forgive himself for biting the Formorian, he'd never forgive himself for hurting Jewel. He was supposed to be her protector, not her tormentor.

The air was cooler than usual and soaked as she was, Jewel had to be cold. A droplet of water snaked from her forehead and onto her upper lip. She licked it away, exactly as *he* wanted to do. His cock had hardened the moment he'd pulled her out of the water—or maybe he'd never lost his arousal—and hadn't lessened since. At the sight of her pink tongue, he hungered for her all the more. His mind flashed a visual of all the things he'd like her to do to *him* with that tongue.

"You need to change into something dry," he muttered, his tone rough. He found and tossed her his shirt.

Her eyelids dipped to half-mast, the excitement of the fight becoming sexual. Breath emerged from her choppily. "Maybe we could…you know, and—"

"Change. Now."

After a heavy pause, her gaze devouring him the entire time, Jewel moved behind the trees to remove her wet clothes and don his shirt. A few moments later, she returned, and the sight of her hit him like a well-placed punch in the gut. The camo shirt hung to the middle of her thighs, but it was *his* shirt and *she* was wearing it and the sight nearly undid him.

Sweating now, he dug inside and withdrew two energy bars. His supply was running low. If he didn't get out of this underwater hellhole soon, he'd be forced to hunt and eat the creatures here—and a Formorian soufflé was not his idea of a good, nutritious meal. Unfortunately they couldn't risk going back into town.

"Time for breakfast." He handed one of the bars to Jewel and plopped onto a rock.

She eased beside him, enveloping him in her sweet scent, and nibbled on the edges of the bar. He gulped his down, staying the urge to escape her appeal.

"Thank you," she said finally, though she sounded anything but thankful. "I do believe these energy bars are the most horrid things I've ever eaten."

"It'll keep you alive, so eat."

"I have berries and meats I bought in town."

"We'll save that for later."

Nose wrinkled, she finished off the bar. They took turns sipping water from his canteen. She continually cast glances in his direction. He knew because he could feel the force of it. Finally she sighed, sending a small puff of air against his shoulder, and looked away. Sighed. Looked at him again. Sighed.

What the hell was going through her mind?

He popped to his feet and paced to the far tree, unable to handle the closeness. Her calves were bare, but her ankles were crossed. She folded her hands in her lap. A very ladylike position. Her eyes told another story, however. They were filled with sadness and desire, hope and need.

"Listen, Jewel," he bit out. "I want to be—"

Without warning, dark, eerie shadows fell over the forest. The insects ceased their chatter. The air thickened with salt.

"Ah, hell." Gray groaned. "Guess we aren't having

a heart to heart out here." This very thing had happened his first night here, so he knew what was coming. "I should have expected this. Whatever can go wrong, *will* go wrong. Fucking great. Anyone ever tell you you're a bad-luck charm?"

"Yes."

He heard the hurt in her voice and swore under his breath. "I'm sorry. I shouldn't have said that."

"Why apologize? You've known one disaster after another since meeting me."

"It hasn't all been bad." Some of it had been amazing.

With a bittersweet snort, she moved to his side. He bent down and hefted up his backpack and her wet things, then linked his fingers with hers and tugged her to the shelter he'd erected. Thank God he hadn't taken it down yet.

"You built this?" she asked, a bit awed as she studied the lean-to of twigs and sapling.

"Yeah. And before you get any ideas, it isn't the Love Shack." He pulled the robe from the backpack and rolled it into a pillow, then tucked the pack in the shack's corner. "Climb in."

They had to lie down and crawl with their elbows, but they both managed to get inside, where there was more room to move around.

The crystal dome creaked open, booming like thunder, and drenched the entire land with ocean spray. Gray knew he should keep his hands to himself, but trapped as they were in the tent, it was no use even trying. He'd give in eventually and better now than later.

He couldn't *not* touch her when they were so close. He wrapped his arm around Jewel's waist, the sound of the rain creating a lulling rhythm.

"Why don't you get some sleep?" he said. "You've had an eventful day."

She traced her fingers over his cheek. "Thank you," she said softly.

"For what?" Everywhere she touched, his skin burned hungrily.

"For saving me from the mermen. For…everything."

The rain pitter-pattered against the leaves as he contemplated her words. He'd saved her life a few times, yes. But it was *he* who suddenly felt thankful.

# CHAPTER SEVENTEEN

THE RAIN LASTED several hours, and Jewel somehow managed to doze off and on, despite her sizzling awareness of the man next to her. Her robe had thankfully dried and was spread over their legs. Sometime during the storm, she'd turned her back to Gray, and he'd draped his arm over the dip of her waist. Being cradled in his protective embrace proved as intoxicating as she'd always dreamed, providing the sense of contentment she'd always craved. Not to mention utter carnality.

As his warm breath caressed her neck, she studied his hand. His fingers were long and thick, the ends callused. There was a light dusting of pale hair below each knuckle.

Those hands were capable of lethal violence as well as the greatest tenderness.

Gods, she wanted that tenderness with every ounce of her being.

Why hadn't he touched her since they'd left the city? Why hadn't he attempted to make love to her? They'd come so close. So wonderfully close. As she remembered, her lips plumped, her mouth watered, and moisture pooled between her legs. He'd kissed and touched her hungrily. *She'd* kissed and touched *him* hungrily. His decadent flavor had teased her mouth, and the strength and warmth of his embrace had surrounded her in a sultry haze of pleasure.

She wanted that again.

She wanted *him.*

Had he lost interest in her?

"What's wrong, Prudence?" Gray asked, his voice husky and rich with sleep. "You went stiff on me."

Jewel forced her body to relax. She needed to get her mind off Gray and sex and kisses and nakedness and—

She'd talk about Dunamis. *That* always sobered her. "What if I told you Dunamis doesn't actually exist? Not the way you think, at least."

Now *he* stiffened, his entire body tightening around her. "What do you mean?" His tone wasn't angry, merely hardened with curiosity.

The darkness was so thick, she didn't try to turn and glimpse his expression. "What if it's not a gemstone?"

He remained silent for a long while, and his hand began kneading her hip, sending ripples of pleasure through her blood. "You wouldn't be asking me these questions without reason," he said. "So, let me ask *you* a question. If Dunamis isn't a gemstone, what is it?"

A cold sweat broke over her body. She'd just had to get her mind off Gray, hadn't she? Now look what she'd done. How could she answer him without admitting the very thing she didn't want him to know? "I wish everyone would leave it alone. Perhaps any hands, even those of your government, are the wrong hands to own it."

"That's a chance I'm willing to take."

How she'd feared, and still feared, that very answer. "You never answered me," she said softly. "Would you still destroy it?"

"I can't answer your question until you answer mine." He kissed the back of her neck, his lips lingering over the sensitized cord of her shoulder.

She almost cried out in relief and need at the first brush of his lips, everything forgotten except him. Except Gray. There was no reason to keep her mind off his loving if he planned to give it to her. "Do that again," she whispered.

"I shouldn't. I've tried not to. But I can smell you, smell your sweetness, and I'm tired of trying to keep myself in check. Tired of thinking all the reasons not to." Lightning brightened their tent for the briefest of seconds, blending light with shadows. "You lied to me earlier, you know," he said, his fingers inching up and cupping her breast.

Her nipples hardened. She arched her back, arched into him. "Mmm, I most assuredly did not."

"You most assuredly *did* lie to me, Prudence."

"I didn't." She groaned as he licked the edge of her ear. "I swear I didn't."

"You didn't bathe naked. Yes, you had a good reason to dress, but that doesn't change the facts. Don't worry, though," he said, his voice husky and rich. "I can help you fix that."

"Right now?" she asked breathlessly, trying not to beg. "You're going to touch me? Like before?"

"Do you want me to?"

"Yes. Please." Her tongue flicked out in an attempt to lave her parched lips with moisture.

"I've been meaning to ask." He slid his hand lower, lower still, until his fingertips played at the hem of her shirt. "Why are you still a virgin, sweetheart? What were you waiting for? Marriage?"

"You," she admitted on a moan. "I was waiting for you."

Gray's cock jerked in reaction to her words. His mind roared in possessive wonder. For hours, he'd been waging a desperate war—touch her/don't touch her.

Guess who won?

He'd been hyperaware of her every move, every sigh. Desire hammered through him. Hell, when had it ever left? He craved her like a drug, and he was helpless to resist. He was becoming addicted to her, wanting her constantly, *needing* to mark her as his, to watch her when she came. To hear his name on her lips.

Every male instinct he possessed wanted every man who came into contact with her to know that she belonged to him.

Being with this woman right now was a mistake. He'd told himself a thousand times. If it weren't for the storm, they'd be out in the forest right now, headed for the Temple of Cronus. But it *was* storming, they *weren't* in the forest, and at last sinking inside her would be the most pleasurable mistake of his life.

He wouldn't bite her. He wouldn't let himself. If the need came upon him, he'd control it, no matter how uncontrollable it seemed. At least, that's what he told himself to ease his conscience.

"If you don't want me to finish this, say so now." He ground himself against the cleft of her ass. "Once I start, I'm not going to stop. Not this time."

"I want you more than I've ever wanted anything else in my life. I won't let you stop."

He flipped her over, sucking in a breath of salt, foliage and aroused woman, and meshed his lips against hers. She opened her mouth and his tongue dove inside, their teeth clashing together with the force of his entry. He cupped her jawline, and told himself to be gentle though all he wanted to do was brand her. Hard. Fast. Forever.

His need for her grew with every second that passed, intensifying dangerously. Her palms caressed his naked chest, flattened against his nipples, then locked around his neck.

"I love your heat and hardness," she gasped out. "Do you think I'll ever get enough?"

"No, never. You taste so good." Sweat dripped from his brow, and his skin pulled tight, urging him to do more. Begging him to increase their pace. He traced his hands over her shoulders, her back, her breasts, pinching her nipples.

She moaned in pleasure-pain and hooked her legs around his waist, cradling his erection as intimately as possible while still dressed. Her tongue continued its battle with his. Her fingers traveled all over him.

"I want to be naked," she panted.

"I want you that way, too." He nipped at her chin, at the corner of her mouth, all the while rubbing against her. "How do you do this to me? How do you make me *need* you so badly?"

Sheer pleasure sizzled in her veins when he hit the exact place she needed him. "Again," she gasped. "There."

He drew back, pushed forward. This time they both gasped at the headiness.

"Sometimes…when I saw you in my visions with other women…" She lifted her head and sucked one of his nipples, reveling in the male taste of his skin. "I pretended you were—" she licked her way to the other side and sucked "—with me instead."

A raw moan tore from him. Another beam of lightning exploded in the sky, chasing away the darkness for a split second, and in that second, their eyes met. Blue ocean water against warrior steel. Fire and passion blazed from his expression.

He stared down at her, and his brow furrowed. "We've kissed like this before," he said, his voice strained. "Not in the tub, but—"

"In your mind. Yes." She reached for him, wanting to jerk his mouth back to hers, but he gripped her hands and pinned them over her head.

"I thought I'd dreamed it, but you were actually there. We fought a demon and a vampire, and then we kissed. It really happened."

"Yes," she said, never breaking their gaze. What did any of this matter now? She needed him desperately and didn't know if she could stand it if he refused her. In these last few days she'd been aroused one too many times without reaching fulfillment. "Does that upset you?"

"Hell, no. I just— Thank you."

A shiver raced through her, vibrating into him. "You're welcome."

"You're the most beautiful thing, sweetheart." She loved him, he realized, shock still hammering through him. He'd known she desired him but had failed to realize she'd given him her heart. Until now. When she'd entered his mind that day he'd been injured, he'd read her thoughts and she'd been unable to hide her love for him.

Love... Far from making him want to leave her, Gray found himself irrevocably drawn to her, needing her so much more.

He wanted to hear her say it. He *had* to hear her say it.

He bent his head to kiss her neck when the scent of her sweet, sweet blood wafted to his nostrils. He gulped. The need for blood, her blood, had awoken with more fervor than ever before.

He needed to slow things down, bring it to a controllable level while he pleasured her so thoroughly that loving him was the only thing she knew. The only thing *he* knew.

He delved his hand along the curve of her hip, along the length of her long leg, then up her thigh until he reached the hem of her shirt. Up...up...he lifted the material. Slowly—it nearly killed him to go slow. He tantalized her nerve endings with barely-there touches, and when the material was bunched at her waist, he paused. Silence encompassed the tent. Not even the sound of their breathing could be heard. Perhaps they both waited, breath bated, for his next move.

His blood sparked with electricity as his fingers played at her waist again. Her skin was so soft. So perfect. She was silk and roses. "I don't want to scare you," he whispered huskily, already knowing she was far from afraid. "Tell me if I do something you don't like."

"I'm not—"

"I'll explain everything I'm doing to you," he added, neatly cutting off her protest. She might think nothing could scare her, but he didn't want to take a chance. "Right now, I'm simply going to explore you. Your legs, your stomach, your every curve and hollow, every sensitive place that makes you gasp for more."

"Yes. All right."

"We'll learn what you like together."

"Every time you touch me, I feel flames licking me, burning me. I like that."

He uttered a strained chuckle. More sweat trickled down his temples. "If you didn't feel that way, that would mean I was doing something wrong. It's my job—no, my privilege—to make the fire become an inferno." As he spoke, he traced his name on her thigh.

She was his, that's all there was to it. Only his.

"Oh, yes." Her low, needy moan blended with a sigh of pleasure. The sounds combined, emerging more like a purr.

A man true to his word, Gray introduced himself properly to her body. "I'm going to touch your breasts."

"Like before?"

"Like before." He lingered there, kneading and rolling her nipples between his finger and thumb.

Her hips arched, her body bowed. Her head fell back, her silky hair tickling his chest. Thunder boomed and the rain increased in pressure, pounding against the shelter. He'd never again see another moonlit, stormy night without thinking of Jewel.

She was passion incarnate and just as wild.

When he'd kissed her, she'd erupted. Just like that. Her hands had moved over him, her lower body had arched into him. When he touched her...

"I'm going to make a mental note that we both enjoy this area." His voice was strained, so strained he barely managed to get the words out. Had he ever been this on-edge before? He didn't think so; he couldn't remember a time when a woman had ever invaded his mind so thoroughly. Had they always been meant to be together? He'd wondered before, had denied it. But only Fate explained this...obsession.

Jewel's stomach quivered when he stopped to dabble at her belly button. So soft, so sexy. He could have spent the rest of the night there, but continued his exploration. "I'm going to touch your bottom."

"Yes. Please." She whimpered, a mewling heavy with anticipation. When he reached the rounded curves, she arched her hips. He massaged.

He called himself a million kinds of fool as his gaze fastened on her neck, watching the pulse there.

"Between your legs now." He delved his hand

exactly where he'd promised. When he began working his fingers up the inside of her thigh, she cried out.

"Gray, I need— I don't know! I watched you a hundred times but I don't know what I need."

He gave a desperate chuckle. She was writhing against him, silently pleading. "You need a more intimate touch, baby. Like this." He tunneled his hand through the tuft of hair guarding her wet folds, then sank one finger inside her tight sheath.

Her hips instantly shot toward the sky. "Oh, gods."

"Do you love me?" He pulled his finger out and spread her moisture with circling strokes. The final vestiges of his control were slipping. A sense of urgency was overtaking him. Always overtaking him.

"Gray. Gray! Do that again!" she commanded, ignoring his question.

His mouth stretched tight with the strain of his own arousal, his need for blood. Sweat no longer trickled; it dripped from his temples. God, he loved hearing his name on her lips.

"Did you touch yourself like this often?" he asked her. So easily he pictured her splayed out on a bed of silk and satin, blue like her eyes, pleasuring herself, bringing herself to climax while she pictured his face.

The image alone was enough to make him spill, so he blanked his mind.

She hesitated. "Only that once. In the tub. My skin had grown so hot and tight. And I wanted to experience your possession so badly."

Using his thumb on her clitoris, he sank two fingers into her. "Do you love me?"

"Ohh," she moaned, another purr. Ignoring the question again. She threw her head back, her pelvis arching and caressing his groin.

He stilled at the consuming pleasure, the sheer bliss of that one touch. He was as hard as a rock, his breathing ragged. When he worked a third finger inside her, she cried out his name, the sound a broken sob. Her body spasmed and tightened around his fingers. Heat radiated off her, surrounding him with her luscious scent.

*Finish it,* his mind shouted.

Slowly he removed his fingers. He ripped at his boots and pants and kicked them off, his cock finally freed. He would be her first. Her first man, her first lover. His possessive instincts roared to life, a powerful avalanche tumbling through him.

He couldn't fight her allure, and he'd been foolish to even try, whatever his reasons had been. They were from different lands? So what. She'd read his mind? Who cared. He might make her pregnant? God, yes. He wanted her to have his baby. He wanted to fill her with his seed. He might bite her? Mmm….

"There could be consequences. A baby. Do you love me?" Gray fit himself at her entrance, and her legs locked around him. His gaze moved to her neck, his mouth watering. "You're mine, you're mine, you're mine. Tell me you're ready for me. Tell me you want me no matter what." The way he wanted her.

"Now. Please now. I want you."

Rocking forward, he worked himself inside her inch by tormenting inch. "Take it all."

"Yes—yes—"

"All of it." Finally her hymen gave way, and he shoved the rest of the way in, seating himself to the hilt. He roared at the pleasure, somehow managing to hold himself still. "You're mine, you're mine, you're mine. Are you hurt? Did I hurt you?"

"More, I want more."

Another roar of satisfaction burst from him, and he began moving in and out. Quickening his pace, he increased the exquisite sensations. She was arching and moving with him, against him. She kneaded and squeezed his back. She clawed. She bit the cord of his neck.

She was feral with her need.

He could barely see her in the darkness, but what little he could make out filled his mind. Her lids were at half-mast, her color high, her teeth chewed on her bottom lip. Raven locks of hair spilled around her shoulders. She was the very picture of eroticism.

She was his.

His orgasm rocked him, and he shouted her name, pounding into her as deeply as possible. He hit her in exactly the right spot because she cried out, too, her second climax springing to instant life, her inner walls tightening around him. All the while, he fought the urge to bite her and won. The need was there, but his need to protect her was greater.

He stayed where he was until the last tremor abandoned him, then finally collapsed beside her, more sated than he'd ever been in his life. A long time later, she peeked at him through the thick shield of her lashes.

Something in his chest tightened, seeing her like this. So satisfied. So lovely.

He couldn't give her up, he thought then. Ever.

"Well, shit," he said. He worried one hand over his face, and pulled Jewel atop his chest with the other. She hadn't told him she loved him. Did she still? Had he misread her?

"Is something wrong?" she asked shyly.

"Go to sleep, baby. We'll talk in the morning." His body was already on fire for her, ready for round two.

He loved her. He did. She was the one for him, the only one. His soul mate. Here in the darkness of the night, there was no denying it. No dressing it up with "maybe" and "probably," or even the standard "I care about her but…" He had never felt more replete, more sated, than he did at that moment.

Just what he needed, too. Another complication for this easy fucking mission.

# CHAPTER EIGHTEEN

JEWEL FLOATED through the clouds, so in love with Gray she might never come down. A smile curled her lips. What Gray had done to her body…pure magic, leaving her decadently content. Memories of the way he claimed her would fuel her dreams for the rest of her life. Making love with him had given her a sense of completion and contentment she hadn't dreamed possible.

Night had fallen and the rain had stopped. The ground beneath her was hard, softened slightly by moss and leaves, but Gray's presence more than made up for any discomfort. She sighed, sated, loving the way she was cradled in his arms, cuddled against him.

This was the life she'd always craved for herself. Every time she'd been punished, every time someone was killed because of her predictions, she'd pictured herself tucked in the safety of Gray's embrace.

She'd come so close to screaming out her love for him. He'd asked her if she loved him, several times, and each time she'd had to fight to hold the words back. If he'd pulled away from her…she shuddered.

He uttered a string of unintelligible words, cutting

through the nighttime silence. His body jerked and Jewel jolted upright.

"Oww!" she cried when her forehead slammed into the shelter ceiling. She lay back down and edged to her side. It should have been difficult, if not impossible to see in the darkened tent; after all, the dome cast absolutely no light. As she stared down at Gray, she saw every nuance of his face, and her jaw dropped open on a gasp.

His eyes were open—and glowing that bright, eerie red again. His skin was pallid, and sweat poured from his overheated body. Her stomach knotted into a thousand different loops. More changes were occurring inside him.

"Gray," she said. What could she do? How could she help him accept what was happening? If he fought, he would only make himself weaker. Leaning down, she whispered in his ear. "I'm here. I'll keep you safe. Nothing bad will happen. I promise."

Slowly his muscles relaxed.

"I'm here," she repeated. "I'm here."

Color spread over his skin, returning him to his natural bronze. His eyes ceased glowing, dimming in gradual degrees. The tent darkened, and she breathed a sigh of relief.

"How do you feel?" she asked him.

"I can see in the dark," he said flatly. "And as you can tell, I'm not wearing my night-vision goggles. I've got to get out of here."

Gray quickly dressed and scooted himself out of the tent. A cool, salty breeze kissed him, taunting in its sweetness. Without bothering with his boots, he grabbed his transmitter and stalked to the river, gazing out at the beauty of the land. Pitch-black greeted him, yet he saw everything as if it were the bright light of day. Leaves shook and wafted on the bright green trees. The clear river water rippled against the wind. A school of rainbow-colored fish swam past, their fins splashing at the surface.

Seeing in the dark was a cool superhero trick, yeah, one he knew he'd come to enjoy. That wasn't what bothered him. As he'd lain in the tent, Jewel in his arms, his body sated from their loving, he'd been hit by another desire to bite into her neck and drink her blood. This time, the need had nearly been unquenchable. Unstoppable. Stronger than ever before. With Jewel, the more he touched her, the more he wanted to bite her. Yet once again, the need to protect her had won. Would that last, though, if his longing for blood continued to grow?

He was human. A man. Not a demon or a vampire, the epitome of evil and all he fought against. At least, he hoped.

*I'm too close to the edge.*

"Santa to Mother," he said into the transmitter. Maybe his boss could help.

Jude Quinlin came online moments later and they discussed *Ra Dracas* and the list Gray had wanted. Apparently vampires loathed fire, demons hated the cold, Formorians could see in the dark, and on and on the list went. Things he'd discovered firsthand already. Shit.

"Is there a way to change vampires back into humans?"

"Not that we've found, but we're only halfway through."

"Keep digging." Gray ended the transmission and jerked a hand through his hair. He paused. There was no pain in his arm. No pain in his neck. He moved his hand to his neck. No wound. His gaze jerked to his arm. No wound there, either.

They were completely healed.

A gasp sounded behind him, and he whipped around. Jewel's mouth hung open, and her other-worldly blue eyes stared down at his feet. She held a glow stick, her features illuminated by its halo of light.

"You're floating."

"What?" His gaze snapped to the ground, and his own mouth fell wide open. My God. His feet were hovering inches above the grass.

"How do I get down?" he barked.

"Visualize your feet touching the ground?" A question, not a statement.

His attention snagged on her. "You don't know?"

Without offering an answer, she tentatively closed the distance between them, wrapped her fingers around his ankles and tugged. He floated down until gently hitting a solid foundation.

"I thought I could handle the changes as they came," he said rawly.

"You're alive. Nothing else matters."

"I'm becoming one of them."

"No, you're still Gray. My Gray."

Unbidden, his gaze traveled to her neck, to the erratic pulse there. "You wouldn't say that if you could get inside my head right now."

Her hand reached out and moved up his chest, sliding along the ridges of stomach muscles, making him suck in a breath. Making his skin tingle. Just as he'd done to her, she found his nipples and rolled them between her fingers. "You're Gray," she said again. "You're hard and hot and wonderful. You're not a monster."

His blood heated with desire and simmered with need. More desire, more need than even in the tent because all of his senses were suddenly heightened. Her mystical scent drenched him; her heat throbbed at him. Her own desire and need blasted him, swimming and blending with his own.

His mouth watered. Maybe, if he allowed himself one taste, just one taste of her blood... He jerked away from her. Hell, no. Too much temptation. Allowing one taste would be like opening floodgates and expecting most of the churning water to stay put.

Hurt and embarrassment crossed her delicate cameo features.

He almost drew her back, but managed to resist. "Don't touch me again. It's for your own good."

Her eyes widened with hurt surprise, and she stumbled backward. "But...why?"

The dome began to emit a slight ray of light, sweeping over trees and rocks. He ignored her as determinedly as she'd ignored his questions of love last night. "Let's pack up. We need to get moving if we want to reach the Temple of Cronus on schedule."

As he spoke, the hairs on the back of his neck rose. The corner of his eye caught a flicker of movement, and every instinct he possessed screamed to duck. He grabbed Jewel by the forearms and propelled them both to the ground. A spear sailed through the air, slicking the spot he'd stood and slamming into a thick tree trunk.

"We want Dunamis, human. If you give it to us, your death will not be so painful for you." The deep male voice boomed as loud as thunder—and came from the water.

Gray forgot everything but protecting his woman. All at once he catalogued his escape route and sized up his enemy. There were at least fifty mermen in the water, spears raised. If there'd been more light, Gray knew those spears would be embedded in his back. The urge to fight them was there, but he wouldn't risk Jewel getting hurt.

"Let's go," he told her, jumping to his feet and jerking her up with him. He kept her body shielded with his.

He pushed her into the shadows of the forest, grabbed her wrist and started running. Rocks dug into his bare feet, but he kept moving. "This is my fault. I knew better than to go to the river."

"I should have known they would come back," she babbled. "I should have at least known what they were planning."

"At least they have to stay in the water." A naked limb reached out and slapped his cheek. He grunted, skidding to a halt just in front of their tent.

Jewel shook her head almost violently. "After a storm, they can walk on land."

Of course they could.

"I can't believe this is happening," she rasped out.

"You have to keep your voice down. Okay, baby? I don't want to make it easier for them to find us." Motions quick and precise, he disassembled their tent and hooked it to his backpack. "How long do we have?"

Jewel remained eerily silent.

Gray jerked on his boots and raced around the camp, grabbing all of their stuff and cramming it into his bag. "Which way should we go?" He clasped Jewel's wrist and bolted toward the trees. He did his best to make their tracks as invisible as possible.

She didn't answer. Her body was stiff, and she was barely moving, slowing him down, practically making him drag her. He flicked a glance over his shoulder. The blue of her eyes swirled, a fathomless pool.

"They are even now leaving the water."

Her voice was as otherworldly as her eyes. Surreal. Like a thousand voices layered into one. Her features were so blank she appeared to be in a trance.

"They plan to scour these woods until you are found and destroyed."

"Sweetheart, I know that. What I don't know is where to go. Can you direct me?"

Silence.

Her feet tripped over a fallen limb, and she stumbled forward. Her body was too stiff to bend and ease the fall. He caught her, absorbing her weight. Good Lord. What was happening to her? Not knowing what else to do, Gray hefted her onto his shoulder. He broke into a sprint. "Jewel?"

Again silence.

He swatted her bottom. "Snap out of it, baby, and tell me where to go."

She instantly responded to the direct command. "Travel into the Inner City. There you will find a shield to protect you."

"A shield? What are you talking about?" Turning toward the city, he quickened his speed. He didn't even think about putting her down. She was as still as the dead, her voice still layered with that weird inflection. He was worried about her, wanted to assure himself she was okay, but he couldn't slow down.

Something the merman said bothered him...but what? He replayed the conversation in his mind as he maneuvered around the trees and ducked under limbs.

*We want Dunamis, human. Give it to us.*

He blinked. They thought he had the jewel. His suspicion last night, when he'd been talking to his boss, rang in his head. Dunamis could breathe, Jude had said.

Gray's arms tightened around the woman on his shoulder. Like Dunamis, Jewel knew what his enemy was planning and knew how to direct him to safety. And she'd told him Dunamis was protected by a man who wanted to destroy it. Protect. Destroy. The two were complete opposites. Gray wanted to protect Jewel, but he wanted to destroy Dunamis.

He shook his head. He didn't want to believe it, which had to be the reason he'd taken so long to reach this point. God. What the hell was he going to do?

The woods were becoming brighter, but Gray did his best to stay in the shadows. He'd been running for what seemed an eternity. His breath emerged ragged, and he hated that Jewel bounced up and down on his shoulder like a sack of potatoes. Was he hurting her? She never uttered a protest.

A spear sailed past her ear, then another, barely missing him. Only his new, lightning-fast reflexes saved them. Gray slanted a quick, backward glance. The mermen were closing in on him. Fast. Their tails had split in two, giving them glistening, scaled legs. How the hell was he supposed to outrun them?

"Where do I go, Jewel? Where will you be safe? How do I get us out of here?"

"Fly. Mermen cannot fly," she said. "You can."

Fly? At the river, he'd floated, but it hadn't been on purpose. He didn't know how to do it on his own.

Another spear whizzed past him.

He actually heard it cutting through the air and was able to slant to the side before getting hit. Down here, like this, Jewel was in danger. That clinched it. He had to try.

"Oh, shit," he muttered, then pictured himself flying.

# CHAPTER NINETEEN

"THE MER KING HAS SENT US a messenger." Layel stroked his jaw and arched his brows as he awaited Marina's reaction.

The demon queen lounged across her makeshift bed of furs, her arms folded behind her neck. Instead of armor, she wore a soft, gauzy gown that barely covered her dry, green skin.

They were in the forest, just outside the Inner City, planning to make war with the dragons, and she looked ready for bedding. Never had Layel encountered a more vain, repulsive creature. Her army was just as bad. They knew the fundamentals of war, but were even now busy gorging on animal flesh, everything else forgotten.

"So?" she finally said, at last acknowledging his presence. Sighing, she eased to her stomach, exposing small horns. "What did he say?"

"The mer king found the human who destroyed your palace and absconded with your favorite pet."

Marina jerked up and twisted to face him, her evil features fairly sparkling with excitement. "Where are they?"

"On their way into the city."

Within seconds, she was on her feet and closing the distance between them. "We cannot allow the mers to find them. *It* belongs to me, and *he* will die by my hand."

Overwhelmed by the cloying scent of sulfur that always surrounded the queen, Layel glided back one step. Two. Across the entire city would not be far enough, really.

This woman he faced and pretended to hold in some regard was partially responsible for the death of his beloved. She hadn't struck the deathblow, no. The dragons held that sin. But some of Marina's people had watched those fire-breathing bastards roast Susan alive and had done nothing except laugh.

She would pay mightily for that laughter.

Layel had no other purpose in life than to destroy those who played a part in Susan's death. She had been—and still was—everything to him. She'd been human, a child of the humans cursed here by the gods to be food for the city's inhabitants. More important, she'd been his.

"The man possesses Dunamis. Do you really think the mers will catch him?" Layel drawled. "That's why the king sent a messenger. He requests our help in the man's capture because he knows he cannot battle the owner of Dunamis on his own." Layel ran an elegant hand over the black shirt he wore, a shirt that covered a fire-resistant breast-plate. "I doubt *we* can capture him, to be honest."

Her sharp teeth ground together. "We have our armies at our disposal. Of course we can capture him."

"Why waste our time and energy even trying? Together we can defeat the dragons, and that is all that matters to me." He loved taunting her.

Her lizardlike tongue flicked out in a hiss. "Our victory will be assured if we capture the jewel."

While Layel himself would love to own the powerful jewel again, he did not want the damn thing close to Marina. The queen had owned it over a year, and was the only reason Layel had never acted against her. Now, he could use her—and betray her—and she would never suspect. Until it was too late.

"I will not be able to fight the dragons to my best ability without it," she simpered. "I will be too distraught."

He had to force his expression to remain neutral, instead of grinning at her obvious try at manipulation. "Then, of course, it is my pleasure to attempt to capture it for you."

"I'll send my men through the city, as well. I wouldn't want you to forget to tell me you've acquired it." As she smiled with satisfaction, Layel glided from her tent. Demons were everywhere. They spilled from the circular glen, their laughter and noxious scent making his muscles tense.

He stalked to the cliff at the edge of camp. Full light greeted him, stinging his skin. Some of his people could not tolerate the light. The older ones, like himself, could walk in the day, but not comfortably. He and Susan had lazed days like today away, staying in bed and making love hour after hour.

Gods, he missed her. The music of her laughter, the

softness of her touch. The love in her forest-green eyes.
Her sweet innocent blood. His lids slitted and he sent
his gaze below, into the city. His vampires were strate-
gically placed atop buildings and hidden along the
streets.

They were warriors, his men. And they were hungry
for demon blood.

Soon. He grinned. Soon.

# CHAPTER TWENTY

"JEWEL."

The voice called to her from a long, dark tunnel. She tried to respond, but her lungs refused to cooperate.

"Jewel."

She opened her mouth, surely the most difficult thing she'd ever done, but again no sound emerged.

"Jewel. Come on, baby. Talk to me."

Gray. She'd recognize that sexy drawl anywhere, anytime. He sounded worried and very upset. The fog blanketing her mind was thick, but she managed to push her way through it and—

Her eyelids popped open.

Gray crouched in front of her, his silver eyes swimming with a wealth of emotion: concern, relief, fear.

She blinked and licked her lips, orienting herself. Where were they? What was he afraid of? Pale locks of hair tumbled on his forehead. Dirt streaked his cheeks.

He caressed a fingertip down her nose. "Don't ever do that again, or I'll— Just don't do it. Understand?"

Do what? She glanced around her, noticing the stone

buildings flanking her front and back, the gravel she lay upon and the robe draped over her head. The sounds of chattering people, pounding horse hooves, and the scents of meats and fruits drifted into her awareness.

"We're in the Inner City," she said. She remembered being by the river, the mers attacking and then... She'd had a vision, she realized with a shake of her head. She always lost track of time and place. "How did we get here?"

His cheeks burned bright red. "I, uh, sort of flew us. First class," he added dryly.

"With wings?" She jolted up and only experienced a moment's dizziness. "You grew wings?"

"I did the levitation thing." His chin canted to the side with an I-dare-you-to-contradict-me air. "Those walking fish men are everywhere. They followed us here." He cupped her jaw and turned her head toward him. "You were catatonic, and said we'd find a shield here." Sighing, he leaned back on his haunches. "We've got to get to a safe place. I spotted demons and vampires, as well."

Her brow puckered. "I knew they were headed this way, but so soon? Are you sure?"

"I never forget a creature that wants to make me breakfast." His wry expression matched his tone.

She chuckled, but her amusement quickly faded. "I shouldn't be laughing. We're in danger."

"It's good to find humor at times like this." His arm snaked around her waist and hefted her up. "You all right?"

He was watching her so intently, searching her face for...something. What?

"You want to tell me what happened to you?" he asked.

She swallowed, licked her lips. How could she explain what had happened to her without revealing too much? "Sometimes I lose awareness. I—"

A splash sounded, and Gray's head whipped to the side. A small bird drank from a puddle. When he realized they hadn't been spotted, he said, "You don't have to explain now. I shouldn't have asked. There'll be plenty of time to talk later."

The words *I hope* hung unsaid in the air, drifting on the breeze with a slight hint of unease. She knew he was not afraid for himself. The man lived for danger. Thrived on it. How many missions had he thrown himself into wholeheartedly, eager for the trials that awaited him? Countless.

Which meant—he feared for her? Oh gods, he did. He cared for her. Shock and pleasure and happiness held her immobile. He'd pushed her away earlier and she'd thought he had learned of her love and wanted nothing to do with her. But he'd been trying to protect her; the knowledge was there in his eyes, shining brightly.

Kings and queens fought to own her, to enslave and direct her, to use her, but this man sought to protect her. To give her pleasure.

"Let's get out of here," he said.

Jewel gave him no indication of her intentions; she simply threw herself against him. His breath whooshed out even as his strong, muscled arms enfolded her.

"You are a wonderful man, Gray James." She kissed his cheek. "I know where we can find shelter for the day."

He offered her a tender smile, but stepped away from her as if he didn't dare hold her too long. "I would have been shocked senseless if you didn't know where we should go."

Jewel stepped back into the curve of his body and moved her hands low, cupping his buttocks. Awareness sizzled along her nerve endings. She would have happily remained where she was for the rest of her life, but she gave a gentle squeeze before releasing him. "We'll survive this if for no other reason than for me to get you into bed."

His pupils dilated and his gaze settled on her neck. He swallowed and stepped away again, his expression hardening. Just like that her gentle, teasing lover was gone, and a cold warrior stood in his place.

"Follow me," she told him, not allowing herself to experience hurt over his sudden change. He cared for her. That was all that mattered.

As they entered the heart of the city, the alley shadows faded, and they were surrounded by bright, illuminating light. Mer soldiers marched from the threshold of one building to another.

Knowing how recognizable she was, Jewel tugged her hood lower over her face, then cast a quick glance over her shoulder to make sure Gray had done the same. He had. But she could see that his eyes were slitted and watery, as if the brightness was too much for him to bear. Probably was. Some vampires never learned to tolerate the light.

She intertwined their hands. His strong fingers wrapped around her delicate ones, his skin rough where hers was smooth. The city pulsed with activity, just like before. Taverns, inns, and shops lined the streets, each bursting with creatures of every race. She paused as two centaurs pranced past, their whooping laughter echoing behind them. Stalls flowed with silks and robes of every color. Vendors peddled roasted fowl.

"One day I will not have to guard my every move," she said with determination.

"One day," he agreed.

Gray's eyes burned against the light. He found himself staring at Jewel, as usual. Her face was partially covered, but what he could see of her features radiated life, wistfulness, and resolve. As slender as she was, she should have appeared fragile and dainty. Yet, there was a core of strength that radiated from her.

Three demons darted down the street, shoving their way through delicate-looking sirens, muscled Cyclopses, and tail-chasing griffins. The demons continually scanned faces. Gray straightened his shoulders, his every kill-or-be-killed instinct going on instant alert. He didn't slow as he shifted his knife from the folds of his robe, his grip tightening on the hilt.

A minotaur woman whose furry bull face was familiar to him skidded to a halt when she saw Jewel. Her gaze widened, and she shifted her bundle of clothes from one arm to the other.

"Erwin," Jewel said, forcing Gray to stop. "How is your boy?"

"He is well, thanks to you." Erwin smiled. "They came for us, just as you said."

"Ladies, can you continue this conversation later?"

As discreetly as possible, Gray positioned Jewel behind him.

One of the demons several yards in front of them stopped and sniffed the air. He whipped around, his red eyes searching, searching. His gaze locked on Gray.

"Human!" The scaly creature released a snakelike hiss.

Not waiting around for a welcome-to-town party, Gray jolted into motion, dragging Jewel with him. "We've been spotted, baby."

People gasped as he pushed through them. What he would have given for a few hollow-point bullets. Maybe a grenade. Unfortunately he was out of both. His only weapon was his blade. Demons could fly, so there was no reason for him to attempt that little feat again. Plus, they would do better if they lost themselves in the crowd. If he could find a vendor selling robes, he could steal two, changing the colors he and Jewel wore.

The crowd was thinning at a fast rate. Centaurs galloped away. Minotaurs burrowed in the ground, finding shelter under mounds of dirt. Pebbles flew from beneath Gray's boots.

The woman, Erwin, had followed them, racing at his side. "Keep going," she said. "I will distract them."

"No," Jewel said at the same time Gray said, "Thank you."

"We're in deep shit, so we'll take all the help we can get," he added, leaping over a fallen food cart. "Jump," he commanded.

She jumped, her robe billowing around her like a storm cloud. Her hood fell, and her hair spilled down her back, a black, glossy river. She looked over her shoulder and saw Erwin throw her armful of cloth at the demons, momentarily shielding their vision before she ran away.

Gray continued sprinting between buildings and alleys. He knew the demons were getting closer. And closer. And shit! They were doubling in numbers with every step. Their teeth were yellow and razor-sharp, dripping with saliva.

"There," Jewel cried, pointing.

He followed the direction of her finger and spotted a female centaur trotting ahead, completely unaware of the turmoil behind her.

"No," Gray said, knowing what she wanted him to do.

"Yes. It's the only way."

He scowled.

"Just hop on and ride. Don't be a baby."

If he didn't know better, he'd swear Jewel sounded excited, rather than fearful for her life. He could not believe he was contemplating this… He didn't mind riding a woman, but holy hell. He preferred it be Jewel.

Increasing their speed, they sidled up to the horse-woman. Her pale-as-moonlight hair streamed behind her. Without giving any warning, Gray grabbed a fistful of that hair and pulled himself up, dragging Jewel up behind him. Immediately the centaur tried to buck them off. When that didn't work, she reared up.

"Giddy-up, horsey," he said.

"Get off me." She twisted, trying to bite Gray's leg. When she saw him, her eyes widened and she stilled.

"Adonis! My deepest apologies, Great Lord. Thank you for this honor. I shall never—"

"Just move."

Without another word, she kicked into gear, her lithe body spurring into motion. Wind tangled in his hair as she raced stealthily around people, through alleys and over carts. Adrenaline surged in his veins, flowing with the force of an avalanche. He'd experienced more adrenaline rushes since entering Atlantis and meeting Jewel than he had in his entire two years with OBI.

Just thinking of his employer made his hands sweat. They were getting antsy, he knew they were. It was only a matter of time before they sent someone else through the portal, looking for him. What would happen to Jewel then?

The female centaur stopped, her hooves digging into the rocky ground.

He frowned. "Keep moving. Go!"

"My Lord of Lords. There are vampires blocking the path in front and demons blocking the path in the rear." Her voice trembled with fear.

"Layel," Jewel gasped.

Gray dismounted, keeping his gaze locked on the trio of vampires. They wore black, and the dark material eerily offset their too-pale skin. Their otherworldy blue eyes were…just like Jewel's, he realized. What the hell?

He blinked, but shook off his unease. Jewel tried to dismount. He stopped her with a firm grip on her thigh. A chorus of hissing laughter erupted behind him.

"When I say so, take off," he mouthed to the centaur. "Take her to safety. I'll find a way to repay you."

Her only response was a frightened whinny.

Shoving his hand away, Jewel slipped off and stood beside him. "If you stay, I stay."

Their eyes met, locking, clashing. In the next moment, the vampires and demons flew into action, heading straight toward them.

# CHAPTER TWENTY-ONE

GRAY SHOVED JEWEL to the ground and threw himself protectively over her body. When she regained her breath, she flailed, trying to make herself the shield. His strength prevailed.

"Damn you," she cried.

He merely meshed his lips into hers for a quick kiss, twisted, and raised his blade. Ready to attack and defend. The vampires' speed was incredible, almost faster than his eyes could see, making them a blur of movement. He didn't know how he was going to fight all of them, or how he was going to save Jewel. He only knew he'd fight to the death if needed.

And it looked like that might be needed.

They were almost within reach, murder in their eyes…almost… His body tensed, readied for impact and battle.

Neither race touched them.

"What the hell?" Shock pounded through him.

The vampires had flown past them and caught the demons midair, crashing together. Hisses rebounded, followed by the sound of sucking. The smell of sulfur blended with a metallic twang.

The centaur bolted into motion. Gray jumped up, pulling Jewel with him, and tried to follow the path the horse-woman had taken.

"Wait," Jewel said, trying to jerk him to a stop.

"Where's that safe house you mentioned?" He tugged his hood back over his head, covering his pale locks, determination propelling him onward. After a quick left and right perimeter check—and spotting several mers—he ushered Jewel to another alleyway.

"Wait!" she repeated.

This time, he spun and faced her. Half of her face was shadowed by the hood, but her lips—those soft, pleasure-giving lips—were perfectly visible. "Baby, this is life and death. We can talk when I've got you tucked away safe."

"I read his mind."

His brow furrowed. "Who?"

"Layel. King of the vampires. I read his mind."

Understanding dawned. He dragged her inside a nearby cart and slithered the canopy over their heads. He didn't like remaining sedentary, but flattened himself on top of her, pressing her back into the splintered wood. "All right, I'm listening." He kept his voice quiet, not wanting the sound to carry. "What did you learn?"

She shivered at the contact. "Layel wants to help us."

"Why?"

"I don't know."

He leaned into her until their breath mingled, the light in his silver eyes piercing her with its intensity. The hard length of his body fit perfectly against hers. "How can you know one and not the other?"

Jewel licked her lips and liquefied against him. Gray had been so distant with her since awaking this morning. He'd barely touched her. And now that he was, she couldn't control her reaction. She wanted him again.

"Concentrate, baby."

"People do not think in sequential ways," she said, forcing her mind on the task at hand. "I want to help them because of this reason and that reason."

He cursed under his breath. "You're right. I'd feel a lot better knowing his motives, though."

"Yes." Her hands itched to slide up his chest, to have his hands slide down hers. "His men are keeping the mers and demons away from us. He wants us to stay here."

"Are you certain he won't hurt you? You can't predict danger against yourself."

"I'm sure about this. Very sure."

He shifted, his erection pressing between her legs. She gasped. He wasn't immune to their contact, either.

"All right," he said. "We'll wait for him."

She brushed her lips over his jaw line, tingling erotically when his beard stubble teased her. Hands climbing up his back, she spread her legs and welcomed him deeper.

He stopped her action with a shake of his head. "Don't. We can't do that here."

"We're perfectly safe."

"Doesn't matter. I don't want to get caught with my pants down and besides that, our physical relationship is over."

"Why?" she whispered, freezing inside. A hollow beat drummed in her chest. "You're touching me now."

"You know what I mean." His stark tone lashed out.

"No, I don't."

His teeth ground together, and he remained silent for a long while. It was clear he loathed the subject. Finally, he snapped, "I'll hurt you, damn it."

Hurt her? "The only way you'll hurt me is by *not* touching me."

His mouth twisted in a scowl. "Things are different now. *I'm* different." His fist pounded into the cart, right beside her head. "Damn it. I want to drink your blood. Every time I get close to you, I can smell your blood and I want to taste it."

Her eyes widened. He expected her to be horrified, scared. Disgusted. How could he know she was not like the women of his acquaintance? She had been raised in this world, where vampires were the norm.

His desire excited her.

She'd never been bitten before, but she wanted to share a deeper part of herself with Gray, wanted to be the first and only woman he drank from. Perhaps it would link them, far stronger than they were already linked.

"I want you to bite me." Not giving him a chance to protest, Jewel meshed her lips into his. He groaned then opened eagerly, without protest, his tongue quickly taking control. His flavor, male and heat, invaded her mouth, a welcome conqueror. Their teeth scraped together as their bodies strained for closer contact. Her breasts pressed into his chest. His hands cupped her bottom and jerked her hard against his erection.

Desire rocked her, hot and hungry.

"You taste so good," he muttered raggedly. "We shouldn't be doing this."

"I want you so much," she breathed.

He kissed his way down her face, her chin, her neck, and his tongue flicked out, laving the sensitive skin. She felt his teeth elongating, readying for insertion. "*I* shouldn't do this."

"Please, do it now." Her body was crying out for all of him. She'd loved him for so long, desired him longer. Craved him. "Maybe my blood will ease the changes inside you and help you conquer them."

"I can't. I shouldn't. I… Stop me if I hurt you." He opened his mouth against her neck and applied a slight pressure. Just about…

"Now, now, children." The flap covering them was whipped aside. "You should take that somewhere private."

Gray sprang up, facing the intruder with a feral growl. Everything about him, from his posture, to his clenched fists and his glowering red eyes, screamed his intention to attack.

Jewel drew in a shaky breath and hopped beside him, her legs almost buckling under her weight. She curled her hand around his forearm. Instantly he relaxed.

"Layel," she said, straightening her shoulders.

The vampire king inclined his head in acknowledgement. His handsome features were so perfect they could have been chiseled from stone. "Leave the Inner City," he said. A drop of black blood trickled from the side of his mouth. He licked it away with a shudder of distaste. "The demons always taste sour." He flicked Gray a glance. "I don't recommend them."

Another low growl purred from Gray. "State your purpose, vampire."

Layel arched an uncaring brow. "Marina is determined to have the girl back."

"She's mine."

Layel chuckled, the sound filled with rich masculine humor. "Neither of us wants the queen to recapture her. For different reasons, I'm sure. My men will see you to safety."

Jewel opened her mouth to protest, but he cut her off. "You know you can trust me in this."

She nodded. "However, it is your motives I question."

"You do not have to fear for your human," Layel said. "While I'm sure he would make a tasty snack, I'm quite full. And besides that, he has a bit of demon blood, does he not? I'm only interested in dessert at the moment, not more of the same rotten meal."

"Give me your hand," she persisted, "so that I can assure myself—"

He backed away hastily. "You will not touch me."

And in that moment, Jewel felt his fear. He was hiding something and did not want her to know it, but she sensed that it had nothing to do Gray. She dropped her hand to her side. "Very well."

"I don't trust him," Gray said, stating the words

loudly. He struggled to get himself under control, to dim the bloodlust rushing through him. He'd almost bitten Jewel, had almost drunk her blood after he'd fought so hard to ignore the craving.

He should have been disgusted with himself.

He wasn't.

He was only enraged that he'd been interrupted.

He didn't like this vampire king and didn't like the way the man watched Jewel, as if inviting her to be his friend. But more than that, he didn't like the fact that the evil creature was swooping in and becoming the hero. Irrational, yes. But it was Gray's job to protect Jewel, and he'd be damned if he'd allow anyone else to get near her. Especially a vampire.

The irony of that didn't escape him.

The woman was hunted like a prized twenty-point buck during deer season, and he didn't dare trust anyone with her.

"Without me, you'll lose her," the vampire said.

"I will allow your men to see us out of the city." Better to keep them close and use them to escape the demons. "After that, they must leave."

"Or what?" Layel asked with amusement.

"Or I'll do to your men what I did to the demon castle."

Layel lost his smile. His ice-blue gaze narrowed menacingly. "Very well. If Marina captures you, however, I will kill you both before I allow her to use the—"

"Layel!" Jewel shouted, nervousness blasting from her voice. "You cannot kill me, and you know it. Now be on your way. Marina is looking for you and she is not pleased."

The vampire actually grimaced. "Until next time."

And then he was gone, two other vampires standing in his place.

"Let's go," one of them said. "We don't have much time."

# CHAPTER TWENTY-TWO

THREE HOURS LATER, Gray found himself alone with Jewel and safe in the forest. True to their word, the vampires escorted them safely through the city and left them in peace.

"This is far enough," one of them said. "We must go now. Do not return to the city."

Before Gray could respond, they vanished in a flap of movement.

"Wait here," he told Jewel. He sprinted through the trees, their trunks blurring because of his own speed. He wanted to make sure the vampires didn't double back and attack. He caught sight of them only once, their white-blond hair whipping past the foliage.

Satisfied they wouldn't come back, he retraced his steps. Jewel was exactly where he'd left her, spreading out the meal they'd purchased before leaving the city. She glanced up at his approach.

"I hope you're hungry."

"Starved." He plopped down. The air was cool and fragrant with summer scents. Birds soared overhead, and the river trickled beside them. The perfect picnic setting. He could almost forget he'd been chased by crazed mermen and revenge-minded demons.

He gazed at the food hungrily. After having only a tasteless energy bar for breakfast, he would have sold his soul—maybe he had already and that was a moot point—for a single bite of that succulent meat.

"Shall we eat?" she asked, as proper as ever.

He didn't take time to respond, simply ripped off a piece of meat and popped it into his mouth. He almost groaned at the sheer pleasure of it.

Jewel did groan. "I don't think I've ever tasted anything quite this good," she said. "Well, except you."

She kept saying things like that, and such boldness from her shocked him enough that he paused, his fowl-filled hand poised just in front of his mouth. "I can say the same of you."

Since their last kiss, there had been a heavy tension between them. They were going to make love again; they both knew it. He couldn't resist her; he just couldn't. Every time he tried, he only succeeded in driving himself insane. So he was done denying himself. His desire to bite her excited rather than repulsed her. A blessing he wasn't going to question.

He didn't know with one hundred percent surety that she was the Jewel of Dunamis as he suspected. Didn't know if he'd have one more night with her or many. None of that mattered. He loved her, and he *was* going to be with her.

When, he knew, would be sooner rather than later.

His gaze drifted to her. Dirt and blood specks smudged her cheek. Black-as-night hair cascaded in tangles down her back. And yet, with the vitality sparkling in her ocean-blue eyes, she'd never looked more lovely. More exquisite.

This tenderness he felt for her, this ferocity. This need to be near her. This furious passion and unquenchable hunger.

This protective obsession.

Only his sister, Katie, had ever brought out his protective instincts like this—and now Jewel. But he felt anything but brotherly toward her.

His sister would love her, he knew.

"You're thinking about your family," Jewel stated. She nibbled on a soft loaf of bread stuffed with cheese.

His brows arched. "And just how do you know that, oh non-mind reader?"

"Your expression is wistful. Tell me about them."

"You already know about them."

"Tell me, anyway."

Between bites, he said, "Brian is the unflappable one, always strong, always steady. Erik is the peacemaker and hard to rile, but once he's mad," Gray gave a mock shudder, "the wrath of Erik is a terrible thing."

As he spoke, everything inside him relaxed. That had been Jewel's purpose, he realized with admiration. "Denver is probably on a date right this minute with the World's Biggest Ice Queen."

"Madison or Jane?" Jewel asked with a grin.

"Madison."

"I remember her. She never smiles."

"I don't know what the boy sees in her. She's emotionless and probably as much fun as an alien probe in bed."

Jewel gasped in scandalized shock. "What a horrible thing to say."

A laugh escaped him, and he was surprised by just how genuine it was. "Maybe warming up a prude is more fun than I realized."

Her cheeks reddened. "I am not a prude."

"Believe me, Blaze, I know." He reached over and squeezed her hand. "Nick is probably causing trouble somewhere with his warped sense of humor. Katie's probably giving her husband, Jorlan, hell, and my dad is probably giving my stepmom, Francis, hell. It seems to be a family tradition."

"I wish I could meet them in person."

Her words instantly flashed an image through his mind—an image of Jewel surrounded by his brothers, sister and father. They would welcome her with open arms, would love her candor and honesty, and hell, he'd love to watch her face as his sailor-mouthed family shocked her.

"I've always wished I had Katie's strength," Jewel sighed wistfully. "When she first met Jorlan, she could have easily been crushed by his sheer maleness. But she ended up conquering him instead."

As Jewel had conquered Gray. Overhead, the dome breathed an amber glow and that glow dripped onto her features, casting her in a perfect frame of radiance. His chest constricted. "Dusk is falling, so we need to finish eating. I want to wash up before lights out."

They finished their meal in silence, and Gray pushed to his feet. He held out his hand. "You ready?"

"To bathe?" Jewel looked at him, her gaze unsure. "Together?"

He nodded. "If you get in that water with me, we're going to make love."

"Finally." Reaching up, she curled her fingers through his. He helped her to her feet. A rosy flush of excitement colored her cheeks as they strolled the short distance to the river's edge.

"Are Mermen going to attack us?" he asked, the thought just now occurring to him.

"They are still in the city, and I do not sense them."

"Did you last time?"

She nodded. "That's why I was dressed and was not naked as promised. I'd hoped they would pass me by. We are very much alone here."

When she released his hand to unlace the knots on the waist of her robe, he stopped her with a huskily muttered, "Let me."

Movements deft, he worked at the material. The dirty covering soon floated to her ankles, leaving her in undergarments. Those he pushed to the ground, too. And then she was suddenly, gloriously naked.

He drank in the sight of her. Pink, pearled nipples, smooth-as-silk belly, a small thatch of dark curls, and long, tapered legs. Everything he remembered, yet so much more beautiful, framed as she was by his love.

Perfection.

Jewel stood completely still for Gray's perusal. Because the people of Atlantis wanted her for her psychic skills, they saw her as an object. A thing. They even called her "it" upon occasion. They'd never seen her as a sexual being. But the way Gray looked at her…she felt achy. Erotic and craved.

"You are so beautiful," he breathed. His eyes were heated, his voice husky.

"Thank—thank you." She didn't know what else to say. Need thrummed through her, and she reached out, peeling away his clothing piece by unwanted piece. Her hands were shaky. His chest was wide and laced with muscle, and his nipples were small and brown, hard points against her hands. A thin trail of blond hair led past the waist of his pants all the way to his penis. The long, thick length of him jutted up.

She'd seen him like this before. Proud. Aroused. Not in the tent, too dark, but for other women. This time, he wanted *her.* Was hard for *her.* Her blood heated with the power of that knowledge.

"We were made to pleasure each other, I think," he said, lifting her by the waist and walking straight into the water.

She wrapped her legs around him as cool liquid enveloped her, making her shiver. Gray's heat kept her warm and provided an erotic contrast. Her arms wound around him. Breasts to chest. Erection to woman.

"I've wanted you for so long," she admitted breathlessly.

"Then take me," he said, his voice rougher, harsher than she'd ever heard it. "I'm yours."

She kissed him then, softly at first. The moment their tongues met, she nearly cried out at the sudden rush of intensity between them. All strength deserted her. Had his arms not been around her, she would have sunk bonelessly to the bottom of the river. One of his hands gripped her thigh, keeping her leg around him.

The feel of his erection pressed directly against her, ready for penetration—yet just beyond reach. He rocked against her. She whimpered at the indescribable burst of pleasure as every nerve ending in her body awoke.

"That feels so good. Do it again."

He uttered a strained chuckle. "First, I need to wash you. Your breasts…they're filthy. Just filthy."

He sounded so wicked.

"Drop your legs," he added.

When she did, his hands cupped the water and he poured it onto her chest. He watched with barely a breath as each drop slid over her plump breasts, catching on her nipples.

He licked the first droplet away, then the other. "You're just so dirty. I need to wash you all over."

"Are you dirty?"

"Oh, yes."

He kissed his way down her stomach, not stopping until he was kneeling. The water just reached the apex of her thighs. Darting out, his tongue found the heart of her. She screamed at the pleasure of it, and her head arched backward. Her hands gripped his head, holding him in place. On and on her tasted her.

Minutes—hours—later, Jewel was desperate. She had to have him inside her. Now. She clawed at him with her nails. He jerked up and they tumbled into the water, their mouths locked together as the liquid washed over them, covering them. Their bodies tangled and strained as their tongues dueled.

Her head grew light just as Gray gave a powerful kick of his legs, sending them above the surface. She gasped in air, taking his breath. He gasped in air, taking hers. The need to have him, all of him, pounded through her.

"Don't make me wait any longer," she gasped.

"Now?"

"Please."

He surged up and into her, going deep.

Her inner walls held him tight, and when he was sheathed completely, giving her body what it had craved all these many days, her pleasure exploded. She spasmed around him. Stars winked behind her eyelids, and heat spread like wildfire through her blood. Because he was inside her, a part of her, her rapture was so much more complete.

"Shit," Gray groaned. He rocked in and out of her, and she clung to him. "So good."

"More." So much more. She might never get enough of him. Already the hunger was building again. "I love you." Unbidden, the words ripped from her throat. They were imprinted on her every cell. Shouting them was as natural as breathing.

"Tell me again," he growled.

"I love you." He wasn't upset?

"Again."

"I love you. Gods, I love you."

In and out he moved, fast, so fast, droplets splashing around them. She bit the cord of his neck, hard. She tugged at his hair, her need becoming too great to control. She needed…she needed…

His teeth sank into her neck.

Exactly that. Instantly another orgasm consumed her. Intense. So intense. "Yes. Yes!" And as she writhed against him, riding the waves of pleasure, he drank from her. His thrusts deepened, grew even faster, harder.

Faster.

Harder.

When he came, a hoarse cry ripped from his throat and the sound echoed through the forest.

# CHAPTER TWENTY-THREE

JEWEL LAY fully clothed in the crook of Gray's arms. She had wanted to stay naked with him all night, but he'd insisted they be prepared for any unwanted night-time visitors, as trouble seemed to follow them.

Right now, his deep, relaxed breathing assured her that he slept peacefully. Her body was sated and relaxed, but her mind refused to quiet. What they'd done together had been wonderful. So wonderfully satisfying. When he'd bit her, oh, the pleasure! Nearly too much to bear. But something about their couplings was beginning to bother her.

He didn't linger over her body like he did with other women. He took her savagely, quickly. He didn't whisper erotic words in her ear; he grunted and growled and uttered guttural things. She loved it, gods, she loved it, but she couldn't help but worry that perhaps he didn't like her as well as he'd liked the others. But why then hadn't he panicked at her declaration of love?

Jewel sighed and forced herself to sleep. He was here, in her arms, and he did care for her. That would have to be enough for now.

GRAY SLOWLY came to wakefulness, images of making love with Jewel fresh in his mind. He lay on a mossy riverbank, his woman tucked securely in his arms. He loved the way he'd gone wild for her. He loved the way she'd gone wild for him, loved the way she'd clawed and bit at him. Loved the way she'd ferally growled his name.

He loved her. Period.

He wasn't going home without her. He'd find a way to take her with him; he had to find a way. He couldn't live without her. She might even now be carrying his child; they'd taken no precautions, this time or before. Maybe Atlantean and human could procreate, maybe they couldn't. Either way, she belonged with him.

Staying here wasn't an option. OBI would send in another agent. The only reason they hadn't yet—or had they? Damn, he just didn't know. They wanted as few people as possible to know about the jewel. Hopefully that concern was still holding them back. They wouldn't want to take a chance that another government, or even regular people, would learn about it.

Later, he and Jewel were going to have themselves a serious conversation. Could she be happy on the surface? Was *she* the Jewel of Dunamis? If not, what was her connection? And there was a connection, he knew there was.

Constantly he wavered between yes and no. Yes, she was Dunamis. No, he didn't want her to be so she wasn't. She was a woman, for Christ's sake, a living, breathing, sensual woman. Not a stone. But she could predict when their enemy approached, knew that enemy's battle plan, as well. She could read minds and knew truth from lie.

Everything Dunamis could do.

Shit! Frustrated, he raked a hand through his hair.

"Do not move again, human."

The deep, raspy voice echoed through the darkness. Remaining perfectly still, Gray sent his gaze throughout the night. He'd been so lost in his musing, he'd allowed someone to sneak up on him. Fucking hell!

Soon he spotted the intruder as clearly as if the sun glowed overhead. His blood ran cold. The golden-eyed warrior had a sword pointed at his heart.

"Let the woman go," he said. Slowly he shifted, pressing his skin against the blade's tip. It pricked and stung, but he was able to settle Jewel beneath him, guarding her with his body. He inched his hand to his waist and the blade strapped there. "Maybe I'll let you live," he said, hoping the boast would serve as a distraction.

The dark-haired warrior chuckled. "I like your spirit, human. Or vampire? Or demon? You smell of all three. Now, awaken the woman. I wish to speak with her."

"I'm awake, Renard."

Gray released a breath he hadn't known he'd been holding. Jewel sounded calm, completely unafraid, and the fact that she knew the warrior by name eased his worry for her safety. That didn't stop him from gripping his blade and holding it at the ready.

"Remove your weapon from Gray, please," she said,

sitting up. "If you hurt him, I will find a way to make your life miserable for all eternity."

Noticing the way her white robe flowed over her exquisite curves, Gray was immensely grateful he'd insisted that they dress after their explosive lovemaking in the river. He wanted no one viewing her nakedness but himself.

The warrior Renard did as commanded and sheathed his weapon with a long, drawn-out sigh. "Am I allowed to have no fun?"

"Not with my man, no."

Gray liked those words on her lips.

"Did you come to steal me away?" she asked.

"Actually, no."

Jewel relaxed. "Truth," she said.

Gray jumped to his feet, not wanting the brute to have any type of advantage. "You want to explain why you're here and threatening me at sword point?" he asked, keeping his voice conversational.

The large warrior, who stood as tall as Gray, grinned. "Not particularly, no."

"Renard," Jewel said, her expression as stern as a schoolteacher. "Tell us, or I'll read your mind. Then I'll tell all your secrets."

He shuddered. "First, you enter dragon territory. Then we see you in the Inner City with mers following you. *Then* demons attack you, and if that isn't enough, we see the vampires save you. Have you joined with them?" The question lashed out, sharpened with a dangerous edge.

"Of course not."

"Then tell us, please, what is going on."

"We? Us?" Gray demanded, already scanning the forest.

Light began to seep from the crystal dome, chasing away the shadows as four other hulking warriors stepped from behind the trees. Gray rolled his eyes. Not only had one man sneaked up on him, but four of his friends had, as well. Why not post a sign on the trees that read, Human This Way. Follow Path.

"Brand," Jewel squealed happily, jumping to her feet. She raced over to the men, throwing herself in their arms one by one.

"Jewel!" Gray started to go after her, every possessive and protective bone in body shouting a protest. He wanted to jerk her away from them, but he didn't. He forced himself to remain in place, entranced by the sight of her happiness. The men were gentle with her as they passed her from one to the other. Still.

He didn't like anyone else—especially these testosterone filled warriors—putting their hands on his woman. And she was his. She'd purred her love and he'd claimed her, so she might as well get used to it.

When had he become such an alpha?

Renard's golden eyes lit with amusement. "Lucky for you she doesn't want to part with you."

He crossed his arms over his chest. "Exactly how long have you been hanging around here?"

Smile growing, the warrior said, "We gave you privacy for your mating, if that's what you want to know." His amusement died quickly, however. "What kind of creature are you?"

Gray shrugged, not about to answer or explain. "Jewel," he called, done with the stranger. She'd been away from him for too long. "Come here. Please."

Steps light, she reclaimed her position at his side. Her expression radiated bright, illuminant bliss. "These men belong to Darius en Kragin," she explained. "He's the king of the dragons, and the dragons are the closest things I've ever had to friends."

He almost groaned. He did frown. "Dragons?" Too easily he remembered how one of their race had welcomed him those first few nights in Atlantis.

"These men are honorable." She looked to the tallest blond. "How is Darius and his new bride?"

The warrior, Brand, raised sandy brows, saying pointedly, "You will soon see for yourself."

Her smile faded. "Renard said you were not here to steal me. There was truth in his words."

"I will not steal you. You will simply come with me willingly. Darius bid us to find you and bring you to him."

"No," Gray said. "We won't go."

"We need to reach the Temple of Cronus," Jewel added.

"The Temple of—" Renard, who now stood next to the blond, frowned. "The temple was destroyed months ago when humans came through the portal."

Jewel's body went completely still, her lungs refusing to take in air. Surely he was mistaken. Surely she would have known, have felt something. "You're wrong," she managed to gasp.

"It was decimated, and there is nothing left. I speak true."

Yes, he did, she realized, her stomach knotting pain-fully. An image of crumpled stone flashed in her mind, and she almost cried out. This was what her feeling of foreboding had been about when she'd asked Gray to take her to the temple. She'd ignored it, had refused to contemplate it because then she would have had to give up hope of finding her father.

But all this time, her hopes had been for nothing. She raised a shaky hand to her mouth, covering her trem-bling lips. She wanted a family so desperately, wanted to find her father and feel his arms around her. She wanted something like Gray had with his brothers and sister.

A strong arm wrapped around her waist and tugged her into an equally strong chest. Gray's masculine scent reached her nose. "I'm here, baby."

White-hot tears burned her eyes, and the trembling spread to her chin. Sinking into him, she drew from his strength and swallowed back her anguish. She would not break down emotionally in front of these men. She was strong, damn it. She would survive. Right now she had Gray, and she would cherish their short time to-gether, letting nothing taint it.

She gave him a lingering hug, then forced herself to disengage. She faced Brand squarely. "Why does Darius wish to see me?" There. Switching the conver-sation to the dragon king almost, *almost* drowned the knowledge that she no longer knew where to search for her father.

Brand tsked under his tongue. "You know only he can tell you that. Are you ready to leave?"

Gray stiffened, and she knew his blood was heating, preparing his body for battle.

"I have promised to do something for Gray," she said, "and that promise comes before your king."

"Whatever it is you must do for your man, you can do at our palace."

Yes, she could, she realized with both joy and dejection. That would give her more time with Gray, and she grasped on to the reprieve. She faced him. "I know you're in a hurry to find Dunamis," she whispered, "and I know your people need you back, but can you stay? For one more day?" Sucking in a breath, she added, "Dunamis will be yours now or later, whichever you decide."

He searched her face, his expression guarded. She expected him to ask how he could acquire the stone now that Cronus was destroyed but he didn't. He nodded and said, "One more day."

Relief swept through her, blanketing her sorrow and her fear. "Thank you."

"Gentlemen," he said, never taking his gaze from her. "It appears we will be joining you."

"Too bad you agreed so easily," one of the dragons said, the tallest of the group. "I would have loved to convince you some other way." The man actually sounded disappointed.

"You will be safe with the dragons." Jewel linked her fingers with Gray's. "They are a fierce lot, but very protective and Darius—" She paused, her words grinding to a halt. A dark premonition slithered through her mind. "Darius is in trouble."

The dragons didn't question her knowledge of this. They knew her powers firsthand and knew she never lied. Simultaneously they roared, growing wider and larger, morphing into their dragon forms, claws, tails and wings sprouting from their bodies and ripping away their clothing. Scales replaced skin, sharp fangs replaced teeth. Fire spewed from their mouths.

Gray tried to grab her and push her behind him.

"It's all right," she said. "They will not hurt us."

"My God. I've seen some weird shit, but this…"

"They will fly us to the dragon palace." She guided him forward. "Climb on and enjoy the ride."

"Dear God." He grabbed his backpack from the ground and slung it over his shoulder before tentatively climbing on the dragon's back. Thankfully it remained unmoving, allowing him to settle on top. His every action was slow and measured.

"What's taking you so long?" Jewel's lips twitched, a smile clinging to the edges.

That smile eased the ache in his stomach, an ache that roared to life when she'd been told about Cronus, and he'd watched her go pale, watched tears fall from her eyes. He'd been helpless to do anything for her.

"Like I really want to touch something I'm not supposed to. I'm thinking we should walk." Even as he spoke, he was swinging his leg around, ready to hop off.

She laughed, the erotic sound of it washing over him in sensual waves. "You are such a man. Just remember, the quicker we get there, the quicker I can have my wicked way with you."

Faster than she could blink, he reached down, grabbed her arm, and hoisted her behind him. "Kick it into gear. We're ready for takeoff."

# CHAPTER TWENTY-FOUR

GRAY HAD DONE some crazy shit throughout his life, but this topped the list. After today, if anyone told him he didn't have balls of steel, they'd be wrong. Usually he enjoyed flying. He'd jumped out of planes, for God's sake. Hell, he'd levitated and flown himself into town.

Right now, as the wind roared through his hair and the crystal dome emitted a soft golden glow above, all he wanted to do was vomit. His only anchor against free-falling to his death was his kung fu grip on a dragon. An actual, fire-breathing dragon. Behind him, Jewel leaned her head against his shoulder, soaking up the experience like they were in first-class accommodations aboard the Concorde.

"There it is," she said, pointing straight ahead. "Darius's palace."

Sure enough, a huge crystal fortress loomed, a jagged and glistening monstrosity of uneven towers. All the colors of the rainbow glittered from the edges. Brand flew closer and closer to it, and a cold sweat broke over Gray's skin. There were no doors that he could see. No windows. And the stupid dragon wasn't slowing down.

Was, in fact, gliding his thin, nearly transparent wings faster.

Someone should have told him the plan was to crash into the wall and bust it open. He would have come up with plan B.

"Jewel, hold tight to me. Get ready for impact."

But the top of the domed ceiling opened, quickly becoming wider. Sea water cascaded inside the palace. The dragons flew straight into the waterfall. Salty liquid rained on him, and he reached behind him and pulled Jewel's face into his back.

Moments later, the dragons glided softly to the wet, tilted floors, the water draining at the sides. Water dripping from him, Gray hurriedly hopped down and helped Jewel do the same. He would not admit to having shaky limbs.

"Thank you." Her wet hair clung to her face and shoulders. Now that they were here, there was a sad gleam in her eyes and a melancholy layer in her voice. Was she thinking about the ruined temple? Not knowing what else to do, he kissed her lips.

She blinked up at him and slowly smiled. Damn if his chest didn't constrict.

"What was that for?" she asked.

"Just 'cause."

He turned his attention to the dragons. Because Jewel trusted them so completely, he was able to relax his guard more so than usual. And wasn't that ironic? He couldn't trust the human partners OBI sometimes stuck him with, but he could put his life in the hands of a fire-breathing beast. For the first time since entering Atlantis, he didn't feel chased or hunted. Or like the next item on the menu.

As he watched, the creatures' scales disappeared beneath their bronzed skin. Their elongated faces shrank, their tails and wings retracted under small slits of human skin, and they were once again completely human. Of course, they were also completely naked.

"Don't stare, Blaze, or I'll cover your eyes."

She snorted.

"This way," Brand said. Without waiting for their agreement, he and the others stalked from the room.

Side by side, he and Jewel followed them into a hallway. Sconces lined the walls, illuminating the glistening wealth. He didn't know what he expected of a dragon palace, but what he found wasn't it. Diamonds, sapphires, emeralds, and rubies adorned the walls. Gold and silver provided the glue that held the gems together.

"My God," he muttered. So much wealth… He'd never seen its like.

Forcing himself to look away proved difficult, but he couldn't allow himself to be distracted. "If anything happens, get behind me. Okay?" He might trust the dragons in this room, but he didn't know what lay beyond these doors. Steadily he moved the knife from his waistband and tucked it under his shirtsleeve.

"I hope you remember being this protective in the morning."

The morning…when she would give him Dunamis? When she would give him herself? "You can count on it," he said, trying to assure her that no matter what she told him, he would not hurt her.

She bit her lip then opened her mouth to say something. She closed it with a snap. "I...like you, Gray."

That wasn't what she'd wanted to say. He would have preferred to hear "I love you" again, but those words would do for now. *He* really liked every damn thing about her. "I like you, too, sweetheart."

"Can you two not shut up for a few seconds?" Renard said on a sigh. "You are just like Darius and Grace. Sweetheart this and sweetheart that. We are sick to death of such nonsense."

"Where are you taking us?" Gray asked.

"To meet Darius," Jewel answered for the dragon.

Brand pivoted on his heel and approached the far right wall. For the first time, Gray noticed the medallion hanging at the warrior's neck. It was small and round and now emitted a slight blue glow. As if sensing its presence, two panels immediately opened.

"I spent two years here," Jewel said. "Javar was leader then. Darius was but a hatchling, learning the dictates of a Guardian."

"And a Guardian is..."

"A protector of this city. When humans try to enter, Guardians kill them."

"Darius doesn't do as much killing these days," Renard said. "Grace gets mad. So now he takes the traveler somewhere on the surface and clears his memory."

"I was not killed or redirected," Gray pointed out.

"Yes," Brand said. "And we are curious as to why. Darius has every intention of finding out."

They finished their walk down the wide, long hall in silence, leaving a trail of water. They turned a corner—and stepped into a dining room of utter decadence. A dragon-clawed table, ivory walls, ebony floors. A large bay window opened in back, overlooking the entire span of the city. His sister, Katie, restored homes and would have killed to own this room. Hooks lined one section of the wall, each dangling a piece of clothing.

A big warrior sat at the head of the table, a dainty redhead on his lap. She whispered something in his ear and the beast laughed. Even laughing, Gray had never seen a more imposing figure. A scar slashed from the man's left eye to his chin. He looked like he dined on small children for breakfast and glass shards for dessert.

"We bring news, Darius," Brand announced. He stopped in front of the still laughing male.

Color bloomed bright on the redhead's cheeks. She popped to her feet, giving Gray his first full look at her. Her hair curled around her shoulders and freckles adorned every inch of visible skin. She wore jeans and a T-shirt.

He'd seen nothing but robes and togas for the past week, and the modern surface clothes shocked him.

Darius frowned, standing and skidding his chair behind him. "Dress first. Then tell me what you have learned." He braced his feet apart and locked his hands behind his back, prepared, awaiting bad news.

The warriors dressed, taking clothes from the hooks. Unlike every other dragon Gray had seen so far,

Darius did not have golden eyes. His were blue and swirled like a morning mist, as otherworldly as Layel's. As otherworldly as Jewel's. In fact, both Jewel and Darius possessed the same silky black hair. Gray's gaze shot from one to the other. Jewel had traits of the demons, vampires, and now dragons, yet she appeared human. What did that mean?

Renard straightened to attention. "Vampires and demons have joined forces. They were making their way here when they stopped in the Inner City to give chase to this human and—"

"Me." Jewel stepped around him.

All eyes focused on her.

Because he felt a sudden rush of pride for her, Gray didn't try to push her behind him this time. She stood strong in the face of danger and accepted the consequences. Even though he hated doing nothing, he would not take that away from her. Especially when he sensed these men would not harm her.

His dad had raised him to believe women needed safeguarding, that they were weak and vulnerable without a man. His strong, capable sister, Katie, proved that theory wrong every day. Jewel, too. She sought to guard and defend his life, to place herself in danger in hopes of saving him.

"I had heard you escaped from Marina, so I sent my men to fetch you," Darius said. His voice was as hard and unbending as his expression. "I am unsure whether to trust you. Are you here at her bidding?"

A wave of hurt flickered in Jewel's eyes, but she quickly doused it and returned the dragon leader's frown. "No. Do you truly believe she would have let me leave for any reason? Even your downfall?"

Darius studied her and nodded. "You are right. I have many questions for you. The human, though—"

"Is my only reason for coming with your men. If he leaves, so too do I."

The dragon growled low in his throat. "Very well, then. If he hurts, destroys or steals anything, I will personally see to his death."

"I'd like to see you try," Gray said without fear.

Unused to insubordination, Darius advanced toward him. Anger darkened his eyes.

The redhead stepped forward with a smile, blocking his path. Her smile seemed genuine despite the tension growing in the room. "I'm Grace, the big guy's wife. It's so nice to meet you."

As she stretched out her hand to shake Gray's, Darius growled, "Touching Grace is not permitted, human. You will keep your hands to yourself."

"Oh, hush up," she said without turning around. She and Gray shook. "I, for one, am glad to see another human."

Darius threw up his hands in exasperation. "You see your brother every day."

She only smiled again. "Can you really consider Alex a human?"

Darius's lips pressed tight as he fought a grin of his own.

"Don't let Darius fool you," she told Gray. "He's nothing but a softie." Grace turned to Jewel. "We're so happy to have you here. I've heard so much about you and have been eagerly awaiting your arrival. Why don't I show you to a room, and you can prepare for lunch. We'll all have a nice conversation after we've eaten."

Darius stalked to the petite woman's side. "I do not want you taking part in this. You—"

Grace turned her attention full force on her husband. She batted her lashes and curled her hands over his chest. "I seriously hope you're not trying to send me away, because you'd be in a shitload of trouble."

The man melted, that was the only way to describe it. His expression softened and he reached out and brushed a red curl from Grace's temple. "Take them to their rooms, then. After lunch, we will question them together."

Grace planted a swift kiss on his lips before beaming up at Gray and Jewel. "As I was saying, I'll show you each to a room."

"We'll share." Gray shifted to battle stance. No way was he going to be parted from Jewel. "Only one is needed."

She looked to Jewel for confirmation. Jewel nodded, her cheeks bright red with color.

The blue-green of Grace's eyes sparkled with knowing. "You can bathe, rest or...whatever, and we'll meet back here in one—"

"Two," Jewel said, looking down at her feet.

Gray's lips twitched.

"Two hours."

# CHAPTER TWENTY-FIVE

THEIR ROOM BOASTED a large bathing pool, an even larger bed, and so many velvet pillows they could drown in them. Vases burst with diamonds, and an array of jewelry sprawled atop a marble vanity. A lamb's fleece carpet lined the floor.

"The sheer amount of wealth is amazing," Gray said, pivoting on his heel to take everything in. He stood in the middle of the room.

"I've lived in many such rooms throughout my life." Jewel stood a few feet away from him and kept her back to him. She gripped the material of her robe, bunching it between her fingers. The time had come to admit who and what she was. She couldn't wait till morning. Worry over his reaction had slammed into her, consuming her, the moment they'd shut the door. *Do it.*

"I'm sorry about the destruction of the temple," he said before she could open her mouth. "I know how much you wanted to discover your father's identity."

"Perhaps one day, my father will find me. Perhaps I'll have a vision of him. Perhaps I'll stumble upon a clue that points me in the right direction." Her eyelids squeezed shut, and she straightened her shoulders, gathering her courage. "We need to talk, Gray. I must tell you—"

"Later."

The huskiness of his tone made her shiver. "But you need to know—"

"I want you on a bed." He moved behind her, his arms winding around her, his hands finding her breasts. "We can talk later."

She twisted, facing him, and he lifted her. He carried her to the silk-covered bed. Gently he laid her on top. Her eyes were already closed, her lips parted as she purred her growing pleasure. Her black hair spilled around her delicate shoulders.

God, he loved this woman.

He took her hard and fast, almost savage in his need. He was surprised the urge to drink her blood remained dormant as he hurtled them over the edge of satisfaction. Immediately afterward, he grew hard again. He couldn't get enough of her, but at least the urgency was gone. Now he could play and savor.

He kissed his way down her body, lingering on her ankles, the insides of her knees. Soon she was writhing beneath his mouth, crying out his name.

"You didn't go this slowly last time," she gasped out.

He heard a tinge of upset and stilled. "What do you mean?"

"You usually go slowly with your women. Like this."

A strained chuckle escaped him, and he hugged her close to him, loving the feel of her breasts against his chest. What an innocent she was. "Baby, that just proves

I want you more than any other. With you, I lose my control. With you, nothing matters but being inside you."

"Oh. Ohh."

He licked his way into her mouth, feeding her kisses. She tasted sweet and womanly, the absolute essence of desire. Passion. Hunger. His cock was already throbbing with need for her, but he was going to go slow this time if it killed him.

As soft as feathers, he moved his fingers down her stomach and glided them to her silky, wet warmth. Teasing her. Taunting her. Pushing her to the edge before pausing.

"Gray!" She shouted his name like a prayer. "Let me finish."

He circled her clitoris with his thumb while two of his fingers moved in and out of her. When she tensed, readying for orgasm, he stopped again.

"Gray!" She shouted his name like a vile curse. "Finish. Please. Hard and fast."

How could he deny such a delicious request? Request? he thought. No, the woman had ordered him. But deny he would. "I thought you wanted me to go slow."

"I changed my mind."

"I'm glad, but I'm still taking this slow." Gradually, inch by inch, he entered her. She writhed against him. Her nails sunk into his back, her hands tugged at his hair and pulled his mouth to hers for a kiss. "I won't have my woman feeling left out or slighted."

"Faster," she gasped.

"Slower," he intoned.

"I already need…I need…"

"Me. You only need me." And he needed her. Inch by slllooow inch. When he was in her to the hilt, he pulled out just as slowly as he'd entered, than sank back in. Her hips arched in response. Everything inside him screamed to quicken his pace, to find release, but he didn't.

"I'm going to savor you," he vowed.

"Savor me faster." Her nipples were pearled against his chest, rasping against him with his every movement.

"Tsk, tsk. So impatient." How much longer could he hold back? Out. In. So slowly. When she gasped his name, his control almost broke. His muscles were bunched with the strain.

"I love you," she moaned.

That was all it took; his control snapped completely. With a growl of need, he slammed inside her, quickly drawing back, only to pound deeper inside her.

Over and over, again and again, he sank into her depths, loving the feel of her hot wetness. And when she screamed her release for a second time, he spilled deep inside her, his orgasm shaking his entire body.

NAKED ATOP THE BED, Jewel lay cuddled in Gray's arms, quite positive she'd never been more content. Even the knowledge that the Temple of Cronus was destroyed, her father still a mystery, couldn't dampen her lassitude. Then…

"Now we talk," Gray said, his voice raspy from all

the growling he'd done. He rolled to his side, facing her and propping his head on his upraised hand.

She sighed, mentally saying goodbye to her relaxed mood.

"What did you want to tell me earlier?"

Dread curled in her stomach, but she forced the words from her mouth. He deserved to know the truth. She'd promised him the truth. No matter his reaction, no matter what he decided to do to her, she'd promised to tell him. "I am—I am the Jewel of Dunamis."

She expected him to gasp, to push her away, or to snort in disbelief. Every muscle in her body tensed, waiting for his horrified reaction.

It never came.

He sighed, and the sound echoed hers. "I thought so."

Confused, dazed, she jolted upright. "You thought so? You thought so! I've been sick with worry and you thought so? Why didn't you say anything to me?"

"Honey, it was just a matter of sorting through certain facts." He tugged her back into his embrace. "Plus, I'm a genius. You said the stone's protector wanted to keep it safe but would willingly hand it over for destruction. That protector is me, right?"

"Yes. You're not angry?" she asked, softening, still unable to believe he accepted her so readily. "You don't want to destroy me?"

"Of course not. For an all-knowing being, you sure can overreact. You're the jewel. We can deal with that. I'm not going to kill you, and I'm not going to give you to OBI. They would hurt you, and that I won't allow. I love you too much for that."

"What?" Heart thumping in her chest, she jolted up again. "What did you say?"

"I love you."

Her eyes widened. Ribbons of happiness curled around her every cell. He loved her. Gray James loved her. He'd never said those words to another, and she heard the truth in his voice. Of all the things she'd imagined happening, this had never entered her mind.

"This is—this is a dream, right?" She rubbed her eyes, blocking the momentary glimpse of wonder she knew gleamed there. "I'll awaken soon."

"Uh, excuse me," he said darkly. "Don't you have something you want to say to me? You've said it before, but that was at the height of pleasure, so it doesn't count."

With a whoop, she threw herself into his waiting embrace. "I love you. I've always loved you."

He reached between them and cupped her jaw with his palms. "That's better." One of his hands twisted her hair, banding the locks around his fingers. "You realize you're coming to the surface with me, don't you? Don't even think about saying no. I'll think of something to tell my boss, even if I have to steal one of the jewels here and give it to him, claiming it's Dunamis." He paused, his expression guarded. "You still want to come with me, right?"

"I'd follow you anywhere." She licked his collarbone, reveling in the sound of his sharp intake of breath. "We have some time before our presence is required. Think I can keep you busy until then?"

"I think you could keep me busy forever."

## CHAPTER TWENTY-SIX

JEWEL RIFLED through the only closet in the room and found several robes. She withdrew a sheer blue one, lace jagged across the hem and small, glistening sapphires sewed into the bodice. They'd bathed and Gray was already dressed in the leather pants and tie-shirt of the dragons. He looked delicious.

He'd radioed his boss several moments ago and told the man that he had Dunamis in his possession. After minutes of the man's excited whooping, minutes of her heart skipping multiple beats, Gray pried a sapphire from the wall and gave her a secret, tender grin before stuffing it in his bag.

How they were going to get her past OBI, she didn't know. She only knew she was going to the surface and she'd never been more excited!

"What do you think?" she asked, holding the glittery material up to her body.

"I think I prefer you naked."

She laughed and shimmied the material over her head, covering her nakedness. "I refuse to go to lunch naked."

"Too bad."

Just as she was fastening the ties of her new light blue robe, a knock sounded at the door. "Enter," she called.

The doors slit down the middle and slid apart. A blond warrior stood in the entrance, the dragon medallion hanging from his neck aglow.

"Brand," Jewel said with a smile. "Nice to see you again."

"And you. Come," he said, his golden eyes averted to keep him from seeing anything he shouldn't. His hair hung in disarray around his shoulders, giving his amused features a roguish quality. "Lunch is served."

Jewel sighed, already mourning the loss of this wonderful reprieve. Of the soft touches Gray liked to slide over her body, of the hot kisses he liked to climb up her legs. As if he couldn't stand letting her go, either, he strode to her side and placed a kiss on her lips, their tongues daring a quick mating.

"Gods above," Brand muttered, spinning on his heel. They followed him down the hall.

Gray linked their fingers and gave a gentle squeeze. "Everything's going to be okay. You'll see. I won't leave your side." Releasing her hand, he anchored his palm to her neck and massaged, shifting strands of her hair. "If there's any trouble," he added, staring into her eyes, making her feel warm and cherished, "I'll go all demon on Darius's ass."

THE DRAGON-CARVED TABLE was piled high with food and drink, wafting a mouth-watering aroma in every direction. All of the warriors Gray had met in the forest were there, plus a few more, sitting impatiently, waiting for him and Jewel to arrive. Darius claimed the head of the table with a formally clad Grace on his right. A ruby necklace draped her neck, her red hair was piled high on her head, and she wore a soft pink gown.

The only two available chairs were on Darius's left. Gray claimed the one closest to the dragon, and Jewel eased in beside him.

"You may eat," Darius said.

Immediately the men dug into the food, a meal that consisted of honey-glazed ham, cranberry turkey, and some kind of white pudding. Each recipe came from the surface, Jewel realized, for she'd seen Gray eat each of these dishes. She spooned a bite of the pudding into her mouth and closed her eyes in surrender as the rich, decadent flavor spread on her tongue.

"I hope you found the room satisfactory," Grace said after swallowing a bite of ham.

"We did. Thank you." Jewel offered her a soft smile.

"Darius explained that you have no name." The pretty human wore an expression of utter perplexity. "He said most people call you 'it' or 'slave'."

"She has a name," Gray said, his tone flat and hard and brooking no room for argument. "It's Jewel."

"See." She tossed Darius a smug glance. "I told you she had a name. A beautiful one, at that." Smiling, she returned her attention to Jewel. "I think it's so cool you can predict the future. Darius and I could have used that kind of ability when I first came here. You could have told him how much he loved me, so he wouldn't have fought it so hard."

Darius arched his brows, his only reaction to his wife's taunting. He tossed back a drink of wine. "What know you of the vampires and demons…Jewel?"

The room tapered to absolute silence; everyone present waited with bated breath for her answer.

Stomach knotting painfully, Jewel said, "I would like to discuss that with you in private."

She meant the discussion to come after lunch. Darius took her words to heart. "Leave us," he told his men.

Though his tone was conversational, the dragons reacted immediately, grabbing their food as they jolted to their feet. Their chairs skidded behind them, creating a screeching symphony. Besides Jewel and Darius, Gray and Grace were the only ones to remain.

Darius looked pointedly at Grace.

"You told me I could stay, remember?" she said stubbornly. She leaned back in her chair, pinched a piece of turkey from her plate and nibbled on the edges, the picture of relaxation.

Darius turned that look on Gray.

"Don't even try it," he said, rolling his eyes. "I'm staying. End of story."

Jewel drew in a deep, cleansing breath, and met Darius's piercing stare as he next turned it on her. "I have an impending sense of doom for you. Marina once asked me what I knew of the Atlantean Mists."

Fury blazed in the blue depths of his eyes. "What did you tell her?" he growled.

"Watch your tone, Lizard," Gray snapped, "or the conversation ends here."

At first the dragon king flashed his teeth—sharp

and lethal. Then he nodded stiffly and repeated his question in a gentler tone.

"You know I cannot lie, so I gave her no answer at all. She does know about the mists, however, and hopes to gain control of them."

Little by little, the dragon relaxed. He snorted. "As if her puny army could match mine."

Tapping a finger on her chin, Grace frowned. "Why would this Marina want control of the portals? Atlantean creatures cannot survive outside of Atlantis. They die within days. Even Darius was not impervious."

"What!" Gray straightened. "Atlanteans die outside of Atlantis?"

Jewel paled. Oh, gods. Having always felt connected to Gray and the surface world, she'd forgotten about her connection to Atlantis. If she traveled to the surface, she would die. She covered her mouth with a shaky hand, hoping to cut off her moan of horror.

"Jewel," Darius prompted.

Would Gray stay here? He claimed to love her, but would that be enough to keep him here? She was too afraid to look at him, judge his expression.

"Jewel?" Darius said again.

Gathering her composure nearly proved impossible, but she did it. She squared her shoulders and forced her next words to form steadily. "Marina doesn't know she will die if she leaves. None of the creatures do. Remember, no one even knew of the portals except the dragons until a group of humans came through and struck a deal with Layel. Of course, Grace and her brother solidified the knowledge of them, since they were not sent by the gods. Now most of Atlantis is aware, yet none know of our vulnerabilities. Marina assumes she can live on the surface without any problem."

"In case you're wondering," Grace said to Gray, "the Atlantean Mists are the portals you used to get here."

Jewel finally looked at him. Gray's skin was pallid, the lines around his mouth taut.

"Speaking of the portals," Grace added, "how did you get past Darius?"

Finally he snapped back to attention, though his expression remained grim. "You have a portal here? This isn't the palace I entered."

Darius's lips dipped into a fierce frown. "You entered Javar's. The guards posted there obviously didn't see you. Did you hurt them?" He leaned forward on his elbows.

"No, I didn't hurt them. They never even knew I was there. They were busy with something else."

The war with the nymphs? Jewel wondered. She didn't mention it to Darius. Not yet.

Two darks brows slashed upward. "You must be a fine warrior, then," Darius said.

"I am," Gray answered matter-of-factly.

"Did anyone else enter with you?"

"No, just me."

"What about after you?"

"No one that I know of."

"I knew better than to send such an army of hatchlings," the dragon king muttered, "but I had to give Kendrick a chance to lead."

"Enough." Grace kissed his cheek. "We can deal with Kendrick and the other portal later. Right now we need to discuss vampires and demons and this sense of doom Jewel has."

"I do not know what they are planning," Jewel stated. "Yet."

"You will find out." A demand, not a request.

She nodded.

Gray shook his head. "If she has to do anything dangerous, the answer is no."

"Nothing dangerous," she promised. "Just exhausting." Without another word, she closed her eyes and blanked her mind, ignoring everything around her.

Gray watched her, ready to spring to the rescue if she even grimaced. Her features began to relax, her breathing evened out, steady, but slow. Too slow. Several moments passed in surreal expectation. And then she spoke, her voice layered with other voices, the sound eerie. Like a legion of ghosts. It was the same way she'd spoken to him when they'd been chased by the mers.

"Your enemies hide in the forest, making their way to the border of your land. In three days, they will sneak inside this palace. The demons will attack first, your fire unable to hurt them. While you are distracted with them, the vampires will move through the shadows and conquer the caves beneath us."

Darius's jaw twitched once, twice. "Do they know we possess Dunamis?"

"Not at this time."

"How can I stop them? How can I prevent this from happening?"

Her expression never wavered, and she continued in that odd voice. "You must attack first. When the third morning dawns, fly into the forest and surround them, then quickly close on their ranks with fire and ice."

"I don't understand." The dragon king shoved to his feet and paced. "How do I use both fire and ice?"

My God, Gray thought. This was exactly why men fought for this woman. Why she was so dangerous in the wrong hands. She could outline an enemy's entire battle plan—and exactly how to defeat it. He'd known, even glimpsed it before, but this…

If anyone on the surface discovered Dunamis was actually a woman, greedy human hands would always be reaching for her. Hunting her. Like she was hunted here, but worse.

Finding out he couldn't take her to the surface with him because she was physically bound to Atlantis had been a blow he had yet to recover from. Watching her in action was yet another blow, driving home the fact that she would never be safe, no matter where she resided.

"While the dragons breathe fire, the human must use ice."

Darius's hard blue gaze flicked to Gray. "Do you have ice?"

"No." He frowned in confusion.

Grace snapped her fingers, her eyes growing wide. "She means the fire extinguishers. The ones brought in from the last human invasion. The ones you have stored here, but your men can't use because dragons are weakened by cold."

Jewel slumped in her chair. Gray caught her and drew her limp body into his arms. "Sweetheart," he said.

She didn't respond. Her eyes remained closed, her expression soft as if from sleep.

"I'm taking her to the room," he said, concern overriding all else. "She's had enough."

Darius nodded. "Will you help us, human? Will you carry the ice when we attack?"

He didn't have time. He needed to get home. But the thought of three more days—and nights—with Jewel was an incentive he couldn't resist. "I have two conditions."

Darius arched a brow. "The first?"

"Jewel was desperate to search the Temple of Cronus for information about her father, but your men stopped us. Send someone to the ruins to search for anything she might find useful."

"Consider it done. The second?"

"When I leave, I want you to keep Jewel here. Keep her safe. You lost her before, and that—"

"Will not happen again. We are stronger now and no one, no one, will harm her. She will be safe with me."

Gray fought past a haze of fury and sadness and relief, and inclined his chin in acknowledgement of their deal. "Then consider me the Ice Man."

AFTER GRAY TUCKED a still sleeping Jewel into bed, smoothed her hair from her face, and placed a soft kiss on her lips, he gripped his transmitter and hunched over the edge of the bed. "Santa to Mother."

Several seconds passed in silence.

"Santa to Mother," he said again.

"Mother here. Has something happened to the package?"

"Package secure." He'd hand them the sapphire in his bag without a twinge of conscience.

Before he could tell his boss the reason for his call, Quinlin said, "Did you figure out that little riddle about the jewel being able to breathe?"

"It was buried under a mound of rocks." Lie. "I figure the text was referring to its lack of air." Bigger lie.

"Makes sense."

Hallelujah. Bringing them back to the business at hand, he said, "I wanted to let you know I'll be home later than planned."

Crackling pause. "Should we send in a cleaning crew?"

"No." He ran a hand down his face. "I've got everything under control. I'm just having to take the long way home to avoid detaining." God, when had he become such a liar? "Over."

## CHAPTER TWENTY-SEVEN

"I'M SORRY, my queen, but the dragons...they have Dunamis."

"Are you sure?"

"Yes. I saw it with my own eyes, walking along the parapet."

If Darius had Dunamis all was lost. Marina would never be able to defeat him—he would already know of their plan. "Layel," she screamed. "Layel!"

Within seconds, the vampire flew to her side, his expression weary. "What now?"

Panicked, she ranted and shouted out the information she'd just been given.

The vampire king frowned. "So we must assume they know our battle plan."

"What are we going to do?"

"We will attack."

"Now?"

"Now." He nodded.

"They must know and will have planned some way to stop us."

His frown deepened. "That is a chance we will

have to take. I, for one, will not walk away from this
war. Let's prepare our men."

GRAY AND JEWEL LINGERED in their room for the next
two days, making love and enjoying each other. They
were naked, and holding on to each other tightly. He
couldn't stop touching her. He planned to make enough
memories with her to last him a lifetime.

"I'm scared for you," she said softly. "You're only
one man, and I don't want you to fight the demons
alone. I don't want you to leave this bed."

"This is something I have to do, baby." He trusted
Darius to keep her here, and in return he would do
whatever the dragon king needed of him.

"What if—"

"Baby, I've been fighting in wars my entire life.
First with my dad, then my brothers, then for my
country. I'll be okay."

"Will you go home?" she asked softly, hesitantly.
"After? Without me?"

"Yes." His tone was finite, leaving no room for
argument.

Tears glistened in her eyes. Hell, he felt his own tears
burn in *his* eyes. "At least we've got now, this moment."
His hand explored the hollow of her back and she
shivered. "Let's not waste a second of it."

LATER, when their passion was sated, Gray taught
Jewel how to best defend herself. He'd put it off long
enough, knowing it would depress her. She'd done ex-
cellently until this point, but he wanted her better

prepared. He wanted to know she could save herself from any situation. Just in case.

She stood in the center of their room, and Gray walked around her, his hands locked behind his back like a military leader. "When I'm gone," he stumbled over the word, "Darius is going to keep you here. But he won't always be around, so I want you well able to take care of yourself."

"I've done quite well so far."

"Yes, but I want you to do better. You're not someone who can scream for help because the people you draw to you might be interested in keeping you for themselves. You have to learn to rely on yourself."

Her lips dipped, giving her a sad, vulnerable expression.

"Quick question. You're walking through the city alone at night and a group of men approach you, intent on forcing you to leave with them. Do you run away or try and fight them off?"

"Fight them off?"

"Wrong. It was a trick question. You don't walk through the city alone at night. That's lesson one. Understand?"

She nodded, her eyes following him as best they could as he continued to circle her.

"Lesson two," he said. He needed to cram months of instruction into a few hours, and urgency was riding him hard. "Any room or building you enter, you scan immediately. You study the occupants. You study the best way out. And you don't let anyone know you're doing it."

"How?"

"Keep your expression casual and your interest focused. Do it now. Scan this room without looking guilty or purposeful."

Her gaze darted left and right, and he shook his head. "Slower," he said. "Combine a look with an action, but never let your gaze linger too long."

She tossed her hair over one shoulder and turned her head, looking directly at him. She grinned, still a little sad, then looked away.

"Good." He wrapped his arms around her waist. "Now tell me what you saw."

"You."

"Describe me. My expression, my stance."

"Your lips were taut and hard, and your eyes were determined. You had your hands at your sides, and I think you had an erection."

He laughed, his first moment of amusement since realizing he had to go home without her. "That's good. Real good. People who seem to be in the wrong place should trigger your suspicions. If you see a centaur in the demon side of town, you'll know he doesn't belong. Therefore you'll know to avoid him. And by the way, I don't want you to ever go into the demon side of town. That was merely an example."

"That, I promise you, I will never do."

"Good. Always remain calm. Emotions cause people to do stupid things. If someone calls you a bad name, don't let it upset you. What does the bastard's opinion matter anyway?"

"You're right," she said with a nod.

"If someone comes after you, try to get away from them. Don't try to fight them if you don't have to."

"And if I can't get away?"

"Then, and only then, do you fight," he said, stepping in front of her. "Go for the most vulnerable part of the body first."

Her gaze strayed to his groin.

"That's a good place, but not always the best. If you poke your assailant's eyes hard enough, he won't be able to see well enough to find you."

She grimaced but nodded.

"Anything can be used as a weapon. A rock off the ground. A stick. If you have them, use them. You can shove a thin stick inside the assailant's ear and slow him down. The eardrum is sensitive and busting it hurts." His stomach was knotting as he thought of her needing to use these techniques.

He closed some more of the distance between them, and her gaze traveled up, up, until their eyes met. She gulped. Her intoxicating scent surrounded him as he reached up and traced a finger down her windpipe.

"This is where air goes from your mouth to your lungs. It's sensitive and fragile. If you punch someone here, you'll disable them." He didn't mention that she would probably kill them if she punched hard enough. He didn't want her worried about that; he only wanted her concerned with her own survival.

His hands lowered, caressing down her arms and spanning over her ribs. "If you're close enough, if someone is holding on to you like this, you can knee or elbow him in the stomach. That will make it difficult for him to breathe and help loosen his hold on you."

She licked her lips, her eyelids dripping to half-mast.

"You already know about the groin," he said, trailing his fingertips down her stomach and cupping her.

Her mouth parted on a shaky gasp.

"Use your knee or your foot and don't hold back your strength. Hit as hard as you can and it will paralyze your attacker for several seconds."

"What do I do if he's gotten his hands around my neck?" she asked breathlessly.

Gray drew his arms up and gently wrapped his fingers around the area in question, but he didn't apply pressure. "If that happens, you have to act immediately because their intent is to make you pass out. And the longer you're in that kind of hold, the more light-headed and weak you'll become. If you've tried to poke his eyes, have tried to kick his groin and neither of those worked, you reach up outside his arms." When she did so, he added, "Now slam your fists down on the middle, at the inside of my elbow."

She did it, but used a touch as gentle as his. Her gaze once more locked on his, and the sexual awareness intensified between them. It never left them, really.

"Your goal isn't to beat up your attacker, but merely to disable him and escape."

"There's a difference?" Her nose nuzzled the underside of his jaw.

He almost threw her on the bed and claimed her then, but refused to end her lesson. This was too important. "In the first scenario, rage is your primary emotion. In the second, survival is your only concern. Next time you punch someone like you did the merman, make sure to load your punch."

"How?"

"Pull back and get as much distance as possible between your fist and your target before you slam forward. Also, if you can shove your palm into your opponent's nose, that's even better." He clasped her hand in his, opened her fingers, and placed her palm inches from his nose. "Hit up and hit hard."

She nodded, and he dropped their hands. He didn't release her, he couldn't. Touching her provided the link he craved, a link he needed as much as he needed to take his next breath.

"If you can't get your palm to their nose, use your forehead. Your purpose is to distract the attacker and free yourself from his clutches."

She leaned into him and licked the seam of his lips. "I'll practice everything you've shown me."

His tongue pushed past her lips, her teeth, and swept inside her mouth. Her flavor filled him, sweet and wonderful and all Jewel. God, he was going to miss her. He wasn't sure he could survive without her.

"Take me to bed, Gray. Drink from me like before."

And he did.

A HORN BLARED.

Gray jerked upright in bed, jolted from a peaceful sleep. "What the hell is that?"

Beside him, Jewel was pale and shaky and it had

nothing to do with the fact that he'd drunk from her neck a little while ago. She was afraid. Very afraid.

As she pulled herself up, the sheet fell to her waist, revealing the perfect mounds of her breasts. "This is the third day. The demons and vampires are closing in on the palace. I just sent a mental warning to Darius."

By the next heartbeat of time, he had already jumped out of bed and grabbed his military fatigues. He slipped them on quickly, then strapped his knife to his belt.

The horn blared again.

Beyond the door, he heard the shuffle of feet, the angry growls of men. Gray stalked over to Jewel, who still sat in bed, her features devoid of any emotion. He bent down in front of her and reached inside his bag, where he still kept the armband he'd bought for her.

"This is for you," he said.

"Me?" Her eyes grew wide and watery, and her lips trembled as he slid the band up her arm. "You bought it for me in the city? Why?"

The horn sounded yet again.

"Because you wanted it," he rushed out, "and I knew it would look lovely on you." He reached up and swept her hair off her shoulders, then anchored the gold band in place. It gleamed bright, the sapphire as enchanting as her eyes. "And because you are the love of my life."

Without another word, he stood and strode from the room. He didn't allow himself a backward glance as he followed several men into some sort of training arena. An army of dragons were already there, lined up, Darius marching in front of them.

"Show no mercy," Darius was saying. "We will de-

stroy the vampires once and for all with our fire, and
the human will vanquish the demons with his ice.
Dunamis has proclaimed it."

Their cheers echoed off the walls.

"These creatures think to surprise us with an attack,
but we will show them the error of their ways. The three
of you," the king said, pointing. "Carry the ice makers
for the human. Do not let the contents touch your skin
or you will be weakened. You will stay with him and
hand him the equipment as needed."

As Grace said, the ice makers were actually fire extinguishers and there were at least sixty of them. He'd
done battle with quite a few weapons, but never with
liquid nitrogen. He would have preferred a few
grenades, maybe a case of C4, but he would take what
he could get.

"Become dragons, my friends, and let us fly."

A legion of roars sounded, echoing through the
rounded enclosure. Clothes were ripped away, faces
were elongated, wings and tails and claws grew. He'd
seen this change before, but he still couldn't tear his
eyes away. The men had become snarling, fire-breathing beasts. One of them—he thought it was Brand—
motioned him over with a long claw and onto his back.

While his mind shouted, "Hell, no," he climbed
aboard. "Let the war games begin," he muttered.

WITH A FIRE EXTINGUISHER anchored firmly on his back
and a black hose in his hands, Gray prowled through
the forest trees. Morning had yet to dawn, so he was
immensely grateful for his superior night vision.

Brand had dropped him off about a half mile back before leaping back into the air. The dragons carrying the fire extinguishers silently descended to his side. Up ahead, he could hear the pounding footsteps of the demon and vampire armies as they drew closer.

The murmur of voices soon drifted to his ears. He heard the clang of metal and the whoosh of footsteps. Gray stopped behind a thick tree trunk and crouched low, preparing to strike. He waited…waited…waited…

Above him, Darius emitted a war cry.

Hose raised, adrenaline high, Gray burst into the enemy lines. He sprinted straight to the demons, spraying white foam. Fire spewed from the dragons, white-hot beams of flashing light and scorching rays, a Fourth of July barbecue gone awry. The heat of it instantly wafted to him, and he did his best to remain out of its path.

Torturous screams echoed through the coming dawn. Amid the cries of pain rose the scents of dying flesh and sulfur. Gray continued to spray, avoiding vampires, keeping the liquid ice trained on the demons.

When a demon flew at him, he tried to spray it but his tube sputtered. Empty. Shit. He whipped out his knife, and the bastard jumped on him. Before he could make his first slash, it was jerked off of him and tossed onto the ground. A dragon, Renard, cut its throat with his claws.

"Work on those reflexes," he told the dragon. "Any slower and I would have been a goner."

His only reply was a grunt before Renard flew back into the fray.

At Gray's left, a vampire spied him and attacked. They clashed and tumbled to the ground. The vampire was about to bite him, about to sink his teeth into Gray's neck, when he paused.

"Dunamis?" the bloodsucker said, shocked and reverent. He released Gray as if he were poison and backed away, disappearing from view.

They smelled Jewel on him, he realized.

Someone handed him another extinguisher, and Gray popped to his feet. The rest of the dragons descended from the sky and attacked the remaining army on foot. Their steady steam of fire never slowed. Staying low, Gray crept through the rest of the camp, searching through the shadows. Over and over, he repeated the same action: spray the extinguisher, slit a demon's throat. Sweat dripped from him and soaked his clothing.

He could scent the blood around him, and it made his mouth water. However, he kept a tight rein on his impulse to drink, concentrating instead on the task he'd been given. Eleven times he was forced to exchange one extinguisher for another.

"Damn you, Darius," he heard a male voice lash out.

Gray spotted the speaker immediately. Layel. The vampire king who had saved Jewel's life, as well as his own. Darius suddenly materialized and swooped in. The two men grappled. Gray hated to admit it, but he was torn. He was here to help the dragons, was indebted to Darius, but was also indebted to this particular vampire.

He heard a growl behind him and spun around, spraying foam. The demon hissed and tore at his skin. Wincing, he shouted, "Darius, let him go," then quickly dispatched his attacker.

Darius shot another round of fire, but the vampire king quickly dodged it.

"Do your job, human," Darius gritted as Layel snarled, "I need no help from you, human."

"This is an old war," someone said beside him. Brand, he realized. "Do not get in the middle."

The two men continued to fight, and Gray watched helplessly, killing any creatures who came along to interfere. Neither man was winning, for they were equally matched.

"You!" a female screeched.

Gray pivoted, his eyes narrowing. Marina, Demon Queen, hovered in front of him, her red gaze slitted and glowing. She bared her teeth at him.

"You stole Dunamis from me. *You* are the cause of this hell." She launched herself at him.

His fingers squeezed the hose trigger, but no foam emerged. Empty yet again. Great.

She slammed into him, tossing him like a doll. In the next instant, she was on top of him, pounding a fist into his nose. He heard the cartilage snap, felt the sharp sting and the warm trickle of blood onto his lip. Her claws ripped into his shoulder.

Unfucking believable. His ass was being kicked by a girl. Still, he felt the cartilage in his nose move back into place, felt the claw marks closing. One of the perks of belonging to the dark side, he supposed.

He shoved her off him, but she flew at him again. He'd never hit a woman in his life but he was drawing back his fist to do just that when she was dragged off him. Layel sank his teeth into her neck, the action fierce, lethal, and as wild as any animal.

Marina's body jerked and spasmed once, twice, then stilled completely. Her head fell lifelessly to the side. When Layel finished feeding, he rose and faced Darius with quiet fury. Blood trickled from his mouth. He looked around, seeing the many men he'd lost, seeing the dragon army now surrounding him.

"I concede this victory to you, but things are not finished between us."

"They never are," Darius said. "Take the rest of your men and go. And know that I allowed you to leave only because you saved the human."

Layel grinned, the action devoid of humor. "We've done this before. I save one of your humans, and you send me on my way. That will not always be the case. One day, I *will* feast on your blood. Since you are being so generous, however, I will do you a favor and tell you the nymphs have overtaken Javar's palace."

"You lie. My men guard it well."

"Go and see for yourself. We meant to take it, too, Marina and I, but they beat us there. Our battle was with you, so we left them to it."

A low growl emerged from Darius's throat, and he took a menacing step forward.

"Tell your woman I said hello. I still remember the taste of her," Layel said, his humorless grin growing wider. "Until next time."

The vampire king vanished.

All around him lay demon, dragon, and vampire bodies. The living dragons gathered around Darius. "You," Darius said, pointing to a group of them. Fury darkened his features. "Go to Javar's palace and find Kendrick. Do not let yourselves be seen. I want to know if the nymphs are truly there."

Gray's shoulders slumped wearily, and he blocked out the rest of Darius's instructions. With this battle finished, his time with Jewel ended.

He wasn't even close to being ready to let her go.

# CHAPTER TWENTY-EIGHT

As ALWAYS, Jewel's visions never told of her own danger.

Jewel and Grace had sneaked atop the palace parapet, hoping to catch a glimpse of the battle. Jewel paced. Her nerves refused to settle, and she couldn't rid herself of a sense of apprehension. Was Gray all right? Had he been hurt?

She couldn't see the battle in her mind. What good were her gifts if she could not help the man she loved? Constantly her fingers rubbed the armband Gray had given her, trying to take strength from it.

"Tell me again that they will return to us unharmed," Grace said, her nervousness as great as Jewel's. "This is what I hate most about being a warrior's wife. I love Darius with my whole heart. He's a part of me, but he fights these wars and I almost die of worry every time."

Jewel paused and gave her a half smile. "Your husband will live a long and healthy life. As will you and your children."

Grace studied her for several minutes, then breathed a sigh of relief. "I'd rather die myself than have anything happen to him."

"I understand. I love Gray with all my heart." She sighed. A gentle night breeze danced around her, tangling her robe and hair. "But I am destined to lose him, it seems."

"Why? There's no reason for two people in love not to stay together."

"I would die on the surface, and if he stays here, humans will continually come through the portals, plaguing our land in an attempt to steal or destroy me."

"Okay, that's a reason. I'm so sorry." Grace gave her a quick hug before Jewel continued her pacing.

"Distract me. Tell me of you and Darius."

"My favorite subject," she said with a grin. "I remember when he and I were first dating." She laughed. "I call it dating, he calls it duty."

Somehow, Jewel couldn't picture the fierce dragon courting anyone. Demand she wed him, yes. Bring her flowers and ask her on dates, no.

"He was determined to kill me, you see."

"What!" Jewel stopped midstep and faced the delicate-looking woman. "He wanted to kill you?" She paused. "I don't know why I'm surprised. That is Darius for you, a man who does his duty no matter the circumstances."

"Darius even had his sword raised, ready to strike. I had just passed through the portal, and it was his sworn duty to silence me permanently. But he didn't. He couldn't. He helped me find my brother instead, and in return, I like to think I've filled his life with the emotions he had always denied himself and love." Her head canted to the side thoughtfully. "Gray needs that, too, I think. He's got that same hard look Darius sometimes wears."

"What am I going to do?" Jewel asked dejectedly.

Neither of them had an answer.

"Do you think the battle is over yet?" Grace asked, her hands wringing together. "I won't be able to rest until Darius is in my arms again."

Jewel closed her eyes and once more tried to send her consciousness outside of the palace and through the forest. Just as the scene was at last forming in her mind, a sense of being watched flittered over her. A menacing shadow covered her mind, and a sense of danger rocked her.

"Grace," she said, looking to her new friend. "We're in trouble."

Grace paled, making her freckles all the more obvious. "What do you mean?"

"There are demons on their way to the palace. They stole a dragon medallion and plan to use it to get inside the palace." Jewel glanced around for a weapon, intent on using anything, just as Gray had showed her. She found a long stick and several fat rocks. She handed the rocks to Grace, her hands shaky. "They cannot die without their throats cut, but we can try to hold them off until help arrives. Come on, let's go down and warn—"

It was too late.

Six demons swooped onto the parapet, their wings flapping furiously. Their claws were elongated and their teeth glistening with saliva. Without their queen around, they would not be concerned with keeping Jewel safe and unharmed.

Death gleamed in their eyes.

Grace raced beside her, determination hardening her expression and washing away her fear. "You take the three on the right, and I'll take the other three."

"Deal."

All at once, Jewel heard their thoughts. *I've wanted a taste of Dunamis for a long time. The human smells sweet, and so does the babe in her belly.*

"You're pregnant," Jewel told her, fearing for them. "Just stay behind me."

Grace gasped and her hand went to her belly. She hadn't known she was pregnant, Jewel realized, not wanting the woman to fight now. "Stay behind me," she repeated.

Grace hesitated only a moment before shaking her head. "No. We do this together."

Jewel leapt into action. Grace didn't heed her words, but was right beside her. The demons realized what was happening and their eyes widened. Jewel swung her stick, aiming for its nose. She heard it snap and watched the creature's head whip to the side. Blood poured down his face. Grace threw one of her rocks and it slammed into one of the demon's temples. He hissed in pain and shock.

Grace threw another rock and it slammed into his same temple. This time he flew backward and into the wall. Two others tried to fly at her, but Jewel jumped in front of her and swung her stick.

She aimed for their groins. Demons might not look like humans, but they procreated the same way. Contact. The bastard howled. She continually swung the stick, keeping the creatures at bay.

In English, so the demons couldn't understand, she told Grace, "Back up. If we can reach the door, we can run to a room and hide."

"Step with me."

"Okay." Together, they backed up. The demons followed, lashing out with their claws and legs, but Jewel managed to fend them off, never letting her swing grow lax.

"We're at the door," Grace whispered. "I'm wearing my medallion so it opened on its own." The dragon medallions acted as sensors, opening and closing all the doorways.

"When we cross the threshold, cover your medallion so the doors will close quickly. They'll have to wait for them to open again. On my count. One, two. Three!"

Jewel spun around and stepped past the door, right beside Grace. The doors slammed closed behind them. She heard the demons grunt as they knocked into the thick stone, the medallion they'd stolen probably—thankfully—hidden underneath a shirt, unused to the sensor-abilities as they were. "Run! Faster," she shouted.

But all too soon they figured out the problem and opened the door. They raced inside, hot on her heels. Anything in her path, she threw behind her, happy when she heard it thump against their pursuers.

One of them reached her and grabbed her by the shoulders, jerking her backward. As she fell, she lifted her stick and stabbed upward. Her momentum gave her added strength, and her impromptu weapon imbedded in the demon's throat. He hissed and jerked, then collapsed.

Grace was nowhere to be seen; she'd disappeared beyond the staircase. The remaining demons hovered around her, growling low in their throats.

"You will pay for that," one of them said.

In a flurry of movement, Grace suddenly appeared at the bottom of the stairs. "Use this," she shouted, tossing a dagger.

Jewel caught it just as a demon spun and launched himself at Grace. The other flew at her. She kicked out and nailed him in the stomach, and while he gasped for breath she finished him off. He fell at her feet and she searched the bottom of the stairs for Grace. The petite woman was holding off the remaining demon with a long sword.

Jewel leapt on top of him, wrapping her hands around his throat. Her blade sliced. He was dead within seconds.

And then it was over.

She stayed where she was, panting, while the dragons who had remained behind to guard them pounded down the stairs. "What happened?" one of them shouted. "Why didn't you call for help?"

"I thought my scream of terror was enough," Grace snapped. She doubled over, gasping for breath.

Jewel gazed at the blood on her hands. She'd done it. She'd proven she could protect herself, no matter her enemy. That knowledge should have made her happy, but it didn't. Gray would leave her now.

A few seconds later, Gray, Darius and the dragon

army strode inside. They wore expressions of smug victory…until they took in the scene of blood and death. Darius rushed to Grace and Gray rushed to Jewel, and both men jerked them into their arms, holding tight.

"What happened?" the two men demanded at once.

"You're safe," Jewel said, tears filling her eyes. Her knees weakened with relief. "You're safe. Thank the gods."

His hands trailed over her, searching for injuries. "Are you hurt? Tell me you're not hurt."

"This isn't my blood." She locked her arms around his neck.

Beside them, Darius was running his hands over Grace, kissing her and scolding her and shouting orders to his men to clean up the mess and kill the demons all over again.

A sense of urgency rose inside Jewel. Her time with Gray was at an end; she felt it all the way to her bones. She should inquire about the battle, she should allow him time to rest. But she did neither of those things. "Take me to our room, Gray. Right now. Please."

He didn't hesitate; he felt the urgency, too. He swooped her up and into his arms. "Don't come looking for us," he said over his shoulder.

# CHAPTER TWENTY-NINE

"I DON'T UNDERSTAND what this means," Jewel said.

It had been two days since the battle and Gray hadn't found the strength to leave her. So here he was, ensconced in the dragon palace, sitting atop the bed with Jewel while she studied broken, faded tablets the dragons had found at the ruined Temple of Cronus.

She'd spent all of last night fitting the small pieces together like a puzzle, working painstakingly through the long hours.

"Do you see these words?" She pointed to a line of jagged symbols.

She looked so lovely. Her hair tumbled down her back. Color bloomed bright in her cheeks, and her lips were lush and swollen from their recent loving. "I see them," he said.

"They say I am dragon."

He wasn't surprised. "You do have Darius's eyes."

"But here it says I'm vampire."

Brow furrowing, Gray sat up.

"And here it says I am Centaur. Here, a minotaur. Here, a mer. Here, a nymph. Here—"

"I get the picture. Shit, baby, you're everything."

How many times had he looked at her and thought she possessed certain qualities of the different races?

"I don't understand," she repeated.

"You're made up of every creature."

"That's…that's impossible."

"Ha! I've learned that nothing is impossible. What else does it say?"

"That I am the daughter of Cronus. Gray," she said, turning wide, shocked eyes to him. "He is king of the gods. Or he was until his son, Zeus, killed him and used his blood to make us." The last was said on a sad, broken gasp. "He's dead. My father is dead. But…how did I see him that day? He hugged me. He held me in his arms."

"Perhaps it wasn't your father who held you."

"Zeus," she said. "It was Zeus. My…brother. He told me he was sorry and I assumed he meant for ignoring me. But Zeus apologized for killing our father. How could I not have realized? It's so clear now." She rested her head on his shoulder, and he felt the warm liquid of her tears slide down his arm. "This is so hard. I expected so many things, but not that. Never that."

He hugged her to him for more than an hour, simply holding her and letting her cry. He whispered things into her ear, sweet things, loving things, all the things he wanted her to know but would never have another chance to tell her.

When her tears died, he squeezed his eyes tightly shut. *I have to leave.* His chest constricted. Now everything was complete. She knew about her past, her greatest enemies were defeated, and she was safe. It was time to tell her goodbye. How he would have loved to spend his life beside her, making her forget her sadness about her father. Comforting her. Simply loving her.

He must have stiffened or stopped breathing because she suddenly pulled from his touch, not looking his way. "You're leaving now."

How could he live without this woman? She was everything to him, and he wasn't complete without her. But he forced himself to say, "I have to."

Her gaze remained straight ahead. "Take me with you."

"No."

"Stay here, then."

If only he could. "I've got to leave. I won't let you be hunted by another agent. I can't."

"Come back to me."

He cupped her jaw and lightly kissed her lips. He felt ripped apart inside. She possessed his heart. To save her, however, he would do whatever was necessary. Even leave her. "I'm going to close the portal, baby. I'm going to make sure no one else ever enters it."

And then, before she could say another word, he made love to her one final time, moving in and out of her slowly, savoring everything about her. Her taste. Her scent. Her feel. Branding her essence in his every cell. Afterward, when she fell asleep, he quietly dressed. His stomach felt like a lead weight had taken up residence, churning with nausea.

Forcing his feet one in front of the other, he walked from the room. Tears filled his eyes. He hadn't cried since his mom died, but he cried now. And he wasn't ashamed of his tears. "Goodbye, Pru," he whispered, and it almost killed him to say it.

He didn't allow himself to look back as he hunted down Darius. The dragon king was waiting for him and escorted him to the portal. Gray stepped inside.

Home.

Misery.

SURPRISINGLY the portal he exited did not take him to the same location he'd entered from. Gray found himself in Brazil. OBI didn't know about this portal, and he planned to keep it that way. For days he worked furiously, blocking the portal entrance with rocks. Afterward, he sneaked his way to Florida and radioed home base to be picked up as if he'd washed up to shore and he did not know how they'd missed him, since they had men posted in the water. When they reached him, he handed his boss the huge sapphire he'd stolen from Darius's wall and with a straight, deadpan expression said it was Dunamis.

They asked him about his mission, and he lied. Hooked to a lie detector, he lied his ass off. And he passed. He told them of the monsters, just to keep them from sending someone else inside. But he mentioned nothing about Jewel, nothing about the vast wealth, and nothing about his new vampire tendencies.

They were so excited about Dunamis, they sent him on his merry way, giving him the vacation he'd been due for the past year.

His vacation sucked. He never left his house. And

now, two weeks into it, he was standing in his basement gym, pounding the hell out of his punching bag.

He had no life without Jewel. Hell, he didn't want a life without her. What was she doing? Was she safe? Did she miss him? Did she spend every night lying awake, imagining his hands on her, wishing his lips were all over her?

"What's wrong with you, man?"

Gray stiffened. He pounded a few more punches into the bag. His brothers had descended upon him en masse this morning and refused to leave. "Nothing," he growled. It was the same answer he'd given them the other thousand times they'd asked.

They kept at it, though, and several times he'd come close to biting them. He thought his eyes might have turned red once because his brothers had also asked him—a thousand times—if he needed to see a doctor. He still craved blood, yes, but only Jewel's. Only her sweetness.

At least he hadn't levitated. Wouldn't *that* have been fun to explain? He'd wondered a few times why he hadn't weakened since leaving Atlantis, since he now possessed some very Atlantean characteristics, but the only answer he could come up with was that he had been born a human and his greatest ties were here.

"I believe you," Nick said. He glanced to Erik. "Do you believe him?"

"I think it's woman trouble."

"Gotta be," Denver said. "Nothing else could shake him like this."

"Shut the fuck up."

"Well, finally he says something other than nothing."

Gray couldn't tell them. They knew nothing about OBI. As much as he wanted to describe every detail about Jewel's loveliness, he couldn't.

God, he had to get her back.

He rested his forehead on the punching bag. He'd meant to do something, anything, to block the portal in Florida but he hadn't been able to do it. Maybe he hadn't tried. He hadn't wanted to sever that final tie with Jewel and destroy all hope of ever seeing her again.

The second day he'd been home he found a rock with her picture on it inside his bag and had punched a hole in his wall. He'd been so filled with longing he'd almost torn his entire house down.

Screw it, he thought in the next instant. He'd had enough of this torture. He was going back in. He was going back to Jewel. OBI didn't know about the portal in Brazil; maybe he could find it again. He'd have to be careful, though. They kept a close watch on their employees, always cautious of leaks.

If he did this, if he went this route, he'd have to say goodbye to his family forever. Could he? Yes. *Yes.* For Jewel, he'd give up everything. *I'm going to do it. I'm going back to her.* He smiled for the first time since returning.

"Will you look at that?" Nick said. "What caused the change?"

He was just about to answer when a wild-haired seductress burst into his gym.

"Gray James," she said, black hair flying behind her. "I've been here for two weeks and survived. I *can* live on the surface." She saw his brothers, smiled at them weakly, and muttered, "Hello," before whipping her focus back to Gray. "Now what do you have to say to that?"

His knees almost buckled as shock pounded through him. Was this a hallucination? "Jewel?" Heart pounding, he raced to her and jerked her into his arms, closing his eyes as her scent surrounded him. God, she was real. "What do you think you're doing? You should never have risked your life like that." He was unable to put any heat behind the admonishment.

"I told you," Erik murmured.

Before she could answer, Gray slathered her face with kisses, happier in that moment than he'd ever been. Praise the Lord for women who rebelled. "I was coming for you, sweetheart. I couldn't stay away from you." More kisses. "Now, you have a lot of explaining to do. Where have you been staying? Why didn't you weaken?"

"I sneaked through the portal and followed you here. Darius realized what I had done and found me. He took me into the nearest town and rented me a room. He checked on me every couple of days but I never weakened, so he finally transported me here." She paused for breath. "I'm part of every creature, which makes me part human and must allow me to exist on the surface. And this human wants to be with you."

His lips slowly inched upward. How he loved this woman. "How did you follow me without my knowledge?"

"How do you think? I finally used my powers for something *I* wanted."

His brothers were muttering about the weirdness of the conversation. Humans? Transported? Powers? They didn't know their brother-in-law was an alien, either. Gray would have a lot of explaining to do later, but for right now, he had Jewel and that was all that mattered.

"Marry me." It wasn't an order, but it was pretty damn close. It *was* a prayer.

"You mean it?" Squealing, she jumped up and wrapped her legs around his waist. "Yes, yes, yes! I love you."

"And I love you, Jewel, Prudence, Blaze."

"That's Mrs. General Happy to you."

He chuckled. "How about Jewel of Atlantis, Jewel of my heart?"

\* \* \* \* \*

*You asked for Layel's story...*
*And now the wait is over.*

*Turn the page for your sneak preview!*

NIGHT HAD LONG since fallen.

The air was warm, fragrant and fraught with danger. The insects were eerily silent, not a chirp or whistle to be heard. Only the wind seemed impervious to the surrounding menace, swishing leaves and clicking branches together.

Delilah's every survival instinct remained on high alert. No telling where the other creatures were. She'd spied a few here and there as she'd gathered stones and sticks. And then they had disappeared, hiding amongst the shadows. She could have hunted them down, could have challenged them, but she hadn't.

The god's warning refused to leave her mind. What if she killed one of her own team members? To begin at a disadvantage would be the epitome of foolish. She'd been foolish a little too often lately.

She and Nola had opted to sleep in the trees, making them harder to find, harder to reach. Right now she was stretched atop a thick branch, legs swinging over the side, handmade spear clutched tightly in her palms. Wooden daggers were strapped to her legs, waist and back.

Sharp bark dug into her ribs, helping keep her

awake, alert. What were the other creatures doing just then?

What was *Layel* doing?

Layel…beautiful Layel. She'd only interacted with him twice, yet that had been enough to utterly, foolishly fascinate her. He was like no one she had ever encountered. Constantly she found herself wondering what his body looked like underneath his clothes, what his face would look like lost in passion, what he would feel like, pumping and sliding inside her.

*He despises you. He is best forgotten.*

Forget that his skin was pale and smooth as silk? Forget that his eyes were blue like sapphires and fringed by black lashes that were a striking contrast to his snow-white hair? Forget that he was tall with wide shoulders and radiated a dark sensuality women probably salivated over? Impossible.

What kind of females did he enjoy? What type of females had he allowed into his bed?

Sparks of something…dark flickered in her chest. Jealousy, perhaps. She wanted to deny the emotion, but couldn't. *Mine,* she thought. He might want nothing more to do with her, but no way in Hades would he be allowed to have another woman. Not while they inhabited this island.

*What's come over you?* Men were no longer something she prized. To her, they were something to destroy, a threat to her loved ones. Since her one and only mating had ended so disastrously, she had not thought to find herself possessive of a male. How many times had she watched her sisters fight over a particular slave? *He's mine,* they would shout. *It's my bed he will warm this night.* A clash of daggers always followed, as well as cut and bleeding warrioresses. How many times had she watched those "prized" men leave when the loving was over? Without a backward glance at the brokenhearted they were leaving behind.

Delilah had thought herself immune. Until now. She'd straddled the vampire's shoulders and he'd looked between her legs with undiluted heat. A shiver followed the thought, drowning her in another wave of that deep and inexorable desire. What would it be like to be bedded by Layel? Would he be gentle, taking her slowly? Or would his passion be as ferocious as his wild, blue eyes promised? Perhaps even a little wicked?

"You're aroused, Amazon. Why?"

Layel's whispered entreaty was so close, so husky, she wasn't sure if she'd imagined it. She stiffened, fingers tight on the spear, as she searched the darkness for him. Only treetops and night birds came into focus. Not even where thin slivers of golden moonlight seeped through the canopy of leaves overhead did she make out the form of a man. Slowly her muscles released their vise-hold on her bones.

*Why am I aroused? Because of you,* she wished she could tell this fantasy.

"Well?"

She gasped. Too real, too real, too real…

Before she had time to react, however, a hard hand settled over her mouth while another shoved her to her back. A heavy, muscled weight slammed into her body. She lost her breath, barely managing to remain on the branch.

In seconds, Layel had her stretched out and her legs restrained. Her eyes widened as her spear was torn from her grip and thrown to the ground. A mocking *thump* echoed in her ears. She balled her hand and moved to strike him, but he released her mouth to catch the action. Next he caged her arms between their bodies.

"You will not hurt me," he said.

"I'll do anything I want."

"Try."

One word, but it was so smug she longed to slap and kiss him at the same time. She didn't panic. Yet. Nola was nearby. Probably sneaking up on Layel…now. But no. A moment ticked by, then another.

Nola never arrived.

Delilah's heart began to drum erratically in her chest. Her blood rushed through her veins with dizzying speed, and need quivered in her belly. Here was her fantasy, in the flesh. Hers for the taking.

*You are an Amazon. Act like one.* Forcing herself into action, she raised her head and sank her teeth into his neck until she tasted the metallic tang of blood. He hissed in her ear, the sound one of pleasure and pain. *You are biting him to escape, yes? So why are you writhing?*

Mmm, so good… Her tongue flicked against his racing pulse.

His hands now free, he fisted her hair and jerked her away. He was panting, anger and arousal bright in his eyes. "Think yourself a vampire, do you? Or are you half vampire? I know your kind consorts with all races and your father could belong to any of them."

She opened her mouth to respond but he shook his head, stopping her. "Scream and you'll regret it."

"As if I would scream," she muttered, offended that he thought so little of her abilities. *You did allow him to sneak up on you.*

*Oh, shut up.*

He blinked in surprise, as if he'd expected her to scream despite his threat.

Her irritation intensified, and she glared at him. "Did you hurt my sister?"

"She was gone when I reached you. I did not touch her."

"Then I will allow you to live. For now. But very soon I'm going to grow tired of letting you overpower me."

He snorted.

"Be thankful I haven't already killed you."

"Do not fool yourself, Amazon. You would be dead right now had I not stayed my hand."

There was fury in his voice and hate in his expression. Stayed his hand? So he *had* come here to kill her? Bastard! Except, despite everything he had said, despite the genuine loathing directed at her, his legs were between hers and she could feel the length of his shaft hardening, growing, filling.

Just like that, her blood sizzled another degree. Blistered her veins. *I am callous, and I care for no one but my sisters.* If they were in Atlantis, she might agree to take him as her slave. If only for the month males were allowed inside the Amazon camp. But here on this island, with a dangerous competition in the works, they might very well be enemies.

"Afraid, Delilah?" he asked silkily.

Her name, spoken on those red lips...a hot ache bloomed between her legs, moisture pooling here.

"Of what?" The words emerged breathless, wine-rich.

"Dying. Pain."

"No," she answered honestly. Dying didn't scare her. Pain didn't scare her. But her reaction to this man petrified her. He made her feel vulnerable, as if she couldn't rely on herself. As if she needed him to survive. He'd already overtaken her thoughts.

"You should be very afraid," he said....

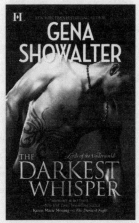